Molten Flux

Book One of The Flux Catastrophe

Jonathan Weiss

Helixic Books

COPYRIGHT

DEDICATION

For my wife, Kayla, and anyone else who has put up with my chaotic aspirations.

CONTENTS

CHAPTER ONE

CANYON CAPTIVES

R YZA COULD TASTE SAND at one corner of his lips and blood at the other. He glanced at the man who'd just struck him. He was shirtless, scarred and covered in filth.

Typical smelter.

The man brandished his scrap metal club at Ryza, threatening another blow if he didn't get moving. In order to avoid being knocked senseless, he bitterly obeyed. Ryza's gift from the smelter was a set of box-like cuffs that bound his wrists, sharp wire biting into his skin. The blood running down his temple made his cropped hair redder than usual. The smelter that had cuffed him shouted something guttural and shoved Ryza into the line of similarly restrained men.

Walls of red rocks reached high on either side, the last signs of daylight brushing over the cliff's edge. The sky had been blue when their trade caravan entered the canyon, now it was a bruised purple. In hindsight, the decision to travel this route was extremely foolish.

They'd been halfway through when a single man holding a dagger stepped from the shadows and brought the whole procession to a grinding halt. Smelters had appeared in front and behind them, ten in total, all with makeshift weapons in one hand, a bag of cuffs in the other, and a hungry grin on their faces.

The line of docile merchants shambled forward and Ryza moved with them. Leaning to his right, he could see what was happening at the front. Each man's cuffs were being threaded with a long length of chain before the chain was passed to the next prisoner. Ryza looked down at his restraints.

It was a small square of thick metal with a slot on each side for wrists to be bound by thick wire. In the middle, a small hole had been drilled for a chain to be passed through. The damn thing was more rust that iron, but no matter how much Ryza struggled against it, he couldn't break free on his own.

The smelter with the chain slapped the man he was attending to on the back of the head, sending him stumbling into the group of the restrained traders, then beckoned to the next man.

The line shambled forwards. Ryza was now next to the caravan's carts. Three men with crowbars busted them open with glee and rummaged around, looting anything they perceived as valuable. Sacks of reels, bundled furs, glinting jewels, and most importantly, water.

Legend had it people once drank the precious stuff. Eons ago when it still rained in this desert land. But one day people just stopped needing to. It was all in the air. Now water was scarce, used only for the concoction of magical inks, inks that would be painted as runes onto the skin where their meaning could be cast as axioms into the world, axioms that could set him free.

He looked down at his wrists. One blocky green rune peeked out from under the restraints. This one could manipulate the magnetism of a piece of metal if he was touching it, enough to break him out of these damn cuffs. In his mind, he could picture the metal wires holding his wrists snapping like twine. But then what would he do? Get beaten to death by ten smelters, most likely, but at least he would die a free man. There was a small vial of green ink stashed in his underpants, but by the time he had painted another rune on his arm, his head would be inside out.

The line shuffled forward again. There were only three people in front of him. He needed a plan, fast. Unconsciously, he began chewing his top lip. He'd done this ever since he was small, it just seemed to help him think. Ryza could still remember when his father had taught him that some animals could be instantly calmed by holding their upper lip. Maybe he was right about that, but he'd also been wrong about a whole lot else.

The chainer pulled the next man into position. Two left until it was Ryza's turn. He glanced around quickly. There was no way he could outrun the smelters. He might be fast and lean, but they would catch up to him before he made it out of the canyon. No matter which direction he chose, there would be at least a mile until he hit open desert. That wasn't an option. The cliff walls would be working against him. But what if he could use them?

His train of thought was interrupted by a shout from the caravan's half-looted carts.

'Water!'

Whoops of delight echoed through the canyon and the smelters swarmed to it. The caravan had set out with an entire bucket of water, enough to trade for a town's worth of reels. Now it would just go to waste in the hands of these wretches. Ryza didn't care. They could have it. That bucket of water may have just bought him his escape. Three men ran past him from the front. Four men were already on the carts.

Ryza looked over his shoulder. Having run out of cuffs, the smelter that had all but concussed him was idly standing guard at the back of the halted convoy. There were now only three men he needed to get past. The chainer, the smelter corralling the chained merchants, and the man who had stopped the caravan in the first place, who was standing about twenty metres away and playing with his pathetically small dagger.

The chainer had paused for a moment in the commotion but was now turned back to the man in front of him. Ryza watched his every motion closely. First, the chainer placed his club down, leaning it against his leg as he fumbled the excessively long iron coil through the cuffs. Once that was done, the man in question received a quick tap from the club to move him along. The whole process took maybe a minute at best.

The man ahead of Ryza stepped forward and he followed. If he could pop the cuffs off fast enough, he could get to the club before the chainer could grab it, then he'd have to dart back to avoid being grabbed. The chainer would still have that length of chain to swing with, but that wasn't a match for the vicious looking weapon. The only problem would be that Ryza would have to fight the other man at the same time. Even if he could dispatch both, the rest of the smelters would be on him.

'Cuffs,' the chainer grunted at the man ahead, placing down his club and holding out his hand.

But the man hesitated. Ryza watched his shoulders tense. Maybe he was thinking of an escape, too. Ryza swore under his breath. It didn't matter if this man made it out or not, Ryza's plan was now ruined.

'Cuffs!' the chainer demanded.

'You can have 'em!' the man roared. He followed through with a vicious upper cut, aiming the edge of his cuffs at the chainer's chin.

But the chainer was quicker, deftly dodging the blow with a step back, scooping up his club as he went. One swing would have been enough to put the man in his place, but the chainer seemed to think a bit more discipline was needed. Each lumbering blow came crushing down on the man's skull, cracking into bone before squelching through brain, sending an explosive burst of blood and giblets in every direction.

By the time the man's lifeless corpse collapsed, both Ryza and the chainer were covered in blood. Ryza could feel the warmth of it soaking through his shirt. He could feel his breathing quicken. If that was the result of a failed plan, he might as well ask to be clubbed too.

The nearest smelter approached them, giving the body a light kick and grunting.

'Bit of a mess there,' he said to the chainer.

The chainer croaked with laughter. 'Yer' telling me! A bit o' flux ain't fixing that!' He turned to Ryza and offered him a toothless grin. 'Sorry 'bout the mess. Looks like we'll both be this filthy for a week.'

Ryza shuddered at the thought. Packed in a cage with the others while covered in a dead man's blood. He'd rather die. They'd kill him anyway once they were ready, only to pump his corpse full of molten flux and make it walk once more. It's how the bastards got the name "smelter" in the first place. Ryza shuddered again. The silvery substance was unnerving enough to look at in a glass vial. He couldn't imagine it coursing through his veins.

The chainer beckoned him forward, but Ryza hesitated. The chainer still hadn't put down his club. He glanced over at the other smelter. He was too close. Ryza could attack the chainer, but the other man would be on him before he was out of the cuffs.

The smelter moved closer, his shoulder almost bumping against Ryza's. 'Wouldn't be thinking of doing the same, now would you?'

Ryza resisted wincing as the man's breath engulfed his face, the scent of long rotted meat. 'I've got enough blood on me for the day,' Ryza said, struggling to keep his voice level.

The smelter and the chainer cackled, throwing their heads back. Ryza glanced over his shoulder while they were distracted. None of the other smelters had noticed the commotion. They were still too busy with the looted cart.

The chainer moved closer, his left shoulder just next to Ryza's right.

'You're a funny one, I always like that in an automind,' the chainer said. 'Hope the flux can bring that back with ya.'

The chainer placed his club down, resting it against his right knee and Ryza swore inwardly. The chainer and the smelter were facing each other in front of him, they'd have him by the neck before he could dive for the weapon. Ryza glanced at the smelter on his left. He was holding his own club loosely in his right hand. If he could just get to it first.

Ryza began concentrating on the rune inked into his left wrist, imagining it sliding into his clenched fist. Almost hearing the loud *ping* the cuffs would make as the wire snapped out with deadly force. Ryza's eyes widened.

That was it!

'Now let's not have any more trouble here. Let's see them cuffs.'

'Of course,' Ryza said with a grin.

He whipped them up to neck level and clamped his eyes shut, forcing the rune in his hand to burn white-hot.

Feel the metal.

Become the metal.

Revel in it.

His father's words ran through his head as an ethereal feeling flowed into the wire, as if it were an extension of his hands. It was his. His to control.

The wire whipped through the air and Ryza's fists flew apart, bursting out of the cuffs and slamming into the faces of the men on either side. It would have been a stunning blow to each of them, enough to send them staggering back, roaring in pain.

But when Ryza opened his eyes, it was to a gurgling silence. His fists were drenched in blood. On either side of him, the men were clutching at their throats, metal wire embedded in each of their necks. Ryza couldn't believe his luck.

That's what they get for giving a Kretatic enough metal.

The club was in Ryza's hands before the chainer's body hit the ground and he sprinted at the smelter still playing with his dagger. They only looked up when Ryza was two paces away, but it was far too late for him.

Ryza made a wide, one-handed swing with the club that would devastate whatever it hit. The blow landed right in the centre of the man's face, the weighty club head caving his skull in with ease. They collapsed into the dust, but Ryza had already sprinted on.

He was scanning the cliff walls as he fled, looking for that one bit of extra rocky surface that he could scramble up. As a child, he'd climbed and subsequently fallen off enough things that he considered himself as nimble on a wall as he was on the ground. He only had to hope that the smelters weren't similarly gifted. And that they didn't find the crates of pristine rifles hidden in the rear carts.

A shout of alarm filled the canyon behind him. The smelters had caught on. But it didn't matter, Ryza was already a good two hundred metres away from them and he'd found exactly what he was looking for. On one side the cliff creased in on itself, just enough to form a narrow rocky shaft that went all the way to the top.

Ryza began climbing it with ease, finding handholds and footholds without even looking. It was only when he was halfway up that he looked down and realised just how much blood was on his hands. At least it wasn't his.

Not yet.

Down below, the remaining smelters had caught up to him. Some of what they were shouting at him might have been words, but Ryza wasn't focused on them. If he turned back to yell at them, if he got cocky, he might as well just let go and fall to his death. However, his focus shook as a loud clang came from somewhere below.

One of the smelters hurled a freshly pillaged rifle at him, the improvised javelin only making it halfway up the cliff before clattering back down harmlessly. The idea caught on and soon all seven of them were hurling their own clubs and machetes at Ryza, none of them coming nearly high enough to hit him. He allowed himself a smirk, but it was wiped off his face when a dagger bounced off the piece of rock he was about to put his hand on. He scrambled higher, a little faster than he was comfortable with, but soon he was clambering over the edge of the cliff.

There was no chance of the smelters following and by the time they reached the top, Ryza would be long gone. He looked to his right at the now unattended caravan. The few men that hadn't been cuffed were now attempting to unchain the rest.

Now they work together.

Ryza hadn't heard a single friendly word for the two weeks since the caravan had left Breggesa. Every single person down there had been out to make their own fortune. He hadn't even learnt any of their names because of how little they spoke about anything that wasn't reels.

At least they weren't trading in molten flux.

They could fend for themselves now. They would probably be recaptured once the remaining smelters realised what was going on. But Ryza was free. All he had to do was find the next trading post and hitch a ride.

Ryza turned around, ready to set off west, but was met with a sight that made his jaw drop. There was no horizon. Instead, all he could see was a tumultuous wall of sand, as high as the sky itself. It was rapidly bearing down on him, sucking up the dunes as fuel. Ryza could feel the oncoming gusts on his tongue. This one would be vicious, more vicious than the smelters down below. Suddenly, the canyon was looking mighty inviting.

Ryza swore to himself. He needed shelter. A cave would be perfect, but as he scanned the land, the only thing he saw was a rocky outcrop. He looked back up at the sandstorm. It seemed to have doubled in size in the time he hadn't been watching it. Enormous dark shapes were shifting in the belly of the thrashing haze.

Ryza began sprinting again, almost losing control of his legs as he belted down the sandy slope for the rocks. Before, it had been a simple race against the wits of some smelters, but now he was competing with the fury of the desert itself. If he hadn't secreted among those rocks by the time the storm hit, he'd be flung sky high by the howling wind. Ryza could feel it pushing against him, slowing his stride as the dunes began to shift under his feet.

He was almost there, but the sandstorm was closer. The rocks disappeared in an instant, but Ryza kept running. The wall of dust was upon him now, stretching over him like a monster's jaws, tendrils of sand reaching out for him.

Ryza burst into it.

He felt his feet leave the ground.

CHAPTER TWO

THE CONSCRIPT'S COLLAR

E VERY SINGLE ONE OF Ryza's senses disappeared the second he entered the sandstorm. He had to squeeze his eyes shut against the gale, but he could feel tiny grains of dust already worming through at the corners. Breathing was near impossible; his nose and mouth were clogged with sand. He couldn't even feel his own skin from the blasting it was taking.

When his feet had left the ground, he thought he was done. That he was sky-bound for good. But he had come crashing down a moment later, sprawling on all fours as he struggled against the wash of sand. It would bury him if he couldn't get to his feet. But try as he might, he could only crawl through the shifting ground.

He had to find those rocks. They had to be somewhere ahead of him. He began moving, progressing inch by painful inch. The further he went, the more exhausted he grew. A shadow darkened his vision. The ground continued to rumble, the sound warping from howling wind to grinding of metal as the sun itself was blotted out.

When Ryza next opened his eyes, he wasn't met by the endless wall of sand. Instead, he was lying on a metal cot in a small room, so cramped he could barely stretch his legs out. There was an odd smell of oil in the air and Ryza could feel the sandstorm still gusting outside.

Ryza sat up with a groan, rubbing his head with both hands. Someone must have dragged him out of the gale and into their shack, although he hadn't seen any kind of structure when he was first searching for cover. His palms felt red raw, but at least they were scrubbed clean of blood. Whoever cleaned him up hadn't been gentle about it. His clothes weren't in a much better state. There were so many rips in his shirt he might as well have been naked.

The room was spinning around him slightly. The smelter's beating was still swirling in his head. He coughed out some sand and made to rub his throat, his fingers only finding something metal. His fingers scrabbled at it, finding seams and messy welds but nothing he could prise apart. He yanked at it with both hands, but it didn't budge.

Secured tightly around his neck was a steel collar of some kind, so tight it almost stopped him from swallowing. There was something on his wrist as well. A flat metal bracelet, the face of it possessing two different dials. The first was a red one that spun wildly in all directions. The second was black and stock still.

Panic was rising in his throat, only to be met by the barrier that was the collar. He needed it off. *Now.* But the room he was in offered him little help. To his left was a bare metal wall, made of a patchwork of scraps that had been slapped on over the years in a shoddy fashion. To his right, a shelf full of rusty medical instruments, some still encrusted in bits of some other unfortunate soul.

They better not have used those on me.

He ran his hands over the collar again. Something was off about it. There was no notch or loop on it. Why collar someone if not to chain them to something? He wriggled a finger under the collar, running it around until he felt something pointed. He tried to swallow. Do something wrong and that might end up in his neck. He shouldn't mess with it, at least not using magic.

He could only wonder who'd brought him here. Ryza twisted in his cot and swung his feet to the floor. His head started to spin faster and before he knew it, he was doubled over, ready to puke. A grumble in his stomach told him not much would come out, spare for bile.

After gathering himself, he planted his feet firmly on the floor, wincing as his bare soles touched the grimy metal. He'd always lamented having tender feet because he was useless without shoes. He scanned the room again, hoping for a sign of his boots.

Nothing.

Nevertheless, he stood up, rolling on the arches of his feet as he hobbled to the door. He tried the handle, but it didn't yield, rattling the lock that rested on the other side.

I went from being a prisoner to a prisoner. What a deal.

He was hungry, battered, and lost to boot. How long would he have to wait until someone came to tell him why he was here?

Ryza paced the room, replaying this thought in his mind over and over while his feet grew accustomed to the ground. This is what happened when he went out on his own into the world. His father had warned him repeatedly of it. He should have stayed in Breggesa. A trading caravan was a stupid idea, anyway. Following his father's footsteps, his business—

No! I'm never doing that!

The thought felt like a lightning strike, a flash of vindication. No matter how bleak being trapped in a strange room with a quaking sandstorm outside, it was better than the alternative. Ryza's resolve hardened again, just like it had when he'd joined the trading caravan. He had to get out of here and he had to do it alone.

But other than the rusty tools, there was nothing else in the cramped room that would aid his escape. He checked the door. There was no visible locking mechanism on the inside. The door must have been bolted from the out. He patted down his pockets.

Emptied. It was all trinkets, anyway.

None of what he had would be useful now. Except... He checked his underpants. The vial was still there! He held it to the dimly glowing orb of light on the ceiling. Half full of a deep emerald green liquid and likely more valuable than anything his saviour had stolen, it was his key to escape. He glanced back at the shelves again, spotting a battered brush and grabbing it.

Perfect.

He sat back down on the cot, carefully unstoppering the vial and dipping the brush in. Ryza only let the tip touch the surface of the precious liquid, just long enough to draw ink before he whipped it out and stoppered the vial. He stuffed it back in his underpants and turned to his left wrist, painting two blocky runes on his skin, just below the metal band. The pair made up a single axiom, each rune carrying its own meaning and purpose. One was to find metal, the other to control it.

Both were dry in a matter of seconds and Ryza went over to the door and pressed his hand against it. Just like before, he shut his eyes, concentrating. The first rune slipped into his palm, burning white-hot, expanding his reach to the other side of the metal door. The next one burned and he took hold of the sliding bolt. With a flick of his hand, it unlatched and the door swung open slightly.

Ryza couldn't believe his luck. Manipulating metal had never been his strong suit, it was something his father never wasted a moment in impressing upon him. It almost defeated the point of being a Kretatic.

Almost.

It was a bitter thought, but Ryza didn't care. He'd just taken his first step to freedom. He was about to pull the door open when it was shoved from the other side, throwing him backwards. Before he could gather himself, a hand was planted square in his chest, pushing him down onto the cot.

'I hate it when you metal mouths start fucking around with the doors!'

It was a woman's voice. Deep, brash and impatient. Ryza looked up at her. She would have been in her mid-forties, a mane of wild brown hair tied back in a rough tail. Easily taller than him by half a foot. Her face was wrinkled and scarred, accustomed to a scowl.

She wore a tunic of thick black leather with an armoured mantle that covered her shoulders. Her pants were lined with pockets, but that didn't seem to be enough for the woman. Strapped around her hip was a small leather satchel, bulging with whatever its contents were. However, Ryza was paying the most attention to the massive rifle slung over her shoulder. With an entire metal body, the weapon was a metre long and looked to weigh enough to be used as a battering ram.

'Didn't know if you were a smelter or not. It's why I locked you in here,' she continued. 'It's not often we drag the half-dead out of sandstorms, so count yourself lucky.' Suddenly she was in his face.

'You better not be carrying any molten flux on you neither!'

'I never would,' Ryza blurted.

'Good. Almost lost a leg to that once.'

Ryza's head was spinning again, and what the woman had just said barely made any sense. 'Why did you save me?' he blurted like an idiot.

The tall woman snorted. 'When we dragged you out of the storm, you were covered in blood and sand, so we took you in either as a killer or a dead man. You're still breathing, so you best come through on the other thing, conscript.'

'Conscript?' Ryza said quickly. 'Why did you just call me conscript?'

The woman whipped a sheaf of battered parchment from behind her back and glanced over them. 'What's your name, boy? And where were you born?'

He hesitated. Should he tell her? He probably wouldn't have a choice. She could cave his head in just by swinging that rifle down.

'Ryza and I'm from Breggesa.'

She propped the rifle against the wall and scrawled something on the front page. 'Ryza of Breggesa... Description: Cropped red hair, green eyes, cheek bones... fresh scar on left temple... bit underfed and pale.' She glanced up at him over the papers. 'That's you?'

He nodded slowly. Right now, underfed was the most accurate word for him. He waited as she scrawled down something else. This didn't seem like a woman who liked to be interrupted. Eventually she looked back to him, her dull yellow eyes measuring him up.

'I'm going to give you the quick and dirty version of things, Ryz.'

He frowned at this. Was she really in such a hurry she couldn't bother with the extra syllable of his name?

She continued. 'When you got pulled into the healers' bay, they thought you were so torn up that you would only be worth fixing if you were one of us. I made the decision to slap a collar on you and take a gamble you'd come good or at least you'd mix in with the rest of the conscripts that just came from Breggesa. I am First Recruiter Yuvet. You'll call me ma'am and you'll call anyone above you sir or ma'am. Right now, that's everyone.'

Ryza shook his head to clear it. 'I... I don't get it. Where am I?'

An open palmed blow struck the top of his already pounding head before he could blink and Yuvet barked back at him: 'Where am I, *ma'am*?'

'Sorry,' Ryza said on reflex. He took a deep breath. 'Where am I, ma'am?'

She drew herself up to her full height, even taller than at first.

'You're aboard the walking fortress of Revance. Currently, you are its newest conscript. That collar you have 'round your neck is connected to that shiny new bracelet. Don't ask me how, you've got to find another metal mouth to tell you that. The red dial on it will point you home to Revance and the black one tells you how much time you've got left to make it back. You've got twelve hours before that collar chokes you to death. Only way to stop it is touching either it or the wristband to Revance.' The tone in which Yuvet recited this was tired and rehearsed, as if she'd said it a million times before.

It took a long while for Ryza to absorb all of this. Yuvet stared him down as he did, but for once she didn't seem like she was in a rush. He'd heard of Revance before. A semi-mercenary force that rode on the back of a massive metal castle, walking back and forth across the dunes and fuelled by the magic of a creator long dead.

It was the way most cargo was hauled across the Droughtlands. If one could afford it. Whenever his father had mentioned it, he said they'd fight for whoever would throw a sack of reels at them. Either way, Ryza never believed the stories. They all seemed too grand, too fantastical.

What he was more focused on was the collar around his neck. The constricting metal, cold whenever he shifted, was closing in on his throat. He checked the bracelet. The black needle was already edging down, threatening to spin out of control. Yuvet's scarred hand grabbed it and slammed his wrist against the wall.

'You're going to have to learn to do that yourself,' she grunted. 'Get up and come with me. If you're well enough to try to break out of here it means this bed is wasted on you.'

Not wanting to be hit again, Ryza stood up and followed her out of the cramped room, hobbling as the ground seemed to stab at his bare feet. The mixture of grime, dried blood and the constant, strange rumbling that pulsed through the floor didn't make it easy to keep up with Yuvet's brisk pace.

She led him out to a larger room, the walls lined with more cots and chairs. Half were occupied by injured men and women, the other half by the bloodstains they'd left. Healers wearing dirty aprons tended to the patients. They all possessed yellow eyes, a prime sign of being a Curiktic, their magic drawing from the sun. Light and fire. Right now, the latter was being used to mend grizzly wounds.

Flashes of light appeared at their fingertips to fuse skin together and incinerate infection, producing a pitiful whimpering from whichever poor sod was on the receiving end. Ryza almost felt sorry for them. He'd been fixed up like that before. It was just as painful as the cuts themselves and left ugly scars to remember them by. But he didn't spare the wounded a second glance. Instead, he quickened his pace to stay by Yuvet's side.

'Look, I don't know what's going on here, but I didn't sign up for this.' He jabbed at the metal collar on his neck. 'So, I would appreciate it, *ma'am*, if we could get this collar off and I could be on my way.'

Yuvet snorted at him in response. 'You getting cold feet, conscript? We'll get some boots on you soon enough.'

They exited the healer's bay through a propped open door, turning left into a corridor so narrow that Ryza had to slip back behind Yuvet. On the left they passed countless other doors, most sealed shut. The rumbling grew louder in the corridor, mixing in with the disembodied calls for soldiers that emanated from pipes on the ceiling. On the right, at about eye level, were narrow viewports, giving way to blue sky outside. Ryza ignored them, still trying to keep Yuvet's attention.

'But I don't want anything from you. I want out!'

Yuvet halted and spun, fury across her face. 'Fine!' She grabbed his collar and roughly jammed his face against the nearest viewport. Wind whipped against his skin, so strong it forced him to squint. The dunes yawned out before him, the distance to the ground more than a deathly fall.

The fortress was massive and the way it moved… Now he knew why the room had been rocking and shaking. He could remember the first tiny arcanite he'd ever created, the one his father had taught him to make. He'd called it the scarab, something Ryza still hadn't mastered. It had a bulbous, dome-like body with a single horn that protruded from the front, made to sense where it was going. This was held up by four legs, straight rods attached to the body by vertical pistons and small cylindrical feet at the other end.

Revance was the same concept, coated in rust and enlarged a thousand-fold. Ryza watched in awe as the leg ahead of him lifted with a scream of metal and compressed air twenty metres above the sand. Then it began swinging forward, the air it displaced throwing a sweeping wave of dust across the dunes. It froze for a moment as it reached the end of its stride before lowering itself back down to the ground. The corridor shook from the impact and Ryza watched open-mouthed as the other leg lifted and followed suit.

'Now I can either toss you out there and let you fall to your death, or you can follow some bloody orders!' She pulled him away from the port and set off again, leaving him to regain himself and follow. 'But before you do decide to jump ship and let collar death take you, I want to confirm something.'

CHAPTER THREE

COLD AND CALM

Yuvet led Ryza through corridors and hallways, flocked with armed soldiers that gawped at him, then down rickety stairs so steep they might as well have been ladders. Eventually they were under the shell of Revance, negotiating their way along mesh catwalks towards a network of cages in the middle of the underside.

Yuvet practically danced her way across and Ryza wished he could do the same, but it would be impossible while he didn't have any damn shoes on. The metal weave underfoot was loose, catching his toes on every second step and threatening to snap them off and Revance's swaying had him clinging to the precious few handrails he could reach.

Each cage had only enough room for a man to stoop in it. Their feet would rely on wide-set metal bars made to show the perilous drop below. Attached to the side was a rusted lever, which Ryza could easily guess the purpose of. Only one held a prisoner. Half-naked and heavily bruised, the man was a pitiful sight. He was asleep, having wedged himself into the corner of his confines.

'This is the only smelter we picked up from the group that ambushed your caravan,' Yuvet grunted. 'The rest didn't want to come quietly.'

Ryza glanced around. It seemed strange that the other cages were empty. 'You don't usually take prisoners?'

'None of them survived the sandstorm down here. Saves us the trouble of finishing them off.' Yuvet let out a dark chuckle and leaned closer to the cage of the sleeping man.

'So, why did you want me to see him, ma'am?' Ryza asked slowly.

'I don't care about you seeing him. I want him to see you!'

She rattled the cage with the butt of her rifle, the vibrating clangs making the man jump and his legs slipped through the bars below him.

'Don't do it!' he blurted.

Yuvet ignored him. 'See this whelp?'

The smelter looked at Ryza and nodded hastily.

'Is he the one who escaped?'

He nodded again. 'Killed three of us before he took off and your lot showed up.'

'That's a shame, I was told four,' Yuvet muttered under her breath. 'Were your men carrying molten flux?'

The smelter shook his head rapidly. 'We were just sent out to grab more people. Only the traders carry it! They'd be just as bad as you lot are if they caught us taking it!'

Yuvet shrugged, her expression unchanged. 'Well, that's all we need you for.'

'You're letting him go?' Ryza blurted.

'In a way.' She reached over and put a hand on the lever. The smelter's eyes flew wide.

'No! Please! I can tell you—'

'Don't care.'

'There's a camp to the north-west—'

'There's a lot to the north-west!' Yuvet bellowed back at him.

'But even—'

Yuvet yanked the lever down hard and the bars under the smelter swung open, dropping him with a scream. But he wasn't gone yet. Clinging to the side of the cage, his desperate pleas turned incomprehensible as he dissolved into a blubbering mess.

'Looks like we're doing this the hard way,' Yuvet said. She swung her massive rifle to bear and pulled the trigger. A cannon blast deafened them all and even though Ryza wasn't holding the gun, the recoil still shook him.

The shot left a hole the size of a fist in the centre of the smelter's chest, a bloody cavern Ryza swore he could see straight through. The man's face paled as it turned to shock, his arms still flexed in a desperate grip around the bars, his mouth moving without making a sound.

'You wanted to kiss him goodbye, Ryza?' Yuvet shouted. 'Dead smelter. Nothing more pure and good in this world than this man's soon to be corpse.' She clapped a hand down on his shoulder. 'This is what Revance does. And I got a gut feeling you'll fit right in.'

Yuvet's words echoed into his head as if from a mile away. He was too stunned and horrified to say anything back. But each one of them had rung true, resonating deeply in his core. His whole life had been spent in fear of molten flux. The stuff was practically haunted. Liquid metal that could almost bring corpses back from the dead.

Almost.

In the back of his mind, a flaming rage he'd pushed back was starting to flare. It felt good. It warmed him. It was right.

With one last gasp, the smelter finally gave in and fell to the dunes below. The sound of his corpse thumping into sand didn't reach him over Revance's grinding cogs.

A part of Ryza wished he could have been the one to pull the trigger. For a long time, he'd been able to define the relationship he'd had with smelters and the flux they traded in as reluctant at best. His father had said they were a necessity. Letting Kretatics like themselves achieve more. But Ryza's discontent had been growing for a long time.

It was dirty work. When the flux was injected into a fresh enough corpse, it would knit the wounds, replacing what was once flesh with a strange and malleable silver coloured metal. Just enough that the body could stand without a hint of the person who'd once lived in it. They called them autominds. Kretatics could use them to make larger and larger machines, but they'd need more and more autominds. A few more of his father's words drifted into his mind.

What do we do when we run out of corpses? We make some more.

As Yuvet led him away, he suppressed a shudder. No matter how much that smelter begged or pleaded, he still deserved what he got.

Back inside Revance, they were climbing again, ascending to what had to be the upper decks. Thick fumes of engine oil made Ryza lightheaded and he had to time his breaths for whenever he walked past a gunport that leaked in merciful draughts of air. The people up here seemed older, more experienced, but that didn't stop them from staring at Ryza as they walked past.

Yuvet brought them to a stop at a counter built into the corridor's wall. Ryza could see dozens of racks of rifles in the room beyond it, where each weapon was in various states of disrepair, only three or four escaping the rust that plagued the fortress. Buckets of ammunition lay with them, brimming with slugs and spilling a few across the floor with the rocking of Revance's unsteady footsteps.

Ignoring the mess, Yuvet rapped on the counter with her bruised knuckles and turned to Ryza. 'This here is one of the many armouries of Revance. When you need ammo, you buy it here.'

Ryza frowned. 'I have to buy ammo?'

Yuvet didn't answer his question. She was too busy rummaging in her coat pockets. 'That reminds me...' She pulled out a satchel, gestured for him to hold out his hands, then poured a small pile of reels into them. 'Your recruitment dues.'

Ryza had always been able to count the tiny metal rings quickly. Half useless talent, but he could already tell this wasn't much. Maybe a day's wage in Breggesa. Before he could figure out what he was going to do with the pittance in his hands, a man approached the counter.

Short, squat and ugly, he didn't look like he'd even be happy to see his own mother. His hands were stained by the gun grease he'd long given up wiping away and when he breathed, it was with an open mouth. By the looks of it, his teeth and fingers were competing to see who there was less of. It was a tight race.

'What?' he grunted at Yuvet.

'Lovely to see you too, Prethy,' she replied.

He jabbed half a thumb at Ryza. 'Who's this?'

'A new conscript in need of new conscript things.'

Prethy held out his hand to Ryza. 'Reels.'

'How many?' Ryza asked.

Prethy barked something that would have been comprehensible if he had more than gums.

'He means all of them,' Yuvet translated. Before Ryza could protest, she'd taken his hand and tipped the contents into Prethy's. Satisfied, the man shuffled out of sight.

'And get him some new bloody clothes as well!' Yuvet called after him as she glanced back at Ryza's still stained rags. 'You pay for your ammo, clothes and equipment here. It means you take care of what's given to you and make your damn shots count. Same again with the food and anything else.'

'What if I don't have any reels?' Ryza said. 'Ma'am,' he added quickly as Yuvet's hand went up.

Yuvet leaned in closer and replied with a hiss. 'Then you figure out a way to find them.'

A slam of metal next to him made him jump. Prethy had returned and a pile of items now lay on the counter. A slightly fresher set of clothes, a small satchel that Ryza guessed contained some ammo, and on top of it all, a rifle. Yuvet grabbed it with one hand and offered it to him.

'You carry this with you everywhere you go. If I catch you without it I will personally hurl you off Revance.'

The rifle almost fell out of his hands it was so heavy. Most of its length was attributed to the heavy-set barrel enclosed in a thick-wired, square frame. Two-thirds of the way down were the important bits. The trigger, the sights and the loading action.

The trigger guard was large enough to fit his whole fist, the trigger comfortably resting two fingers and Ryza's hand felt right at home in it. He gave the trigger a few quick flexes, feeling the tough click roll from within. The sights were as simple as could be, a low post at the end of the barrel and a notch above the trigger to line it up.

The mechanism of the rifle was just as straight forward. Running across the right side of the rifle, between the trigger and the sights, there was a seam in the metal. This must be where the rifle broke apart. The two sections were held in place by an embedded metal slide, controlled by a round bar that could fit in his closed fist.

Ryza pulled it back, feeling an internal spring resisting him. Once it was all the way back, there was a click from within, holding it in place. The rifle broke open, swinging in towards his waist, supported by a wide hinge welded onto the left face above the trigger. The inside of the barrel was revealed, along with the hammer that would send the slug on its way.

Ryza snapped it shut, the hand-bar slamming back into place. He chewed his upper lip. Something wasn't right about it. He opened up the rifle and snapped it shut again. He'd heard two clicks. One had been when the hand-bar had locked back into place, but what had been the other one? He repeated the action, this time with his fingers on the trigger. Then it dawned on him.

'This one's broken,' he said unconsciously.

'How?' Prethy grunted.

'Shutting the rifle knocks the trigger enough to set off the firing mechanism.' Ryza actioned the rifle one last time just to make sure.

'Good spotting,' Yuvet murmured, unable to hide the slightly impressed tone in her voice. She looked to Prethy. 'Get him another.'

Prethy disappeared and there was a loud clang from beyond the counter as if he'd thrown the rifle across the room. Ryza leaned in slightly and spotted a small scrap heap that it now lay on top of.

'You've used a rifle before?' Yuvet asked.

'Never shot one. But I've seen them made.'

She hesitated, eventually giving a slow nod as a frown grew on her face. It was as if she suspected something, but she wasn't quite sure what. Prethy returned a minute later, handing him a more truncated rifle.

When Ryza picked it up, it had seemed lighter, but only if he wasn't thinking about it. He ran his hand across the trigger guard, his eyes shut as he searched for a feeling. It was... calm. Cold and calm. There was a magnetic resonance in the metal. It had once been enriched by a Kretatic like him, leaving a signature feeling only others of their kind could sense.

It made sense. Imparting one's resonance into metal, even if its function was purely mechanical, still allowed a greater reliability and control of the device. Just holding it seemed to slow his heart, steady his shaking hands. It was as if he were fully in control of the rifle. Ryza gave the trigger one last pull, savouring the almost silent click it produced.

'Perfect,' he muttered.

CHAPTER FOUR

LOST AND FOUND

O NCE AGAIN, YUVET WAS leading Ryza through a maze of iron corridors. People still gawped. He couldn't stare back at them. It was like he was either a prized beast or one being led to slaughter. The way Yuvet was telling it, he was now as much a soldier as they were. He had a gun, slugs and a strict lecture to never keep the latter inside the former in case of the seemingly common event of shooting out a comrade's kneecap. Though she never mentioned if it was by accident.

Now he was armed, he had an escape. He had no need to be a prisoner on this metal monster with his throat bound by iron. All he had to do was slip away, find something to break off the collar and fade into the sands. It was simple. Hell, he'd done something similar a few days before, which was how he'd ended up here.

Is running and escaping just going to be the rest of my life?

For a moment, his mind flashed back to the smelter, trapped in the cage and about to fall to his death. The fear in the man's eyes, the bloodlust howling in Ryza's head. Just the taste of it left him wanting more in a sick and twisted way. Was it wrong of him to want to stay here? Not just to fight, but to hunt down more smelters?

He needed to think in the moment. Ryza set his eyes searching. He'd already passed a hundred branching corridors and there had to be a hundred more. The key was finding the right one. One that would lead to a pair of bolt cutters and not a dead-end. He began to lag behind Yuvet. She never once looked back to check on him. Fear must keep her conscripts in line. Fear of her or the collar.

Five steps.

Ten steps.

Then he was gone.

A chute with a ladder had presented itself on a crowded thoroughfare. His footsteps were lost in the racket of shifting cargo and he could simply clamber down into the curling corridor below, his path now set for the belly of this mechanical beast. The forge rooms —as Yuvet had called them— would be the place to find tools. Big tools. Magic wasn't an option to get the collar off. Getting through the resonance instilled in it would take him hours and that was if the damn thing wasn't attached to his neck. Brute force would be quicker. It always was.

Navigating Revance at Yuvet's back was hard enough, but doing it alone was impossible. Every path was busy. Stopping for even a moment would have him run over by foot traffic, yet keeping the rapid pace of the others soon had him lost. Picking a path was futile. They either led in loops or dead ends and he didn't want to be caught by Yuvet down the latter. He stopped in a small nook, taking a deep breath to suppress a shudder.

What would she do to me now?

Ryza knew he'd never find his way anywhere on his own, but others might. All he had to do was follow them. He watched the crowd dashing back and forth. Conscripts looking probably just as scared as he did, still uncomfortable with their collars. Grizzled veterans, herding groups of them along. Men and women with crates of food, supplies and gods knew what else. And then he saw her.

A woman barely older than him walked past. She wore a heavy chainmail apron, with shallow pockets that attempted to hide an array of pliers and other tools. Her hands were covered by thick black leather gloves that seemed to smoulder from fresh welds. Her brown hair was streaked by sweat and grease, kept in by the heavy metal mask that was propped on top of her head. But most importantly, her eyes were green.

Ryza began to trail her. Out of all the people of the Droughtlands, Kretatics —like him— were the most likely to be working on some sort of machine. It was their lot in life to make the blasted things. Others tended to trust them for little else. The woman walked with a strong gait, all square shoulders and big strides, but the way she gave everyone who passed her just enough side-eye threw him off. It was what someone paranoid would do when they were ready to lash out at anyone in their way.

Just like I'm doing.

He focused his eyes on the ground, only glancing up every few seconds to make sure he was still on the woman's trail. The path she took somehow became busier than before. But this was good. Less chance of him being noticed. All the people staring at him before must have only been looking because he was with Yuvet. The corridors widened into service tunnels and then...

Ryza stopped dead in his tracks. All thoughts of escape temporarily vanished from his mind as his mouth dropped open. Before him was a cavernous space, walls of patchwork metal and a floor crawling with workers, until even that gave out for a gaping hole right in the middle, open to the shifting dunes below.

Near the edge of the hole was a mountain of scrap metal. Workers were taking from it, using either tools or magic to bend it into shape, then affixing it somehow to the inner walls of Revance. The supporting arches that ran across the ceiling were the most unnerving part. They groaned and flexed with each step of the fortress, expanding and retracting like it was all about to collapse.

Whatever space wasn't occupied by workers was instead filled by roving arcanites. Magical constructs of magnetised metal, these ramshackle creatures took whatever form their creators could be bothered to make. Most were little more than two small wheels and an arm with a pincer on the end. Enough to get around and drag something small with it. They moved in packs, patrolling back and forth between workstations and scrap piles, or following the more important looking Kretatics as they went about their business.

These machines were the magical domain of Ryza's people. No matter how big or small, an arcanite could be made from just a few pieces of metal and a well-placed axiom. All it required after that was a portion of the creator's mind. The more complicated, the more of one's mind it needed to have loaned to its ongoing existence.

One of the small, two-wheeled creations rolled past him. It would be powered only by an idle thought. A bigger creature followed it, with four creaking legs supporting a brimming trough of tools. Someone would be wandering around half-drunk to control that.

He'd never been too great with arcanites, his father had said he lacked the focus. There were ways of remedying that, but they were now unspeakable to Ryza. It was for this reason that he always marvelled the big machines that Kretatics could control on their own and why he could barely comprehend Revance's existence. But he wouldn't have to for much longer. His escape was near.

Ryza tore his eyes away, spotting his quarry further down the hall and set after them. He passed a dozen workstations where people hammered away. The combined racket of this place was loud enough that he didn't have to worry about his footsteps being heard. The woman ahead of him stopped and took her place at an empty forge, flipping down her mask. Now Ryza could see the back of her collar.

She was a conscript, too.

Her workstation was made up of a small cauldron of molten iron surrounded by charred tools. She took a few hunks of metal and began dipping them in, pressing them together and working an axiom into them for good measure.

The process occupied her completely, enough for Ryza to dart forward and steal a pair of bolt cutters on the perimeter of her workspace as she tended to the forge. He retreated into darkness, wedging himself between half an upturned buggy and a sheet of chain-link fence. From here he could see out, but no one would have a chance at seeing him, unless they were specifically looking for him. He took a quick scan of the forge room. No sign of Yuvet.

Perfect.

Wedging the bolt cutters around the collar nearly choked him. The only way he'd get enough leverage was if he wrapped his leg around one handle and kept the other pressed against his body. He braced himself. If this collar was as deadly as Yuvet had said, he'd have to do it quick and clean. His body tensed and he was about to squeeze when a muffled voice made him jump.

'Please don't do that.'

Another woman was standing in front of him, arms crossed, head cocked slightly to the side. She took off her mask, revealing a short crop of white-blonde hair. Her face was pale, pointed and elegant, the kind not meant for hard work, but she seemed to have missed that notion.

'Take that off him,' she grunted to the arcanite at her foot. It rolled forward and snatched the bolt cutters from Ryza's grip, easily strong enough to overpower him. 'Last thing I want to do is clean your corpse out of here. Even then, the smell of the blood...' She wrinkled her nose in disgust. 'Makes everything rusty as well.' A smirk crossed her face, which Ryza could register was her default expression. 'That's what I'll call you! Because of your hair!'

He clambered to his feet, pushing out of his hiding hole. 'My name is Ryza.'

'It's Rusty to me. I'm Holm and— Ferrick! Get over here!'

The woman he'd been tailing looked up and approached. She took her mask off, revealing dark patches under her eyes and cracked lips as she breathed heavily. Both of their eyes were green, but there was a stark difference. Where Holm's were radiant and piercing, Ferrick's were dull and murky. It was the toll that too many arcanites and not enough rest could take on a person.

'Can you explain to Rusty here why we don't try and take the collars off?'

Ferrick adjusted hers unconsciously, revealing a glimpse of a rather purple bruise underneath. 'Break the collar and it breaks the timer on it, sending four bolts of metal straight through your throat and spine.' Clearly she'd said it one too many times.

'Then how can I get it off?' Ryza asked her quickly.

'Only Forgemaster Tyrag can do that and only when he's good and satisfied you're one of *us*,' Holm said.

Ferrick pointed to an empty dais at the other end of the room, marked out by the four curved pillars that arched over it. 'He's usually up there.'

'But now he's down here,' Holm said, a note of foreboding in her voice. 'It was nice knowing you, Rusty.' She gave him a quick, forced handshake, her other hand giving him a hearty slap on the hip. It must have been some kind of tradition aboard Revance. She took a step back and sat herself on Ferrick's workstation, ready to witness the spectacle.

Marching along the cleared aisle was a bald and weedy man. The stubble cresting his chin was grey like iron and the wrinkles in his face were carved deep into a scowl. Something had displeased him and Ryza could guess why he was looking straight at him.

'What the hell do you think you're doing distracting my workers?' he roared, pointing a single, crooked finger at him. Trailing off his wrists were heavy golden manacles, a short length of chain hanging off each. Bizarre to some, but Kretatic superstition had gold as the key to greater control over an arcanite.

'Rusty here had cold feet and decided he'd rather not be able to breathe than serve with us.'

Tyrag was in Ryza's face now. Three inches shorter than him, the man still managed to tower. 'Let it be known, I don't like rust on my fortress,' he growled. 'What is your real name, boy?'

'Ryza, sir.'

'Well, Ryza, if you're looking for an easy way out, there's a nice hole over the way you can jump out of any time. Spare us all the mess. But if you happen to survive whatever the hell Yuvet is about to do to you and you feel like doing some real work, come down here to the forge rooms and get your hands dirty. We can always use more Kretatics. We never have enough idle minds around here.'

On a normal day, Tyrag's last words would sicken him, but there was something far more concerning coming his way. With mounting dread, he turned to see Yuvet storming through the forge rooms, utter fury in her eyes.

Ryza only remembered the first half of Yuvet's beating. She'd single-handedly redefined the idea of physical punishment to him. Gun stocks, walls, fists, boots and whatever else Yuvet could reach was slammed into every part of his body, all of this managed while hauling him through the corridors of Revance for everyone to see.

An eternity later, Yuvet was dragging him upright, pulling his swollen face close to hers. 'Listen close, Ryz. People I'm about to throw you in with are your squad and you'd better not let on that you just tried to desert us. Next time, I'll save myself the trouble of beating you and let them do it.'

A door with a large number "5" carved into it opened behind Ryza and Yuvet shoved him into the room. His legs wobbled under him for half a second before he collapsed in a pile.

Everything hurt and the probing boot that poked his shoulder felt like a steel-toed kick. A pair of hands grabbed his shoulders and pulled him up, eliciting a pained groan from him. He leaned heavily against the wall, for the first time feeling the cool metal soothing his bruises.

It was only now he sensed Revance's magnetic resonance.

A wave of exhaustion began to flow into him and he could feel his mind slowing. His eyelids began to droop. All he could focus on was how the metal felt. It was just so... tired. That could only be expected. Yuvet had said Revance had been walking for years. But it was more than physical fatigue. There was something missing, some part of this feeling that didn't let it be complete.

A slap across Ryza's face snapped him out of it and he opened his eyes.

The room was downright claustrophobic. Where he was standing was barely wide enough for his shoulders, the ceiling just a few inches over his head. On either side of him were bunks built into the walls, narrow and without coverings. There were three on his left and two on his right, the bottom slot there occupied by a row of five metal drawers. Ahead was a small room with only enough space for four wobbly looking chairs and a table that was little more than a shelf jutting out of the wall.

Standing in front of him was a haughty woman, looking to be five years older than he was. She stared him down with a set of yellow eyes and for a moment Ryza thought he was staring at another version of Yuvet. The only difference was the slightly more youthful appearance and the buzz cut she sported. In the bunk to his right at eye level, another girl was staring at him. She was much closer to his age, if not younger. She'd rolled over only to regard him with bleary blue eyes. Her sun-bleached hair was tied into a rough knot, the colour seeming to blend in with her tanned skin.

How could she sleep when the entire room shifted every minute?

There were two boys, also his age, sitting at the table. The one on the left had a mop of curly black hair, just enough to hide his eyes when combined with the fact he was hunched low over the book spread out before him, his nose only an inch from the page. The other boy leaned back lazily in his chair, a raised eyebrow and a friendly smirk directed at Ryza. Like Ryza, he had green eyes.

The woman took a half step closer, just enough to make Ryza move back slightly. She tilted her head.

'Is this him?' the girl in the bunk said as she rubbed her eyes.

'Can't be, you heard the state of him,' the boy with the book mumbled.

The cocky looking boy stood up and peered over the tall woman's shoulder at him. 'Looks like he took a few extra blows than we first thought. They're calling you *Bloodfist*, lad.'

Ryza's eyes snapped to the boy. *Bloodfist?* What the hell did that mean? He looked down at his hands. They were still red raw from the sandstorm, with flecks of blood hardening under his fingernails. Ryza's stomach lurched as he remembered that the blood wasn't his.

'What's your name, boy?' the woman growled.

'Ryza,' he mumbled through a busted lip.

'Smelters beat you that bad?' the cocky looking boy said.

He gave a weak nod, glad for the opportunity to lie and the boy gave a low whistle. 'I wonder what the other guys look like.'

'They're dead and that's what Revance pays us for.' She clapped him on the shoulder. 'I'm Ditric. Welcome aboard.'

'Ruka,' the girl on the bunk said. She gave a lazy wave then closed her eyes to doze.

'Gry,' the boy with the book muttered.

'And I'm Haven,' the cocky looking boy said. He reached past Ditric and did his best to give a bone-crushing handshake to Ryza, but all he could feel was a numb throbbing from his knuckles. Ditric gave Haven a sharp elbow to the gut to force him back, then motioned to the bottom bunk on Ryza's left.

'Your bunk. Your drawer is on the other side.' She flicked a finger to the low ceiling. 'Rifles live up there.'

Ryza followed her gaze to see a few suspended hooks bearing the others' rifles. They were as battered and scratched as his, the muzzles burnt and charred. Either they saw frequent action or they were never cleaned. He looked back down. Ditric had already turned her back to him, now sitting opposite Gry and his book, peering out a narrow gunport.

'What a warm introduction,' Haven muttered. He sidled forward, regarding the full view of Ryza with a smirk.

'She's always like this.' The sound was a whisper from Ruka, barely making its way into his ears over the distant, grinding mechanics of Revance's limbs. It was the magical talent of Reythurists like her. Marked by blue eyes, they could control the air itself, sometimes even without an axiom. Ryza tried to keep the suspicion out of his eyes as he regarded her. They always knew more than what was said.

And I'm the shifty one.

He glanced over at Gry. Under his mopped and matted hair, his ears had probably pricked too.

Haven gave him what was supposed to be a warm punch on the shoulder, perfectly striking a bruise Yuvet had just laid there. 'They messed you up *real* good. What's your story, then?'

'I was with a trading caravan—'

'Traders ain't fighters,' Ditric said. He flinched, but she still didn't look at him.

'It was a lucky escape. I had an axiom ready and metal and those smelters were stupid.'

A grin cracked on Haven's face. 'You know, I was about to join a caravan too.' He drew himself up a bit more. 'But Revance was a-calling! The pay seemed a whole lot more promising, too. Me and Ruka joined at Breggesa. That's where you're from, right?'

Ryza nodded.

'Gry's from a place called Lautis—'

Months away. No wonder he was so dirty.

'—and Ditric started in Iroka, but she's from all over the place—'

'Used to be a mercenary,' she cut in. 'Got paid for protecting rich kids like you, Ryza. Was hoping they'd pay more here, even that I could skip this stupid collar shit... Even the pay though, most of that goes right back into Revance. I'd kill to have a few reels on the side.' She glanced over at him, measuring him up one more time. 'You may sound it, but I ain't ever seen a rich kid so skinny. What's your story?'

'Just... had to make a run for it.'

'What a terrible lie,' Ruka muttered. She turned over.

The others ignored him now, except for Haven.

'It's alright, mate. We're all just here for the reels, eh? Look, you're beat, have a rest and you can tell us in the morning.'

Ryza's knees were beyond functioning, so he was forced to collapse backwards while clinging to the bunks beside him, before rolling sideways into his. It was a joke of a bed, a piece of cloth covering a sheet of rattling metal. He bunched up his coat into some semblance of a pillow and shut his eyes. Chatter continued around him, indistinct over the never-ending grind of Revance. The constant shifting movement would haunt him for every day he was trapped aboard this damn fortress.

CHAPTER FIVE

TARGET DOWN RANGE

Tʜᴇ ꜱᴏᴜɴᴅ ᴏꜰ ᴀ loud clang coming from right next to Ryza's head made him wake with a lurch. On a well-trained instinct, he sat bolt upright, only to slam his head into the bunk above him. A stream of curses escaped his mouth as he rubbed his forehead. He could hear the *tap-tap-tap* of a boot kicking against metal.

When he opened his eyes, he was greeted with the sight of exactly that, knocking against the frame of his bunk, inches from his head. He leaned out and found the smirking face of the girl from the forge rooms, but she wasn't looking at him.

'So Ditric, looks like you finally found yourself a fifth!'

Ryza watched as a fist swung out from the bunk above him, which Holm deftly side-stepped.

'Get the hell out of here, Holm!' Ditric spat.

Holm put on a face of mock hurt. 'I just wanted to check up on my old friend! Came as soon as I heard you got a full team. Anyway, who's your new boot-licker down there?'

'See for yourself,' Haven's voice said, carrying a note of loathing for the woman Ryza hadn't thought possible.

Holm looked down at Ryza and her face lit up like a firework.

'Rusty! I wasn't expecting to see you here!' She glanced back at Ditric's bunk. 'We're already friends, you see,' she said in a gloating tone. 'I guess I'll be seeing you lot around. I'll have to look in on your training too, so I can make sure you're still as good as you say you are!'

Before anyone could say anything, Holm had given the bunk one more hardy kick and skipped out of the room, slamming the door behind her.

Ryza swore under his breath, feeling the muscles in his shoulders relax. He could only hope he wouldn't be waking up like that every day. And what did she mean by boot-licker? Or friends!?

Ditric's boots suddenly hit the floor and she was crouched in front of him, her jaw locked.

'So, you and her are friends?' Ditric said. 'Thinking of chasing after her, are you?'

Ryza propped himself up on his elbows. 'I am definitely *not* her friend.'

Haven's face appeared, hanging from the bunk above. 'Can't blame you for chasing that, she's all there on the outside,' he said with an upside-down grin.

'I am definitely not going after *that*, either!' Ryza said quickly. 'I only met her when I was lost and ended up in the forge rooms.' It was a slight lie, but it was better than revealing himself as a deserter. 'They all seemed unstrung down there.'

'Probably because they are,' Ditric said, standing up with a groan. 'But she's worse. You better stay well away from her. I knew her before Revance. She was always rotten. I swore I'd never see her again after—'

'Oh, come on Ditric, we know the story,' Ruka complained as she slipped out of her bunk. 'Tell it again and my ears will fall off.'

Ryza glanced between the two as they stared each other down, silently wishing Ditric would prevail. Why he wanted to hear more about Holm was beyond him, but this seemed like tantalising gossip.

Ditric grabbed her rifle from the ceiling hooks and groaned. 'Fine! We have to get moving anyway. But if I ever catch you hanging around her again...' She gave her rifle two firm slaps, causing something inside it to rattle.

Message received.

After pulling on boots and collecting rifles, they left their room, beginning the winding journey through Revance to the food halls. Breakfast was in order, whatever form that took. Ryza made sure to follow the others closely, noting every turn, ladder and staircase they passed. If he was going to be stuck here, he might as well know his way around.

More conscripts streamed through the corridors, jostling along as they dragged their heavy wristbands against the walls. According to Yuvet, it only needed to be tapped once every twelve hours, but Ryza couldn't help but join the rest.

Trudging boots and scraping metal. The chorus of Revance.

When they reached the mess hall, the long tables were half full, the number of those seated slowly increasing as people trickled in from a dozen different side doors. They queued up for food, the uniforms turning the crowd into a swaying mass of worn brown leather. More than half were weighed down with metal collars just like his.

Revance seems to be more conscript than commander.

Some could be veterans and leaders, for all Ryza knew, but he couldn't tell here. If they were back in Breggesa, they'd blend in with the peasants that lived at the outer walls. Spare for the rifles. The guards that kept watch over Breggesa were outfitted in robes of brilliant blue with shining silver breastplates over the top. He turned to Ruka, who was in the queue behind him, and raised the point.

'Haven't you figured it out yet? We don't get nice things here, even these coats... on the outside we would have got ten of them for what we had to pay. At least we all end up looking the same. Harder for anyone to get singled out.'

'But how would we know who's who?' Ryza asked.

Ruka shrugged. 'I guess that's all in the training. When I got recruited, they just told us to come with as little else as possible. Anyway, get your reels ready.'

They shuffled forward, eventually reaching the front of the line. He'd been expecting to see a team of cooks crewing a canteen, however all that was there was a slot in the wall, through which a small tray of food was shoved. Ryza passed through the three reels Haven had lent him, took the tray and stepped to the side as Ruka received hers.

They found seats halfway down the hall and, once he was settled,

Ryza looked down at his meal. There wasn't much. Just a bowl of coarse grain that looked like half-crushed biscuits and two more hunks of cured meat which he didn't know the origin of. If that's what three reels bought, he'd be starved by the next pay. Ryza glanced around. Gaunt cheeks worked to get the meal down as fast as possible.

Probably to make it taste better.

It only took them minutes to be done with it. Following Ditric's lead, the five of them got up and began making their way out of the dining hall. For a moment Ryza had been expecting them to be heading back to their cabin, though Ditric quickly informed him that they were heading for the firing range. Apparently it was their day for rifle training, though how this was scheduled seemed arbitrary at best.

The range was bare bones. It was a single long room with the far wall missing, giving a distant view out the rear of Revance and the vibrantly blue sky beyond it. After a morning inside the fortress, it was the first colour Ryza had seen that wasn't that of drab metal.

Round metal targets stood at intervals along the way, their surfaces dented from use and the posts supporting them bent. A bench ran across the room near where they had entered, separating them from the range itself.

Yuvet was there, leaning against it with her arms crossed, rifle propped against the wall at her side, nearly as tall as she was. She fixed each of them with a steely gaze as they filed in. It was enough to make Ryza shiver.

She remained silent as other teams of conscripts gathered in the room, the more nervous members of the groups pinning themselves against the wall, as far away from Yuvet as possible. Ryza had half a mind to join them. As Yuvet's eyes scanned over the collective, about thirty of them, she lingered on Ryza and let out a grunting chuckle.

Probably happy with the good work she'd done on me yesterday.

An absolute shiner of a black eye had well and truly bloomed on the left side of his face and a dull ache in his left wrist made it hard to hold his rifle without looking like an amateur. Though most around him seemed to have the same problem.

'Organise yourselves! One group per booth, revolving,' Yuvet barked.

There was a rapid shuffling as they split into loose lines and Ryza found himself standing with his squad ahead of him.

'I want you each to take it in turns to step up to the bench and fire five slugs at the closest target down range, then step back. I'll provide instruction as I see fit.'

Ditric was the first up, though she wasn't there for long. Not even a minute had passed before her rifle had discharged five rounds, four of them bouncing off the designated target. The fifth missed, ricocheting off the walls a few times before flying out the far end of the range.

With an audible grumble, Ditric stepped back, Gry taking her place. He took his time, methodically loading his rifle with excruciatingly deliberate gestures, to the point Yuvet barked at him to hurry up. His timed and careful aim resulted in only two hits and when he was done, he stepped back without a word.

By now, Ryza's ears were ringing, the tang of acrid gun smoke stinging his eyes. Haven approached the bench, managing a respectable three hits. Next was Ruka and while she struggled to load the rifle, even dropping the slug once or twice, she still hit the target four times.

Now it was Ryza's turn. He stepped up, swinging his rifle off his shoulder. When he caught it, he hesitated for a second, letting the calm resonance of the metal flow through him. The air around him felt thinner and his head grew slightly lighter. He reached for the slugs in his new pouch. They were just waiting for him, each one almost as thick as two of his fingers. He picked one and held it close to his eyes, turning it as the bronze casing caught the light. He noted the thick, spiralling grooves worked into the length of the round itself.

Ryza cracked the rifle open against his hip and slipped the slug into place, then snapped it shut and brought it to his shoulder. The sights lined up for him and his fingers found the trigger. It was a natural motion, as if the gun had taught him.

BLAM!

As the smoke cleared from the end of his rifle's barrel, he tilted his head and squinted at the target. There was definitely a solid dent that hadn't been there before. Ryza reloaded and levelled the rifle again.

BLAM!

Another direct hit. He glanced out of the corner of his eye at Yuvet, who was beginning to look impatient. She'd been all too keen to criticise the four before him, but she was yet to say a word.

Ryza fired off two more shots and he could feel a grin creeping across his lips. He couldn't suppress it. He was having too much fun. He lined up his last shot. If he could get this, he would be five for five! He pulled the trigger and he hadn't even felt the recoil before he knew it would be a hit.

He turned to Yuvet as he lowered his rifle, doing his best to wipe the smile off his face. However, she did not look impressed.

'You can operate it, conscript, but let's see how well you do when your target is fighting back.'

At least his squad looked suitably impressed. Except for Ditric. She was glowering at him, grinding her teeth. Her knuckles were clenched so tightly around her weapon that Ryza thought it was going to snap. She wouldn't meet his eyes, her attention firmly fixed on the rifle in his hands.

'Looks like you picked the right rifle,' she growled.

'All rifles are built the same,' Yuvet barked. 'Now, I want you all to—'

'Oh, come on!' Ditric burst out. 'You know these metal mouths are always doing something screwy! There's no way he could have hit all those shots by himself.'

Ryza had flinched at the term "metal mouth." He'd never said the words himself, they seemed too ugly for his tongue, but plenty had spat the phrase at him. Even Yuvet, just because she'd seen his green eyes. He clenched his jaw. He wouldn't rise to it. It wasn't worth the trouble. By the looks of it, he wouldn't need to.

Quick as a flash, Yuvet was in Ditric's face, nose to nose and somehow towering over her, even though they were nearly the same height.

'You will *not* interrupt me again, conscript!'

'Yes, ma'am!'

'Nor will you disrespect me, or any other superior soldier aboard Revance. Which, need I remind you, is everyone. Got it?'

Yuvet finished with a quick jab to the solar plexus, a blow that would likely leave Ditric winded for hours. She wilted slightly before straightening up, her face stoic.

'Call that settled,' Yuvet muttered as she stepped back, once again surveying the groups. They still stood gathered in their squads, only Ditric standing away. She was still fuming and glaring down range.

Yuvet began walking among them, barking the day's orders at each group of conscripts. Some were sent to the motor pool to protect cargo runs to nearby towns or meet for patrols.

They'd probably only be combing through wasteland out here.

Others, guard duty or arduous physical training. Whoever was assigned this seemed the most disappointed, but Ryza had already prepared himself for drudgery. After Ditric's outburst, Yuvet was probably saving the worst for last. To them, she only said two words.

'Dust off.'

Each member of his team reacted differently. Ditric gave a solemn nod. Haven hid a theatrical groan. Ruka let out an odd sigh of relief and Gry was emotionless.

Yuvet sent them off with a wave of her hand and they left, Ryza trailing behind the group. How Ditric had reacted earlier was fresh in his mind. He was the last to the door and was about to go through when a bark from Yuvet called him back.

'Ryza. A word.'

He froze. Had she believed Ditric? Was it against some kind of rule to enchant your gun? He hadn't even done it. It was just like that from the last person who used it. How would she even prove it? Slowly, he walked back over to the bench, where she was still leaning casually.

'Yes, ma'am?'

'I figured I should do this once all the others were gone because I don't want them thinking you're getting any special attention.'

'I won't need any, ma'am,' Ryza lied. In actual fact he was clueless. He was already praying that the rest of his team was waiting just outside for him, because he wouldn't be able to find them otherwise.

'You're completely wrong there, Ryz. Remember that you're missing two weeks of training. I can't have you blundering around without it because you will get yourself killed, which would be a shame after that display of marksmanship. You look to have some potential, whether it was from you or your gun.'

'Part of me wishes I had missed a shot or two...'

'Because of Ditric? Don't mind her, she's still trying to prove herself for some reason. The ex-mercs are always doing that. Here's what I want you to do. In the evenings, 'bout three hours after the last meal, report to my cabin. I'll make sure you get filled in on what you've missed. Healers are still having a tantrum at me for taking you on. I want to prove 'em wrong. Prove you're a killer.'

A grin was crackling along his lips, but something told him he had to keep a straight face. 'Thank you, ma'am,' he replied.

'Starting tonight. And make sure no one sees you. Anyway, get on your way, conscript.'

Ryza turned and headed for the door, letting the smile spread across his face. Yuvet would probably be crass and short tempered with him in her lessons, but that was better than being left in the dark. For the first time, someone cared about him.

CHAPTER SIX

FRIENDS AND RIVALS

A FEW HOURS LATER, Ryza was stretched out in the sun on an almost hidden deck, positioned somewhere on the rear shell of Revance. The jagged and pockmarked hide of the fortress made it perfect for climbing and Ryza had scaled it easily, slipping out through the motor pool undetected. Now he sat with his legs dangling off the edge of the small platform, his chin resting on the low guard rail that surrounded it. The only way someone would see him was if they were running along behind Revance or if they flung open the locked door behind him.

It turned out the "dust off" had just been clean up duty. Swapping their rifles for brooms, they'd been sent up and down the corridors of Revance, clearing the sand that had leaked in from the most recent storm, the same storm he'd been pulled out of. Watching others do the more interesting work as he swept —albeit the more dangerous work— he couldn't help being relieved. He'd never lived a life this wild. Not outside of Breggesa, not outside of those walls.

Watching the dunes go past, it was only now he realised how alien they were to him. How deadly. What if there had been no sandstorm?

No Revance nearby to pick him out of it? He leaned back and let out a long breath. He was safe here, with a gun and all these walls of metal.

Heeding Yuvet's advice, he'd decided to give Ditric some space. The last thing he needed was to be stuck in that tiny cabin while she fumed silently at him for the precious hour they didn't have anything to do. She was menacing enough as it was.

Ryza felt himself chewing his upper lip. When he'd escaped the smelters, he'd made a choice. Anything would be better than becoming an automind and Revance had been there to take him in. Even if it would kill him to leave, at least he was alive and, most importantly, he still had his own mind.

He felt himself shudder as he remembered the first time his father educated him on molten flux. It was like liquid metal, a sloshing conduit that seemed to expand to whatever container you put it in. Inject it into a dead body and it would *almost* bring it back to life, leaving nothing but a physical shell, one that would be malleable to a Kretatic's bidding. An extra mind for the control of arcanites. He pushed it from his thoughts. All dwelling on that had ever done was give him nightmares.

The door behind him burst open and he nearly fell off the deck.

'Rusty!' a voice exclaimed.

Oh no, not you.

Before he could get up, Holm had plonked herself down next to him, a wide grin on her face.

'Fancy seeing you out here.'

'How did you find me?'

She shrugged. 'Was just walking past and saw you out the window.'

'This is pretty far from the forge rooms to just be walking past,' Ryza said, looking away.

'It's also pretty far from the conscript's quarters,' she shot back.

There was a short pause, no doubt her attempt to elicit something more from him.

'What do you want, Holm?'

He flinched as a playful punch hit his arm.

'We're friends, aren't we?' she teased.

I don't think so.

'Just wanted to come by and congratulate you on your shooting this morning. Heard you beat out Ditric.'

Ryza frowned. 'You weren't there, were you?'

'Word spreads fast, Rusty,' she said. 'Anyway, she'd be mounting a bit of a grudge against you by now. She could never hit all her shots when I was around, always said I put her off.'

Ryza glanced out of the corner of his eye, spotting a goading smirk on her face. He stayed silent. This girl wanted something from him. He wasn't sure what, but he wouldn't give it to her. He knew nothing extracted the truth like a well-timed silence. When he had first been learning the ropes of trading, this trick was used on him many times. Unfortunately, it had been to great effect. He'd only been able to last five heartbeats before he had cracked.

Six heartbeats later, she stood up, brushing the dust off the back of her pants.

'Well, since you don't feel like talking, I'm going to get back to doing something useful,' she said. Ryza could hear the mock pout in her voice. 'It's a shame, you know. There's a good place for you in the forge rooms, plenty of ink to play with and some *other things* too. We protect our own. Send Ditric my regards.'

Ryza heard the high pitch scrap of hinges behind him and he couldn't help but turn. Holm was still looking at him, an eyebrow raised.

'Yes?' she said.

'Why don't you carry a rifle?'

She smirked again. 'Locusts don't *need* rifles.'

The door slammed and Ryza was alone. What had she meant by not needing them? According to Yuvet, everyone on Revance was *required* to carry one at all times. And what were Locusts? The name sounded like some kind of cult. Though why would she be asking after him? This was only the third time they'd met and he'd never said a friendly word to her.

It had to be something to do with Ditric. Holm must have been planning to befriend him to continue her little game. Ryza could feel himself beginning to fume. This is where it would stop. He was not going to be a tool here, not like he'd been under his father.

His last thought had dropped a lead weight in his stomach and he leaned heavily on the guard rail.

No more being used.

Shifting to get sensation back into his legs, he felt something poke at his hip. Something small, metal, hidden away in one of his many pockets of his greatcoat. He frowned as he reached for it, pulling out a small tin card. It was blank on both sides, but it didn't need anything written on it to tell him what he needed to know. Commonly scraps like these would be a Kretatic's calling card, a token that could allow them to learn each other's distinct resonance.

He could feel Holm's in there, full of dancing, shouting chaos as he turned the metal over in his hands. She would've just had to follow her own resonance to find him here. Without a second thought, he threw it as hard and as far as he could, watching as it bounced off Revance's carapace before disappearing from sight.

He sat for a while longer, mulling it over in his head, planning how he was going to approach Ditric. Eventually the door burst open, once again jolting Ryza out of his trance. Ditric was standing there, her hard stare fixed on him.

'And how'd *you* find me?' he said, turning his back on her.

'Saw you hanging out here with Holm a while ago, spotted you from outside our cabin.' There was a suppressed rage in her voice, like she was waiting to unleash something on him.

'Wasn't by choice,' Ryza said. 'She found me. I figure she's just trying to use me to get to you. I hope it's not working.'

He risked a glance over his shoulder, catching sight of her looking completely dumbfounded. Ryza had been planning that line since Holm had left him.

After a moment, she let out what sounded like a fake cough. 'You see through her too?'

'Like she's glass.'

They shared a small chuckle.

'Mind if I sit?'

'It's more your fortress than mine.'

She took this as invitation enough and perched herself on the guard rail, leaning out over the edge a bit more than Ryza would be comfortable with himself.

'Sorry I called you a metal mouth earlier.'

Ryza shook his head and grinned. 'It's not like you said anything bad about me in particular, just about the *supposed* underhanded nature of my people.'

'Yeah, well... call it a lived experience.'

'Tell me about it,' Ryza said flatly. He paused for a moment. 'You never told me where you were from...'

Ryza watched her carefully as she drew a deep breath, looking up as she did so. 'My parents... they used to be ammo makers in Iroka. Most of it went to Revance. Hell, I still have a few slugs of theirs. Saving them for, well, I don't know what. Anyway, short story is that they were taking me to Kyrea, thinking the factories there would pay better.

'Our travelling caravan got hit by smelters and I managed to escape. They didn't. Somehow, I made it back to Iroka and at the time all I could really do was join in with some mercenary work. I was young and stupid. A perfect fit and there ain't much that's changed, now I think about it.'

'Smelters? You're sure?'

She nodded solemnly. 'I heard 'em talking about the flux.' Ditric spat. 'Their corpses are still out there somewhere, rotting after being... *used*. I wish I could have found them. After I got my shit back together, I went out looking in the factory tunnels where they would've ended up, if only just to bury them, but...'

Bile was gathering in Ryza's throat. 'You wouldn't have found them. The flux consumes them eventually.'

'And what makes you sure of that?' Ditric snapped at him.

He could feel the bitterness rising in him, there was no resisting it. 'My mother got turned into an automind,' Ryza said quietly, 'and my father is one of the richest smelters in Bregessa. A flux trader.'

Ditric turned to look at him, wide-eyed. Ryza could see the anger, the lust for revenge. He knew it would be there.

'And you were a smelter, too?' Ditric's shaky voice said.

'You think I would do that?' Ryza spat. 'My father raised me to be nothing more than a tool to keep his outfit running! Imagine having a mother that doesn't even know you exist because she died giving birth to you! Imagine the thought of your father not even mourning her, but instead chucking her body in with the rest! I saw smelters bring back the dead before I could even talk! Worst part was when I found out where the bodies came from.'

He took a deep breath and leaned back, letting all the repressed feelings wash over him. The horror of what he'd witnessed, the guilt of not having done more.

'You know what he kept saying? He kept asking, "What do we do when we run out of corpses? We make some more." Every automind was someone. Had names. Lives. And I saw it all stolen in the name of a few more reels.'

Next to him, Ditric let out a low whistle.

'And I thought I was the tortured one. You joined that trading convoy to get away, then.'

'I didn't have much of a choice. He wanted me to go out and start meeting the smelters that brought in the would-be autominds. Negotiating over corpses by the cartload. He never let me forget I was practically the offspring of an automind. Still don't know what he meant by it, but I can't stop wondering.'

'Doesn't make any sense, does it? Considering he meant to make you and all,' Ditric said with a smirk. Upon spotting Ryza's doleful look, she wiped it off her face.

'It's about control. To him, it was always his way or else. Think about it this way, wearing this collar that's supposed to choke me to death is the freest I've ever felt. And the fact I'll be getting to put a stop to some of this shit? A bonus.'

She was silent for a while and Ryza watched for a response. What if he'd said too much? News aboard Revance that he was the son of a flux trader wouldn't go well.

'Why would you tell me this? About your father?' Ditric eventually asked.

'Because we've suffered by the same hands. I know you don't trust me, but I've seen enough to make me want to end it all. I need you to know I ain't a smelter.'

She nodded slowly. 'You're right. On all fronts. But you'll need to prove yourself.'

They talked for a while longer about their upbringings, Ryza fascinated by the ordinary life Ditric had led before she'd lost her parents. They'd been ammo smiths and Ditric assured him she could tell the difference from a properly charged slug and one liable to cause a misfire by touch alone.

For Ryza, it was easy to let her talk. Ask a few questions here and there, then letting her set off on a tangential yarn on something she could reminisce about. Any time the conversation began to redirect itself towards him, he deflected it as subtly as he could. He'd revealed enough for today. If he were to put it into words, it felt like his memory was bleeding.

They were still out there when the sun began nearing the horizon and it was Ditric who noticed it first.

'Best get inside before all the mission crews come back,' she said as she stood up, stretching her stiff legs. 'Part two of dust off is cleaning up whatever mess they drag back in.'

Ryza was about to stand up when he remembered something.

'You mind if I see your rifle for a second?'

'I do mind, unless you've got a bloody good reason.'

He gave a theatrical shrug. 'Well, you haven't quite been shooting straight, have you?'

Ryza held out both hands and she reluctantly handed over her rifle. As soon as his fingers touched the metal he could feel the same screaming chaos he had felt earlier that day. This rifle had Holm's magnetic resonance all over it, that was for sure. How it was making the rifle not shoot straight was beyond him, but undoing it wasn't. He reached into his pants, fishing out the vial of ink he'd stashed and then rummaging in his pockets for an ink brush.

'Is that... ink? Where the hell did you get the water for that?'

'Stole it from my father,' Ryza grunted as he found the brush. He unstoppered the ink carefully, making sure not to spill a single precious drop. He then dipped the brush in, drawing out just the right amount of the green ink for what he was doing. As soon as the liquid had pooled in the bristles, he resealed the ink and began etching a single rune on his wrist. This axiom was simple. All it needed to do was neutralise the metal.

Without knowing the controller's magnetic resonance, it would've been all but impossible. But Holm had made the mistake of handing him the very thing he needed. Even if the metal card she'd planted in his pocket now lay in the dunes of Revance's trail, he still perfectly recalled the dancing chaos that was her signature.

Ryza watched the rune slide into his palm. The moment it burned white-hot he touched it to the rifle, instantly smiting the unruly resonance it held.

'Holm did something to it. She'd hinted it to me earlier, saying that you couldn't shoot straight when she was around. I'm guessing meddling with your gun is what she was talking about.'

Ditric chuckled. 'I don't know why she would bother. Last I checked, she couldn't hit Revance from the inside.'

Ryza held it out to her, but she didn't go to take it. Instead, she rummaged in her ammo satchel and held out a slug. 'See that red post over there?' She nodded towards one of Revance's legs and Ryza saw it. Some kind of long forgotten warning sign, barely attached to the bent post holding it. It was about forty yards from them, swinging in wide arcs with the articulation of Revance's leg.

'Reckon you can hit it?'

'Is this about the range this morning?'

'I just want to make sure you haven't put your own tricks into it.'

'Can't trust me then?' Ryza said with a smirk. He jammed the slug home roughly into Ditric's rifle and brought it to his shoulder. He was acutely aware of the rusty trigger under his finger, resisting the urge for it to twitch as his aim swayed with the target. The feeling of cold and calm didn't come, instead it felt like his heart was pounding in his ears. He could feel Ditric's eyes boring into him and his hands started to quiver.

It's fair enough, I wouldn't trust a metal mouth either.

He jerked the trigger, his heart dropping as the shot careened out over the desert, missing the mark abysmally. Ditric clapped him on the shoulder with one hand and took her rifle back with the other.

'So it was beginner's luck this morning,' Ditric quipped. 'I would've been suspicious if you'd hit it. Thought you'd put your own tricks there in place of Holm's.'

Ryza felt himself turn red.

'Still, I wasn't going to make that shot, either. Come on, rest of the squad reckons you've jumped ship.'

Ryza didn't respond for a moment. He was staring at his rifle leaning against the railing next to him. What was so special about the resonance in it that made him such a good shot? He grabbed it and stood up, feeling the cold energy against his palm.

Who made this?

CHAPTER SEVEN

BOUND BY DRUDGERY

T HAT EVENING, RYZA PROCEEDED as discreetly as he could to Yuvet's quarters. He didn't want to risk being questioned by the occasional patrols within Revance's corridors, but the rickety catwalks of the fortress' outer layers were far more threatening. Powdered rust gathered under his fingernails as he scrabbled for handholds. Every second or third one snapped off in his grip and the precious few that held firm groaned as if they were about to do the same.

Yuvet had told him to keep this a secret, but from the cold outer shell of Revance, Ryza cursed himself for not telling his squad. He couldn't be sure what to expect. How often was it that she took people aside to give them private lessons? Or with this just another beating in the works? As he clambered into a passage on the upper decks of Revance, Ryza's hands wouldn't stop shaking. This was supposedly the officer's quarters, but they looked just as drab as where he'd just come from.

He found Yuvet's door and knocked tentatively. A warm glow washed across him as it swung open, emanating from an orb of light fixed to the ceiling. It was just bright enough for him to see, but not quite enough to keep him awake.

The room itself was tiny. It seemed nobody aboard Revance had the luxury of space. The walls were hidden behind dozens of marked maps, shelves bristling with lists and files and racks of weapons and armour, each piece grimy from misuse. "Improvised" was the only way to describe the latter two. Each piece was unlike anything Ryza had seen yesterday at the armoury, so he guessed they were the trophies of distant battles. The only furniture in the room was bolted down, a small bed and a stool.

Ryza sat down as ordered, and what followed was a two-hour lecture where he couldn't get a word in edgeways. Yuvet explained the countless pieces of jargon used around Revance, the almost endless chain of command and the near unlimited number of things expected of him not only as a conscript but also in whatever role he fitted into once he was fully trained.

There was potential for him to be anything from one of the lowly cooks to the commander of Revance itself. He could find himself looking after the ammo and weapons stockpile, or the vehicles in the motor pool. He could be training conscripts much like Yuvet did or ordering them around on small scouting missions.

However, it was most likely he would end up in Revance's infantry wing, which consisted of the bulk of the crew. They were the ones that crewed the numerous cargo runs between Revance and the various villages and towns the fortress passed by, fighting off smelters along the way. The fortress had started its life as a merchant platform and had since struggled to shake the legacy.

The list went on and on, but one thing stuck out in Ryza's mind.

'Whatever you do, try not to end up in the forge rooms. Never have I seen a place drive good conscripts bad like down there.'

'Why, ma'am?'

'They slap so many bits onto the fortress that they start to think they can control the damn thing. They get out of line real fast after that. Never have to crack more heads than down there.'

He couldn't help but relate this to Holm. Had she always been as manipulative as he'd seen her? Or was her work making her this mean-spirited? Ryza brushed it from his mind. Even the girl that was with her, Ferrick, looked halfway along the path of losing it.

Yuvet dismissed him after two full hours and Ryza managed to sneak back to his cabin undetected. The door groaned as he pushed it open, but no one inside stirred, so he slipped out of his boots and crawled into his bunk, the overload of information from Yuvet still swirling in his head.

This was how every day for the next two or so weeks would go. He would wake up along with the others and after eating with them, they would be training, either in the range rooms or completing physical conditioning and hand to hand combat exercises that were meant to make them faster and stronger, but the only effect they had on Ryza was to exhaust him to the point of collapse.

The afternoons took the form of maintenance, drudgery and whatever other mind-numbing busywork that needed doing. Their first memorable task was to hang off the side of Revance from thick metal coils. Swapping their rifles for buckets of grease and hand pumps, it was a vain effort to keep the fortress' leg joints from rusting over.

Dust-filled flurries of wind battered them as they worked. Every now and then a strong blast would send them spinning and bouncing painfully across the metal shell, but Ryza counted himself lucky he was hanging next to Gry.

'How do you know when it's about to happen?' Ryza shouted, clinging to a welded shut hatch through a particularly bad blast.

Gry tapped at his temple, pointing to his eyes.

'Reythurists can feel the winds, even the most distant ones,' he said.

They kept working in determined silence and Ryza soon found a growing appreciation for the castle's workmanship. Gry had told him about the strange way Revance shed its skin. It was what kept the forge rooms busy, hastily slapping together new rooms as Revance got rid of the old.

'You know things, Gry,' Ryza said, attempting to make conversation. 'Why's the metal all smooth like this?'

Gry shook his head. 'Constant sand blasting. Many people think Revance will last forever, but nothing is forever on these sands. Not as long as they shift and blow.'

'How do you know that?'

He looked at Ryza, wearing an unusual grimace. 'By waking up every day to find a little bit more of my family's home has chipped away. At least Revance doesn't do that too fast.'

'Is that why you joined? Tradition of getting out of the house before it topples?'

Gry managed to force a chuckle a moment too late. 'Our mother always made sure we were strong. Never stopped us when we were fighting and Revance seemed to be the next logical step to show that to her.'

'Doesn't quite sound like you really wanted to join. More the circumstances like me, eh?'

This time they shared a heartier laugh. 'Something along those lines. My two older brothers joined a while back, but when we got the news they'd carked it, my mother cried because they hadn't been strong enough.'

'I'm sorry,' Ryza said. Out of the corner of his eye, he could see Gry wearing a hollow smile.

Ryza lost sight of him for a second as he swung into one of the shifting joints of Revance, only hearing the squeaking of Gry's grease pump before he reappeared, narrowly avoiding being crushed.

'It's alright. We've lost a lot through the years,' Gry continued, unfazed by the fact he'd nearly been squashed. 'That's why our mother always raised us strong, to take on whatever would take from us, she'd say. I just need to tough it out long enough until my last brother can get settled here, so I can make sure he's okay.'

'And then what?' Ryza couldn't help in asking. So far, he hadn't met someone aboard Revance who had a plan for when —or if— they got out. Hell, he'd never had a plan further than doing whatever was ordered of him, by his father's hand or by Yuvet's. 'The Academy of Breggesa?'

Gry nodded. It wasn't a hard guess. Anyone that spent that much time with their nose buried in a book was bound for something scholarly.

'A part of me wishes I'd just tried to go there first. It wouldn't have been tough, but it feels like the right place for me, you know? But family legacy comes first.'

Gry's last words made Ryza sick to his stomach and he didn't want to think about why. He couldn't bring himself to continue the conversation and with Gry's quiet nature, he didn't need to.

Thankfully, dangling next to the business end of Revance's workings wasn't a common occurrence. More often they were assigned to fill one of the many two-man watch posts that sprouted out of Revance like thin metal mushrooms. Ryza could hazard a guess that it was more for somewhere to put them, out of the way from any actual work they'd probably screw up. It was dull, but at the very least, safe. Aside from the perilous fall.

All the stories of Revance heroically fending off massive attacks were probably just to bring in battle-hungry fighters like Ditric, who had been grumbling for weeks now about not having anything but metal targets to shoot at. Luckily, Ryza didn't find himself holed up in a guard tower with her. Instead he was paired with Ruka, whose small frame left him enough room in the watch post to stretch out.

'I feel like a vulture in a nest,' Ryza said, stifling a yawn. It was three hours into their watch and dawn was only just starting to break. If they were lucky, they'd be able to see the ground by the end of their shift.

Ruka giggled. 'Funny way of putting it. I remember spending a couple days in a set up like this and it never struck me that way.'

'That's your idea of a camping trip?'

She shook her head. 'Was probably a couple years back when I was first in Breggesa. Wasn't quite this high up, either. Only had the clothes on my back and some street kids took me in. We were one and the same, really. Lost.'

She rested her chin in her hands, leaning against the watch post's railing which creaked in the effort of holding her up. 'No one wanted to be on the rooftops in the baking sun, so no one was there to chase us off. It was always safe up there.'

'Yeah,' Ryza murmured. He knew the exact thing she was talking about. It was a place in the northern reaches of Breggesa, where clay hut after clay hut were jammed against each other and whose residents defended what little real estate they had with ferocious intent. As a child, Ryza could remember straying up to those parts often —his father would never search for him there— and being chased by the locals before he'd even done anything. The only way to get away from them was to get onto the buildings.

'They never took kindly to Kretatics,' Ryza said, the thought slipping out of his mind.

'Course they didn't! Half of the kids were on their own because of the smelters.'

'I... what?' It took Ryza a moment to realise they were talking about different things. 'Kretatics and smelters aren't the same!'

'Can't explain that to a kid that's not even ten years old,' Ruka snapped back. She was looking up at him with a glower she'd have to had learned from Ditric. 'If Kretatics are the ones that *use* autominds, then it's them *wanting* autominds that drives the smelters.'

Ryza felt frozen in her gaze. Did she know? Had Ditric told her about him? If she did know, she'd done a bloody good job keeping it quiet. Before Ryza could come up with an answer for her, she looked away.

'I guess I can't blame you. Sorry, I just...'

'It's alright. It was hard,' Ryza said. 'Growing up, I mean.'

'Yeah.'

'I've a gut feeling all of us had something like that, one way or another.'

Ruka nodded. 'Can't really change it. Taught me a whole lot, even if I didn't get to go to the schools. Can only really go after smelters now and stomp it out, right?'

'Is that why you joined?'

She shook her head. 'I was running out of options. You know where girls like me end up once they get old enough, right?'

Ryza felt his heart sink. Best not to delve any deeper. They'd simply had such different upbringings, everyone on Revance, all converging here for a couple of reels. Maybe that was just how Revance worked. Take the dregs of the lands and forge them into an army in through countless mind-numbing errands.

Luckily, Yuvet didn't seem to think they were ready to see fighting yet. At least this was the main thrust of Ryza's ongoing private lessons with her. He couldn't get a word in edgeways at the best of times, but she still believed him inadequate. It was only when she was showing him how to best clear a jammed rifle that he found the guts to speak up.

'What was it like on Revance when you first started? You know, as a conscript, ma'am?'

'Stupid question. How's that going to help?' She hadn't even looked up from the rifle she was showing him. This lesson was unusual, nestled deep in the armoury of Revance rather than in Yuvet's cabin. The only reason they could be in there was a favour from the toothless quartermaster, who'd leered at Ryza as they snuck in. 'Revance has always changed. It was more a cargo hauler than a fortress a bit before my time, but we still move goods between Breggesa and Iroka.'

'But even these collars,' Ryza tapped his own with his finger for emphasis. 'Have they always been put on conscripts?'

Yuvet slammed the rifle shut and looked up at him. 'You not like yours?' she snapped.

'Well... I mean, it's fine, but–'

'Wrong answer!' Yuvet barked, slapping him over the top of his head. 'It doesn't matter if you like them. The point is they keep you from running off.' She put the rifle back on the rack with all the others and Ryza decided not to tell her she'd left it jammed to save himself another slap.

Yuvet instead leaned on the nearest workbench, casting her gaze over a broken collar that the quartermaster had been working on. It was cut clean in half and was coated in dried blood.

'The batch of conscripts I came in on was the first to wear them, I think.' She picked up one of the collar halves, inspecting it with a hint of nostalgia. 'They weren't nearly this comfortable.'

'But what did you think of them, ma'am?'

Yuvet shrugged. 'I knew by signing up I was signing myself away, so I half expected something like this. But most of the others weren't too pleased. Couple dozen died thinking they could beat the collar. Looking back, it made sense. Before my time, half the conscripts only came in to get a rifle before jumping overboard to start raiding and thieving. Only a hardened core of troops remained and it was insanity back then. There were days when the smelters came at us and outnumbered us seven to one. I've heard there were talks to abandon Revance.'

'Abandon it?'

'Well, it would be impossible to *abandon* Revance, wouldn't it? Every other soldier could go their own way but there'd still be a thousand conscripts bound here by their collars. But it's... different. To put it in a way I can say to a whelp like you, the dropout rate ain't high enough. There are too many soldiers onboard, too many mouths to feed, too many bodies to coordinate. And then there's the things that get overlooked.' She pointed sharply at him. 'Be wary if you find yourself being overlooked.'

Like the Locusts.

With that, he was sent on his way, Yuvet saying he'd learnt enough for the night. She was right. Ryza was sure he'd be able to take apart and reassemble every weapon aboard Revance, spare for the massive cannons arrayed along the prow.

As he crept through the silent corridors, his mind kept shifting back to Holm. What if she was one of those overlooked elements? Maybe Yuvet knew what the Locusts were. Ryza kicked himself for not asking, but he probably would have got a slap if he had.

Stinking of gunpowder, he made his way back to his squad's cabin, ready to perform the usual silent song and dance of trying not to let on that he'd been getting any kind of special attention. It took him a while to sink into that fitful sleep he enjoyed inside Revance's shifting rooms. This time it was plagued with the single question.

What if?

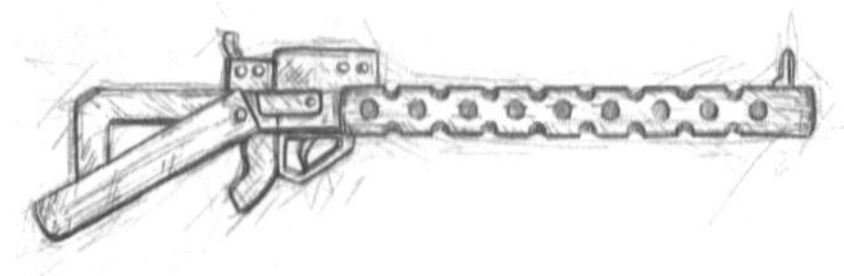

Chapter Eight

Scrapyard Smoke

I T WAS EARLY MORNING when their cabin door was kicked open. Ryza sat up, banging his head on the bunk above. Swearing under his breath, he leaned out to see Yuvet standing in the doorway.

'Squad five... You've got a mission today!'

Ditric was the first on her feet, leaping from her bunk to stand to attention.

'Don't get too excited. You're just helping one of the metal mouths from the forge rooms retrieve some lost goods.'

Yuvet slammed the door before any of them could say a word. A moment later, Ryza heard the clang of the next cabin being kicked open.

'Finally, we get to bloody prove ourselves,' Ditric said as she reached up for her rifle.

'What will we be doing?' Ryza asked.

'Just as Yuvet said, a simple salvage run,' Gry said. 'They always need more scrap metal to replace the pieces Revance sheds.'

'Why don't they just pick up the bits that fall off?' Ryza said.

'You wanna try ask that?' Ditric said. 'Just do what you're told.'

Rifles in hand, Ditric took the lead as they stomped through the corridors. Ryza started filling with a nervous tension, an energy that started in his feet and wormed its way up his body. He was finally getting off Revance, even if it was for a few short hours. It would be a break from the ceaseless clanking of the fortress and the strange, tiring resonance the metal of it possessed.

The only thing that worried him now was the collar around his neck. He'd managed to make it two weeks without choking in his sleep, an occurrence common enough to warrant warning. Out there he was at the mercy of the tiny black needle on his wristband. He brushed it against the wall for good measure, sending it ticking back a few degrees.

Entering the motor pool, Ryza heard Ditric swear from up ahead. A moment later Haven copied her and Ryza could see why. Lounging in the nearest vehicle was Holm, who was already eying him off. The contraption was little more than an engine with four wheels and half as many seats, held up by the wide trailer it was attached to.

Yuvet had taught him the buggy was called a lead-better. The name came from the heavy, supposedly slug-proof plate of cast lead affixed to the front and the fact you'd be gambling to get any protection from it.

Holm was dressed much lighter than they were, wearing nothing more than a thin cloth tunic, the trousers of her forge leathers and boots. She looked less prepared for a skirmish with smelters and more for a light bit of city shopping. Ryza found himself suddenly leading his team as they approached, the rest avoiding making eye contact with her.

'Fancy seeing you lot here!' she called out. 'Looks like we're going on a day trip together.'

'You can't be serious,' Ditric growled.

'And since I outrank you, you'll call me "ma'am," as well.' She climbed into the driver's seat. By the looks of it, she'd be controlling the whole contraption with only a single steering vane.

'So, who's sitting up front with me?'

There was a clatter of movement and by the time Ryza looked around, his entire team was wedged in the back of the trailer, the front seat next to Holm still empty. Reluctantly, he climbed into it, catching Haven mouthing *"sorry mate,"* out of the corner of his eye.

'Must be the boot-licker's lucky day,' Holm said. 'We've not talked for a while have we, Rusty?'

'Not necessarily a bad thing,' Ryza replied.

Holm began cranking the ignition and soon the buggy was vibrating with a low whir, jolting and sputtering as she eased it forward onto a platform at the edge of the motor pool. Ryza quickly realised that this machine ran on oil, rather than Kretatic axioms like he'd expected.

This way, anyone could work it and they wouldn't have to be concentrating the entire time they were driving to stop the damn thing from falling apart. As they neared the edge, Holm waved to a burly man and he jumped into action, throwing a lever that made a tightly wound winch spool out.

Slowly, the platform began to lower towards the sands, swinging with the momentum of Revance as it moved. When they were only a half metre above the ground Holm gunned it, bouncing the buggy onto the dunes. They skidded to a halt and Holm turned in her seat.

'Didn't lose anyone?'

'You wish!' Haven called back.

Ryza had to chuckle. Holm rolled her eyes as she turned back to the steering vane, accelerating until they overtook Revance. He twisted in his seat as they pulled away from the colossal stamping feet. It was the first time he'd properly seen the fortress from the outside.

An enormous cannon, with a bore wide enough to drive the lead-better down, hung low from the prow. Numerous other guns bristled like thorns at the base of the cannon. They looked miniscule in comparison. Belching smokestacks lined the spine of the fortress, with ramshackle networks of ducts and pipes sprawling across the patchwork metal side. It was a tapestry of dull browns, chipped oranges and oil-stained greys, but no matter how hard Ryza tried to focus on one colour, the whole thing seemed to blur into a mass of rust.

The only distinct colour sprouted from Revance's very highest point. A tendril of ethereal green smoke emanated from it, reaching into the sky and somehow beyond it. Ryza couldn't see its source, but he guessed it was from what Yuvet told him was the control room of Revance.

Soon the fortress faded into the distance, becoming little more than a rusted grey blob. Rolling hills of fine red sand surrounded them and overhead, the blue sky was tinged in places with faint ripples of green. When he'd asked Gry about it in the past, he'd explained it was to do with the strength of Revance's resonance. Not that it made any sense to either of them.

'Where are we going?' Ryza eventually asked over the noise of the engine.

'There's a whole region north of here that's all just scrap lands. Somewhere in the middle of it is a gathering point where people leave behind the good stuff they can't carry. Copper, gold, k-ore if we're lucky. The place has always been abandoned. I don't know why they insisted I take you lot along with me. We always hit it each time Revance swings past.'

Ryza frowned. 'What do you mean, "Revance swings past?" You make it sound like no one has control of it.'

'That's because no one does.'

'What?'

'Story I heard is Revance was just found wandering the desert one day and we've just been adding to it ever since. There's a route that it follows, no one's sure why, but it stops at most major towns we need to stop at. Maybe those towns popped up because Revance went past it!'

'That's utterly bizarre.'

Holm nodded. 'Makes it tough for us down in the forge rooms. It's hard enough adding to an arcanite that isn't your own, even harder if you've never met the maker. Forgemaster Tyrag's been pushing for a change for ages, but he doesn't think he can do it without the whole damn fortress falling apart.'

'Is it even possible?'

Holm glanced sideways at him, hesitating. 'Maybe. But anyone who's taken control of something even a tenth of the size of Revance died trying.'

'So how would Tyrag do it?'

'Only the Locusts know,' Holm said, tapping her nose.

Ryza twisted in his seat, but the four behind him hadn't heard her. The way Holm said it made him uneasy, like it was some dirty secret. The last time she'd said this, it was to dismiss having to carry a rifle like everyone else. She still didn't have a rifle, but she did have a long line of green runes running down each arm.

Where the hell did she find all the water for that many axioms?

The land turned from fine sand to mounting piles of garbage and debris until they were steering through canyons of time-worn scrap, with only Holm seeming to know the way. Framed by rocky cliffs, their destination was a heaping maze of twisting metal, a path cutting through the middle.

As they pulled up to the torn chain-link gate, Ryza caught sight of a few shacks tucked into the centre of the jumble and frowned. He swore he'd seen a puff of smoke coming out of a chimney, but as the buggy had lurched to a halt, he'd lost sight of it.

Holm was the first one on the ground, striding through the gate as Ryza jogged to keep up. The rest of the team shambled along behind them, rifles held lazily. At least they didn't seem worried about an ambush.

But something seemed off to Ryza. He followed Holm as she began rummaging aimlessly through one of the scrap mountains, keeping an eye on the nearest shack. That was where he could have sworn he'd seen the smoke, like that of a flame recently extinguished. He sidled closer to it, sniffing the air for the acrid scent charcoal left behind. But he could smell something else.

Burnt meat.

Meat doesn't burn on its own.

Ryza turned around slowly, gently slipping a hand into his ammo pouch and loading a slug into his rifle. Holm was still elbow deep in salvage and the others were picking through similar piles of scrap.

Why would such good pickings be unguarded?

There was a slamming of metal behind him and he spun, catching sight of a woman bursting from an open shack door. Her hair was matted, her scarred body clad in torn leathers and she wielded a long, rusted axe in hands with bruised and bloody knuckles.

Ryza had seen hands like that before. They were the kind that beat dead flesh just for the hell of it.

Smelters.

He locked eyes with the woman, trading a glare of hate and fury. She let out a howl of rage, a fearsome battle cry that made Ryza take a half step back. Before he knew it, she was barrelling towards him, axe raised and ready to maim.

He raised his rifle in a fluid movement, feeling its cool resonance flow through him, steadying his hands and his heart. As he aimed, the trigger readied itself. She ducked and weaved, shouting something Ryza couldn't hear, but there was nowhere for her to hide.

Ryza fired. He didn't even feel the recoil, only saw the golden muzzle flash that blinded him for a fraction of a second. His vision returned and the woman hit the dust, a bloody wound blooming on her back as she slid in the dirt. The slug had gone clean through her, tearing organs apart indiscriminately.

Good.

Ryza reached for his ammo pouch, his hand beginning to shake the moment it left his rifle. It made getting hold of the next slug all the more difficult, but he couldn't afford to drop a single one. He'd only managed to muster the reels for twelve slugs yesterday.

Eleven now.

The familiar metallic snap that came when he reloaded his rifle was blocked out by the ringing in his ears. He began grinding his jaw to clear it, a trick Yuvet taught him. It wouldn't do much, but it was enough to make out the wild calls of alarm from around the scrapyard.

Ryza turned. His squad had already formed a well-trained firing line and he could see the gap where he was meant to be. Properly coordinated, they could unleash nearly a hundred rounds in a minute. He took a step towards them, quickly scanning the piles of metal before he hesitated.

Where the hell was Holm?

The last he'd seen, she was searching through a scrapheap, but now there was no sign of her. She must've run before he fired, hiding somewhere in the valleys of twisted metal.

'Ryza!' Ditric bellowed. 'Get in the line!'

He could hear the roars now, the war chants and the clatter of weapons, but he still couldn't see where it was coming from. Holm was bound to encounter one of the raging lunatics at any moment. Ryza swore to himself. As much as he disliked her, she had to be found before the smelters got to her. Especially since she didn't even have a bloody rifle.

Ryza sprinted between the scrap heaps, making sure not to look at

Ditric who was waving furiously at him. Later he could just say he hadn't heard her, missed in the heat of battle. But as he disappeared into the maze of bent steel, Ditric's barked order rang out after him.

'Open fire!'

CHAPTER NINE

THE SMELTERS' LAIR

T HE SIGNATURE CRACK OF rifles split the air as Ryza rounded the scrap pile and a chorus of enraged shouts rose in response. There had to be more than a dozen of them, it was like they'd kicked a smelter's nest.

He skidded to a halt at the corner of an upturned buggy, peeking around the corner to see four smelters sprinting past. Another volley of rifle shots responded and three of them fell, the surviving man scrambling out of the line of fire, making a beeline for Ryza.

The smelter made it to the alley before Ryza could shoulder his rifle. He barely caught sight of Ryza and made a desperate swing with his axe. Ryza ducked, the blade biting into the rusted vehicle behind him as he darted away. He'd put ten feet between them before the smelter let go of his now useless axe and locked eyes with him. They were bloodshot, his irises yellow.

A *Curiktic.*

He aimed his rifle, hesitating when he saw a grin spread across the man's cracked lips. Ryza's eyes darted to the man's hand. A rune was burning white in his palm. Whatever simple axiom the smelter had in mind, it couldn't be one of healing that Curiktics were often known for.

Ryza dived sideways and a gout of fire burst forth from the man's hand. He kicked at the ground as he fell, twisting his body as the flames washed over the back of his greatcoat, singeing the hairs on his neck but doing nothing more. Before the smelter could ready another axiom, Ryza was on one knee, his rifle shouldered.

BLAM!

Crimson gore exploded from the man's stomach, shock and pain washing over his face as the slug burst out the other side of his torso. Ryza didn't waste the moment, springing to his feet and charging. He swung hard with the solid metal butt of his rifle, caving in the smelter's skull with a satisfying crunch.

The smelter crumpled and Ryza ran past him, plunging further into the scrapyard. He reloaded his rifle as he ran, then slipped an extra slug into his cheek, a trick Yuvet had taught him in their private lessons. Why waste time fumbling with your pouch when you've got a perfectly good mouth?

He slid to a halt at the corner of a shack just short of the scrapyard's main row. Down the street, smelters were taking cover behind whatever they could as they advanced on the firing line. Each time one of them dared to dash forward, the unfortunate sod in question was downed by a volley of slugs. A brutish smelter rose to his feet, still hidden behind a rusting silo, and began shouting at his underlings.

'We take them together! We have the numbers!' the brute roared, slamming his axe against his iron breastplate.

Ryza felt breath catch in his throat. It didn't matter how well drilled the other conscripts were, there was no way they'd be able to fend off all the smelters at once. There were still a dozen smelters on the main street and who knew how many more out of sight.

'We charge on three!'

Ryza stepped out, levelling his rifle. The brute had to be fifty metres away, further than any shot he'd made in the practice range.

'One!'

No, he could do this! Coolness flowed through his hands, steadying them. His breathing slowed. The sights on his rifle aligned.

'Two!'

BLAM!

'Thr—'

The brute was cut off as a cloud of red mist ballooned from his shoulders, the blood hitting three of the nearest smelters. But it was too late. With a mighty battle cry, the rest of the smelters rose as one and hurtled towards the firing line. The first volley of slugs took out three. The second, another two. Just before the smelters reached them, Ditric and the others scattered, disappearing into the scrap alleys as their attackers gave dogged pursuit.

Ryza ducked behind the shack and broke his rifle open on his hip to reload. He hadn't seen the blood-covered smelters charge with the others.

'Where'd that shot come from?' he heard one of them shout.

He snapped his rifle shut and paused.

'It was that shack! They're behind us!'

Shit.

Ryza ran, pelting across the main street into another alley. Just as he reached it, he turned, only having enough time to shoot from the hip.

BLAM!

The slug flew past the first two smelters, hitting the third in the foot. They tumbled, screaming in agony as they fell. Ryza swore to himself again as he dashed deeper into the scrapyard, weaving down the narrowest alleys he could find.

The whooshing of a wildly swinging axe was quickly replaced by the clangs of it rebounding off protruding iron bars. Ryza glanced over his shoulder to see the first smelter wrenching his weapon from a tangled scrapheap, the second attempting to shove past him.

Perfect.

The narrow confines gave him just enough time to reload. From his ammo pouch he pulled out one slug, stuffed it into his gun and...

BLAM!

The first smelter crumpled with a howl of pain. His comrade stepped over him, hefting a fearsome war hammer over his head as he charged. Ryza danced around the smelter's ungainly swing as it slammed into the ground, responding with a sharp blow to the face with the stock of his rifle. The smelter staggered backwards, the mace flailing wildly as he went and catching Ryza's knee. He fell with a sharp gasp, his rifle falling from his hand as he clutched at his leg.

Before Ryza could even think about recovering, a kick to the ribs flipped him onto his back. Every ounce of air was knocked out of him. The smelter was over him now, the massive hammer raised. Ryza forced himself into a lurching roll and the hammer landed with a thump that quaked the ground. His rifle was only a metre away. If he could just reach it...

'Come on you whelp, get up and fight!'

Ryza glanced over his shoulder, almost incredulously. The smelter was just standing there, war hammer propped casually on his shoulder and a wicked smile on his oil-streaked face.

Why the hell are you so confident?

The smelter seemed to have read his mind. 'You've lost your little purse,' he jeered, pointing to his feet.

The smelter was right. His ammo pouch lay open in the dirt, half a dozen slugs scattered around it.

'Get up, get your gun and we'll do this properly, eh?'

Ryza began crawling towards his rifle, letting out an audible groan for good measure. It had cracked open when he'd dropped it. Still with his back to the smelter, Ryza coughed into his hand and reached for his rifle, fumbling with it for a moment as he snapped it shut. He rose to his feet, holding his rifle by the barrel like an unbalanced cudgel.

'Good,' the smelter grunted. He let out another howling battle cry and charged forward.

Ryza didn't hesitate. He flipped the rifle in his hands and pulled the trigger.

BLAM!

The smelter stopped dead in his tracks, a look of surprise and utter betrayal flashing across his face before he fell, landing face first in the dust.

You said you wanted to do it properly.

Yuvet's trick had come in handy. The lucky part was the smelter's hubris. Ryza stepped over the now lifeless body and gathered his ammo pouch, reloading his rifle as he did so.

Now what?

He listened hard, grinding his jaw to mute the ringing in his ears.

The gunfire had ceased, so he could guess that the rest of the smelters had been put down as well. The only thing he could hear was Ditric's distant shouts. But where had the smelters come from? Holm said this place would be abandoned. Had she known? Was that why she'd disappeared as soon as the fighting had started, to join them? Where was she now?

Ryza stepped onto the main street and looked around at the bodies that lay silently along it. All smelters by the looks of them. He couldn't help the grin spreading across his face.

They deserved it.

'Ryza!' Ditric's voice barked.

He looked up. Ditric was marching towards him, fury in her eyes. The others were following her, along with Holm. Ryza frowned. Surely she would've been deeper in the scrapyard after fleeing the smelters.

He didn't get a chance to expand on the thought. The moment Ditric was close enough, she clenched a fist and swung it at Ryza's jaw. The blow made his skull ring like a bell.

'You stupid metal mouth!' she roared. Another punch and Ryza fell. 'You trying to get us all killed? Where the hell did you go?'

From the ground, he looked from her to Holm and back again, still trying to piece it together.

'Holm... she'd gone, I thought—'

'The second all hell broke loose I threw her behind our firing line. The one *you* were meant to be a part of!' She swung with her iron-capped boot, delivering a kick to the guts that knocked out his last breath. 'You never run from your squad, boot-licker.'

He couldn't help but look up at her in shock. She'd never called him that before.

'You could have killed us all.'

Before Ryza could respond, Ditric turned and stomped away, fuming under her breath. Gry, Ruka and Haven helped him to his feet.

'Why'd you run off?' Ruka said as she brushed the dust off his shoulders. 'And why do you smell like... smoke?'

'I thought Holm had run off, hid somewhere in the scrapheaps, but she'd be in danger there.'

'So, you went charging after her?' Gry said bluntly.

'I wasn't thinking,' he muttered, eyes fixed on the ground.

A sing-song voice pierced the air and Ryza groaned inwardly as Holm approached.

'Not even thinking and you still come running? I'm beginning to wonder if you have a thing for me.'

'Oh, shut it, Holm,' Haven moaned, rolling his eyes. He turned back to Ryza. 'Anyway, what about that smoke?'

'One of them caught me by surprise with an axiom. Never heard of a smelter being important enough to be allowed water.'

'One of them? How many did you take on?' Ruka asked.

'Must have been about five or six. I wasn't keeping count.'

Haven gave Gry a nudge, his usual grin spreading on his face. 'There you go! Told you the Bloodfist was on our side.'

Ryza frowned at him. 'What do you mean by that?'

'We were all taken by surprise when the smelters attacked us. When you ran off, I believed that you had gone to join them and that this was a set up orchestrated by you,' Gry said. 'Word around Revance is you were once a smelter. I didn't want to believe it, but what happened just now gave me pause for thought.'

Before Ryza had a chance to respond, Ditric's voice cut the air. He looked up at her. What if she'd told the others?

'We're getting this job done before more smelters show up. Grab some scrap and load the trailer. Then we're leaving and if you're not onboard, you can try walk back.'

'She *is* rather insistent,' Holm said.

The others groaned quietly as they set to work, splitting up and heading towards the scrap heap. Ryza made to join them, but stopped when he felt a hand grab his arm.

'You come with me. I want your help with something.'

Ryza shrugged Holm off and glanced towards the others. They hadn't seen her grab him, they were too busy rummaging through the junk again. There was a hidden mischief in Holm's eyes. Did she have something planned?

She interrupted his thoughts by drumming the metal collar on his neck with her fingertips. There would've been a sound of tapping, but her nails looked too chewed down.

'Remember this thing? Remember that I'm in charge while you're wearing it?'

'Lead the way,' Ryza said reluctantly. He was being ridiculous, after all. The only reason he didn't trust her was due to of how grating he found her entire existence.

They began making their way towards the other end of the scrapyard. In the shadows of the cliff face, Ryza could make out a small cave mouth, flickering gently from unseen firelight. Every time Ryza passed an open shack, he glanced in, only to find it filled with rotting bodies.

Expired goods. At least they didn't have the flux.

Ryza checked his rifle was still loaded, his eyes now firmly fixed on the caves.

Holm noticed him. 'You're keen. Hoping for another chance to show off?'

'I'd rather not,' Ryza lied. Her question put the image in his head of blasting away one more smelter. Just the thought of it sent a blood rush surging through his body.

'Either way, I'd be lying if I said I wasn't impressed,' she said nonchalantly.

'You what?' Ryza blurted. Another thrill shot through him and he hoped it wasn't what he thought it was. 'Call it getting lucky.'

'You got lucky how many times, five?'

'Six,' Ryza corrected before he'd thought about it.

'Seems like it's more than luck. If I'm not mistaken, you're quite the talent. Especially after only a few weeks onboard.'

'Why are you telling me all this?'

She shrugged. 'A simple compliment for a job well done.'

The cave's entrance looked like a tear in the rock face, only just wide enough for Ryza, yet three times as tall. Standing before it, he could see a small oil lantern sputtering away some ten metres into the cave, nestled into a small crevasse in the rock wall at head height. He felt a small nudge in his ribs from Holm and he took it as his cue to go first.

He was painfully aware of how the cave's walls scraped at his shoulders. Moving this slowly was frustrating to say the least, but any quicker was downright impossible. As he proceeded towards the lantern, he could feel Holm's hand on his shoulder. Either it was resting there to let him know she was right behind him or it was to gently keep pushing him forward.

He took the lantern with his left hand, keeping his rifle level by wedging it against his hip. Each step made the tiny flame sputter, casting flashes of orange light down the passage. More cramped corridors branched off from their path, so dark and tight Ryza didn't even think to look down them. His stomach lurched as he passed them. One last hidden smelter could leap from the shadows and drive a knife into his back.

Holm would probably let them do it.

The path began to slope upwards bit by bit, eventually giving way to an almost cathedral-like cavern, the roof too high for Ryza's lantern to reach. A wide plateau lay before them, furnished with the ransacked contents of what could have been a rich merchant's home and surrounded by a sharp drop into complete darkness.

Rugs, chests, beds and couches lay scattered around with no concern for organisation, all overturned or damaged from sheer carelessness. Anything that looked usable still bore the scars of having been sawn apart and clumsily reassembled in their new home. Lanterns, just like the one Ryza was holding, sat on the floor at odd intervals, just far enough apart so there was a sinister border of blackness between them.

'What the hell is this place?' Ryza uttered. He couldn't see what was in the darkness, or what his voice was echoing off. Staring into the black below unnerved him most. It was a steep fall. He was only a foot from the edge and even though he could move away, he found himself frozen in place.

'Looks like it's been turned into a smelter den. Found this cavern the last time we did a scrap run here, back when I was a conscript like you. But all this junk is new. No idea how they got it all in here.'

'It's quite luxurious. Better than what we have on Revance, eh?' Ryza said, keeping his tone casual.

Holm smiled sideways at him and an odd chill ran down his spine. He dismissed it. It was all in his head.

'You know, some luxury does exist onboard Revance. Have I told you about the Locusts?'

Ryza struggled to keep a straight face. 'You've mentioned them...'

'All Kretatics. Skilled, talented and very well rewarded for it. We're always on the lookout for any set of green eyes coming through the ranks with a certain spark, something a bit extra. You've managed to make quite a name for yourself, Rusty. I thought you might like to be rewarded for it.'

He began chewing his upper lip, making sure not to meet her eyes. 'What's the catch?'

'Catch?'

'There's always a catch. Good only comes from something bad.' He felt himself cringe. He'd just used one of his father's most repeated lines.

'Well... We keep things under wraps. Certain activities and pleasures we're afforded wouldn't exactly fly with one or two of the higher ups and it would be terrible if there was a foul smell about things. Otherwise, it would be a good future for you aboard Revance. Prime positioning to rank up, plenty of extra reels and as much ink as you could think to use as well. You wouldn't even have to hang out with all those dropkick conscripts you've been thrown in with.'

Ryza felt his ears twitch. 'They aren't dropkicks.'

'You would stick by them? Even by Ditric? After the way she treated you for almost single-handedly winning that fight?' she said. 'She called you a metal mouth. Not exactly something our people take kindly to.'

'*You* aren't my people,' Ryza growled.

'You're making a big mistake, Rusty.' She moved closer to him, only half a foot away.

Ryza held his ground despite his racing heart. 'I think it's quite the opposite.'

'Suit yourself.'

Without warning, Holm shoved him square in the chest. Ryza felt the ground disappear from under his feet and suddenly he was plummeting into the abyss.

CHAPTER TEN

UNDER THE SURFACE

RYZA STIRRED WITH A groan, pain rippling across his body. It started in his spine, spreading to his ribs before it throbbed intensely in his legs. His ears rung as if a rifle had been fired next to his head and his stomach was churning like he'd been poisoned.

What the hell just happened?

He could only remember the push. The way Holm stared at him with blank indifference as he fell, then there was nothing.

Ryza opened his eyes. Or at least he thought he had. Lying on his back, all he could see was darkness. Something flickered in the corner of his eye and he rolled over, regretting it as a wave of nausea boiled in his guts.

A small pile of flames danced on a pool of oil a few metres away. In the firelight he could see his rifle lying on the ground and next to it, the lamp he'd been holding. It had been shattered into a dozen pieces.

Shit.

Oil lamps were all well and good when the oil was *inside* the lamp, lasting for hours, days sometimes. But the flames were dying down as a panic surged in his heart. He clambered to his feet and scooped up his rifle, whirling around as he desperately searched for another source of light. There was only blackness. Not even the lanterns on the plateau were visible.

Looks like Holm wanted me to die in the dark.

Ryza swore under his breath. Maybe he could hear something? Ears straining, all he could make out was the hiss of the fading flames. But there was another sound beyond it. Something between a ticking clock and tiny footsteps. Something metallic.

A glinting metal figure was moving towards him, each lurching step bringing it closer to the fire. He almost screamed. In the darkness, Ryza couldn't tell how tall or close the thing was.

But it was getting closer.

'What are you?' he shouted, his voice cracking.

The thing stopped abruptly, just out of the firelight's reach.

'Origin.'

The voice was deep and metallic, as if it had been produced by two pieces of finely machined steel grinding together. The thing took another step closer and Ryza jerked his rifle down to it, then frowned.

It was an arcanite, only a foot tall, with two wire thin legs supporting a metal body the size and shape of a brick. Similarly thin arms hung limp at its side, protruding from flaps mounted at its shoulders. Its head was rounded and flat on top, made up of two half spheres stacked atop one another, the top piece possessing wide holes where eyes would be.

Ryza chewed his upper lip as he crouched to examine the arcanite. Where had it come from? Who was controlling it? And why could it speak? Suddenly its head shifted, the lower half now jutting out. Ryza almost yelped again.

Is it mimicking me?

He glanced back at the fire. His new metal friend was all well and good, but he'd only be able to see it for another thirty seconds before the flames died.

Gears whirred from within the arcanite and it took another few steps towards the oil puddle, stopping just short of it.

'What... What are you doing?' Ryza asked. He wasn't expecting an answer, but he just couldn't hold the thought in either.

Suddenly, the arcanite toppled face first into the fire. There was a splash of oil and Ryza leapt back. He barely landed on his feet, only just catching a glimpse of the flames licking the contraption before they were snuffed out.

Darkness rushed back and Ryza dropped to a crouch, feeling around with one hand for where the arcanite had fallen. The silence of the cave was interrupted after a few seconds by a strange slurping noise, then a scraping of metal. A flash of light blinded Ryza and the little arcanite was standing again, though its eyes now glowed brightly, tongues of flames licking out of them.

'How the hell are you doing that?'

In response, its head split in half and flipped up, revealing a wavering spout of fire.

'You understand me?'

The head flipped back. Was that a nod? Ryza crouched down closer to the arcanite.

'Well, Origin, was it?'

'Origin,' it replied.

'Only say one word?'

'Origin.'

'I'll take that as a yes,' Ryza muttered under his breath. 'Can you get me out of here?'

Origin stared silently at him for a few seconds before it marched away, cutting a path through the gloom. Ryza followed, making sure to stay as close as possible. This arcanite was his saviour, but who had sent it? Was someone watching him down here? Maybe that's what Origin was leading him towards.

After a few minutes of leading him over rocky ground, the cave floor evened out, the walls shrinking to a narrow passageway. Soon there was a glow of firelight ahead, enough for Ryza to step over Origin and move quickly towards it, rifle raised.

The corridor led him into a small room, dimly lit by a lantern that hung from the ceiling. More tattered furniture sat under it, surrounding a small table in the centre that was cluttered with leather-bound ledgers, loose notes and crumbs. Ryza walked over to the desk, ignoring Origin as it wandered about the room. Judging by the still lit lantern, it had been occupied at some point in the last day.

Why was this place so far away from the rest of the smelters?

Ryza flipped open one of the ledgers and felt his stomach drop. He'd seen notes like this before, in books just like this one when he'd snuck a glance at the papers his father always worked on. Rows upon rows of numbers, prices, dates and recipients. All to trade one thing.

Molten flux.

Just leafing through the pages made his jaw clench. Each page had around fifty entries, one for each vial of flux, marked with a serial number to make sure no one exceeded the allotment they'd purchased. Flux might be all but self-replicating, swelling in volume to fill whatever container it sloshed into, but roving bands of enforcers were more than happy to take back the loss by turning the would-be profiteers into autominds themselves.

Nearing the end of the records, the pencil appeared to get bolder. These were the recent trades. Ryza leaned in closer, paying close attention to the column listing where the flux was going. Mostly far-flung factory towns, places where any sense of humanity was sparse. But then his eyes landed on the last entry.

Revance.

A single vial had been purchased by someone aboard the fortress. These ledgers never listed the name of the buyer, instead hiding them like the cowardly bastards they were. Ryza scanned across the row.

The date of the sale was recent.

The price was extremely high.

There must have been some special conditions about this one, just to get it aboard. Was that why Holm had wanted to come into this cave? Could it be an entire automind as well? He checked the ledger's contract number.

C316.

If he could find the flux, he could find the buyer. Then he could put a slug in that traitor's head. But first he'd need to find his way back to Revance. The lethal resolve flowing through him drained in an instant.

The tiny black needle on his wristband that counted down to collar death had snapped off, broken in the fall. He racked his brain, trying to figure out how much time had passed. He'd touched Revance just before they'd left, but how long was the trip to the scrapyard? How long had he fought the smelters for? And how long had he been down here?

Holm would've left the cave after she'd pushed him, telling the others he'd slipped and fallen, never to be seen again. Maybe they would've protested, insisting on searching the cave for him? Ryza shook his head. Even if they did, they wouldn't have found him in the darkness and after the way Ditric was, she probably *wanted* to leave him here.

Ryza leaned heavily on the desk. This was the end and he couldn't even fight it. He'd happily take the smelters for another round rather than this. He wouldn't even know when it was about to happen.

There was a metal whir to his left and Ryza glanced at the sound. Origin's spindly metal arms were struggling to clamber over the edge of the desk. The arcanite made it up after a few more attempts, pushing itself to its feet and looking up at Ryza.

'Don't suppose you could do something about this?' Ryza said weakly, shaking his wristband.

Origin took a step closer and reached out, batting at the metal a few times before it gave up.

'Well, thanks for trying.'

'Origin.'

Ryza chuckled to himself.

My last words are going to be with an arcanite that can only say its own name.

No, he couldn't let it end like this. Not yet. Maybe if he found his way out, then someone would find his body. If he took the ledger, they'd find that too, then expose whoever on Revance had bought molten flux.

Justice would find them, even if he was dead. Dead and turned into an automind. It was a sickening thought. The resolve returned and he scooped up the ledger before turning to Origin.

'Do you know the way to the surface?'

'Origin.'

What else could I have expected?

But much to his surprise, the arcanite trotted towards the edge of the table, hurled itself off in an almost suicidal manner and landed with a clunk. Ryza skirted the table to see Origin getting to its feet, the fire in its head flaring brighter than ever. Setting off at what was a dawdling pace for Ryza, Origin headed for the rocky corridor they'd come in from, quickly disappearing down a route Ryza hadn't seen on the way in.

Twisting and turning, the only thing consistent about Origin's path was that it was leading up. Ryza soon lost track of time. All that mattered was getting the ledger out. He began to consider just giving it to Origin, telling the arcanite to find a way to deliver the book to someone important. But he dismissed the plan.

I am NOT dying down here.

After an age, a crack of light twinkled up ahead and Ryza rushed past Origin. He burst out into a blazing sunset, the surrounding rocks washed with red and orange hues. A strong breeze filled his lungs and it was only then he realised how rotten the air underground was.

His eyes took some time to adjust to the fierce light, his vision eventually being greeted with a sweeping view of sand and detritus. He was high above it all, standing on the cliff that towered more than fifty metres over the scrapyard. His heart sank at the absence of a lead-better waiting for him.

They would have saved themselves first. Better four live than five die.

In the distance Ryza could see the outline of Revance, walking along a horizon that wobbled in the heat haze.

I just have to scale this cliff and make it to the horizon before I choke to death.

Ryza felt something nudge at his leg and looked down to see Origin standing next to him, the flame in his eyes now snuffed out. A single arm was tugging at the hem of his greatcoat.

'You want to come too?'

It tugged again.

'Alright, but you keep quiet.'

Ryza picked Origin up by a small handle that was roughly welded to its back and its arms and legs retracted into its body with a whiz as soon as they left the ground. The arcanite turned out to be just small enough to stuff into the cavernous inner pocket of his greatcoat.

With Origin weighing against his chest, Ryza set off down the cliff. Eons of eroding winds had carved a jagged chute through the centre of it, allowing him to hit the ground in minutes.

From the ground, he couldn't see Revance. The mountains of scrap and garbage made sure of that. He looked down at his wristband. The red needle on it was a spinning blur. The damn thing must've broken in the fall as well. It didn't matter for now. Revance was a hard thing to miss seeing in the barren Droughtlands.

Ryza set off at a light jog, carefully pacing himself for the long journey ahead. Yuvet's rigorous training regime was to prepare him for situations like this, but right now he could only feel the burning exhaustion in his legs from yesterday's routine.

The sunset soon gave way to night and scrap lands to red sand. Dim stars were the only thing to light the dunes as Ryza plodded along their flowing crests. The grinding metal of Revance echoed across the sky, filling his ears long before it came into sight. He'd grown used to the sound in his time aboard the fortress, but never truly noticed it until he was out here.

The only sign of Revance was the spectacular green ripples of light that dashed across the night sky, painting his path home. He made a mental note to ask Yuvet what really caused it, because it certainly wasn't any axiom he was familiar with. Then again, asking about unfamiliar magics was a sure-fire way to be thrown into the Academy of Breggesa's dungeons.

Ryza was getting close now. He quickened his pace. It would be a cruel twist of fate if he were to die only steps from safety. His lungs heaved as he trudged up one last massive dune, but it was all worth it. Revance was ahead, walking slowly through a shallow valley of sand.

Ryza didn't waste a moment, taking a short run up before skipping onto his back, sliding all the way down the dune on his greatcoat. He came to a stop near one of Revance's massive legs and slammed his wrist into it.

A breathless whoop of joy escaped him.

He'd done the impossible.

He'd lived.

Ryza latched onto the colossal foot just as it lifted from the ground. It flew forward through the air and the rust on the ledge under his fingers started to slip. He'd barely recovered when the foot slammed down, sending him tumbling into the sand. Unperturbed, Ryza restarted his ascent, finding a porthole he could pry open just as the leg began to lift again.

He tumbled into an empty corridor somewhere on the infirmary decks, where it was only a short wander to his squad's cabin. What would they think when he walked in? Maybe they were still awake, mourning his loss. Ryza chuckled to himself.

Be a little bit humble.

He pushed the door open and was greeted by a chorus of snores. Right now, he wanted nothing more than to join them. Closing the door quietly behind him, he stuffed his greatcoat, Origin and the ledger into his drawer. With a small *clank,* his rifle was holstered too, leaving him to quietly flop onto his bunk.

The full force of his aching legs hit him as soon as he lay down. The only escape from it would be sleep. Ryza shut his eyes and felt himself begin to drift. However, one thought was plaguing his mind. The molten flux aboard Revance. In his mind's eye, he could see the vial and the numbers carved into it.

A gut feeling told him Holm was involved somehow. Her and the Locusts. He felt a grin break across his lips.

Imagine her face when she sees me alive.

CHAPTER ELEVEN

BACK FROM DEATH

R YZA SAT BOLT UPRIGHT as he woke, slamming his head into the bunk above as usual. He swore under his breath, rubbing his forehead. The sound of metal slamming on metal had roused him and now he'd only added to it. Three pairs of legs were standing next to his bunk, though they weren't facing him.

'What is that?' Ruka's voice said.

'It's coming from Ryza's drawer,' Haven said. 'Someone's messing with us.'

'Then I'll make a mess of them!' Ditric said. There was a clatter and one of the legs changed their stance. The sound of a rifle cracking open came next.

'But we don't have any ammo! We used it all yesterday!'

'I always have ammo! Now open that drawer.'

Ryza slid out of his bunk and stood up, but the others still hadn't noticed. He tapped Ditric on the shoulder.

'Best not to fire inside, you'll send us all deaf.'

She whirled around, shock and reflexive rage battling on her face. 'Ryza? But... how?'

'He's back!' Haven cheered, pumping a fist in the air. 'Back from the dead!'

Ryza looked over at Gry. Even he was surprised enough to look up from his book.

Ditric lowered her rifle and fixed him with a stare that made him feel like he'd catch fire under her gaze. 'You were gone for more than twelve hours. How did you survive?'

Twelve hours?

That couldn't be right. Yuvet had said the collar would execute him after that long and he certainly wasn't dead. Ryza looked down at his wrist, remembering the timing needle was still broken. Was that all it took to disable the collar?

'Sheer perseverance?' Ryza said.

Before anyone could reply, his drawer banged again, knocking five times before falling silent.

Slowly, Ditric pointed her rifle at Ryza, the close confines only allowing her to press the muzzle into his left knee. 'Open the drawer.'

He crouched down and gently pulled on the handle, his eyes almost crossing as he looked down the barrel of Ditric's gun.

'Meet Origin.'

Ryza placed the arcanite on the floor of the cabin, where it proceeded to do absolutely nothing.

'Did something happen to you out there?' Ruka said tentatively.

'Yeah, he lost his bloody mind,' Ditric replied. 'A metal ball on a box? Really?'

Dismissive as Ditric's tone was, Ryza noticed her knuckles white on her rifle, which was now pointed firmly at Origin.

It was as if the arcanite had heard her, responding by suddenly shooting its arms and legs out and falling flat on its front. Once it stood up, it attempted to bite the barrel of Ditric's rifle. She shooed it away and Origin began to wander aimlessly, occasionally patting down sections of the walls.

'I think we'll need the entire story,' Gry said, watching Origin's progress.

'A harrowing tale of heroic deeds and struggles for survival?' Haven said theatricality.

Ryza shrugged. 'If only. Holm pushed me down a pit and then Origin led me out. After that I just made for where my wristband was pointing.'

'Holm pushed you?' Ditric said. 'She told us you'd fallen on your own.'

'We waited around for you as long as we could,' Ruka added. 'Eventually Holm was insisting we go back and Ditric didn't refuse.' She tapped her collar. 'These things and all.'

'She must've been getting nervous I would come back,' Ryza said under his breath. He reached into the drawer and pulled out the smelter's ledger. 'Either way, she did me a favour. I ended up in a smelter den. I found this. There's something interesting at the back.'

'Give it to Gry, he's the reader,' Haven said.

Ryza tossed it over and Gry caught it with a fumble before flipping through the pages, his expression growing more horrified by the second.

'There must be hundreds of vials... maybe thousands, just in this region alone.'

'What are you talking about?' Ditric asked. 'What's it got to do with Holm?'

'Molten flux.' The words came from Ryza's mouth sharp and hard. He could almost watch them pierce the air, stabbing into the minds of the others as they flinched.

'There's so much... You could make an army with it all, all in recent weeks too. It's like it—' Gry stopped abruptly as he hit the last page.

'What is it?' Ruka asked.

'Revance...' Gry muttered.

'What?'

'There was flux sold to someone aboard Revance,' Ryza said grimly.

'Can't be,' Ditric said. 'Orders are to kill smelters and destroy autominds at first sighting. It would be impossible for molten flux to get anywhere near Revance, let alone onboard!'

'That might be true, but just before she pushed me, Holm was telling me about a little group called the Locusts. Sound familiar to you?'

To Ryza's surprise, Ditric's face was blank. Just past her, Gry faltered. He leaned heavily over the book for a moment, his eyes shut.

'I've heard of a couple other Kretatics around here disappearing,' Gry said quietly.

'Because of Holm?' Ditric snapped, interrupting him.

Haven let out a disgruntled snort. 'Let him speak for once, would you?'

Gry continued. 'One of them was a friend of mine, before we joined Revance. Just before she... Well, she was a Kretatic like you, Ryza. Good at sensing things in metal, finding the pure stuff. She told me Holm had approached her a few times. Just friendly interactions, nothing overtly sinister, but she knew there was something behind it.'

'There always was,' Ditric grunted.

Haven hissed at her and Gry continued.

'Before we lost her, she came to me and said that Holm had asked her to join something called the Locusts. She didn't tell me what it was, but she left before I could ask. The only thing I knew was that she'd refused to join. I haven't seen her since.'

'And Holm definitely did it?' Ruka asked. 'Disappeared her?'

'Judging by the way she treated me when I refused her offer, I'd say so.' Ryza stepped over to the table, looking down at the ledger.

'What are the Locusts?' Ditric asked.

Ryza didn't answer for a moment. He lingered over the ledger, eyes still fixed on the last entry. 'What I got from Holm is they're a group of Kretatics from the forge rooms, treating themselves to some "extra pleasures." Skimming the good stuff off things we find in raids or from the cargo we're hauling.'

'Why only Kretatics?' Gry said.

Ryza had been wondering the same thing since Holm had last spoke to him.

'Probably to get away from the treatment of a certain few people,' Haven said, giving Ditric a nudge. In return, he received a lightning-fast jab to the guts. Despite being utterly winded, he still couldn't stop chuckling to himself.

'Did Holm mention anything about magic?' Gry asked quietly.

'Said there'd be plenty of ink to go around, yeah.'

An odd gut feeling was telling Ryza that the Locusts and the smelter's ledger were connected, but he couldn't quite join the dots. If these Locusts were the ones that had bought the molten flux, what would they do with it? There were already plenty of people scurrying around the fortress to be ordered into action. An automind was only for controlling a larger arcanite, but Revance was the largest arcanite of all.

'Out of all people, how did I miss it?' Ryza murmured to himself.

'Miss what?' Gry said.

'You know how an automind is used, right?'

Only Gry nodded.

'It's a dead and empty mind,' Ryza continued. 'No resonance, no thoughts, nothing to even keep them alive because the flux does it instead.'

Yet again, he was met by blank faces. He resisted a groan of frustration.

'A Kretatic's resonance is what marks the arcanites they make as their own. No two are the same and no two resonances play nicely with each other, which means Kretatics can't construct and control the same arcanites, at least not properly. Any contraption they make must be controlled *entirely* by one mind, putting limitations on the size or complexity of the arcanite produced. An automind acts as an extra mind. A mind with no conflicting resonance.'

'So, you're saying...?'

'The Locusts would have to be the one trying to get the automind. To make something as big as Revance.'

There was a tense silence in the room, only broken a few seconds later by Ruka.

'But... why?'

'What?'

'Why would they need to build something like Revance? They're already onboard. They've got everything they could want, right? By the sounds of it, it's just some little gang formed so they can giggle about keeping others out and snatch gear from the store rooms.'

Ryza opened his mouth, but nothing came out. What if she was right? Maybe he'd been too desperate to link the flux to something.

'Well, maybe they don't have it. But right now, that's where I'm looking for that flux.'

'It won't work,' Ruka said.

Ryza turned to her, seeing the sullen, almost stern, look on her face. 'Why's that?'

'You really think that you can just wander about and the Locusts would just *tell* you if they had the flux? If Holm's already tried to kill you once, what's stopping them from having another go once you start snooping around?'

'But I'm sure–'

Ruka shook her head, cutting him off.

'You're not sure, are you? If these Locusts are that damn scary, then why don't you just keep your head down and not drag us into it? The only thing you have is a hunch, nothing more!'

She seemed to shrink slightly after saying this.

'Ruka's right,' Ditric said. 'You don't even know if the flux is onboard, you've just been saying it. If you reckon all of this is connected, how does Origin come into it?'

The arcanite looked up briefly at the mention of its name before going back to patting down the walls.

'It's an odd little thing,' Haven said. He crouched down next to Origin and began prodding it. Origin replied with a few attempted snaps of its jaw. 'You haven't put any more power into it?'

'Not a single rune,' Ryza replied.

'Then how is it still active after so long?'

'What do you mean?' Ditric asked.

Haven shrugged. 'Little arcanite this size wouldn't last too long away from its creator. Did you recognise the magnetic resonance? I'm garbage at it.'

'I haven't checked.' Ryza crouched down next to him and put his hand on Origin's bulbous head. It didn't try to bite him and Ryza closed his eyes, searching through his palm. The resonance was a familiar feeling, a kind of tiredness. The metal felt smooth, not from machined precision, but from eons of abrasive sand. Before he could figure it out, Origin jerked away from him, turning back to the walls.

'And why does it keep smacking the walls?' Haven pondered.

'Doesn't matter,' Ditric said, handing out their rifles. 'It's breakfast and then business as usual. After Yuvet chewed us out for losing you—'

'Even though it was Holm that tried to off you,' Haven quipped.

'—she tells us we're going to keep training and undergoing missions as substitutes for the other conscripts they've already lost. She'll be mighty surprised to see you still kicking.'

'But what will I do with Origin? I can't take it with me.'

She eyed the arcanite and let out a disgruntled snort. 'Just stick it back in the drawer.'

At Ditric's words, Origin skittered to the corner of the cabin, as far away from the drawers as possible. Nevertheless, Ryza grabbed it by its head and stuffed the arcanite away.

'You behave,' he whispered as he slid the drawer shut. He frowned. Why was he talking to it like it was his child?

As they made their way towards the food hall, they were blessed with near empty corridors. Ryza stifled a yawn as he took to the serving line. After running all the way back to Revance, he could've done with a sleep in.

When his tray was shoved through the slot, he took it and was surprised to see a set of staring eyes on the other side. They vanished a moment later and Ryza moved on with a frown.

Strange. Turns out there's people making the food after all.

He took a seat with his squad and the food hall began to fill. As usual, everyone entering made a beeline for a tray of rather generously named food. While they waited, they stared around the hall idly. It was only when their gaze landed on Ryza that they started gawping. Whispers flowed up and down the line and those who had been served seated themselves as close as possible, just so they could stare at him between bites.

'Looks like you're famous, mate!' Haven said, slapping him on the back.

'They can stare all they want. I feel pretty ordinary.'

'But you've *done* something extraordinary,' Ruka said. 'First you fought those smelters bare-handed, then kill six more on your own and now you've survived collar death.'

'Surely it happens all the time.'

'Not a single record of it,' Gry said.

'Though it's not exactly something they'd like to keep a track of,' Haven chuckled. 'Can't be giving us conscripts too many ideas.'

'I just want to know why the collar didn't kill you,' Gry said. 'It has to be something to do with that arcanite you brought back.'

'You got any ideas?' Ryza replied.

He pointed to his blue eyes. 'Reythurist, remember? If this was about the flow of the air around us, I could tell you anything. For arcanites, it's up to you and Haven.'

He looked over at Haven, who gave a shrug. 'Got nothing. It looked to me like a stray dune cat that followed you home. We'd need a better Kretatic than us.'

'The Locusts,' Ryza said in a low voice. 'They're all Kretatics, aren't they?'

Ruka groaned. 'You remember one of them just tried to kill you, right?'

'Only one of them.'

'The one that's staring at you from across the room.' Ditric pointed at a distant doorway and Ryza followed her finger. Wearing a scowl, Holm stood against the opposite wall of the mess hall, her arms crossed.

'She does not look happy with you,' Ditric grunted. 'You must have done something wrong.'

'Yeah, you forgot to die!' Haven said.

'What are the consequences for trying to kill someone aboard Revance?'

Ditric chewed for a moment as she thought. 'I'd wish for an execution, but we don't have any proof. A conscript's words don't count for nothing. She's going to get away with this unless you want to do something personally.'

'You'd better not,' Ruka chided. 'Don't give her a reason.'

'I won't. Not yet...' Ryza stared back at Holm and she cast her eyes away.

Not while I have leverage.

'Even going through the Locusts won't be a guaranteed way of figuring out Origin,' Gry said.

'And what is?' Ryza said.

'I've read up on the trail of Revance. As it patrols the Droughtlands, it passes certain places. Sometimes it's next to major settlements or towns. Next one coming is Kyrea. Factory town—'

'Means it's a shit hole,' Haven interjected.

'—that has enough Kretatics in it that one might give you an answer.'

Ditric shook her head. 'No chance on that, conscripts aren't allowed off Revance without mission. Especially not to a town like that. There are enough smelters there that I doubt the full force of

Revance could purge the place.'

'Well, there goes that plan,' Haven said.

Not quite yet.

Ryza was still looking at Holm. He could see something new in her and it wasn't guilt. She was uncomfortable, glancing around the room as if she were about to be attacked.

Maybe he would take Holm up on her offer. He could use the Locusts and their "special privileges" to get to Kyrea, where he could figure out what Origin was and then come back to find the flux aboard Revance.

'I'm going back to our cabin, just to make sure Origin hasn't escaped,' Ryza said. It was a stupid lie, but it gave him just enough reason to stand up.

'Might want to take a long way out of here,' Ditric called after him.

He pretended not to hear, instead heading straight for the door Holm was standing next to. It was partly to see if she would still want him to be one of the Locusts. Partly to see just what she would say to his living, breathing face.

As he approached, she forced a snide grin.

'Fancy seeing you here,' she chimed.

'I hope you're not disappointed.'

She paused, looking at his chest while she considered her next words. 'How'd you make it back?'

'That's something I'd only tell a friend. Now, why have you been staring at me? It almost put me off my breakfast.'

'I was sent by Forgemaster Tyrag. You're to see him as soon as possible. He wants to check your collar. If you're worth his time, you must've done something amazing.'

'And how do I know this isn't just another attempt on my life?'

'Because it's not,' Holm said through gritted teeth.

Ryza frowned. She wasn't frustrated, she was anxious about something to the point she couldn't stop shifting on her feet.

'In the forge rooms, I'm guessing?'

'Yes.' She leaned in closer, her voice lowered. 'The rest of the Locusts still want to meet you, you know.'

'Tell them their invitation wasn't all too welcoming,' Ryza replied, forcing as much venom into his voice as he could muster. He wanted to watch her squirm.

'Please... You just have to meet them.'

He felt an eyebrow go up. Why was she asking, almost begging for this? There had to be something else going on. He glanced over his shoulder at his team. They were still ensconced in breakfast; Haven having helped himself to whatever Ryza had left on his plate.

Meeting the Locusts would get him closer to finding the automind and the molten flux and to working out what Origin was, but what would his squad think? Ditric was guaranteed to ostracise him and the rest would follow her lead.

'I'll think about it. But if I did, you'd owe me Holm. Big time.'

Before she could respond, Ryza pushed through the door next to her and out into the narrow corridors, walking fast towards the forge rooms. It was a difficult fight, but he managed to suppress the vindictive sense of victory rising in his chest. From the very first day, Holm had something to dangle over Ryza. Now he had something of his own.

CHAPTER TWELVE

THE FORGEMASTER AND THE LOCUSTS

RYZA'S JOURNEY WAS ACCOMPANIED by the usual racket of marching boots, clanking iron and the echo of commands bellowed out through the comms pipes overhead. More people turned to stare as he passed, glancing at his hands and whispering the name "Bloodfist."

He picked up his pace, shooting down three ladders to eventually find himself on the lowest deck of Revance. A right turn would take him to the motor pool, but today Ryza turned left. Narrow doors that were carved into the walls led to partition repair shops. The ramshackle workstations inside were vacant, the contraptions in need of mending lying abandoned from the previous day.

It soon turned into the cavernous hall Ryza had found himself lost in on his first day aboard Revance. He'd come out on a walkway on the edge of the massive hole that dropped to the desert floor. On the opposite side was the dais. Ryza swore the four pylons that sprouted from it had grown a foot taller since he'd last seen it.

Sparks would occasionally shoot up from behind it, the air split by the sound of piercing metal. Skirting the catwalks, Ryza approached the dais, finding a massive wire cage the size of a house at the rear. From the outside it looked like a monster's lair, decorated with half-destroyed arcanites that were strapped to the outside like trophies.

The chain gate to it was wide open, but he rapped his knuckles on it anyway. The sound of hammering metal stopped abruptly.

'Enter. Slowly,' a voice declared. Ryza felt himself shiver. The way the sound seemed to crawl out of the air meant it was Tyrag. His first meeting with the man had been unpleasant to say the least and he had a feeling this would be much worse.

The inside of the cage was more organised than anywhere else Ryza had seen aboard Revance. Rows of meticulously positioned work benches filled the space, with equally precise shelves lining the walls. Tyrag moved between them, paying no mind to Ryza. Half-built gadgets were repositioned, tools firmly yet deliberately set back in their places and spare lengths of twisted rebar were returned to the material buckets from where they'd been taken.

Ryza stood in the middle of it all, waiting for Tyrag to say something, anything. But as seconds ticked into minutes, he could feel his heart begin to race.

'Forgemaster Tyrag,' Ryza said, his voice cracking. He swore under his breath. Why were his nerves getting to him now?

'Correct,' he replied.

'You called for me to come see you, sir?'

He nodded slowly, still not looking at Ryza. 'I certainly did. Only I didn't expect you to brave my presence so soon. You are less of a coward than I would have expected of a conscript.'

Ryza bit his tongue. He wasn't sure if it was an insult or a compliment.

Tyrag fell silent again, focusing his attention on his tables for a few moments too long before he spoke again.

'The only reason I *requested* your presence is because you did something rather spectacular. Something I thought was impossible. I do hope you know what it is.'

'I survived collar death, sir,' Ryza replied promptly.

'Up to seven bolts are positioned in specific locations throughout the collar around your neck,' Tyrag continued, as if Ryza hadn't spoken. 'Each one designed not to cause instant death. That would be too kind to a deserter. They push in slowly, so that no matter how the collar happens to be positioned, at least one of them will impact a vital blood line. What follows is a very slow demise, the kind even the hollowest men dread.'

Tyrag paused as he met his eyes and Ryza had to fight against his instincts to hold his gaze steady. 'Why tell me this, sir?'

'Revance is an army formed almost entirely of conscripts that lack discipline and skill. The fear of the collar is one of the only things that keeps them in line. Ever since the collar was instituted, not a single conscript has strayed from Revance for more than twelve hours without meeting their fate. Tales conflicting this risk disorder in the ranks, desertions and wasteful deaths.'

The Forgemaster had barely finished his sentence when he drew close to Ryza, quick enough to make him flinch. He could feel a tug at his neck and realised that his collar was now firmly in the grip of Tyrag's hands. There was a high whiz from just behind his ear and suddenly the bolts began to tighten around his neck, spinning as they attempted to burrow into his skin.

'Judging by your expression of deathly terror, you haven't felt this sensation before, have you?'

Ryza sputtered something inaudible as the bolts pressed harder. If he so much as shook his head, he would be impaled.

'How strange...'

Tyrag squinted, then stepped away. As his fingers left Ryza's collar, it began to loosen and he sucked in a grateful gulp of air. Tyrag turned back to his work benches, moving between them as he scratched his head.

'It works perfectly,' he continued. 'Not a single fault that I can sense.'

'Maybe I hadn't actually been away for a whole twelve hours,' Ryza suggested.

'A plausible explanation.' Tyrag paused, stopping in his tracks as he looked slowly up at Ryza. 'You have a question?'

It was only now Ryza realised he'd been chewing his upper lip.

'Who created the collar in the first place?' Ryza asked.

Tyrag looked down as he let out a low chuckle. 'That would have been my father, a Forgemaster of Revance before me. It was nearly forty years ago, more than twice your lifetime. Not many ask that question. I suspect it was on your mind as you have a certain opinion on the collar. You think it cruel?'

Ryza nodded hesitantly. It was a baited question. 'It's hard to think it as anything else while wearing it, sir.'

'Then you think of it wrong. The collar is a necessity, the kind that builds great things. It has kept the conscripts of Revance in line until such a point as they can be trusted to run this fortress as it deserves to be run. As such, the continued existence of Revance and all the crew aboard it is all thanks to my father's legacy. Cruel, but necessary.'

'But why can't we be trusted, sir?'

'Why take the chance? With the collars, Revance runs much more efficiently. However, there is still a way to go. You understand the strange path Revance takes as it patrols across the lands, yes?'

Ryza nodded slowly, his mind working to keep up with whatever idea Tyrag seemed to be getting at.

'None of the crew hold any control over this path, not even me and I'm supposed to be the one closest to the machine. Until Revance can truly be controlled, it is hardly the fighting force it is made out to be. We are nothing but a beast of burden that wanders the Droughtlands. Just as Revance supposedly was at its inception.'

'But how would you even control it? I've been told it's impossible.'

Tyrag paused for another moment. 'It would be impossible for a young whelp, such as yourself. You may leave now.'

Tyrag turned back to his work without another word. Ryza took a step back, ready to leave, but something in his gut stopped him. It was as if Tyrag had cut things off too quickly, like he was on the edge of revealing... something.

'You speak of cruel yet necessary means...' Ryza started.

Tyrag looked up at him, fixing him with a confused look.

'You wouldn't happen to be referring to autominds, would you, sir?'

A wry grin began to spread across the Forgemaster's face.

'Very perceptive of you, conscript.'

'I thought Revance's mission was to fight smelters, sir,' Ryza stated, trying to hide the heat rising in his voice. 'Does that not go against everything we work for?'

'At this point in time, yes. I take it you haven't met Commander Valtos. He leads Revance. It is his mission. He is... a strong leader.'

'What are the consequences of bringing molten flux aboard Revance?'

'Summary execution,' Tyrag said quickly. 'A shame really. Some great things could be done with tools like that.'

'What do you mean?' Ryza regretted the question the moment he asked it.

'You and I are both Kretatics, yes? Surely you understand. Imagine channelling your mind through another, one that is completely free from thought and preoccupation. So much room to move, to create, to control. No soldier would go idle, even after death.'

'It's abhorrent.'

'It's necessary,' Tyrag snapped. 'For Revance.'

Ryza felt his teeth grind. 'How would you get flux aboard Revance if you would be killed for it?'

'I wouldn't. For now, it is a mere fantasy. A fantasy for creating a legacy to match that of my father's. Nothing more than that. Now away with you, before you ask any more dangerous questions.'

Ryza clenched his mouth shut before any more probing questions spilled out. His legs had been screaming at him to run the moment he'd walked into the cage and now Tyrag had given him the opportunity, he wasn't going to waste it. As he strode out of the cage, he found himself under the watch of half a dozen forge workers returning from their breakfast.

One of them approached him, a burly looking man with a mane of blonde hair flowing from beneath his welding mask. He swept it from his face with his right hand, revealing a gleaming grin and green eyes, the other hand offered to Ryza as he drew nearer.

'I was told that you wouldn't be coming,' the man said. Ryza could hear the wealth flowing through his voice.

'Who are you?'

'I am Maligar,' he stated proudly. He leaned in closer, snatching Ryza's hand to shake it. 'Leader of a *certain group*.'

'I told you I could get him here.'

The hairs on the back of Ryza's neck prickled, sensing the approach of an unpleasant someone.

'Good to see you could make it too, Holm,' Maligar said with a grin.

'Locusts...' Ryza said absent-mindedly.

'Not so loud,' Maligar hissed. 'Not while we're near to the old man.'

He took Ryza's shoulder and forcefully steered him to a small access tunnel that was so dark he couldn't see the tip of his nose. His feet found a set of steep and narrow steps and he proceeded up them gingerly.

'Just a few stairs, Rusty, nothing to worry about,' Maligar said in his ear. 'Anyway, I'm glad you came to meet us.'

'It wasn't exactly my intention,' Ryza muttered.

He felt Maligar's hand clamp down harder on his shoulder. 'You're here now and that's what matters.'

They turned a corner and Ryza could have sworn he'd walked back into the forge rooms. It was a similar layout, though with larger work areas occupied by half-built arcanites whose bodies were pressed against the ceiling. A small feat, considering that Ryza could feel the hair on the top of his head brushing against the bowed iron above.

Towards the back of the room Ryza swore there was some kind of fighting arena, a lowered pit only big enough to allow two combatants to stand at arm's length, but Maligar had ushered him off into another room before he could be sure.

That might explain the bruises on some people around here.

The next chamber was even more compact, giving Ryza the impression that this was all a section of Revance that had been wedged in while no one was looking. At least it had a touch of luxury to it, just as Holm had promised.

Coloured rugs covered almost every inch of the floor, plush couches lined the walls, occasionally interrupted by a door leading off to a darkened room or a shelf displaying radical looking devices or precious jewels.

'So, what do you think? How does this compare to your little cabin?' Holm chimed from his side.

His reply didn't come instantly, the words having to fight their way through gritted teeth.

The best lie is the truth.

'I haven't seen anything like this for a while.'

The moment he had walked into the room it felt as if he'd been thrown back to when he was ten years old. The first time his father had introduced him to one of his little "business dealings." Opulence, greed and gluttony were what Ryza discovered that day and he'd loved every second of it. It wasn't until he understood where this kind of wealth was spawned from that he began to revile it. Now he could only worry as to what had bought all these creature comforts.

'Something concerning you, Ryza?' Maligar asked.

Ryza met his eyes and was surprised to see that he looked genuinely concerned.

'Just... just worried about getting to my squad before they miss me,' Ryza lied.

Maligar let out a booming laugh. 'No rest for the dead! That is a stunning commitment to the cause. I quite admire that, Ryza. Quite a bit.'

'Why is it that you admired me in the first place, then?'

Maligar shook his head. 'It's not me that had an eye on you. You'll have to take that up with Holm.'

She was deep in conversation on the other side of the room with a girl he half recognised, not hiding the glances she was throwing his way whenever she paused for breath.

'Why call yourselves the Locusts, anyway?'

'It's simply what Revance is! We're all a swarm of locusts at our core, passing through the lands almost like a season, stripping bare what little is around for our own needs to the point that the locals think of us as pestilent thieves. At the very least we're honest about it,' Maligar said. 'Our number may invite other Kretatics they see as fitting to our group, those that we think can come around to this fact of life. If they refuse, well, we must be kept secret. Accidents happen all over Revance now, don't they?'

'But why the secrecy?'

Maligar tapped his nose as he smirked. 'Not until you're one of us, Ryza. There'd be a mutiny if the rest of the crew realised we're little more than mercenaries creating our own contracts. Anyway, after you survived your own accident —a tale you'll have to share— I saw fit to reach out to you, as a means of apology. We can't have the legendary Bloodfist out there with a grudge against us, can we?'

'And if I refuse?'

'Why would you?' he declared. Maligar threw his arms wide. 'You could live with a touch of luxury in your life! What possible reason could you have for turning that down? You could be with your own people, you—'

'My own people?' Ryza snapped. 'What do you mean by that?'

'Us, Kretatics, metal mouths, whatever you want to call us. Wouldn't it be so much more pleasant to not have to trifle with the discrimination of the ignorant washouts? I've heard you've already had a run in or two with your own squad.'

'It's not like that!'

'Then what is it like, Ryza?'

He didn't have an answer. He remembered the venom in Ditric's voice when she'd called him a metal mouth and could still feel the bruise she'd left him with, tender on his cheek.

'You seem indecisive, Ryza. I'll make a deal for you. You don't have to commit to anything now, except for coming to a little celebration we're having soon. Holm will come to you, if you're game. She'll be there too, you know.'

He watched Maligar's eyebrow go up as he thought, only realising a moment later that he had been chewing his upper lip.

That's a habit I'll need to break, among others.

Ditric wouldn't take kindly to him hanging out more with Holm, nor would the others. He might as well consider himself an exile from his own squad if he took Maligar up on the offer. But then again, what about the flux? Each time he met Holm's eyes, it seemed more and more likely in his head that the Locusts would have it.

'What's the celebration for?' Ryza asked casually.

'One piece of knowledge we can't have you running about with,' Maligar said with a grin. 'You in?'

Ryza glanced around the room again, still unable to take in the lavishness of it. When he met Maligar's eyes, he nodded firmly.

CHAPTER THIRTEEN

HALF-TRUTHS

A s Ryza negotiated his way to the range rooms, he played his conversation with Tyrag on a loop through his mind. There was something the Forgemaster had said that Ryza was sure he missed. He seemed intrigued by the idea of using autominds to control Revance, but would he actually do it? No, he seemed to know the consequences of betraying Revance all too well. The way he was savouring the concept of collar death certainly showed this.

Ryza unconsciously tugged at the band of rough metal around his neck. He could still feel the bolts pressing into his flesh. He couldn't help but think back to the depths of the dark cave, imagining himself cowering in the dark as each curved iron barb slowly went to work. If Origin hadn't come along, that would've been how he'd ended.

As long as the collar was around his neck, he was an automind, if only one lucky enough to keep their mind and their life. The sooner he got it off, the better.

After running them through their various drills of the day, Yuvet called for them to stop. It was nearly noon and the morning of target practice had left Ryza's arm with the familiar ache of recoil. It wasn't helped when Ditric approached and gave him a less-than-friendly punch on the shoulder.

'Hope you found what you were looking for when you ran off

after breakfast,' she growled. 'Yuvet gave us an earful for losing you yesterday and then another one when you didn't rock up on time with us.'

'Surprised she didn't snap at you when you finally wandered in,' Haven added.

'I found it, don't worry,' Ryza said. It was a half-truth, but it was better than nothing.

'What were you talking to Holm about?' Ruka asked.

'Her pushing me off a cliff.'

Another half-truth.

Ruka glanced over her shoulder at Yuvet. 'You going to tell her? She thinks it was us that lost you.'

Ryza looked up to see Yuvet standing at the doorway, bellowing to another group of conscripts outside.

'No,' he said slowly. 'I want to hold it over Holm's head a bit longer.'

Haven stifled a chuckle. 'And what are you planning on getting from it?'

'A rather serious question, actually,' Gry said. 'Something Locust related?'

Ryza shook his head quickly. It was as if Gry could see right through him. 'Just a bit of guilt-tripping.'

He glanced at Ditric and she took his shoulder in her grip. 'Whatever you do, don't go messing with them. They can't be trusted.'

'You talking about metal mouths?' Ryza shot back.

'No, I—'

But Yuvet interrupted her before she had a chance to absolve herself.

'You lot! Get over here!'

As they walked over, Ryza glanced at Haven, but he was too preoccupied giving Ditric the foulest look he could muster to meet his eyes.

Lucky that Yuvet was around.

His jab at Ditric had been off the cuff, enough to distract the others from the subject of Locusts. All he needed to do was keep his squad out of the picture until after the Locusts' mysterious celebration and then he'd be able to convince them to help.

'You five, just because one of your squad is back from the dead doesn't mean you get a free afternoon,' Yuvet barked. 'You're out on patrol today. Go to the motor pool and meet up with a driver called Lod. Shouldn't have to fire a shot, so if you manage to lose Ryza again, consider yourself lost with him.'

She looked between them for a moment, an eyebrow raised.

'You waiting for a kiss goodbye? Go!'

The motor pool was a pit of confusion. They had to push through a dozen other squads of equally hapless conscripts to find their driver. They eventually found Lod, a crusty and toothless man whose muttered words were incomprehensible. However, this didn't deter him from claiming to be their driver.

They piled into his skeleton of a lead-better and he lurched the vehicle through the crowded motor pool. His knobbly hands jittered on the steering vane, but they still somehow made it to the desert floor without crashing into a more heavily laden buggy as it was prepared for a cargo run.

As Ryza rode shotgun, he was treated to what could have been the greatest tales of Revance's triumphs, if he were only able to understand it. After nearly an hour of driving, Lod brought the lead-better to a screeching halt and Ryza looked around. There was nothing but sand in every direction. When he turned back to the driver, he was treated to a rotten grin, an encouraging wave, and the first word out of the man's mouth that he could understand.

'Patrol.'

Ditric's boots had hit the sand before the buggy had stopped and by the time Ryza was out, she was a good twenty metres away. The others were jogging to catch up to her and Ryza joined them, feeling his legs moan in agony as they were forced into action.

The minutes stretched impossibly into hours and Ryza could swear they were trudging in circles. It was pointless busy work, just enough to get all the conscripts out of the fortress and yet there wasn't a single soul around to see it. It almost made Ryza regret not joining the Locusts. Holm said they got some special treatment. Maybe it would have kept him out of the baking sun.

He hung at the back of their aimless march, far away from Ditric. She would still be fuming over his jab. To be fair to her, it had been a low blow and he could feel a ball of guilt growing in his stomach for it.

Or it could be hunger.

He pulled some rations from his ammo pouch and set his jaw to work grinding up a handful of grisly, nameless meat.

What I would give for something I could actually call food.

As he ate, Haven fell back a couple of paces to walk alongside him, munching away on his own rations.

'Good this,' he grunted over a mouthful.

Ryza swallowed a chunk of what he was sure was crushed bones and glanced over at him. This was the first time he'd heard anyone give praise for Revance's so-called food.

'What's good about it?' Ryza asked, his curiosity getting the better of him.

Haven glanced down at his handful of meat. 'This stuff? Nothing. But I've probably eaten a ton of stuff like it since I was born. No, what's good is the quantity Revance's got.'

'What do you mean by that?'

He shrugged. 'Well, you know how it is. Young lad growing up with two parents, they ain't well off, probably far from it, but they don't want him to know. Put four walls around him and a roof over his head and it'll be enough. Keep his belly fed and it'll be enough, teach him one or two things and it'll be enough.

'But eventually the young lad works out where the reels are coming from, or at least, where they *aren't* coming from. Parents always told me they weren't hungry round dinner time, or they'd already eaten.'

'And it starts to weigh on you,' Ryza added.

'Yeah. Before Revance I don't think I'd let myself be hungry for three years. Just kept telling myself everyone's hungry and that's fine. Joining here gives me enough and lets me make some reels for the folks back home, not that there's much leftover after commissary takes a cut. Main reason I signed up, really. Putting my neck on the line just for a feed.'

'It's quite noble of you,' Ryza said quietly.

'If you'd have signed up, what would have made you?'

'Something like yours. I knew where the food and other things were coming from. Just didn't like what bought it all.'

'Think you'd send some money, too?'

Ryza shook his head. 'My father would laugh and send it right back.'

'Prideful bastard, eh?' Haven said with a chuckle. 'And your mum?'

Ryza felt a thousand words catch in his throat as he opened his mouth, but none of them came out.

'Not around?' Haven asked softly.

Ryza nodded.

'I'm sorry.'

'Don't be. She's in a better place than she was.'

They trudged in silence for another half hour before Haven broke it.

'There something going on between you and Ditric?'

'Like what?' Ryza scoffed.

'Like... Something. I don't know?'

'There isn't a thing going on between us. She's as much my squad mate as she's yours. Why would you ask anyway? You thinking of making a move?'

'She'd crack my skull open if I did that,' Haven said. 'Was just wondering from being in the range this morning, with what she said to you...'

Ryza held his breath.

'I don't know...' Haven continued. 'Ever since you rocked up it's like she's taken to seeing us as no-good metal mouths.'

A frown crossed Ryza's brow as his brain whirred into action. What if Haven was right? Previously he'd only thought that Ditric's venom had been directed at Holm, a fair target by all means.

But now he thought about it, there were the little things as well. Any time he retrieved something from the drawers in their cabin, he could feel her eyes burning into his back. She never ordered Gry and Ruka around as much, nor could he remember sitting next to her at dinner or breakfast. The more he thought about it, the more sense Haven's thoughts made.

He looked ahead to see Ditric, Ruka and Gry walking side by side, sharing an animated conversation he couldn't hear. The ball of guilt that had been growing in his stomach began to dissolve and he looked over at Haven.

'Maybe you're right.'

'I wouldn't care either way,' Haven muttered. 'We'll all get split up before we get these collars off. But until then, we stick together, yeah?'

Ryza nodded. 'Definitely.'

'And that arcanite you found?'

'Origin?' Ryza chewed his lip. 'Keep it safe if we can. Make sure either one of us or someone we can trust has an eye on it. Same thing with the ledger.'

'What about Ruka and Gry?'

'That's what I'm wondering as well.'

As the hours wore on and the sun began to set, they found themselves back where Lod had parked the lead-better, their first set of footprints still printed in the sand. He was still lounging in the driver's seat, a makeshift shade cloth propped over his head as he snoozed. Ditric gave the buggy a swift kick, waking him with a jolt.

Spare for the spitting buzz the of engine, the ride back was dead silent. Ditric rode shotgun, leaving the rest of them to exchange tense glances. It was like Ruka and Gry could sense the discomfort in the wind as it whipped past.

After an unusually large dinner —he suspected the Locusts might have been trying to curry favour with him by means of an extra helping on his plate— Ryza excused himself early, giving Haven a subtle nod before heading back for the squad's cabin. Judging by the manner Yuvet treated him with this morning, he could easily assume that it would be business as usual, including his nightly lessons.

Barely more than a minute later he was standing outside her door, rapping his knuckles against its iron surface with the ledger stuffed in his coat pocket.

He heard a violent flurry of movement on the other side before the door swung open, revealing a slightly flustered looking Yuvet. Her wide eyes relaxed as they recognised him and she beckoned him in.

'Ryz. I'd forgotten you weren't dead.'

'Even after this morning?'

She slammed the door behind him and cuffed him around the ears. 'Walking corpses don't get away with snark, neither,' she snapped.

'Yes, ma'am.'

'Sit down.' She pointed to the only stool in the room before she collapsed on her bed. 'What's that in your coat? Light reading?'

'Something of the sorts, ma'am.' Ryza pulled out the ledger and flipped it to the last marked page and handed it over.

'What the hell is this?' Yuvet said before having even looked at it.

'I found it after a skirmish with them yesterday. A smelter's ledger recording the trades of molten flux, including their destinations.'

'And how did you know what that looks like?'

'I've seen these before, ma'am.'

Yuvet finally looked down at the book and her eyes went wide. She slammed it shut and looked at the door, as if someone were about to burst in. But nothing happened.

'How much more do you know about this?' she asked, her tone darkening.

'Nothing at all,' he lied. He wanted to see if Yuvet would play her cards first, because he certainly didn't have any up his sleeve he was willing to use.

'You won't have noticed then,' she muttered to herself. 'Wouldn't have been here long enough. Things ain't right around Revance. Commander Valtos? Barely seen him and he's been leading the charge against smelters before this. Even Revance itself is running out of supplies.

'At the rate we're going we'll be completely out of ammo, food and oil by the time we get to Iroka. We'd be able to stock up there, but I'd hate to think of what would happen if we came under attack. Worst part is no one thinks anything is wrong. Too afraid to point fingers, let alone try fix it.'

'Does the molten flux come into it, ma'am?' Ryza asked.

'How the hell should I know? You're the metal mouth, you know autominds and all the rest. You tell me what someone would be doing with it here.'

'I wouldn't have a clue,' Ryza lied. In reality, there were a dozen things he could think of.

'Doesn't matter. If this is true, it means that Revance has been corrupted from the inside. Fucken' bad news for the both of us, for everyone aboard Revance and, hell, everyone in the Droughtlands. How many other people know about this ledger?'

'It's between us and a bunch of dead smelters.'

Yuvet nodded. 'Keep it that way. You and I, we're going to get to the bottom of this and before you ask me what's in it for you, you're doing it because you're bloody loyal to Revance and if Revance does fall, that collar is something you won't be able to survive, no matter how you did it before.'

'That's more than fine by me, ma'am. How do we start?'

'These meetings? I got nothing left to teach you, but let's say I do. Just to keep our asses covered. I want you to investigate the forge rooms and the people running it. They're the ones responsible for maintaining Revance and because of that, they're the biggest drain on supplies. I'd go myself, but they don't take kindly to anyone without green eyes. If there's anyone taking more than their fair share, it'll be them.'

'And what do we do if we find the one who bought the flux?'

Yuvet shook her head. 'It's a foot note in a bigger scheme, the thread you've tugged to get in. It doesn't matter now, but whatever happens, it's on your head and your head alone.'

'Good,' Ryza said through gritted teeth. 'Because I'm going to kill them.'

CHAPTER FOURTEEN

SPILL THE BEANS

RYZA COULDN'T BELIEVE HIS own cunning as he walked out of Yuvet's cabin. If he was correct in his assumptions, which he generally was, he now had several people tied to his fingers like puppets. Holm would be easy. Outside of the Locusts, she would still be in deep trouble if he revealed her murderous intent. He was almost relishing the thought of holding it over her.

Maligar would only be lightly tied, his persistence in wanting Ryza to join the Locusts would be enough to elicit a small favour or two. Haven was now firmly allied with him, supposedly against Ditric. Ryza now felt his friendship with him was strong enough they'd be as thick as thieves. Maybe Haven could be turned against her.

Only as a last resort.

He caught himself with a gasp. What the hell was he thinking? Manipulating and betraying his friends. It was madness. The kind his father happily participated in. That was not what Ryza was going to turn to.

As he'd had these thoughts, his legs had taken control of themselves, leading him on one of his familiar shortcuts across the outside of Revance. He was now perched on the narrow lookout where Holm had found him on his second day. He'd thoroughly checked himself for any hint of a metal card bearing her resonance, so there wasn't a chance of her finding him now.

Ryza let out his breath slowly, expelling the whirling thoughts from his mind. There was too much going on in his head to focus properly, too many strings being pulled at to make a remotely rational decision. All he needed was a moment to relax, to catch himself.

His mind hadn't stopped racing since the moment Holm had pushed him the previous day. Even his dreams had been punctured by the sensation of falling into the abyss, with nothing but the vision of her smirk to go with it.

There was a gentle creak of neglected hinges and Ryza whirled around, almost falling from his perch.

'Fancy finding you here,' a voice said from the darkness inside. They sounded nervous and Ryza couldn't quite place who it belonged to.

'Who's there?' Ryza said, his hand gliding towards his rifle. Not that it would do much good. He didn't have a single slug on him, but it would make an effective truncheon in a pinch like this.

'What's the matter, Rusty? Already forgotten me?'

He let out a sigh of both relief and annoyance.

'Come on out then,' Ryza grunted as he sat back down on the ledge. 'You outrank me, so you can go where you like, *ma'am*.'

The door slammed and Holm gingerly sat herself down on the other end of the lookout. He glanced over at her, but she was staring at her boots as her feet swung in the breeze.

'How'd you know I'd be here?'

Holm shook her head, forcing a smirk. 'You think I was looking for you?'

'I still haven't heard that apology you owe me from... well, I don't need to spell it out.'

Only now did she meet his gaze. But something seemed off. In the past, her smile danced around her eyes as well as her lips. Today she could only force it onto the latter. It appeared her usual bravado was gone, replaced by a sober mood.

'Then I'm sorry.'

'How sincere of you.'

She shrugged. 'It's all you're getting.'

'More than I usually do,' Ryza grunted. He paused a moment, waiting to see if Holm had anything else to say. Maybe she hadn't come looking for him. Maybe she'd come up here to think, just like he had.

'Something's troubling you. Doubts?'

'It's none of your business,' Holm shot back.

'A regret then? Something you can't really talk about with anyone else,' Ryza continued. 'Or are you finally feeling a tiny bit of guilt?'

'Why'd you think that?'

Ryza felt a smirk break across his mouth as he waved out at the horizon. 'Why else would anyone come up here?'

'Then what's troubling you?' Holm asked.

'Nope, I asked first. Beans. Spill.'

'Only if you tell me what's got you up here next,' Holm said as she held out a hand.

Ryza shook it and then crossed his arms expectantly.

'I'm going to guess it's something about the Locusts?' he said.

'Gods, it's like you already know!' She drummed her fingers on the ledge for a few moments before she looked out at the horizon. 'Yeah, Locusts. Maligar was talking to you about his *celebration* this morning, right?'

Ryza nodded.

'Well, he's been going on about getting a couple of special supplies for it, whatever the hell that means, and I've got a gut feeling that it's got something to do with Revance swinging past Kyrea. You know what kind of place that is.'

'If it's meant to kill someone, that's where it's made.'

And made with molten flux.

'Exactly. I just have a feeling that it might be enough to get a few Locusts executed.'

'Do you know exactly what he's planning?' he asked. 'What even is there to celebrate around here?'

She shook her head and Ryza felt his heart sink. It was like the buyer of the molten flux was about to be dropped into his lap.

'Just wish I could talk him out of it. His ideas... I thought they were all talk but... I don't know.'

'What ideas?' Ryza pressed quickly.

She shook her head again, this time with a grin. 'I've said my bit. Now, what's troubling you? Get your beans out or whatever you said.'

Ryza swore under his breath. Fair was fair, not that Holm was likely to play it that way. He couldn't reveal too much, but it had to be something convincingly bothersome to satisfy her.

'What's the deal between you and Ditric?' he asked.

'That sounds like a question, not beans.'

'Just tell me, I'll get to the point.'

Holm began drumming her fingers again. 'When I grew too old to be house-bound, I set out to be a trader. Like you, apparently. Ran with a caravan, found most of my earnings tithed away from me and one day decided to go solo. Problem is a girl like me attracts a fair bit of attention. I needed a guard if I was going to travel. I found Ditric in Iroka. She didn't seem quite right, young and angry about something, she never told me what. But she was all I could afford. Come to think of it, I probably shouldn't have let her know about that.'

'She ever called you a metal mouth?'

'Most of the time. I probably deserved to be called worse. She always thought I was short changing her on her share of the trade, even though I probably saved her neck as much as she saved mine. What are you getting at there, Rusty? Has she got it out for us Kretatics?'

'It's what I'm starting to think. Even then, I wouldn't know what to do about it, considering she's our "squad leader." Supposedly.'

'Locusts are Kretatic only for a reason.'

'How'd she end up hating you, anyway? Steal a few reels from her and make a runner?'

She chuckled. 'I wish it had been like that. Look on her face would've been priceless.'

'What was it, then?' Ryza said.

He watched Holm carefully as she faltered, her usually witty words catching in her throat.

'Well, I discovered why she was so angry when I found her.'

'What did you do?' Ryza's jaw felt like it had been rusted shut. The words barely made it out.

Holm was dead silent, so much so that Ryza could swear he could hear her heart pounding.

Four beats passed before Holm spoke.

'I got offered a job to pass to her. Good pay, pick up some goods and deliver it, nothing even fucking complicated about it, but...'

'What was it?' It wasn't a question, but a demand.

'I was desperate for reels, we both were... There were only three of them... They didn't even tell me everything until she'd left with the other mercenaries.'

Ryza could already guess. The word slipped from his mouth as a growl.

'Autominds.'

'It's not like that—'

'Then what is it?'

She didn't have an answer for him.

Ryza scoffed. 'I always hated how people would look at a Kretatic and sneer before we'd said a word, but I'm starting to think it's self-inflicted. We're all traitors to ourselves the second autominds come up. Makes me ashamed to be thrown in with people like you. No wonder people think we're all smelters at the bone.'

'There's plenty worse done in this world, smelter or not,' she retorted.

Ryza stood up and pulled the door open. 'Sure seems to take one to know one, if that's what you think!'

Before she could answer, he stepped through and slammed it shut, proceeding at a brisk pace down the corridor and darting around the corner. He risked one last glance to make sure she hadn't followed. There wasn't a sign of her.

Out of unnecessary caution, he proceeded back to his cabin on a much longer route than normal. Revance was so massive that even if Holm had decided to give chase, it was a slim chance they'd run into each other. If they did, he'd have no idea what to say.

Guilt was curdling in Ryza's stomach. Holm certainly seemed like the kind that wouldn't crack often and when she did, it would only be for a moment. Maybe he'd been too harsh. He was on the verge of turning around to find her and apologise, only snuffing out the idea by reminding himself that she'd tried to kill him only yesterday.

What she'd involved herself in was unforgivable. She'd had a choice and he hadn't, he told himself.

But we're both just as guilty.

CHAPTER FIFTEEN

SMELTERS FOR HIRE

IT WAS A DAY of red skies and dusty air as Ryza picked his way through the remains of a skirmish. Two dead smelters lay before him. One caught a slug to the head seconds after Ryza had got out of the lead-better. The other, a Reythurist by the looks of it, lay embedded in the sand after a failed attempt to take flight using an axiom of hastily drawn runes.

It had been a week since he'd talked to Holm. A week packed with so many missions and skirmishes that his squad had been temporarily broken up to fill the ones that hadn't come back with all their members. Each cargo run he'd been assigned to had been forced to fend off multiple hijackings and the raids on known smelter bases felt more like day-long sieges.

The smelters were getting braver and more well-armed, a combination that had Ryza's rifle so hungry for slugs he'd been forced to take a loan from the armoury to keep his weapon fed. He suspected he'd only been allowed the loan through some connection with the Locusts, but he couldn't be sure. There'd been no time to search for the flux aboard Revance as he swore he'd spent more time in the wastes than in the fortress.

The only person he'd met from today's crew of conscripts was Ferrick. She was the girl from the forge rooms he'd briefly spoken with before Yuvet gave him a concussion for his attempted escape. Two of the others were too busy shaking in their boots on the journey from Revance to introduce themselves. The last, proudly named Grud, now strode towards the corpses with a puffed chest, even though he hadn't fired a shot.

High above them, a signal flare hung in the sky. It burned bright, replacing the sun that was hidden behind the recently passed dust storm. The poor bastards that crewed the water pump outpost were nowhere to be seen. It was in a dead-end canyon with high rock walls, so either they'd escaped or smelters had done something worse.

The pump itself was a grand construct. Ryza had only seen one in the flesh once before. Above ground was a massive steel umbrella, positioned over a pit covered by an iron manhole. A Curiktic would drop a ball of super-heated magnesium down the mile-deep hole, where it would hit a deeply buried water reserve that hadn't yet evaporated and turn it to steam.

The umbrella would then catch the vapour, funnelling it into a twisting mass of pipes and valve-sealed tanks before it was lost in the air. Now the manhole lay uncovered, meaning anything down there would be bone dry.

What a waste.

While there wasn't nearly enough of it to experiment, it was thought that the moment pure water sensed the sky, it would disappear. Mixing it into ink would buy a few more seconds, but the act itself was a deeply personal ritual which most preferred to carry out by their own hand.

Smelters may be reckless by nature, but like everyone else in the Droughtlands, they wanted water above anything else. Something else was going on here. He glanced at Grud, who was prodding the closest corpse with the muzzle of his rifle.

'Hey, Bloodfist, come have a look at this,' Grud called.

'Don't call me that,' Ryza said as he walked over.

Nothing seemed out of the ordinary for a man without the top of his skull. Just brain matter splattered across the ground and blood soaking into the sand. It wasn't until Grud pointed at the smelter's weapon that Ryza raised an eyebrow.

It was a rifle, Revance pattern, markings and all. Ryza stowed his weapon and picked up the smelter's gun, turning it over in his hands before breaking it apart to peer down the empty barrel. When he snapped it back together, he froze. He'd felt two clicks. Ryza actioned it again. Another two clicks.

'I've held this rifle before.'

'You what?' Grud said.

'This was the first one the quartermaster tried to give me on Revance. It was faulty, so they gave me another, but how did it end up here? They should have fixed it.'

'You think they just tossed it out?'

'And someone just happened to find it that fast?' Ryza shook his head. 'Something's wrong.'

He glanced around again, catching Ferrick's eye as she nodded towards the only shack in the basin.

'Grud, take the other two and stand guard at the canyon mouth, see if you can get on top of the cliffs. I think there might be more smelters.'

Grud took a big, theatrical sniff of the air. 'Smells like a trap.'

As Grud left, Ryza crept over to Ferrick, taking position with her against the wall of the shack just next to the door.

Silently, she pointed to her ear, held up one finger, then gestured to the door.

She can hear one of them inside.

Ryza loaded a slug into his rifle and moved to the front of the door. Like everything else out in these parts, it was just a piece of scrap, but it would still take a mighty kick to bring it down.

The first kick rattled the frame, but the door held. The second produced a small yelp from inside. With a third kick, the door almost snapped off its hinges, flinging open with enough force to bang loudly on the inner wall. Ferrick dashed in before Ryza regained his balance. Inside, he found her attempting to wrestle another smelter to the ground, a fight Ryza finished by slamming the stock of his rifle into the bastard's head.

By the time the smelter came to his senses, Ryza and Ferrick had their weapons trained on him.

'Look, just... just don't kill me!' the man sputtered. 'You want water? I can get you...'

It was odd that the man wasn't as pitiful or wild as the smelters Ryza had seen before. He was broad and grizzled, a warrior rather than a grave robbing bandit, despite the fear in his eyes. Like the others outside, he was dressed for travelling, all sturdy leathers covered by a cloak. His weapon lay discarded on the other side of the room, another of Revance's rifles.

Ryza nodded towards it. 'Where'd you and your friends get your rifles?'

'We bought them in Kyrea.'

'Who from? The factories making them should only supply to Revance. You aren't getting them from the fortress, either.'

'I don't know... it was just one of the gun merchants there.' The man's gaze flickered down to their collars, then back to them, his eyes filling with panic. 'Look, I'm not a smelter, alright? I know what you lot from Revance are like, but we don't do that, we're just mercenaries, guns-for-hire. Same as you!'

'So, you raided a water pump thinking you'd get away with it?' Ferrick spat. 'Or was this a paid job, too?'

'No, no, we just needed some water on the way back from our last job, it was sent for by someone *from* Revance! We were here to buy, not steal! I assure you we had the reels. This place was already empty by the time we got here. You have to believe me!'

If I believed you, then I just killed two mercs for nothing.

Ryza slowly lowered his rifle and crouched down, eye level to the terrified mercenary. Something was off with him. The pupils of his green eyes were pinpricks, even in the gloom of the shack. His skin was far too pale for someone who spent their days travelling. As he leaned in closer, the man flinched.

'I need you to tell me everything. Who sent you, what for and where?'

'I don't know who sent us. All we got was this little arcanite that rolled up to us with a box on its back. It had a dial and a huge bounty reward for tracking down whatever it pointed to and bringing it to this outpost somewhere near between Kyrea and Breggesa. The guys that the three of us were with, they lit up and we had to follow along if I wanted a piece of the action.

'We bought our buggy, guns and supplies with whatever we had in our pockets and spent about three weeks travelling, following that damn dial into the middle of nowhere. Soon we hit ruins. Those-of-glass, y'know? Huge, massive glass towers like they were from another world, so tall out of the ground but going so deep. The dial pointed down... so... so we went down...'

As the man trailed off, Ryza saw out of the corner of his eye that Ferrick's rifle was beginning to sag.

'How deep did you go?' Ferrick asked softly.

'I have no idea...' The man's eyes began to drift in different directions as he spoke, but he hadn't noticed. 'It took us a couple tries and every time we went down there, everything was different. Sometimes we felt like we were underground for days, when it was only minutes to our lookout posted above. The things we found down there too... Living pieces of metal that twisted like worms, stairs going up that only took you back down and the shadows...'

The man broke, rubbing his eyes and gasping for air as if he'd just been buried. Ryza was about to give him a shove when he felt Ferrick's hand on his shoulder.

'Wait. He's been through more than you know.'

'And how do you know that?' he shot back.

'Because that's what I did before I joined Revance.' She paused. 'But keep that to yourself.'

Ryza turned back to the man and leaned just a bit closer.

'I need to know what you found down there. What was the bounty was for?'

After a long breath, the mercenary responded. 'We weren't meant to screw around with it, it's what we agreed on after our first trip underground. We'd seal it in a box and get our reels. Nothing else. But it was just this little arcanite and it kept saying one word... It just said... Origin.'

Ryza's head swam like he'd just been slapped. Origin was from the ruins, maybe even a relic of a those-of-glass. He'd heard nothing but legends about those places, tales of danger and death. But someone aboard Revance had been looking specifically for the arcanite in secret.

'Tell me the name of who sent out the bounty.'

The man shook his head. 'We got no names, nothing, not even when we dropped off the arcanite. Only a fat sack of reels to divvy up between the three of us made it out.'

Ryza shook his head. His hands moved across his rifle, ready to brandish it. 'There has to be something. Anything!'

'There was the resonance of the arcanite that sent the bounty out! Cold and calm, but... but... but nothing else!'

Ryza's hands froze on his rifle.

Cold and calm.

His rifle.

Whoever had ordered the bounty was the same person who had once owned this rifle and the only people who didn't seem to carry a rifle around Revance were the Locusts. And since Origin had ended up in that smelter camp, then whoever wanted the arcanite had something to do with the flux that had been bound for Revance! All he had to do was find the former owner of his rifle and he would find the buyer of the flux!

'Ferrick, search the shack,' Ryza said breathlessly.

Another wave of panic shot through the mercenary's eyes as Ferrick began moving through the other rooms. He started babbling at a fever pitch, growing paler by the second.

'You ain't going to find anything that you shouldn't already be expecting! More comes out of Revance than you know, boy. Our buggy, out the back, that came from there too. The markets of Kyrea? Loaded with your people's gear. Don't even know how you lot stay supplied with that much going back out into the Droughtlands!'

'And that's why you went back to Kyrea?' Ryza barked. 'Spend your bounty on *our* gear? Or was it to buy molten flux!?'

'Not at all! We'd just heard of this crazy old coot that wouldn't shut up about old arcanites that lived in Kyrea. We wanted to know, no, HAD to know what that stupid little arcanite was!' The man gasped sharply, his left eye fixed on Ryza and his right on the ceiling. 'I see it in you, boy! You know about the arcanite, but—'

The man was cut off as Ferrick called out to Ryza.

'Ryza! You're not going to like this.'

He tried to stand up, but the mercenary kept grabbing at his coat.

'Please, it was the other two, I didn't want—'

Ryza brushed him off and followed the sound of Ferrick's voice through the circular outer passageway of the shack. She came out of the last room, shaking her head as she went back to keep an eye on the still jabbering mercenary.

Only a thin cloth veiled the doorway, the hem of it dancing gently in the draught. Subtle light was coming through beyond it, probably through a hole in the roof. Ryza pushed it aside with the muzzle of his rifle and stepped into the room.

Inside, he saw exactly what he'd expected to see the moment he'd heard Ferrick's call. But it didn't stop the waves of shock and horror pumping through his veins.

There were four of them. Three men, one woman, huddled in the corner of the room, standing there with their clothes torn to rags. They didn't look at him as he entered, even though he was sure he was breathing hard enough for them to hear. They just stood there, motionless as they faced the wall.

Autominds.

Fluxburn scarred their exposed skin, taking the form of a translucent rash with dull, silver liquid pulsing underneath like it was their blood. The backs of their necks were still bare, a bright bruise blooming out from where the needle had gone in.

They're fresh. Less than a day, maybe. Any more and that bruise would look silver.

Ryza slowly stepped forward, keeping his rifle trained on them with one hand while he reached out with his left, placing it gently on the nearest automind's shoulder. They turned with shuffling feet, their blank face staring at him with silver orbs where eyes should've been. The molten flux had taken everything it could, leaving the shell as nothing more than a husk.

He didn't check the other autominds. He didn't want to know exactly how much of a waste the bastards had made of their lives. He was already stomping back through the shack, his nostrils flaring with fury as his heart began to race, the resonance in his rifle doing nothing to calm him.

Ryza could already hear the bastard begging from the next room. When he walked in, Ferrick already had him dead to rights.

'No, please! You don't understand! The reels they were giving per automind, it was almost as good as what we got for the arcanite! The other two—'

BLAM! BLAM!

The acrid stench of gun smoke filled the room and Ryza's vision grew hazy from it. At least that's what he told himself as they both reloaded. He looked at Ferrick, who seemed just as horrified.

'You're not going to speak a word about anything said in here, got it? It'll complicate things with the others too much.'

'What about the autominds in there?' Ferrick asked. 'Can we save them?'

'We leave them. There's nothing we can do for them.'

Ferrick's brow creased. 'How do you know?'

'My hands aren't clean.' Ryza said sharply. 'Go get the others, we're heading back to Revance. Say that he tried to fight.'

Ferrick paused for a moment, considering Ryza before she nodded slightly and left the shack. As soon as she was gone, Ryza nearly collapsed, his hands on his knees as he drew breath after shuddering breath. He'd never wanted to see another automind like that again, but now he'd been confronted with four of them. It didn't even look like the mercenaries had done them the courtesy of killing them before pumping them full of flux.

Once he'd gathered himself, he searched the pockets of the man, looking for anything more about the bounty. Coming up empty handed, he instead collected the extra rifle and headed out to do the same with the other corpses.

Still nothing. Shit. What if he'd been lying about it all?

With three extra rifles clutched in his arms, he then went to the back of the shack, where —as expected— he found a beaten up lead-better, just like the one that had carried them out here. This one's front plate had taken a pounding, but that didn't stop Ryza from throwing the extra rifles into the back tray jond getting in the driver's seat.

The engine hummed pleasantly as Ryza cranked the ignition and he manoeuvred it to the front of the shack. The others had returned by now. Grud was wearing a stupid grin and shouting about getting extra pay for bringing back another lead-better.

Because you did all the hard work on that one.

With Ferrick riding as his shotgun and the other three on the original buggy, they set a winding course through the dunes that would take them back to Revance. It was only halfway through the journey back that Ferrick's voice broke the monotonous thrum of the motor.

'You ever heard of mercenaries taking autominds like that?'

'You think I have?'

'You said your hands weren't clean.'

Ryza couldn't help nodding. 'It happens. A flux trader needs fresh bodies to give to a buyer who doesn't want to deal with the smelters to get them. Wants to operate without making a whole lot of noise. But I never heard of too many going out of their way to do it. Only reason I can think of is if demand has shot way up.'

'Thought you might know,' Ferrick said casually.

Ryza felt his knuckles go white on the steering vane. 'Why's that?' he asked through gritted teeth.

'Ditric's your squad mate, right? She never talked to you about what got her out of mercenary work?'

In his shock, Ryza almost jerked the vane and flipped the buggy. 'What?'

'Holm told me a while back, reason Ditric hates her guts. Back when Holm was a trader, she often hired Ditric as her guard. One day she got wind of a good opportunity to Ditric, put her on to it and the whole thing turned out to be a smelter hit, just like at the pump back there. Holm still doesn't know half the details, but they've blamed each other ever since. I don't know why she'd do it, though.'

'Holm?'

'No, Ditric. Holm said she followed through on the job before coming back to her. I would have just bailed out of it.'

'Sometimes you don't have a lot of choices.' Ryza said, chewing his upper lip. There was that smelter-hating part of him that wanted to immediately blame Ditric for what she'd done, but their friendship was almost starting to repair.

Maybe she didn't have a choice.

Ryza focused his mind on Origin and finding the owner of his rifle's magnetic resonance. Now another connection had come into play. Revance's missing supplies.

Could it all be the same culprit?

CHAPTER SIXTEEN

RUNNING ON EMPTY

WHEN RYZA AND THE others were hauled into Revance's motor pool, the gobsmacked mechanics hadn't been expecting them to come back, let alone with an extra lead-better. Least pleased of all was Revance's master of vehicles, Garrog, a brute of a man for whom the whites of his eyes were just as yellowed as his irises.

From the impression Ryza quickly gathered, Garrog could've spent the rest of the day shouting about how metal mouths never brought back anything good, only mercifully stopping when Yuvet appeared to rescue him.

'Just put it with the rest and fix it up!' Yuvet had bellowed at him. 'Anyway, you're always complaining about not having enough buggies! Go!'

Garrog had grumbled for a moment before turning his barking rage to his own mechanics, while Yuvet had grabbed Ryza forcefully by the shoulder and steering him out of the motor pool, leading him to a large and distinctly empty storeroom. Once they were inside, she bolted the door and began to pace around the room.

'Notice anything strange?'

'No ma'am,' Ryza instantly replied.

Yuvet threw out her hands dramatically as she stopped in the centre of the room. 'Where's all our damn cargo!? Everything in here was bound for Iroka on a contract that was meant to pay for all the other shit that's gone missing! If we don't find it, we'll be making the trip back to Breggesa with nothing but bayonets and bare fists. You made any breakthroughs in the forge rooms?'

'Not yet—'

'Dammit, Ryz!'

'But I've found something else, ma'am.'

'Then tell me!'

He recounted the mercenary's last words, leaving out anything related to Origin. He wasn't ready to reveal the arcanite yet.

'So Kyrea might be where everything's going,' Yuvet muttered. 'Or at least where it's not coming from. I've checked the log books, they've all been marked as if we're receiving goods, but that could only mean that someone onboard is looking the other way for a cut of the reels that the factories are making by selling to someone else. Stupid plan. They'll be busted in about a week or two when we've got nothing to eat!'

'There's one more thing, ma'am. He said the price paid for fresh autominds was high. Only factories looking to ramp up production would ask for that. If it was something high enough to tempt mercenaries, it must have at least tripled.'

'Tripled?' Yuvet's eyes snapped to him. 'Why would you know the price of an automind?'

Now he had to play his last card. It was the only way she would trust his word. 'My father is a... a flux trader.'

Ryza didn't have time to flinch before the barrel of Yuvet's rifle was pressed against his chin.

'Give me a reason I shouldn't,' Yuvet growled, her finger brushing the trigger.

'Because I want to kill him as much as I want to kill every other smelter in the Droughtlands. He was the reason I ran from Breggesa, the reason I'm now glad I've joined Revance and the reason I want to track down the smelter onboard and shoot them just as much as you want to shoot me.'

Yuvet still didn't move. She kept her gaze hard, waiting for him to break, but Ryza stood resolute. He knew what he believed in and there was no way she could shoot him for it.

After eight heartbeats, Yuvet lowered her weapon.

'Go get something to eat, Ryza. And keep searching. I can't help you get to Kyrea, but if you find a way...' She let out an exasperated sigh. 'Only come to me when you find something, not a word before that. I've heard about you out there killing more than enough smelters, but if it gets around that you're the son of a flux trader, it'll be both our heads.'

Ryza nodded as Yuvet waved him out of the room. As he walked the corridors, a cold sensation prickled on his back. There were now multiple people who knew what he was. Ditric might be acting friendly towards him now, but there was no telling who she'd told before. As for Ferrick, he'd just have to hope she kept her mouth shut. Ryza could remember the first day they'd met, she'd looked too exhausted to talk in the first place. But then he remembered who he'd met alongside her.

Holm.

Ferrick had just mentioned the two of them were friends, but how much did they share? He'd have to find her again, swear her to secrecy, or in the worst case...

Kill her?

It was brutal, but Holm had tried to do the same thing to him to stop word about the Locusts from getting out.

No, there has to be another way.

When Ryza got his meal in the mess hall, he scoffed it down so fast he didn't even make it to his seat. Instead, he jogged back to his squad's cabin, arriving out of breath and finding the four of them looking up at him perplexedly.

'Yuvet catch you for more physical conditioning?' Ruka asked.

'Beatings, more like,' Haven cut in.

He let out a chuckle and clapped Ryza on the back as he staggered in.

'Look, just sit down, all of you,' Ryza said. 'I'll explain as much as I can.'

They crammed themselves around the cabin's tiny table, with

Ditric opting to lean against the bunks, having drawn the short straw for seats.

After placating Origin and somehow convincing it to sit down too, Ryza launched into his story of what had just happened, leaving nothing out, not even his conversation with Yuvet. When he was done, Gry was the first to speak.

'So, there must be something going on within Revance and it looks like Origin here is the key to figuring out what.'

'Origin,' it replied.

Ruka sighed and tapped the arcanite on its head. 'That's all well and good, but how do we find out what the deal is with this thing? It ain't going to kill us, right?'

'Other than getting to Kyrea, where they said that old man was, I have no idea,' Haven said.

'Maybe not,' Ryza said. He turned to Ditric. 'Ferrick, the girl I was with, I'm going to keep an eye out for her, I still have some things to ask her about the ruins of those-of-glass. Maybe she'd know more about Origin.'

'I've met types like that,' Ruka said. 'They don't like being asked about that stuff.'

'Well, it's not like he's got a choice, is it?' Ditric said. 'And there's no way he's getting to Kyrea on his own.'

She's right. Maybe the Locusts can help.

But Ryza was in for another week of fruitless searching. There was no sign of Ferrick, nor even Holm. While it quickly became mind-numbing, at least Ditric seemed to be warming towards him. Just yesterday she'd sat next to him at their morning meal.

By this point Ryza would have killed for something interesting to happen. In any spare moment he was stalking up and down the maze that was Revance, searching for a hint of the molten flux or that cold and calm resonance. Other times would find him sitting alone in their cabin, watching Origin wander the room aimlessly.

His thoughts always ended up at the mercenary's mention of the old man in Kyrea and what Holm had said about a trip out there. All he could do now was hope she'd invite him along.

Now I must rely on the most unreliable person I've ever met.

It wasn't until one evening after he'd finished dinner that

something finally happened. He and the others were filing out of the dining hall, carried by the slow push of people, when someone going the opposite way bumped into him. Ryza had managed to turn just in time to catch sight of Holm's white-blonde hair before she disappeared into the crowd.

He checked his pockets and found a single slip of torn paper.

Dawn.

Motor Pool.

No Gun.

Alone.

CHAPTER SEVENTEEN

KYREA

LONG BEFORE THE SUN threatened to rise, Ryza had laced up his boots and tip-toed out of the cabin with a pack over his shoulder. Origin was stuffed inside, along with enough rags to muffle him. He felt utterly naked without his rifle. But as much as he hated it, he had to trust Holm.

Spare for the guard posts, Revance was empty, making it easy to find his way to the motor pool unquestioned. Mechanics wandered from vehicle to vehicle in a haze of their own exhaustion, their tired faces only lighting up when they summoned small balls of intense fire to their hands to patch vehicles back together. In the far corner, Ryza could see one of the workers still tending to the spare lead-better he'd brought in.

Most seemed to focus on the cluster of treadhulks, so Ryza steered clear. These were massive contraptions clad in plates of steel armour at least six inches thick and held off the ground by sets of jaggedly toothed tank treads. Sparks bounded out of their many gunports every few moments as if there was a bonfire within.

The vehicles were intended as cargo vessels, made to haul whatever goods Revance was tasked with to their final destination that the fortress itself wouldn't go near, yet the current works looked to be mounting enormous cannons to them.

Away from the cacophony of works, Ryza spotted Maligar standing at the motor pool's edge, staring out over the dunes. Three vehicles sat next to him, much stranger than anything Ryza had ridden in so far. Lower slung, being barely a foot off the ground, their wheels replaced by odd, bulbous metal domes, the padded seats reclining almost flat and their chassis bizarrely free of any fleck of rust. The middle of the trio was slightly larger, owing to the bulky crate strapped to its rear. Was some of the stolen cargo in there?

'The Bloodfist himself!' Maligar exclaimed, without a care for who might hear. 'I was wondering who would arrive first, though I wasn't betting on you.'

'Why not?' Ryza said as he approached. He glanced inside the vehicle's crate as he passed it, yet it was disappointingly empty.

'Well, all of your known exploits that got our attention have involved you arriving late.'

Ryza could only give a half-hearted shrug.

'I'm guessing you know what's happening today?' Maligar continued.

'We're going to Kyrea,' Ryza said. 'Or at least, the factories, right?'

'You know a thing or two, then! Yes, Kyrea. The Locusts need something from there.'

'Why make the trip? What do they make that we can't make here?'

Maligar paused for a moment, his mouth half open. 'It's not about what they make, Ryza, it's how they make it. From what I've heard, someone like you would already know.'

Ryza frowned.

What the hell did he mean by that?

'Anyway,' Maligar continued. 'I'm sure you'd like to have a poke around the place. It's not just factories, you know.'

'Only out of curiosity. Why do you need extra hands, anyway? Something big?'

'You'll find out when you're needed, don't worry,' Maligar said with a grin. 'I wanted to give you the opportunity to enjoy a few of the perks the Locusts confer, just in case you're yet to come around.'

Before Ryza could press him on the matter another pair arrived, both of them wearing excited grins. Small talk ensued, soon joined by several more members of the Locusts. Much to Ryza's surprise, they were a rather jolly bunch. Cracking jokes and slapping backs like old friends without a hint of anything sinister between them.

There wasn't any chance of Ryza getting a private word with Ferric by the time she decided to show her face. She too was rifle-less, but a serrated machete hung in a sling at her side instead. Ryza kicked himself for not thinking about doing the same. He glanced around at the others. Aside from her, none of them were wearing collars. What could Maligar want from two conscripts?

'By the looks of it, almost all of us are here, so I'll lay out the last details of our mission today. We'll be heading for Kyrea. No need to worry about navigating, whoever ends up driving a skimmer can just follow mine. Once there, we'll have free time to roam as we please until the deal at noon. Afterwards, we'll make our way out to a spot near Revance's predicted path, where we'll wait for the sun to go down before returning.'

'Sundown?' Ryza said. 'You know these collars are on a timer, right?'

Maligar grinned at him. 'Exactly, Ryza! Exactly. In fact, it's the exact reason I had you invited along. I want to see how you beat collar death.'

Ryza felt the colour drain from his face. He'd come here to find who had the flux aboard Revance, but now he was on the back foot. He certainly couldn't back out. If he went on this journey, he'd have to reveal Origin and even then, he wasn't sure if the arcanite actually reset the collar.

'So then why bring me?' Ferrick asked.

Maligar looked from her to Ryza. 'To make sure Ryza shares his trick. If someone knows how to beat the collar, it's knowledge that must be shared.'

One of the other Locusts piped up. 'So, who keeps an eye on the conscripts?'

Ryza already knew it was going to be before he was tapped on the shoulder, but it made him jump anyway.

'Hello, Rusty,' Holm chimed from next to him.

'The last member of our expedition!' Maligar announced. 'Most of you may not know her, but Holm is our most recent member and the one responsible for bringing Ryza and Ferrick into our midst. Come to think of it, she's also partly responsible for Ryza's notoriety.'

'He doesn't thank me for it, either,' Holm said in a tone of mock offence.

'Holm, you'll be keeping a close eye on these two to see how they beat the collar and when the time comes for the deal, you three will act as our lookouts. Gallic, Truden and Poke, you'll be scouting for the people we'll be dealing with and bringing them to the right spot at noon and getting us there too. As for myself and the remaining three, we unfortunately won't have a chance to roam Kyrea, but I'm sure we've all seen our fair share of it and the exquisite delights it offers.'

Everyone but Ryza and Ferrick shared a round of laughter.

'Yes, let the younger folk have some fun,' Maligar said, looking at his folded arms. He whipped them out and clapped his hands together, fixing them all with a grin. 'Let's get moving! Into the skimmers, in the groups I stated, if you would.'

They split up, Ryza reluctantly following Holm and Ferrick as they dashed into the front seats of one of the skimmers.

'These are a few of Tyrag's prototypes he doesn't seem to pay too much attention to, which is why we can borrow them,' she explained as Ryza clambered into the back seat. 'Built for speed, probably more than you can handle.'

As Holm drew an excessively long axiom down her arm Ryza, passed out goggles from the small collection under his seat. If this thing was built for speed, it was also built to fill his eyes with dust. Only question was, how the hell did it move?

He'd barely strapped the goggles on when the skimmer lurched beneath him. He involuntarily grabbed the hull for support, regretting it a moment later as Holm's maniacal resonance danced through his hands like a static shock. Ryza let go and had to suppress the urge to vomit. The buggy was now hovering a clear foot off the floor, an odd, low rumbling coming from underneath.

The skimmer shot off the mark. Holm hadn't even bothered waiting for the cranes to take them down. The floor of the motor pool simply disappeared from under them and suddenly they were soaring over the dunes. Ryza's guts lurched again as the desert below began to pull harder. But they didn't hit the ground. The skimmer shuddered as it neared the dunes, throwing up a spray of red dust. Now they were blasting along the dunes, only an inch between them and the sand.

The dunes eventually turned to salt flats as they went, signalling a relief from the undulating motion the skimmer took as it crested each hill. The land was speckled with derelict pump stations and settlements clustered around those that were still fruitful. Each of the latter was heavily fortified by walls of plate metal, but Ryza couldn't guess where it had come from. Pieces that large only existed in Revance's walls or in the ruins of those-of-glass.

'So Rusty, what are you planning to do when we get there?' Holm shouted back at him.

'Personal business,' he grunted back.

She glanced over her shoulder at him, an eyebrow raised despite her goggles. 'Oh, come on! Don't trust me?'

'Maybe he's too embarrassed to say,' Ferrick said.

Holm thought for a moment. 'Could be... There are some risqué experiences to seek out in Kyrea once you get past the factories. I know of a few if you need recommendations.'

'It's not that,' he said, a touch too quickly.

'Back when we found those autominds at the pump...' Ferrick said. 'I remember you said something like, "my hands aren't clean." That have something to do with it?'

Ryza swore to himself, the word lost in the roaring wind.

'Now that's something to talk about!' Holm exclaimed. 'What have you done with autominds, Rusty? Seen them? Used them? Made them?'

He couldn't say a word. Holm would just twist it.

'Silence is damning, Rusty!'

Then I'll be damned.

The salt flats gave way to barren rock, cratered with the remnants of forgotten mining operations. The large pits formed narrow paths with sheer drops on either side, forcing Holm and the other skimmers to joust with cantankerous arcanites twice the size of their vehicles. Either they made it to the next wide point in the roads or be crushed under the enormous treading feet of the opposing machines.

Ryza could barely get a glimpse of them as they whizzed past, but there must've been a dozen people riding the hides of the hulking beasts. The toll it would take on a Kretatic's mind to control one of them must be immense, unless...

Ryza swore to himself for not putting the pieces together sooner. How could he have been so stupid? Kyrea was a factory town, one which Revance relied upon, yet due to its rather unique positioning, it was overlooked by anyone without a death wish. The description of it as "unique" was another of his father's vague gifts, but it was only now that Ryza wondered if it had something to do with those-of-glass.

Making it a place where flux flowed freely.

These factories wouldn't be a scene like Revance's forge rooms. They'd be something far worse. As Maligar's course took their group descending down the spiralling ridges of one of the pits, Ryza tried to mentally brace himself for what he was about to witness and pray it didn't recognise him.

They dismounted at the bottom of a basin, leaving the skimmers parked between a collection of far more ramshackle "transports." The small crowds of ragged beggars scattered at their presence, lingering thirty feet away.

An acidic stench of sulphur emanated from scattered outcroppings of twisted and dented vents. Foul black smoke billowed from them, raining ash on anything unlucky enough to be downwind. Maligar didn't seem worried about that particular fate. He waved at them to gather near one of the larger manholes that plugged straight down into the earth.

'I don't think much has changed since our last visit, which means you'll need to keep your heads low in the tunnels. I don't need to remind you that Revance isn't a friendly name, but don't go splashing it around or wandering around in too big a pack.'

It took Maligar and three of the burliest Locusts to open the rusted hatch, and Ryza had no intention of helping. They descended the ladder it revealed, Holm and the rest of the Locusts following until Ryza was alone with Ferrick.

'You reckon it's safe down there?' he asked her. 'Being underground and all. I heard this place was made by those-of-glass.'

Ferrick shrugged. 'Seems more a question for you than me. Smelter's paradise down there. Besides, won't matter if you can't pull off your trick with the collar again.'

'Origin,' came the arcanite's call, still muffled in the backpack.

'I'll show you, but you have to help me, got it?'

'Is this something to do with your "personal business"?'

'Sort of.' Ryza shrugged the bag from his shoulders and began unbuckling the straps, explaining as he did. 'You remember those mercenaries we found at the water pump? How they spoke of an arcanite they brought back from the undercities?'

Ferrick glanced between him and the pack, fear mounting in her eyes. 'What have you...'

Ryza freed the last strap and Origin tumbled out, landing on its face with its wire thin arms tangled together. Ferrick leapt back, a hand already wrapped around her machete as she glanced to the nearby bustle of rag-wrapped travellers inching towards them.

'You know where that thing came from, right!?' she hissed. 'I've seen people's skin fall straight off their hands after holding stuff from there!'

'Hasn't happened with Origin,' Ryza said, showing her his rough yet unblemished palms. 'I need to find out what this arcanite does.'

'But why not just get rid of it? Even if it's done nothing to you yet—'

'Because it's how I beat the collar.'

Ryza held his wristband out to Origin, who staggered over and tapped at it a couple times, making something inside it tick over. Ferrick held out her own wristband and watched in awe as the black dial wound its way back at Origin's touch.

'It actually works...' Ferrick said breathlessly. 'You could have left this whole time... Why have you stayed so long?'

Ryza straightened up, scooping his now empty pack onto his shoulder. 'Personal business.'

'Just like now, huh? Keep your damn secrets then,' Ferrick said. 'What's the plan?'

That's a good question.

'You remember those mercenaries at the pump station? He'd said something about an old man in Kyrea who'd know what Origin was, but I've got no idea how to find him.'

'It looks like your friend does,' Ferrick said, pointing.

Origin had already set off, plodding on its tiny feet towards another manhole a hundred metres away. They followed closely, with Ferrick helping him haul the weighty hatch off the manhole Origin had decided to stop at. It was nearly impossible for the two of them and Ryza was tempted to dip into the last of his ink to help free the metal, but thankfully the rusted hinge squealed before that.

The shaft was barely wide enough for Ryza's shoulders, not sporting a ladder as much as a pair of spiralling grooves that ran around the walls in a helical fashion. Before he and Ferrick could debate over who'd have to go first, Origin took two steps forward and simply plummeted into the darkness.

CHAPTER EIGHTEEN

AUTOMINDS AND ORIGINS

THE TIGHT CONFINES OF Ryza's descent didn't let up when his feet finally hit solid ground. The few less-than-accidental kicks in the head received from Ferrick along with complaints of how slowly he climbed didn't help the strange popping sensation in his ears. As he stepped out of the way to let Ferrick ground herself too, the only thing that changed in the surroundings was that the path was now horizontal rather than vertical. The spiral-walled tunnel stretched in either direction, lit by dying glow bulbs and echoing with grating machinery and far-off conversation.

Ryza spotted Origin proceeding down one of the narrow corridors, its tiny body half lost in the twisting smoke that hung on the floor and hastened after the arcanite.

'How can you even trust it?' Ferrick hissed in his ear. 'You don't even know where it's going!'

Origin's head twisted back to face them, letting out a fierce trill of grinding iron like it was mimicking her, not breaking its tiny stride.

'That answer enough for you?' Ryza whispered.

The tunnel led out to a catwalk that swayed underfoot, the fraying cables that fixed it to the ceiling doing little to ease Ryza's worry of the massive drop below. The cavern was almost big enough to fit Revance itself. It was framed by walls of impossibly machined rock and its floor bustling with garish sights that beckoned for Ryza's attention.

Rickety carts overflowed with brightly coloured clothes. Stalls laden with meat still sizzling from the grill cast a pungent aroma into the street. Kretatics surrounded by all manner of arcanite offered their contraptions' services as messenger, labourer or enforcer.

He watched as the purchase of the latter was hastily commissioned by a merchant that was in hot pursuit of a thieving street urchin. The child was weaving through the crowd, clutching close their bounty, a limp sack of grain, but dropped it with an inaudible yelp as an arcanite three times their size stomped after them.

The contraption was a battering ram with legs, but it did not stop when it had the chance to retrieve the stolen goods. Ryza looked away. He could already picture the inevitable. If Ruka's stories were true, it wasn't uncommon, either.

To get his mind off it, Ryza decided to nudge Ferrick into a conversation. He had to yell over the din just to be heard. 'I've heard stories of this place, but I never understood how it was built.'

'Wasn't built,' Ferrick replied. 'They would've found it like this. Those-of-glass —not that there's much glass down here— left it behind. No one knows how deep it goes.'

'Why?'

'No one who found out made it back to say.'

As if the arcanite had heard her words, Origin's path suddenly branched off the catwalk and it tumbled down another chute, forcing Ryza and Ferrick to follow quickly before the arcanite was snatched up by one of the many thieves lurking below.

Among the market crowds, Origin didn't have a chance of taking two steps without being kicked over, so Ryza resorted to tucking the arcanite into his jacket pocket, relying on the spindly arm pointing out of the folds to guide their path.

The tunnels grew smaller —yet still gigantic by Ryza's standards— as the wares on offer grew more illicit, just as Holm had said, yet not an ounce more subtle. Grizzled merchants stood shiftily in doorways, flashing hunks of twisting, living metals in their palms as they met

Ryza's gaze. When he looked again, they were gone.

Entire avenues seemed dedicated to the arms dealers. Racks of rifles were on proud display, carefully watched by hulking guards wielding the cheapest weapons on offer.

He lingered by one of the racks, turning a rifle in his hands and seeing the pattern of Revance stamped across its stock. Despite the gloom, it gleamed as new, perhaps never having once been aboard the fortress before finding its way here. The rifles on either side were identical, all churned out of the same factory. The one that should only be supplying to Revance itself.

A sneering gun merchant approached, but Ryza decided to move off before he attracted too much attention. Other purveyors stocked the more well-loved rifles, which Ryza guessed had been given an early retirement from Revance's armoury.

At this rate, I'll be lucky to still have my own in a week.

He and Ferrick continued on Origin's path for a few more minutes, pausing only as Ryza spotted a column of shambling bodies cutting a path through the crowd. Three smelters strutted at its head, taking vicious swings with their clubs at those who didn't step aside fast enough.

Despite Origin's little arm imploring him to turn left, Ryza followed. Morbid curiosity was driving him to see what they were to be used for. Ferrick came with him, none the wiser of Ryza's detour until they were closer to his target.

Autominds always made an unmistakable sound. Their bare feet slammed into the ground as one and their wrists were shackled so tightly they practically walked on top of each other. Ryza couldn't bear to look closer. He knew what he'd see. Slumped heads and empty eyes. Patches of bruised and broken skin where molten flux filled in the gaps.

The line of autominds was diverted through a cavity in the wall. Judging by the chipped rubble surrounding it, it'd been blown through with crude explosives. A few of the autominds tripped on the rough threshold, yet those they were bound to carried them without hesitation.

'Ryza, we shouldn't be here,' Ferrick whispered. 'This doesn't look right.'

'No... it doesn't.'

Suddenly, the autominds halted just ahead and the sound of an argument carried back to them. It was between the three smelters and a fourth who sounded like they'd been waiting for them. Ryza pulled Ferrick into the shadows behind the line of autominds and the three smelters stomped past. Each had a small sack of clanking reels in hand, but they wore expressions that seemed none too pleased about it.

With the smelters gone, the autominds' march resumed. Ryza followed, forcing a reluctant Ferrick to do the same.

Only a few steps out of the ruined passageway had them presiding over another cavern where a wave of clanging metal almost made Ryza's eardrums burst. It was another one of the tunnels, this time filled with batteries of production lines that weaved among themselves like tangled roots.

The stations were not crewed by humans, but instead by arrays of pincered arms, rapidly hammering drop forges, whizzing conveyor belts, and constantly threshing hoppers. Flashes of iron and brass rushed through the process, glowing with the same heat that smothered the cavern's oily air.

From a distance, Ryza followed the autominds down the steep and winding slope towards the work floor, ignoring Ferrick's protests as he tried to figure out where one machine ended and another began. The only sign of it was the narrow spouts that vomited fresh ammunition into rapidly filling barrels. They were all working in perfect harmony and he estimated they'd be spitting out eight or nine new rifle slugs every second.

But how?

No matter how practised a group of Kretatics could ever be, controlling multiple arcanites in concert like this should be downright impossible. The metal would feel sluggish at the best of times, meaning arcanites requiring lightning-fast commands like these were a fool's errand.

Moving along the line with his hand pressed to the metal casings of each machine, Ryza waited for a different resonance to appear. Just a single break from the droning feeling of dread that emitted from the contraptions. When he caught up to the line of autominds, he stopped, realisation dawning on him far too late.

There must be thousands...

They were lined up in pairs, spaced a metre apart ahead of him, dead still for a few moments before they blindly crawled under the machines. Ahead, the fourth smelter watched them go, their attention only being caught by Ryza and Ferrick's presence once his charges had disappeared into the darkness.

'Oi!'

Shit.

The man started fumbling with something at his belt and Ferrick realised what it was long before Ryza did. Her machete swished out from her side and she closed the distance in the blink of an eye. The smelter only just managed to free his hand cannon —a rifle that'd had everything unnecessary crudely sawn from it— as Ferrick primed her machete for a wild swing.

The hand cannon went off with an echoing blast. Ryza felt a slug whizz over his shoulder as Ferrick vanished into the burning haze of gun smoke. There was a revolting crunch of metal biting bone, the sound splitting the air again as the man's ribs splintered. The smelter collapsed with a dull thud but Ferrick wasn't done.

She reversed her grip on her machete and drove it straight into his lifeless chest, impaling the blade as deep as it would go. Ferrick was still struggling to retrieve her blade as Ryza approached, only managing it by planting a boot on the corpse's neck and cracking a few more bones on the way out.

'Bastard will probably be an automind in a minute,' Ryza muttered.

'He'd deserve worse if it existed.' Ferrick said, breathing heavily. She patted the smelter down, failing to come up with anything worth taking. Even the hand cannon had shattered from being dropped. With one hand, she tore a somewhat clean section from the smelter's trousers, using the rag to wipe the blood from her face.

'Where'd you learn to fight like that?' Ryza asked. He wasn't sure if the feeling he was trying to contain was admiration or horror.

She waved her blood-drenched machete and the hand that wielded it with a grin. 'It's like you say. My hands aren't clean. Hope the mess was worth whatever you were after. Why'd you want to come down here so bad?'

'I'd heard of the factories. I just never knew it took this many autominds to run them. I had to see it for myself.'

A minute later, they were back in the main tunnels and Ryza was dutifully following Origin's prescribed course. The path grew more barren, the only passers-by taking the form of more columns of trudging autominds, along with the smelters leading them.

'Must be thousands of them in the miles surrounding us, maybe more,' Ryza remarked. 'Makes you think about what Revance does, if this is what's still happening.'

She laughed mirthlessly. 'What Revance does? Please, half the time I feel like we're doing *less* than nothing. Pointless patrols of empty stretches of land and chasing something that knows to stay well out of our reach.'

'And by that you mean?'

'Revance patrols the Droughtlands. Sure, it stops in a couple places, but only ever for a few days at a time. Otherwise, it's constantly moving. It always was a cargo hauler, we've just turned it into something it ain't.'

'So? That's good, isn't it? Means we can keep an eye on as many things as possible.'

'It means that we can't establish any kind of control over an area. Doesn't matter if we roll through a place guns blazing, the smelters will come back the moment we leave and know to take a holiday the next time they see us coming. Just think though, what if Revance could be controlled? Actually controlled? We could take it here and just flatten the place.'

'Wouldn't work. Revance is too old for its resonance to be copied and taken over. You'd need to find the creator, but they're probably dead.' Ryza glanced over at her, a frown forming on his brow. 'You really want to flatten this place? Kill all these people? They aren't all smelters.'

'Don't you?' she shot back. 'Thought you'd be in favour of a few more killings. I was surprised I beat you to killing that smelter back in the factory. You *are* the Bloodfist and all.'

'Yuvet's never taught us anything with a machete,' Ryza said, changing the subject. 'All she'll tell us is ways to get back far enough to reload our rifles. Another perk of the Locusts?'

'It's half knowing what to do with it, half what it does,' she replied with a wink.

Ryza glanced at the bloodstained blade slung by her side. Hopefully he didn't find out "what it does" the hard way.

Origin's path turned from sure-footed stone to crumbling rocks. It was as if they'd crossed a forgotten border into a wide and natural cave. Narrow strands of sunlight leaked through the cracks in the cavern ceiling, the largest of which fell on an isolated hovel that sat at the back of the hollow.

Ryza finally cut Origin loose and the arcanite sprinted towards the dwelling. He and Ferrick followed at a distance, only halfway across the cave by the time Origin was pounding its tiny wire fists on the hovel's door.

It swung open, knocking the arcanite over, and a dishevelled old man staggered out with bare feet. Ryza and Ferrick stopped in their tracks, the latter ready with her machete.

'Who's out there!?' the man rasped. His face turned wildly, blind eyes searching for something they'd long lost the ability to see. His clothes were punctured and grey, and if Ryza hadn't heard him speak, he would've mistaken him for an automind.

'How many of you are there? Quickly!'

'Just two of us,' Ryza called, 'and an arcanite.'

The old man gave a yelp of surprise as Origin began gently battering his shins. After a moment, a smile splitting his lined face and he crouched down, placing a shaking hand on the arcanite.

'A couple of lifetimes since I felt that.' The old man straightened up and produced a vial of ink and a brush from his coat. 'Stay there for a moment, would you?'

It took the blind man nearly half a minute to paint two runes on his arm. Once he was done, he lowered his hand until it was an inch off the ground.

Some kind of pressure filled the air, putting a lump in Ryza's throat as his joints started to lock up. A pulsing shiver took him as the sand in the cave did the same, a thousand iron filings rising to hover at their ankles before they shot towards him.

He wanted to duck or run, but he couldn't bring himself to do anything but squeeze his eyes shut. Nothing happened. At least, it felt like nothing. Ryza cracked an eye open.

'Iron filings embedded in your clothes. They'll fall out when you leave,' the old man said, his vacant eyes still somehow meeting theirs. 'My name's Rettic. I don't know how you found Origin, but you've reunited me with a piece of my past I've tried to forget.'

The inside of the tilted shack was dim and musty, and Ryza had to tread carefully as to not trip on the miniature junkyard that had replaced the contents of what should have been a home.

Complex instruments and archaic gadgets lay in tangled piles. Animal pelts hung haphazardly from the walls and buckets of rotten smelling mushrooms Ryza had spotted in other parts of the cave were positioned so that one was always within arm's reach.

The light creeping in through the cracks in the roof wasn't enough to take it in properly and Ryza caught himself wondering if it would be rude to ask for a candle to be lit. He dismissed the thought. He was only here for Origin.

Rettic had sat himself down on the only chair in the place and perched Origin on his lap. He looked blindly between them with faded green eyes, a squint deepening the creases on his brow.

'You know... you know what Origin is?' Ryza said, breaking the silence.

'Of course I know. My memory may be going more than coming, but I could never forget Origin.'

Ryza leaned in to Ferrick, not taking his eyes off the arcanite. 'Not a word of this leaves this room, got it?'

'I feel like I'm not going to understand what I'm about to hear, anyway.'

Ryza walked over and crouched next to the old man. 'Where did you first meet it?'

'Him,' Rettic snapped.

'What?'

'It's a man,' he continued. 'For god's sake, haven't you even thought about what you have here? The two of you sound young enough to not be burdened by such a worry.'

'Then enlighten me.'

'Origin is the result of a pure resonance.'

Ryza stared blankly at the arcanite.

'Of course, you don't follow,' Rettic grumbled to himself. 'Looks like the Academy of Breggesa is still a consortium of filled and decided minds.' The old man rubbed the bridge of his nose for a few moments before turning back to Ryza. 'Magic is bound by axioms, yes? Runes are the words that form the axiom, restrictive, but to the point. Now just imagine if you didn't need the axiom. That for just for a second you could channel your thoughts instead.'

Ryza frowned. It was like Rettic had just asked him what it would be like to grow an extra head. 'Why only a second?'

'Because it kills you and you'd do best not to know why.'

'But Origin is...'

'Old,' Rettic finished. 'The oldest thing in the world, last time I encountered him.' He tapped the arcanite. 'Still are, aren't you?'

'Origin,' he said.

'What do you mean, "the *oldest* thing in the world?" What about those-of-glass, right Ferrick?'

'Yeah, I'm struggling to believe anything could be older than them,' she said. 'How can you even be sure of any of this?'

'A fresh mind is more open for learning than an expectant one,' Rettic mused, poking Origin's now outstretched arm. 'He's... from that world. Between then and now, something happened, killed all those people but somehow didn't destroy their cities, just buried them. Before that there had to be a magic much more powerful than anything we know, something like pure resonance. That much is evident by the fractures of magic you find down there. I visited once. Took something I should not have. It was Origin that tried to warn me.'

'Origin.'

'If he's that old then, why does he have the exact same resonance as Revance?' Ryza asked.

'Because he created it.'

Ryza's jaw dropped. In the back of his mind, he'd known something like this all along, but he simply couldn't allow himself to believe it before. Surely a Kretatic powerful enough to create Revance would be able to sustain himself in an arcanite forever. It was as if the more unbelievable it became, the more Ryza found himself believing it.

Ferrick's voice broke his thoughts. 'But how could Origin still control Revance? It's too big, it—'

'Origin is a mystery that will outlast time itself,' Rettic stated. 'He fears no death, never did. Not even when he was flesh and bone. An unfortunate curse, to say the least.'

'But his resonance could be copied, right?' she asked. 'Someone could control Revance with him?'

'Origin,' the arcanite said.

'You heard what he said,' Rettic chuckled. 'Though I don't know how someone would do it, their brain would burst, if I recall the size of Revance correctly. Damn thing got far too big for its own good.'

'Unless they already had a thousand autominds,' Ryza muttered under his breath. 'And enough molten flux to fill them.'

The old man froze and then turned slowly to face Ryza. 'I take it that's why you're in Kyrea today?'

'No,' Ryza said quickly. 'We're *from* Revance. We want to stop it, if anything! We just—'

His greatcoat suddenly tensed around his body. Rettic's hands were clenched and white-knuckled. Ryza tried to step back, but the iron filings were holding him in place, digging through to his skin.

'Revance does not "stop" the scourge of molten flux,' Rettic growled. 'Never did. I can feel your resonance, boy. It's the kind that leads to bloodshed, but I don't know whether you've come to try and stop something or be the one that starts it.'

He grabbed Origin and shoved the arcanite roughly towards Ryza. There was a clatter of metal on tiles as the iron filings fell from his and Ferrick's clothes.

'Long ago, Origin tried to warn me. But I see no point in warning you. Now get out.'

Ryza stuffed Origin into his backpack and nodded to Ferrick. Under the old man's blind gaze, they left the hovel quickly, trekking back into the main tunnels of Kyrea.

'No idea how a mercenary would have come to know of him in the first place,' Ryza asked. 'Who do you think he even was?'

A wry grin split Ferrick's face. 'I thought you knew all there was to know about molten flux, but I guess you didn't know him.'

He returned a quizzical look.

Did she know?

'Your hands aren't clean, remember?' she added, waving her own theatrically.

'Then spill the beans!'

'The *what*?'

'Just tell me,' Ryza sighed.

Ferrick sighed back, mocking him. 'You heard how he said he "took something he should not have," right?'

'And?'

'Let's just say his hands aren't clean, either.'

His jaw locked as he put two and two together. If not for Ferrick, he would've turned around and beat the old bastard senseless for what he'd blighted the world with. But then again, maybe he hadn't known. Ignorant of the horrors it brought. Just like Ryza had once been.

'Must nearly be noon,' Ferrick said, interrupting his chain of thought. 'We should head back and find Maligar.'

'You two certainly should!' a familiar voice said from behind them.

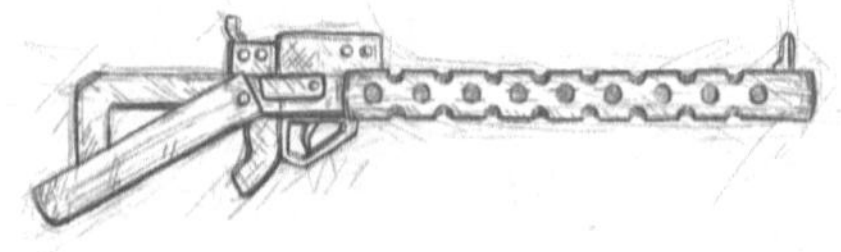

Chapter Nineteen

A Failed Redemption

RYZA SPUN IN SURPRISE, his stomach almost leaping out of his throat as he caught sight of Holm. She was barely three feet away. How had she snuck up on him? How'd she even known he was here? They must've been in the furthest reaches of Kyrea, maybe even beyond that, considering the lack of smoothened rock walls.

'Check your pockets,' she said, almost in answer to his thought.

Ryza gave himself a quick pat down, his hand stopping on a small lump in his coat pocket. It was a rifle slug. He pulled it out and Holm's maniacal resonance danced on his fingertips. A curse escaped with his breath. How could he have fallen for the same trick twice?

'How long have you been following us?' he asked.

'Only started after I got a good look at the dancing girls in the upper reaches,' Holm said. She glanced down at the slug as Ryza turned it over between two fingers. 'Pretty slick, right? You can keep it. Just remember to return the favour for me. What are you doing out here, anyway?'

In the back of his mind, the theory that the Locusts were searching for Origin was slowly growing. Once Holm found out about Origin, she'd probably take him and then leave Ryza for dead here in Kyrea. Ryza looked to Ferrick. She'd spill the beans on everything she'd just heard, he was sure of it.

'Turns out Ryza's a man of learning,' Ferrick said smoothly. 'There's an old Academy kook in there and he dragged me along to find him.'

Holm turned to Ryza, her arms crossed and eyebrows raised. 'And did you learn anything?'

'Gods no,' Ryza lied. 'They kicked us out when I told them we were from Revance.'

'Well, they did you a favour. We've got places to be, come on.'

Holm led them back through the market the same way they'd come, casting a glance back at Ryza each time they passed a column of autominds. He made sure not to meet it. What if Holm already knew about Origin, if Ferrick had somehow told her?

The crowds of the passing markets receded as he pushed the thought from his mind, replacing it with his noble intention of catching out whoever brought the molten flux onboard in the first place. He knew he was close, his lead with the Locusts was surely correct. He just had to make it out of the stinking and narrow tunnels of Kyrea.

The air was no cleaner once they reached the surface. A particle-laden haze had filled the carved basin, a thick layer of factory fumes. Ryza could only see fifty feet with his stinging eyes as he emerged from the manhole. Ferrick and Holm came next, both having been smart enough to hold on to their googles from the skimmer ride for just this purpose.

The skimmers in question lay on the edge of Ryza's vision, a dozen or so figures crowded around the one with the crate as haggling conversation floated through the air. It echoed strangely, each word coming to him out of order, yet he'd already guessed what was being discussed.

Molten flux.

A much larger silhouette beyond the skimmers had tipped him off. It was one of the automind-carriers, its massive, cantilevered legs curled to rest its hulking body on the ground. Its two-tiered decks were little more than catwalks, but they somehow managed to hold thirty or so tightly packed autominds.

'Ferrick, go check if Maligar needs anything from us,' Holm ordered pointedly. 'Rusty, stay here. I want my *saviour* here in case any more smelters come attack me.'

Ferrick giggled as she left and Ryza resisted the urge to follow. There was a nasty grin on Holm's face and he didn't want to find out what was behind it.

'Who's Maligar talking to?' Ryza asked as innocently as he could, nodding over to the congregation.

'Oh, he's not just any old smelter,' Holm teased. 'He's a flux trader. Named Cardan. We thought you might know him.'

He could remember the first time his father had so coolly introduced Ryza as a child and since then he'd been haunted by the flux trader's eerie presence. His ghostly green eyes, his pallid skin that only just resisted the sharp bones beneath that tried to pierce it and the pair of autominds that were always at his side, supporting his frail frame.

He spotted the trio of figures through the mist standing just beyond Maligar. Ryza unconsciously took a few more steps back, his nerves screaming at him to jump back down the manhole and reside within Kyrea for the rest of his life alongside that old kook Rettic.

His father had never stopped enviously talking about Cardan's legendary memory. He'd said it was so faultless he didn't even need to keep a ledger like other flux traders. One glance at Ryza and his past would no longer be hidden as a shameful secret, yet the hungry look in Holm's eyes meant it might be too late.

Sure, he'd let slip to one or two people that he was the son of a flux trader, but that was all. He'd never revealed what he'd seen. What he'd done. How many he'd—

'Ryza?'

He jumped as Holm tapped him on the shoulder.

'Looks like I'm always surprising you,' she said.

'And I'd rather you didn't,' he said.

'We'd all rather have a lot of things differently. Like the fact the last time I talked alone to you, you shouted me down for doing something I didn't have a choice in.' Her tone was cold and bitter despite the smirk she held.

Ryza scoffed but made sure to keep his voice low. 'You had a choice. If you hadn't set Ditric up like that, no lives would have been taken.'

'And how many lives have you taken, Ryza? They don't call you Bloodfist for nothing.' She took a step closer, staring him down with a penetrating glare. 'You know, I can feel it in your resonance. The violence. The relentlessness. It's not a recent thing, either. Resonances may change over time, but this feels like it's been like that for a *long* time. Makes me think you've got a bit more to hide than you let on. It seems odd that you'd shy away from a flux trader. Almost as if you know each other, right?'

'So what?' he said, failing to push the nervousness out of his voice.

But Holm didn't say anything. She just glared and Ryza could feel each heartbeat rattle his ribcage, threatening to tear his chest open. Eight passed before she spoke again.

'It's almost like he'd recognise you. What did you do? Fight him?'

Ryza finally broke her gaze, fixing his attention on a patch of ground three feet to his left.

If only.

'No, you helped him, didn't you? You sold autominds, maybe even made them.' Holm's usual grin returned, more sadistic than ever. 'You're more than just the son of a flux trader, aren't you?'

'I'm not that anymore,' he grunted.

She started drawing closer, each step savoured and deliberate as Ryza stood frozen in place.

'I know you've been sniffing about, looking for flux. I'm still not sure how you caught wind of it, but I can guess it's why we keep running into each other.'

She was nearer now, barely a foot away, but she wasn't stopping.

'But that's not what you're really looking for, is it? Running from what you've done wasn't enough.'

They were almost nose to nose but Ryza couldn't pull away. It was like some kind of magnetic force was sucking him in. He could only focus on her eyes, on the victory burning within them.

'I remember you telling me that I was one of the Kretatics that brought us a bad name,' she whispered.

Ryza could feel the heat of her breath on his face. He was so lost in her eyes that he couldn't look away.

'I think you only said that to make yourself feel better. It didn't work, Rusty, and if you think finding a little bit of flux will right your wrongs, then you're sorely mistaken. Because you've just helped us buy it.'

Ryza couldn't muster a single word.

Not even a breath.

'You'd better play along,' she breathed into his ear. 'Because, just like me, you're in too deep.'

Motion finally found his legs and he stepped back, clumsily enough to make Holm giggle. His head reeled in a stunned daze as he wordlessly followed her back to the rest of the Locusts. She'd just seen through him like he was made of glass. Now all he wanted to do was to shatter and be sprinkled into the ground.

The enormous automind-carrier emitted a haunting groan of strained iron as it lifted to its feet. The lifeless bodies aboard swayed helplessly from the motion. Cardan was the only steady figure among them. Ryza watched as it gingerly manoeuvred past the other empty vehicles without tripping, only tearing his eyes away to glance at the cargo-filled skimmer.

To Ryza, the contents were all but confirmed. The box was now a coffin. A corpse had to be in there, still fresh and in near perfect condition. He could see the vial of flux in his mind, its label bearing a single scribble.

C316.

This had to be the flux noted down in the ledger he'd found. It was all starting to make sense. There never was molten flux aboard Revance. The flux marked in the ledger hadn't been a past purchase, but an order made ahead of time and now he'd watched it happen without lifting a finger to stop it!

At least I threw a spanner in Cardan's works by killing all those smelters before I found the ledger.

A sudden realisation almost stopped Ryza's thoughts dead in their tracks. Cardan didn't use ledgers. Ever.

That was what was so infamous about his organisation. He could sell flux in places where it was punishable by death and deny it if caught, because there wasn't a shred of proof written down. Maligar's purchase was a new trade which had nothing to do with the ledger and, in turn, Origin. Ryza had been following the wrong trail this whole time.

'Back in the skimmers,' Maligar barked. 'Same as before, but Holm, you're with me.'

This left Ryza as Ferrick's sole passenger. Maligar set off their convoy with a single wave, leading them on the same looping path out of Kyrea that they'd come in on.

Salt flats turned back into red dunes as Kyrea receded behind them. By mid-afternoon, Ryza was stretching his arms, surreptitiously tapping his wristband against one of Origin's exposed limbs and making sure Ferrick did the same. While she still had a collar of her own, she had some incentive to keep Origin a secret.

A niggling sense of panic wormed into Ryza's mind as their path weaved and twisted. Revance should've come into view hours ago. Maybe they weren't going there. Maybe they were destined for Maligar's "celebration."

A celebration of flux.

Chapter Twenty

A Celebration Of Flux

It was late afternoon by the time something appeared on the horizon that wasn't an outcrop of wind battered rocks or a burnt-out hut. Glinting glass pillars rose into sight, a dozen or more of them stretching into the sky. They were like the discarded spears of giants, tall and proud, pointing straight up, spare for one that seemed to lean heavily against another.

'Is that a ruin?' Ryza asked as they drew closer. 'From those-of-glass?'

'Never seen one?' Ferrick said.

He shook his head. 'Never thought I would. After everything I've heard, everything you've told me, I've never wanted to, either.'

'Maligar must have some serious balls to be taking us to a place like this. I'm half tempted to head back to Revance now.'

'No,' Ryza said quickly. 'Maligar would think we're going to rat him out.'

And he'd still have his flux.

The skimmers pulled up in the trough of a dune, the ruins just beyond it, out of sight. Maligar's party was the first to dismount, lifting the metal crate between them and marching up the hill in a funeral-like procession as Ryza and Ferrick followed. Upon cresting the hill, Ryza halted. It was like his feet had hit a non-existent tripwire as he realised the sparkling monoliths were actually buildings.

Walls of glass covered every strangely angled surface, ancient cracks spreading across them like spider webs and dangling shards of it in places where it should've lain shattered. Strange arrays of antenna rose out the tops, making each tower at least twice as tall as even the grandest of constructions in Breggesa. Some of the flanks of the buildings were missing or hollowed out, allowing Ryza a look at the white and copper furnishings and walls within. Despite being blanketed by sand, he could tell it was nothing made by human hands alone.

Counting them all was impossible. Each time Ryza swept his eyes over the two circular rows of towers, his thoughts were instantly lost in a curious apprehension of the oddities he sighted. Beyond the two rows of buildings was a perfectly flat clearing. There wasn't even the slightest crease in the sand. He wasn't sure he wanted to find out why.

An impatient crowd was gathered in the sandy trough between two of the closest towers, ringed in by the dozens of parked vehicles that would've carried them here. Raucous conversation flowed like a battering wind between the group, only growing in intensity as their excited eyes caught sight of the newcomers.

'Quite something, isn't it?' Maligar said as he slapped Ryza on the back.

The others had already started making their way down the hill towards the party, eliciting whoops and cheers as they were noticed. This left Ryza and Maligar alone, overlooking the congregation.

'Is this all of the Locusts?'

'Almost. One or two of our number couldn't make it.'

'But what's it all for? Why a place like this?'

'Well,' Maligar said, holding out his arms as if he were presenting a grand vision, 'you have to understand that the idea of the Locusts was always one that hid underground, moving in the shadows, with slight touches of influence here and there to bend things our way but nothing more than that.

'It's time we came into the light, Ryza. To be honest about what we are and what Revance is. Locusts of the land! Scavengers, same as everyone else, yet held back by a mission we've already failed. Time we rose up with our say on how things should be done, instead of the stagnant tenets that Revance abides by.'

'It sounds like you're planning a mutiny.'

'You know, that's exactly what Holm said when the idea was presented to her. You're a lot more alike than either of you would care to admit.'

He placed an arm around Ryza's shoulders, leaning in as Ryza struggled not to flinch.

'Put it to you this way, if you weren't happy with the situation you were in, how things were being done around you, you'd be better off changing things than just running away from it, right?'

Ryza didn't say a word. Maligar had hit too close to home, probably on purpose.

'You see all these people here? See how none of them have collars on? They could all leave Revance at any time they'd like, but they're here because all I had to do was ask. They came today because they all care about Revance *itself*. This gathering is the start of that. Come sundown I'll reveal all.'

'But why bring me here?' Ryza asked.

'Because you're iconic, Ryza! You're the Bloodfist! No conscript has made a name for themselves quite like you, whether you intended it or not. I need people like you to be a part of this, someone that everyone will know. It'll really be the thing that brings the Locusts from the below.

'It's why I picked this place for the so-called unveiling, after all. A whole city lies under these ruins. These buildings, apparently called skyscrapers, go down for at least half a mile. They represent us, reaching up to the surface, breaking through what hid us for years to reach for our time in the light so we may use the tools which we've long had to bury.'

Ryza could feel something coming up from his stomach and he had to resist the urge to vomit. Not only was he stuck as a part of this, but he was to be one of the faces of it.

'Go enjoy the party,' Maligar said. 'Mingle. Make some friends. They'll be more than happy to see you. Just stay clear of the insides of the ruins. We may be safe out here, but I haven't heard anything good of what's in there.'

With that, Maligar began his victorious march down into the crowd, greeted by another round of cheers and warm handshakes. This left Ryza alone on the hill and all he wanted to do was run. He glanced over his shoulder. The skimmers were still there. He had ink. He could be gone within a moment, returning with the full force of Revance. But there was still a Locust or two there.

Maybe the ones that were absent simply weren't important enough to come? Worse still, they could be too important to leave their post. Could it be Tyrag, the Forgemaster? No, surely not. Ryza could still remember what Maligar had said when they'd first met.

Not near the old man.

Ryza scrubbed the idea from his mind along with the notion of fleeing. What Maligar had said was right. He couldn't run anymore. He'd have to change things himself.

Curious stares met his presence as he joined the party, but no one approached. They were too busy with their own eager babble about whatever Maligar had planned or trying to jostle for a better spot in the packed circles of Locusts spectating loosely ruled fistfights.

They fought with a brutal finesse and he couldn't help but cheer and roar along with the crowd. He even spotted Ferrick in a bout, beating the tar out of a man a good half foot taller than her.

When she was done with him, she beckoned to Ryza, forcing a wink through an emerging black eye. He shook his head. Origin was still tucked in his pack and he couldn't risk a moment separated from the arcanite. Besides, he wasn't sure he'd come out in one piece. She shrugged, instead taking on another challenger with furious gusto.

Brilliant rays of orange soon refracted through the glass of the skyscrapers, creating a spectacular show of light over their heads. He stepped back from the still ongoing competition and scanned the crowd for Maligar, having long lost track of him.

Ryza found him standing at the top of the hill they'd arrived at, the metal crate at his feet and a few others standing around him. Even from this distance, Ryza could recognise them as the Locusts who'd come to Kyrea.

Maligar's inner circle.

Others had noticed too. They were looking up, pointing. The fights slowly broke apart and an air of excitement quickly grew among the crowd as whispers shot back and forth.

'Is it going to happen now?'

'What's going to happen?'

'I don't know, whatever's in the box.'

On the hill, it looked like Maligar had noticed. He turned to the crowd, arms raised in an open gesture, forcing a hush upon them.

'My friends! My people! I am glad you've all been enjoying our gathering, but we must take a moment to thank all of you among us who organised it at such short notice.'

The crowd cheered for a few seconds before Maligar hushed them again.

'To all of you down there who've let rumours fly past their ears and through their mouths, I thank you. It has built the anticipation in a way I never could. The excitement in the weeks leading up to this day has been palpable. I've had to dodge countless questions, only being able to promise a change. A change that will better us all. I can now tell you this change will bring us into the light. No longer will the Locusts hide in the shadows of Revance, we shall now *become* Revance!'

Cheers filled the crowd. It was like they were *excited* for a mutiny. Maligar quelled them again, his voice somehow booming over their collective babble.

'I want to clarify this is not a hostile takeover. This change will be diplomatic at worst. Hopefully even welcomed! As a union banded together, we can have a say in the actions of this army, we shall be able to be the rudder that steers our fortress through these perilous sands and finally take control of our lives and our fates.'

He walked over to the coffin, stepping one foot onto it in a triumphant pose like he was to be modelled into a statue. 'I know you've spent half the party wondering what's in this box, but you won't have to wonder any more, for it is a symbol of our first change we are to institute into Revance. It has been acquired at both great risk and effort, which is why I have had to keep you in the dark for so long.'

Maligar reached down for the handle on the coffin and paused for dramatic effect, seeming to relish the collective intake of breath from the crowd. But then he straightened up.

'I don't think I'm quite the right person to make this reveal.'

Maligar's gaze struck Ryza.

Ryza's heart stopped.

No...

'To represent a new age of the Locusts, I think it appropriate to call on our most recent member. Ryza, the Bloodfist!'

He pointed a single finger at Ryza and the crowd turned as one, their eyes quickly finding him. Despite the stunned look his face had screwed itself into, they started chanting his name, quickly changing their chorus to something else.

'*Bloodfist! Bloodfist! Bloodfist!*'

Hands found his back, pushing him forward against his will until he was spat out the other side of the crowd. His legs didn't want to take another step. Behind him, the chanting was growing louder, faster.

Up the hill, Maligar was beckoning Ryza on. He could see Holm at Maligar's side, though she wasn't doing the same. Her arms were firmly crossed and a piercing stare was all she threw down at him.

The chanting reached a fever pitch, loud enough to make his ears ring. Then something terrible happened. They'd stopped. He glanced over his shoulder. The crowd had backed away. He was alone, wishing he'd just sink into the ground.

'What's the matter, Ryza?' Maligar called down. There was a note of concern in his voice, though Ryza couldn't tell if it was genuine.

With straining effort, he lifted his foot, shuffling loose the sand gathered on it. The crowd cheered as he found another step.

'Just a bit of stage fright is all!' Maligar bellowed over the noise. 'Can't expect him to be great at everything, now can we? Come on!'

The walk up the hill took an age and Maligar encouraging his every step didn't help. It just made a lead weight grow in his stomach. Once Ryza reached his side, Maligar silenced the crowd.

'Now we may have our reveal!' he turned to Ryza, motioning towards the coffin. 'The honour is yours.'

Hesitating, he reached down and grasped the handle of the crate's lid. With a twist to the right, the seal was cracked and the lid scraped open. An automind lay inside, his eyes shut and his body bruised and limp. He was middle-aged, balding and slightly more rotund than average, yet his face was gaunt and drained of all colour. Ryza tore his eyes away in disgust. The poor bastard would've likely been killed that very day. He couldn't even see the telltale signs of molten flux on his skin.

'Don't be shy, Ryza, give him a slap and get him moving.'

The sharp order came from one of the nearby Locusts. They were right. Autominds left without orders for a few hours would fall into a coma-like state. The only way to "wake them" was with physical force.

Ryza raised a well-practised hand and brought it down as a hard blow across the automind's face. There was no response.

'Hit him again!' Maligar roared.

A backhand this time. They stirred with a soft moan. For a moment Ryza was thrown off. Autominds didn't feel pain.

It must be because this one was fresh.

The thought had sprung to his mind as a reflex more than a fact, but he didn't spare the time to check it was true. If he did, he'd be reawakening parts of himself he'd vowed to forget. Ryza gave them one last slap and the automind jolted upright, clutching at their face.

Still a few instincts left in them. Maybe too many.

'Good!' Maligar exclaimed. 'Now lift him up so everyone can see.'

With the help of another Locust, Ryza grabbed the automind and hoisted them to their feet, letting them wobble precariously.

'Where... where am I?'

Panic was flooding Ryza's veins. Autominds didn't speak! They never have! Of the dozens, or even hundreds of autominds that had shambled past Ryza's eyes, not a single one of them had managed so much as a syllable!

The man turned around, his eyes dreary and dazed, not the blank look Ryza had been expecting a moment ago. His eyes were blue. Whole. Alive. Not the orbs of silver that an automind should have. Ryza heard Holm gasp but couldn't turn his head to see at her.

'Who are you people?'

Ryza was too shocked to respond. He only realised Maligar had started talking to him when he gave Ryza a small nudge on the shoulder.

'Check into the box, you'll find the tools we need.'

Ryza was beyond hesitation now. Even the mounting horror of what was coming couldn't stop him. He reached in, finding out something gut-wrenchingly familiar. It was an injector gun, his hand already conforming perfectly to the grip. Contained in a bracketed frame of iron, a glass vial sloshed with sliver liquid.

Molten flux.

This was the liquid he'd spent hours and days of his childhood pouring carefully into vial after vial after vial. Watching the strange fluid duplicate itself to fill its container and trying not to think about what it was to be used for. Praying he didn't spill it onto his skin, or worse, to the floor where it would spread uncontrollably.

The needle at the end of the gun, a good four inches long, glinted in the first light of the moon. Every time Ryza had held a gun like this, he'd wondered what it would feel like to press it into his own flesh, to pump the trigger and feel that all-consuming substance race through his veins.

'I was... I was in Breggesa... the Academy... Are those *ruins*?'

The man was talking again. Out of the corner of his eye, Ryza could see Maligar growing impatient. What he was meant to do now was obvious.

Maligar began addressing the crowd again, his arms up and open like he was their saviour. 'I could have brought you all an automind today, but that would've been simple to acquire. Contrary to Revance's mission, they're everywhere! Instead, I wanted to show you. I wanted to show you the daring bravery that we can now possess ourselves. I wanted to show you the first step, in action, of Revance coming under our control! Of our lives coming under our control.'

Maligar turned to Ryza, a hungry grin on his face.

But Ryza still hadn't moved.

I'm not going to do this.

Maligar approached him slowly.

I promised myself.

He was behind Ryza now, placing two hands on his shoulders.

Not again. Never again.

'Ryza.'

Maligar's voice came as a gentle whisper in his ear, only inches away from his skin.

'I know who you are. I've known since I first met you. Cardan told me that you would be the one perfect to execute this.'

Execute.

He would be taking this innocent man's life. Something he'd promised himself he'd never do again. He'd already taken too many in the name of molten flux.

'I know you can do this. Do this for me. For everyone here. They've put their lives on the line for you.'

His shaking hand raised the gun as if Maligar was willing it more than he was.

No...

'Revance is at stake, Ryza. The lives of all its soldiers, too. Only you can save them.'

Maligar released Ryza's shoulders, throwing his hands into the air once more. The crowd roared in approval. Ryza's pulse doubled. Something evil began to burn within. A feeling he'd sworn to never call upon again.

The violence.

Ryza stepped forward, placing himself directly behind the man.

Revel in the violence.

'But why?' the man mumbled. 'Why take me here? This place—'

Ryza cut the man off by wrapping his left arm around his neck, quick and tight. The man began to choke, the force in the crook of Ryza's elbow cutting off his windpipe. Hands scrabbled at Ryza's arm, then started to flail as the man realised he couldn't break free.

Ryza held the injector high as he planted his feet in the sand.

Quick and clean. I can do that much.

He fixed his eyes on the man's neck, the raised hairs, the pale flesh. And then he struck.

The needle plunged deep, striking right at the centre of the man's spine and worming between his vertebrae. The man's entire body seized in response, his legs kicking from beneath him and bringing them both to their knees.

But Ryza didn't relent.

His finger pumped violently at the trigger of the injector, forcing the flux within to bubble and froth. Yet the man still floundered, a gurgling scream breaking from his quivering lips with each burst of liquid that flooded his blood lines. But Ryza couldn't see it. His vision was clouded by all the rage and hatred he'd assembled within himself.

What he'd always needed to get the horrific job done.

He didn't even realise the vial was empty until the man had stopped twitching. Ryza pulled back, dropping the gun as he staggered to his feet.

What if I've made a mistake, done it wrong somehow?

The man wobbled on his knees and ahead of him, the crowd held their breath.

No, I've done this too many times to do it wrong.

He teetered forward. Then back. Then he stopped, caught by his own sense of balance.

The only thing the flux leaves behind.

Maligar now stood by Ryza, his eyes wide. Even he was not immune to the stunned silence that swept across the ruins.

'Is it... is it done?' Maligar whispered. 'Is he an automind?'

Ryza's nails dug hard into his palms, the pain a momentary redemption. The pain always helped.

'Yes,' Ryza spat. 'He's dead. He's what you wanted.'

'Get him to stand up,' Maligar said.

Ryza reached for the automind, but Maligar grabbed his hand. With his other, he handed Ryza two things. Ink and a brush. The vial holding the green liquid held the same design of bracketed iron as the injector gun's container. The brush was just as lavish, sporting not the bristles of a slaughtered beast, but the carefully plucked flight feathers of a hunting bird.

Not this too. Not now.

He didn't have a choice. He began drawing, his memory already overlaying the completed axiom on his blank forearm as he worked. Below, the crowd began to babble, confusion spreading between them like a disease.

They have no idea.

The axiom was ready, the ink dry. Ryza didn't stall any longer. He reached for the back of the man's neck, his palm squelching down on the bloody hole the needle had left behind. He savoured each rune as they burned white-hot in his palm.

Pain. Pain like they can't feel.

To control an arcanite, one would have to force their resonance on a simple piece of metal, yet molten flux behaved *nothing* like solid metal.

It was fast. Unpredictable. Ryza closed his eyes as he pictured the path of the automind's infected blood-ways, laid out before him like the roots of an old and dying tree.

Each beat of their heart, each breath of the lungs, each twitch of muscle, it was all his, yet the molten flux bore that burden for him, leaving his own consciousness to bloom in the empty space this man's mind had left behind. Each thought came twice as fast, twice as clear and twice as loud. Now an arcanite would be child's play. Hell, he could make an army of them!

Ryza eased his focus and opened his eyes again. The automind was a part of his own body, its senses linked to his. He was in two places at once, just like he was controlling an arcanite, but with so much more ecstasy in return.

He looked to Maligar, relishing the flash of trepidation in response to the fury Ryza knew was branded on his own face. If this was who he was meant to be, then Maligar could have it. He glanced back to the automind, regarding it with barely a thought and it obeyed.

The automind shambled to its feet and the crowd erupted once again.

CHAPTER TWENTY-ONE

THE FALL OF ORIGIN

RYZA WAS SAT IN one of the upper floors of the skyscrapers, nestled among debris that must've lain untouched for centuries. To his left was Origin. Neither of them had said a word since Ryza had collapsed into the dusty corner. Origin had simply crawled out of his backpack and sat himself by Ryza's side, his hollow metal eyes staring up at him.

The arcanite would have heard —and probably understood— what Ryza had just done. He could feel Origin's judgement and he deserved it. Hours had passed since the moment he couldn't stop replaying in his head, but the blood from the automind's neck still stained Ryza's left hand. Part of him wanted to cut it off with a piece of the jagged glass that surrounded him.

The sun was gone, lost to the horizon's dunes and replaced by the bonfires of the Locusts. He could still hear the party, distant yet jubilant. With his clean hand, he rubbed his face and twisted to his left, looking past Origin and through the slit of broken glass that had once been a window.

The last time Ryza had opened his eyes —nearly an hour ago by his shaky estimate— the Locusts had been making their fun by testing out the automind. They were building the largest arcanites they could muster or just ordering the damn thing to run senselessly into their friends.

Ryza couldn't blame them. The first taste of it was always the best. The sheer rush of having a mind as sharp as a razor was always going to outweigh anything else.

It'd happened when he was eight. He was just learning to draw runes when his father had decided to introduce him to the "family business." Up until that moment, Ryza had never wondered where autominds came from, or how they were made. From then on, he'd wondered no more.

I made them. They came from me. People like me.

Maligar's words of encouragement still circled in his mind. Why had he gone along with it? He could have just said no. Surely, he wouldn't have been killed for that. Ryza shut his eyes again, chewing his lip until he could taste blood.

I can't run anymore.

Everything had been a blur as he'd slipped away from the crowd, yet as he'd passed through the rows of parked buggies, the glint of an overlooked rifle had been far too tempting.

With steady hands, Ryza pulled the stolen weapon across his lap, almost finding an odd comfort in its weight. He only wished it was *his* rifle, with its calm that flowed into him every time he ran his hands down the metal. His thoughts drifted to the rifle's former master, the one he was sure was searching for Origin and had started this mutiny brewing.

He let out a long sigh as he looked up at the faded ceiling. He couldn't find them now, not with what he'd done. There were a couple hundred people who'd cheered him on, who counted him among their number. Now he was one of them. With well-practised hands, Ryza broke the rifle open. This one was clean to the point it might've never been used.

Probably hasn't, if it belonged to a Locust. The cowards.

The Locusts had never truly been faced with the smelters. Never truly got to know what Revance was supposed to be fighting against. The grave robbing, the kidnapping, the mass slaughter. That's why they ate up Maligar's words. Because they didn't know better.

And they didn't want to.

Ryza patted down his pockets, eventually finding a single slug. He pulled it out, shutting his eyes as Holm's resonance danced through his fingers. She'd been the one to get him into this. She'd said she too was in too deep, but she didn't need to drag him down with her.

Ryza looked over at Origin, finally able to meet the arcanite's hollow eyes.

'I've done a terrible thing, haven't I?'

'Origin.'

'I want you to run. Run down into the ruined city below us, no matter what it holds, and never come back.'

The arcanite was silent.

'I know... that I said I would protect you. Make sure you wouldn't fall into the wrong hands, but it turns out I'm the wrong hands too.' Ryza couldn't stop his voice from breaking. 'You came from down there, right?'

'Origin.'

'Then just go back to where you hid yourself before. To save the few innocent lives left up here. I can't protect you from all of them. What they'd use you for.'

Ryza waited as his heart pounded in his chest. Eventually Origin stood up and began walking towards the strange vertical shaft at the other end of the room. Ryza had glanced down it when he'd first made his way through the skyscraper. It was three metres wide by three metres long and deeper than the eye could see. It had called to him, pulling him in stronger than gravity should.

The arcanite now stood on the edge and turned to face Ryza. They exchanged one last look, a look that said more than the ancient arcanite would ever be able to muster, before Origin tossed his tiny body into the abyss.

Ryza waited for the faintest echo of clanging metal hitting the bottom, but as minutes passed, it still hadn't come. The impossible magic down there must've swallowed Origin up, never to be seen again.

Good.

Without him, Maligar and his conspirators would never be able to control Revance. Even if Ferrick did tell them about Origin, they'd have to search for him somewhere below, but that would be far too dangerous. By the time someone unearthed the arcanite, Yuvet would have exposed them all.

Ryza slotted the slug in place and snapped the rifle shut. His hands twisted the rifle, resting the stock on the ground so his chin was propped up on the muzzle. Cold metal bit into the underside of his jaw, but the hollow space just beneath where his tongue was seemed colder.

It's where the slug will come from. A hot, clean death.

He didn't even deserve that much. Not after what he'd done. If there were going to be more autominds, it was something Ryza couldn't face. His hands began playing down the rifle, tips of his fingers caressing each groove and bump. He found the trigger guard as his hands began to shake.

I can't walk away from this.

He had to end it. Had to! End it all before he stabbed a needle into someone else's spine and stole everything from them. Ryza sucked a deep breath in through his nose and leaned harder on the rifle.

For all I've taken.

His fingers were struggling to reach the trigger. It was almost out of reach.

Almost...

But nothing happened. His fingers hadn't pulled the trigger. They wouldn't. Ryza opened his eyes. Was this some kind of trickery from the slug Holm had given him?

Now that's ridiculous. If she was here, she'd pull it for me.

No, he could put that slug to better use.

He brought himself to his feet, rifle still in hand as he looked out of the shattered window. There were hundreds of Locusts down below, all ready to be traitors of Revance and he had a slug. One slug to take out whoever he chose.

The muzzle of the rifle easily fit through one of the larger cracks in the window and Ryza peered down the sights. He might be a little over a hundred metres away, but he could still pick out each face from the crowd. Maybe if he just took one pot shot at them, they'd be frightened enough to scatter.

A moment of fear stops nothing.

His rifle's sights lingered over Maligar. Even if he were gone, his inner circle would take over and there was still whoever was looking for Origin. He spotted Holm next. Her death would be inconsequential. Ryza's aim hovered on her for a few more seconds before he found his final target.

Circled by the crowd, the automind stood blank and motionless. Shooting it would undo everything Maligar was to the Locusts. His bravado, his promises that they would rise unchallenged, all of it would be gone, replaced by uncertainty and doubt as his newfound toy was snatched away.

Ryza trained his sights for a few more seconds as a calm flowed through him, hands perfectly still. He didn't need his own gun. He could make the shot. He exhaled gently and pulled the trigger.

A flash of light burst from the muzzle. The glass exploded into shards that shot into Ryza's face and hands before he could flinch. The sting of it made him hiss under his breath before another sound reached his ears, a gory splat that was followed by the thump of a body hitting the sand. He squinted down, vision blurry from the blood trickling from his forehead.

The crowd had stopped the moment the shot was fired, all eyes on the automind, each one in utter disbelief as they stared at the corpse, its head blown clean off.

All except Maligar.

'Who was that?' he roared. 'Who the fuck was that?'

Ryza watched, barely resisting a grin as Maligar marched to the automind and kicked it over. He spun, scanning the crowd as he continued to scream. No one answered, but instead of lashing out, Maligar crouched down.

What the hell could he be doing?

Ryza squinted, but all he could make out was Maligar's hunched back. Suddenly, he threw his hand out, his ornate brush displayed in his grip. He was about to use an axiom.

Oh no.

Maligar raised his other hand and slammed it into the ground. The sand shook in a wave, pulsing out from Maligar. It swept like a sandstorm over the ruined skyscrapers, shaking loose glass and making metal groan as it headed towards Ryza.

It was a simple pulse of magnetism, strong enough to rattle even the most distant Kretatics. It was something smelters would do when they wanted to find lost autominds, or victims that were attempting to hide. Every time Ryza had cast one of these axioms, it had felt like he was tearing off a piece of his soul.

Ryza's entire body convulsed as he collapsed, his bones about to vibrate out of his skin, his teeth clattering against each other like they were about to crumble to powder. His stomach curdled, forcing him to twist into a ball as he gasped silently from the pain of it.

He struggled to push the last of the nausea out of his head as he stood up and looked out the window. Led by Maligar, the entire party of Locusts was marching towards his skyscraper.

I can't run now. That's what I wanted. No more running.

When the first of the Locusts appeared at the top of the stairs, Ryza brandished the rifle at them, the vague gesture only enough to make them flinch. As more came, they simply began to laugh.

'You can't shoot us all!' one of them jeered.

'He probably doesn't have any slugs left!'

Right on both counts.

'Who is it, anyway? I can't tell, his face is a mess.'

Maligar pushed to the front and marched towards him. 'I think I know,' he growled through gritted teeth. 'Who do we know that always ends up covered in blood?'

Before Ryza could manage a retort, Maligar was grabbing him by the throat with both hands and pinning him to the wall. The crowd pressed in around them.

'Why do it Ryza?' he grunted. A vein was bulging in his forehead. 'Just throwing your life away like this? You're so young.'

A weak sputter was Ryza's response. The edges of his vision started to blacken.

'You think eighteen years is a lifetime? I could've given you longer than that. So much longer.'

Ryza kicked out, either hitting nothing or having already lost the feeling in his legs. He could only clearly see Maligar now, the rest of the faces were just shifting wads of flesh. His lungs were burning, screaming for air, but Ryza was helpless.

Maligar suddenly released his grip, letting Ryza drop to the floor. He slumped there, gasping for air, barely aware of Maligar snatching up the discarded rifle.

'A slug! Someone give me a bloody slug!'

He was quickly obeyed. Ryza looked up in time to watch Maligar load the rifle.

This is it. Just what I wanted.

Ryza blinked and then he was looking down the barrel.

'We could have been great, Bloodfist,' Maligar said, shaking his head. 'You were going to be one of our heroes. You could've lived forever...'

Maligar lingered on his last words, then fell silent. Around him, the crowd watched, staring at their leader, waiting for his next move. He cocked his head. His eyes had drifted to Ryza's blood-soaked left hand.

'I've got a better idea.'

The words filled Ryza's heart with dread. That phrase had never led to a quick death.

Maligar's finger darted from Locust to Locust. 'You, and you two over there, hold his left arm and hold him still.'

One of the Locusts snatched at his left hand, bending back his fingers until Ryza was forced to relinquish his arm as it was pinned hard against the wall as the other two tackled him, pressing down on his body and not allowing him to move even an inch.

'If you don't like what we need for our axioms,' he said, raising the rifle. 'Then you won't make axioms by yourself.'

Ryza gasped in pain as the burning muzzle was pressed against his forearm. He squeezed his eyes shut and a blast rattled his eardrums to the point he couldn't even hear the scream of agony that left his lungs.

His arm throbbed like it was on fire, each ribbon of flesh in its own distinct hell. His only impulse was to squeeze his fist into a ball as tight as he could, to dig his nails into his palm to replace one pain with another, one that he at least controlled. Instead, he was met with the sight of Maligar waving his severed hand to the crowd like a trophy. From the elbow down, his arm was a bloody stump.

Splintered bone stuck out, strips of juicy raw muscle, tendon and skin clinging to it, each shocked quiver sending a new pulse of pain through his entire body. With each rapid beat of his heart, he could see blood leaving his body. Each ragged breath and involuntarily contracted muscle forced out more.

Maligar crouched in front of him, so close Ryza could feel the wash of his breath against the shards of glass embedded in his cheeks.

'When you die, I just hope there is a next life, just like this one, where you can keep walking around without that hand. An eternal reminder of the lifetime you threw away.' He stood up and turned to the crowd. 'We've got nothing to stay here for, let's head back to Revance.'

'What about his hand?'

Maligar roared with laughter and flung it across the room, wristband still attached, straight into the bottomless shaft Ryza had watched Origin fall down.

As they filed out, Ryza couldn't even move from shock. His vision began to blur into a pinprick and all he could stare at was his arm. He could still feel his hand there, invisible, fingers still twitching as he heard Maligar's voice. It sounded almost a mile away, even though he was just across the room.

'Search the surface. Make sure to find the arcanite. I'll send someone back if it's below.'

Ryza looked up, his head feeling like it had spun a dozen times. The only thing he could make out was the shape of a person standing before him, nothing more.

'Not yet. I want to watch him bleed. I want to make sure he's dead.'

The last few sparks left in Ryza's mind connected and he recognised the voice.

Holm.

CHAPTER TWENTY-TWO

AN UNLIKELY SAVIOUR

R YZA'S FACE STUNG. HIS eyes were clenched shut against a foul paste that was being smeared across his skin. The smell was suffocating, something between putrid meat and burning flesh. Pain washed through his body as his senses came back to him and he could feel his pulse quicken as rough hands danced across his body.

'Easy there. Let's not have a repeat performance, eh?'

It was a man's voice, soft and calm in his ears. But Ryza was still waking, his entire body fighting against itself.

'Just rest,' the voice said.

He tried to open his eyes, but they were practically glued shut under the paste. His lips cracked open and he caught a taste of it.

Just as bad as it smells.

'Rest, rest,' the man repeated.

Between the man's hushed words, he could hear the low thrum of machinery and the faint howling of a distant wind.

'No,' Ryza murmured. 'I need to...'

The words trailed off. He wasn't quite sure what he needed to do. He was still processing the fact he was alive. His last memories appeared in a disjointed parade. The reflections of bonfires dancing off glass walls, followed by the roar of a buggy's engine. Blood lust, a blast right next to his ear, lancing pain that consumed his entire body, then a word.

Just one word.

Origin.

His eyes shot open in spite of the paste and they instantly began to burn harder. His body thrashed, but his limbs were undecided, each attempting to hurl him in a different direction. The narrow cot he was in rocked under him, threatening to tip.

'Fine, we'll do it the hard way,' the man grunted.

A hand clamped down on his right arm and there was a clanging and scrambling as various metal objects seemed to fall to the floor around him. Before Ryza could break free, his face was being assaulted by a coarse cloth.

He struggled, sputtering against it, but it was no use. Soon the cloth was taken away and Ryza opened his eyes. A man ten years his senior greeted him, a broad, unconscious smile on his face as he tended to Ryza. His hair was dark brown, wire straight and shot in every direction, long enough to risk covering his gleaming yellow eyes.

'You're a... a healer.'

'We've got cognition!' he said, raising his arms in mock celebration. It was short-lived and he got back to wiping the last of the paste from Ryza. 'Good thing too,' he added. 'If you woke up without being able to put two and two together, then I would have wasted all the spare blood I pumped into you.'

'What would have happened otherwise?'

'You'd be about as good as an automind to me.' He threw the rag over Ryza and into a bin before offering his left hand to him. 'Name's Greely.'

Ryza went to shake it, lifting up his left arm as one last memory returned to him.

Maligar throwing his hand across that ruined room and into the abyss.

Now there was nothing there but a bandaged stump. Greely was still holding out his own hand, his grin flickering into a grimace.

'Sorry about that, but the old "handless handshake" is better than us breaking the news to you.'

'Where am I?' Ryza's question melted slowly from his numb mouth.

'Revance. Infirmary, second deck. Not surprised you didn't recognise it.'

Ryza looked around the room. Cots like his sat beside surgery bays, all of them unoccupied.

'How did I... Where is everyone? There should be dozens—'

Greely shook his head. 'Not for the past week. I'm worried all the wounded didn't make it and were turned to autominds. At least, that's the chatter I've heard.'

'Hope not,' Ryza said. 'What did you do to my arm, then? And what was that paste?'

'Paste was to lessen the scarring from all that glass I pulled out of you, but since you woke up before it could do its work, you're going to have a few extra marks to show off.' Greely glanced down at the stump. 'Had to seal the skin up. Bit of fire, few axioms, you know the rest. Now it's basically a hunk of scar tissue, with a touch of extra metal built in as well.'

As the healer talked, Ryza tried moving his arm, gently straining against the bandages that held his elbow in place. It was bizarre. He could imagine clenching his left fist, feel his fingers closing in, but they wouldn't be met by the flesh of his palm. He passed his other hand through where his arm used to be and shuddered. All it had done was make him want to scratch what wasn't there.

'It'll take a while to get used to.' Greely's grin disappeared as he continued. 'I've dealt with a lot of lost limbs on Revance. They all get used to it eventually.'

'Really?'

'Well, it's not like it'll grow back, will it?' He chuckled at his own joke. 'On the plus side, you're a Kretatic. Seen plenty of your lot who I've treated fix themselves up with a metal arm like this one.' He picked up something out of sight and placed it in Ryza's lap. 'That plate I sealed off at the end of your stump is what you can attach it to.'

Ryza picked up the metal arm, scrutinising the dozens of joints, hinges and bearings worked throughout the wrist and the knuckles. It was a crude instrument, each part added to it out of an ongoing necessity, made of half-rusted iron with a few flecks of gold here and there. Most would write this off as a hunk of junk, but if it was as well-loved as it looked, something about it must work.

'Who did this belong to?'

'A dead man, as is everything we've got left aboard Revance. Anyway, want to try it out? They tell me it's better we do it while you still feel like your hand is there. Makes the axiom stick for a lot longer. While you still *think* you have an arm, you keep your focus on the arcanite that *is* your arm. If you're lucky, the only thing you'll have to worry about is rust.'

Ryza held out his right arm as Greely began drawing green runes on it. He could feel the last ounces of his remaining pride chipping away with each stroke of the brush. Axioms and runes were meant to be personal undertakings, the intention behind it only belonging to the one who created it. But this was Maligar's retribution. That axioms would no longer be his to use alone.

Once the ink was dry, Ryza wedged his stump into the metal arm's joint and pushed the axiom up his right hand. It burned white-hot in his palm and he pressed it into the prosthetic, yet he didn't feel anything change. Usually taking control of an arcanite involved exploring the metal it was made of, yet...

Ryza opened and closed his new left fist one stuttering finger at a time. He didn't need to control it like an arcanite. The feeling was already there. It was as if his hand hadn't been blown off in the first place!

'Looks to work well enough! I'll fix you up with the straps to keep it attached later.'

Greely got up to leave.

'Wait, where are you going?'

'Yuvet told me to fetch her the second you woke up, so I've already disobeyed her.'

'What about my collar?' Ryza blurted. 'Does it still work?'

'It'll still kill you. Just touch it to the walls if you don't want that. Anything else?'

'No, just... thank you. For saving my life.'

'You didn't thank me the last time, so I don't know why you're starting now!'

Before Ryza could ask him to explain, the healer was gone. He looked back down at his new arm. For some reason he'd still been expecting to see flesh there. He shut his eyes and felt around all the tiny brass pipes, wires, pistons and gears within. There were the shadows of a resonance there, enough to be present, but not enough to be discernible. A dead man's resonance could only last up to a week before decaying.

This arm was fresh.

The thought of it sent another wave of guilt through his system. What he'd done last night. Pointless slaughter he could have refused. All because of the Locusts. Because of Maligar. The guilt turned to fury. The moment he saw Maligar he would kill him.

No, that would be too quick for the bastard. A monster like him needed something slow, cruel and horrifying. Ryza flexed his new hand again, feeling the sheer torque now available at his fingertips.

I've got the exact thing.

His legs still felt numb, but he forced them out of the cot, his head spinning violently as his bare feet hit the floor. Bile rose in his throat. His vision began to dim. Suddenly, the door slammed open and Ryza lurched at the sound.

Oh shit.

He would have said the words, but his mouth flooded with more stinging bile instead. He staggered sideways, throwing his good arm towards the tin tray next to his bed but the wild lunge sent the whole thing crashing down. Ryza followed it, smashing his left shoulder into the floor and only just managing to get a blunt looking scalpel into his hand.

'Such a warm reception, Rusty.'

Ryza could barely focus his vision on the tip of his tiny knife, let alone the figure in the doorway.

'Stay the fuck away from me!' Ryza spat through his teeth.

'Why?' Holm asked, advancing on him.

He used what little leverage he had to try get to his feet, his body wedged against the bolted down bed as Holm came closer and closer.

'You tried to kill me. Said you wanted to watch me bleed!'

She shrugged, indifferent to the accusations.

'You've come to finish me?'

She was just out of his reach. One good lunge and he might be able to finish this fight before it started. But Holm didn't seem to care. She didn't even look at the knife. She leaned in, head cocked, frowning at him like he was a child having a tantrum.

'How do you think you got here?'

'I... I... It doesn't matter! You—'

'I saved you.' Her voice was firm, her frown now a scowl. 'Put down the knife, Ryza.'

He dropped it without thinking. With one hand, she grabbed his shirt and shoved him back into his bed before sitting herself on Greely's unoccupied stool.

'But... but why? Why save me?'

She shrugged again, this time not meeting his eyes. As usual, she was hiding something. Ryza waited out the silence, counting out the heartbeats. Holm lasted eight.

'It was only after the other Locusts left that I could try to move you and by then you were about ready to drown in a puddle of your own blood. I'm surprised you even made it. It was dead quiet when I got you in here, only Greely on duty.'

'Who else knows I'm here?'

'Yuvet, the master of recruits and other than that... nope, nothing. Hell, you could take that funny little arcanite you've got and make a run for it.'

'I could have done that a long time ago,' Ryza said bitterly. He wished he had. He should have run the moment he worked out Origin could reset the collar.

Holm was looking at her knee as it bobbed unconsciously. 'But why stay?' she eventually said.

'After you pushed me in that cave, I found a smelter's ledger. The last sale was from Revance, an order of molten flux identified as *C316*. Do you know anything about that?'

'No.'

Ryza swore under his breath. 'All this time I've been looking for it.'

'Why?'

It was his turn to stay silent. The guilt was back, stronger than ever.

'It's because of what you came from, right? Your father was a flux trader and you more than happily took part in the business.'

'It was the day he told me about my mother,' Ryza said quietly. 'She died just after I was born, but my father brought her back as an automind. Still needed her body, I guess. Wanted to sell it off. Wouldn't be surprised if it was him who killed her in the first place.'

A gigantic weight was pressing down upon his chest, forcing the words out uncontrollably. 'He said he wanted to raise me just right for this, without another's interference.'

Holm licked her lips as she considered her next words. 'Every time I talked to you, I thought you just had a few sins in your past you were trying to make up for. But after watching what you did to that man, it turns out you're just as broken as the rest of the Locusts. You probably thought you could save us all, save Revance. But you can't.'

'What about Maligar then? What if he were stopped?'

Holm shook her head, almost in disgust. 'What he wants is beyond Revance. Save the fortress or let it fall, he won't stop wanting it.'

As he looked at Holm, Ryza noticed an underlying touch of desperation in her voice. She'd always been guarded around him. Maybe her resonance —so loud and chaotic— was a cover for something else? While resonances didn't often change on purpose, over time, subconsciously...

'You don't want any of this, do you? Why the hell did you even keep it all up?'

'I don't have a choice!' Holm exploded. She was on her feet, fists clenched, ready to swing. 'By the time I realised I was in too deep, I had to keep going. And I've watched you and Ferrick do the exact same thing.'

She turned and made for the door, scattering anything in her path.

'Holm, wait!' Ryza tried to move his legs, but after the last attempt, they refused.

She turned at the doorway, fixing Ryza with a furious scowl. 'It's been weeks of you taking cheap shots at me for the things I've had to do! I hauled you back to Revance because maybe, just maybe, you were doing it because you knew better than I did. That you *were* better. But you're so stuck up your own ass that you can't even see that you're exactly the same as me! It's embarrassing I ever thought it was anything else.'

Ryza didn't get another word in before she slammed the door.

CHAPTER TWENTY-THREE

HIDING THE DEAD

RYZA HAD NOW BEEN alone for twenty minutes, but his breathing wouldn't even out. Holm's last words still rang in his ears. They only added to the shame. It was like his entire past, the one he'd so narrowly fled, was finally consuming him.

He was sitting on the bed, staring wide-eyed at the floor, afraid to blink in case the expressionless faces were waiting in that brief moment of darkness. They were the faces of the autominds he'd made. Of the lives he'd taken.

Holm was right. She was the better person. Whatever she'd done in her past was nothing compared to what Ryza did before coming here. The only comfort he could give himself was that Origin was safe, hidden somewhere deep in that undercity, whatever the hell that place was.

The door banged open a second time. Yuvet strode into the room, draped in her usual trench coat with an expression that mixed fury, concern and bewilderment. The rest of Ryza's squad filed in behind her. Ditric's face only bore fury. Ruka at least looked concerned and for the first time Gry was bewildered. Haven brought up the rear, his entire being locked in sheer disbelief.

'I should be here to kill you for dereliction of duty, desertion and probably treason,' Yuvet stated.

'I'd deserve it,' he muttered.

She responded with a sharp slap across his head and Ryza nearly blacked out from it.

'You'd be lucky to get even that. Now tell me everything you know! Every single fucking detail, I don't care how insignificant!' She turned to his squad. 'Sit down and listen carefully because someone needs to tell me when he starts lying.'

Ryza obeyed, starting all the way back at finding Origin and the ledger, then to undertaking the secret mission of searching for the molten flux. His voice began to falter as his story pulled into the ruins where the Locusts' party was held. He wanted to lie, to absolve himself, but Yuvet's unrelenting stare forced the truth out of him. As he told them of opening the coffin, pulling out the dazed man and then the injector, he kept his eyes fixed on the floor.

'Fucking metal mouths never change,' Ditric said in a voice of pure disdain. 'You're a fucking animal.'

Yuvet didn't even bother reprimanding her. 'I'd happen to agree.'

'I know. I'm sorry, ma'am, for everything I've done. But I know that's not enough.'

'You're damn right it's not. The one thing I want to get straight is that Origin, the one thing these Locust bastards need to take over Revance, is currently lost with those-of-glass, correct?'

'Yes.'

'Well, that's one small victory in your months-long blunder,' Yuvet muttered. 'It'll buy us the time we need to nail down who's involved. I'd go after Maligar, but that idiot isn't going to be the head of anything. All charm, no follow through.'

'I don't think we've actually got as much time as you think, ma'am,' Haven said, his tone unusually grim. 'We need to find Origin.'

'Why's that?' Ruka asked. 'You know people don't survive going down there, right? Even if they do, they don't last long after.'

'Origin was found and he could be found again,' Haven said. 'You really want to take that chance?'

'We'd be taking our chances if we went down there,' Ditric grunted.

'And it sounds like the Locusts are more than willing to do the same.' Yuvet let out the deep breath she'd been holding, glancing from face to face before she spoke. 'This is your mess, Ryza. By extension, your squad's too. You've got to go and fix it. Besides, I can't trust anyone else to.'

They all gasped, Ryza especially. He could barely walk! He was in no state to be sent back out so soon.

'But you want us to go... down there?' Gry asked, his voice shaking.

'We can do it, Gry,' Haven said. 'We ain't got a choice.'

'What's the plan then, ma'am?' Ditric said.

Yuvet rubbed her eyes as she thought. To Ryza, she looked like she hadn't slept in days.

'You'll have to stay holed up in here for the day. The less people that know about you or this mission, the better, which means keeping out of sight. We can trust Greely. He'll bring you food, ammo and the best equipment and armour I can get you on short notice. Might even be able to fix you up with some ink. From the stories I've heard about those places, you'll need every drop you can get.

'Tomorrow morning, before dawn, I'll escort you down to the motor pool and get you on a lead-better. Ditric, I want you to lead this mission.' She looked pointedly at Ryza. 'Make sure you all come back alive.'

'Understood, ma'am,' Ditric said with conviction.

'You won't hear from me until then. On top of all this, Commander Valtos has taken ill and a team of eight healers can't find their ass with both hands, let alone figure out what's wrong with him.'

Yuvet left and slammed the door shut behind her, leaving Ryza at the mercy of Ditric's impervious stare.

'If Valtos is ill, it would be an ideal time to attack,' Gry said in a worried voice.

'You think someone's poisoned him?' Haven asked.

'It's possible,' Ditric said. 'But we can't do shit from here, so there's no point thinking about it.' She walked over to Ryza, placing herself on the stool in front of him just as Holm had. 'Tell me everything you know about these ruins.'

He relayed his combined knowledge of them, consisting of what he'd seen the previous night and what Ferrick told him in the form of ominous, cautionary tales. It was meagre, but Ditric found it somewhat satisfactory.

Greely returned three hours later, straining under the weight of a massive crate he struggled to wedge through the door. He dropped it with a pained gasp and breathlessly told them he was needed elsewhere.

How the healer had managed to pick up the damn thing was a miracle. Five sets of plated steel armour, Ryza's dented-up rifle, a never-ending coil of braided steel rope and a slew of strange instruments even Gry struggled to understand. Enough loose slugs to besiege a small town rolled around beneath it all.

As Ryza picked up his gun, it was with a pang of regret. His right hand shook as it touched the trigger, and the metal fingers of his new left hand squeaked and scraped as he tried to grip it. No matter how cooling the previous owner's resonance was, he felt he may never shoot the same again.

The rest of the day was spent either sizing up their arms and armour or covering themselves in runes in preparation for whatever lay beneath the sands. Since his quaking hands were yet to steady from the previous night, Gry and Ruka were kind enough to draw a litany of axioms onto his remaining arm instead. The most interesting was one that would explosively repel anything metal that he didn't control.

'What about my armour?' he asked Gry.

'If you still need it after that...'

Ryza didn't want to entertain the prospect. His new hand seemed to have a mind of its own. The joints and knuckles twitched and flexed with every dull throb of pain that radiated from his stump of an arm, the metal cold against the cauterised flesh. Even the metal plate Greely has concealed under his flesh for the arm to latch onto felt strange.

Each time he looked down at the prosthetic, a glimpse of his real arm's last moments replaced it, before it was all wiped away in a blinding muzzle flash.

'Any of you ever been down one of these ruins before?' Ryza eventually asked to distract himself.

'Had a job take me near there once, but never saw anything of them,' Ditric grunted. She'd managed to fill her entire arm with axioms and was now slowly working on the other one.

'I remember one night I had to hole up in there with a few others,' Ruka said. 'We were stuck between towns in a sandstorm just as bad as the one out there now. The place we found shelter was almost buried, only one room actually above the dunes. We had to make camp a bit below, but none of us slept. There was this big hole in the floor, we couldn't see how deep it went, but something about it...' She trailed off with a shudder.

'Don't worry about that. All we need to do is find the damn arcanite!' Haven declared.

Ryza pointed his metal fingers at him. 'Exactly!' He grinned, ignoring the fact he sounded alarmingly like Maligar. 'We get Origin and we get out. Our wristbands will lead us to him. The red dial doesn't point to Revance specifically, just to the nearest instance of Origin's resonance. Just have to dodge whatever else we find down there. You read anything about these places, Gry?'

'Yeah, you're always ear deep in a book,' Ruka said. 'You have to know something.'

Gry looked up from his own rune work, his axioms copied out of a book, of course. 'The whole subject is pretty taboo. I've heard the Academy of Breggesa keeps a tight lock on any knowledge of these places, just so people won't go investigating themselves. Like Ruka said, they do a good enough job repelling people on their own, so the only things commonly known are the tales of people going down there and simply not coming back.'

'Ferrick told me there's good pickings,' Ryza said. 'Dangerous but just as valuable. Are those the things stopping people coming back? Or is it monsters? Or magic?'

'I haven't a clue. The only rumour that persists—' he swallowed hard, his eyes beginning to waver. 'Of a figure with black eyes called a shadow dancer. I've never known more than that or what it even does to people. Whenever someone tries to tell me about it, they just can't find the words.'

Ryza knew exactly what Gry was talking about. The hairs on the back of his neck stood up at the name and a lump appeared from nowhere in his throat. If just the idea of its supposed name could trigger something like this in him, what would meeting one do? He glanced around at the others. They looked just as uncomfortable.

He tried to flush the thought of it out of his head with the usual whirling cacophony of conspiracy that engulfed Revance. But each time without fail, it was replaced by a pair of looming black eyes.

Unnatural.
Unblinking.
Unstoppable.

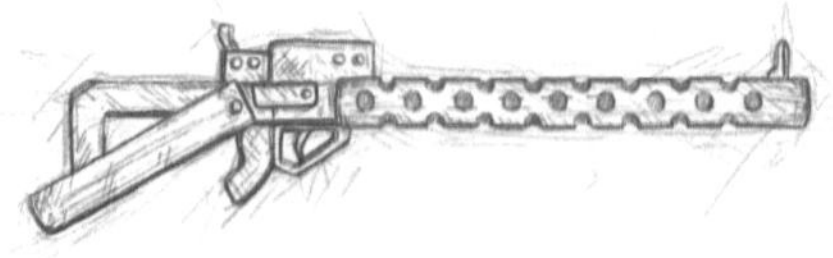

Chapter Twenty-Four

The Old Blood

'For fuck's sake! Ruka! Do something about this bloody sandstorm!'

Ditric's shouts barely were heard over the roar of the sandstorm or the teeth-rattling thrum of their lead-better. The storm was so thick that it didn't matter that the sun hadn't risen.

At Ditric's less-than-formal command, Ruka stood up in the back seat, her stance impossibly stable as she held both her palms forward into the wind, eyes clenched shut behind her goggles. A sharp crack of wind followed, slicing a clear path through the sandstorm and setting their ears ringing. Clear desert lay ahead, but their destination was nowhere in sight. Nevertheless, Ruka kept the axiom focused, her expression locked in a trance-like state.

The five of them had left Revance an hour ago, clad in heavy body armour and armed to the teeth with as many axioms as they had skin to put them on. Yuvet had been their clandestine escort, smuggling Ryza's and their unwieldy crate of equipment to the motor pool. A vehemently reluctant Garrog had been waiting with their lead-better and Ryza recognised it as the one he'd recovered from the derelict pump station weeks ago.

Over the course of the journey, he'd occupied himself by constantly tightening the straps on his armour. Getting it on had been an entire

production. Padded cloth, followed by a stiff leather under-layer, topped off by more steel than he thought a man could carry that took the form of shin guards, gauntlets, pauldrons, a chest plate almost an inch thick and a neck guard that almost reached up to Ryza's upper lip
.

When Ditric was helping him secure the last piece, she assured him he'd survive being shot at point-blank range, as long as he wasn't hit in the head.

They each wore dark tan cloaks around their armour, with the idea it would keep dust out of the pinching joints between pieces. Though it had only been minutes in the gale before Ryza felt a small sand dune collecting in his pants.

'How close do you reckon we are, Ryza?' Ditric shouted over her shoulder.

He needed to lean forward to have a chance at being heard. 'Can't tell. Was too busy bleeding to figure out how far away it was. Just keep following the dial.'

Haven was sitting next to her and tasked with watching the compass on his wristband. Ditric gave him a slap on the chest to get his attention. 'Anything?'

'Unless we've gotten turned around, we're still heading towards him.'

They kept going. Each sideways gust threatened to whip under the lead-better and flip it like a child's toy. Through the haze, Ryza spotted a hauntingly familiar silhouette in the distance.

'This is it!' Ryza shouted.

'Good, we're almost half empty for oil,' Ditric said.

She slowed the lead-better as they approached, pulling to a stop in the shelter of one of the smaller skyscrapers. Here the sandstorm was nothing more than a dust shower, allowing Ruka to finally slump back into her seat, her breathing ragged. The other four hefted the crate off the back of the buggy and Gry began sorting through the various pieces of equipment Yuvet had appointed them with.

He handed one of these to Ryza, a pair of narrow, wire-linked cans he was to wedge in either side of his neck guard.

'These things are rare. No idea why Revance even has them. Detects magic residue. The kind those-of-glass left. If you hear it humming like it's going to break, you're in too deep.' Gry said, attaching his own. 'Pull back or you'll be puking your guts. Literally.'

Ryza gave one of the cans at his neck a tap and it immediately started humming.

At least it can point out the obvious.

'Got your breath, Ruka?' Ditric asked.

She climbed out of the buggy and collected her own rifle. 'As best as I can. I'm ready.'

'Good. Load up and shoot anything that moves,' Ditric said. She turned to Ryza and jabbed a finger at him. 'Take us to where you saw Origin last.'

As they stalked through the ruins, Ryza felt much more secure than the last time he was here. His gun's cool resonance now greeted him like an old friend. Even his new arm had taken to the resonance, his metal fingers finally twisting into the right spots to grip the barrel.

Ryza's trail took them from ruin wall to ruin wall, never straying too far from them in case he lost track in the sandstorm. At some points, they might as well have been in the middle of nowhere for all he could see. In these conditions, everything looked the same. He needed something distinct, a sign that would show the way.

'Is that a corpse?'

Ruka had been the first to spot it. Ryza wanted to turn his squad away, to tell them they'd seen nothing and to keep moving. But he'd asked for a sign and this was it. They approached, their rifles trained on the half-buried body.

'Friend of yours, Ryza?' Haven asked.

'This was the automind.' Ryza's tone was grim, he couldn't help it. He didn't get a chance to look at the body up close. Nor did he need to.

The wind and the storm hadn't disturbed the body. It was simply trying to provide it with a proper burial. A trickle of flux oozed from its shattered skull, an endless fountain that disappeared into the sand. Ryza looked up from the corpse, tracing in his mind's eye the deadly slug's path back to the skyscraper which had been his vantage point.

'Still can't believe you made an automind,' Ditric said, shaking her head in disgust. 'For the Locusts and all. Did you even have a choice?'

'No,' Ryza said. He wasn't sure if it was a lie, but he could lose sleep over it later. He set off towards the skyscraper, the rest following him.

'How are we doing on our collars?' Ruka said, peering at her wristband.

Everyone except Ryza looked at their wristband. His was probably somewhere a few hundred metres below their feet.

'Looks like we're about two hours in,' Ruka said.

'Good, still have plenty of time,' Ditric said.

They crept up on the skyscraper, the sandstorm's ever-present haze now snubbing their view of its peak. It was like it was no longer there. *Maybe it wasn't.*

Ryza dismissed the thought. Of course it was there. It was impossible for it not to be! The world went quiet when he ducked through one of the shattered glass windows. The sandstorm couldn't reach them here. The only noise was the rhythmic thrum of their magic sensors growing with each step.

As he retraced his path, he could remember walking past all these rows of barren shelves, gun held loosely in his still intact left hand, his eyes fixed on a point thousands of miles away as he tried to process what he'd done. Ryza shivered. He already knew these memories wouldn't be pleasant. Around the corner were more shelves, all surrounding the metal spiral staircase he'd trudged up. This time he ascended quickly, his rifle raised.

When he reached the top, he was greeted by that same white hallway. Sand had gathered in the corners since then, but at the end of it, the door was still wide open. Ryza and Ditric moved towards it. The muzzles of both their guns were fixed on the entrance to the next room and a tiny part of Ryza was expecting Holm to jump out.

Nothing came of this instinct and as they stepped into the room, Ryza heard gasps come from his squad mates.

'How much blood did you lose here?' Haven said.

'More importantly, how much did they pump back into you?' Gry added.

The dried remnants of Ryza's blood now stained the torn, dust covered carpet and had painted the clutter of sleek desks pushed against the back wall with vicious splashes. Ditric was the only one unfazed by it, her attention instead drawn by the bottomless pit Origin had hurled himself down.

'So, this is the shaft,' Ditric said, peering down it. 'Seems to go forever. Come over here, all of you.'

They gathered around her as she knelt at the edge, placing her rifle down and holding her hands over the void. A trio of yellow runes flickered across her exposed wrist. She grimaced as they burned in her left hand, a perfect sphere of fire forming between her palms. She dropped it and it fell like a stone. Its light grew smaller and smaller until it was barely a pinprick at the bottom and after a while, it simply vanished. Their magic sensors crackled savagely in response.

'Did you do that, Ditric?' Ryza asked quickly.

'Not at all.'

'Then what did?'

'Two options,' Gry said. 'Some*thing* or some*one.*'

'Could it have been Origin?' Ruka asked. 'He might not appreciate balls of fire.'

Ditric held her wristband above the void, twisting it until the dial spun, now pointing down and to the left.

'If it had pointed straight down, it would have meant Origin was there,' she muttered.

'But if it's something else—'

'Unless we want to waste more time looking for another way down, we don't have a choice,' Ditric barked back. 'Ruka, Gry, you're our Reythurists so you're going to have to float down first and figure out if we've got enough rope, otherwise we'll need to stop in the middle before we go lower. Who wants to go first?'

The two of them glanced at each other and hesitated.

'I'll go,' Ruka said. 'Gry's never been good at magic.'

'I'd be offended, but since you offered...'

Ditric handed her one end of the rope and summoned a smaller, more solid-looking orb of light to wedge into her armour. 'Make sure you come back up.'

Ruka ignored her, concentrating on her runes. In her left hand she held the end of the rope in a tight fist. Her right was held out over the void and Ryza could see the blue runes rearranging themselves on her forearm. Satisfied, she sent the axiom into her palm.

The air tensed and flexed around them, not quite a gust but it still made Ryza's ears pop like he was climbing a mountain. He ground his jaw to ease the pain, but it dropped open the next second as Ruka's feet had left the ground. She floated perfectly still, toes pointed towards the floor two inches below her. He'd seen Reythurists fly before, but only from a distance.

Ruka moved into the shaft and turned to face them, her eyes still shut. A few more runes flowed across her arm and another pulse of wind emanated from her body.

'She's feeling the air of the place,' Gry explained. 'Means she'll see anything that wind bounces off.'

'About thirty metres down, there's an opening like this one,' Ruka whispered. 'I think there are stairs in that room.'

'Do you know how deep this shaft is?' Ryza asked.

Her face scrunched, turning downwards. 'Could be hundreds of metres deep, maybe more. There's... there's no bottom.'

Ruka began her descent, Ditric carefully feeding the coil to her as the light of her glow bulb shrunk into the darkness. Ryza just wished there was something he could do to help.

Soon the rope stopped and after a minute it tensed with three solid tugs.

'She must want us to come down,' Ditric said. She took the remaining length of rope to a nearby column and knotted it as hard as she could. After slinging her rifle under her arm, she returned to the shaft.

'Don't fall,' Haven offered with a grin.

'You wish I would,' Ditric snapped. She sat down, intertwining her legs with the steel rope before she slid over the edge, the back of her armour scraping against the wall. A minute later, there was another three tugs of the rope and Gry did the same. Once he was out of earshot, Haven turned to Ryza.

'If I don't make it out of this but you do, make sure my parents get the reels I've made for them, yeah?'

'Of course.'

'You got any last requests? Kretatics first and all?'

The phrase made Ryza's arm ache harder. 'No, not for me.'

'Suit yourself.' Then Haven slid over the edge.

Once again Ryza was alone in the ruins, a rifle in his hands. A little over a day ago he'd sat here, ready to die. Now he was about to risk his life again. He looked down the hole, watching as Haven slipped from view.

How far have you fallen, Origin?

The rope jerked three times. His turn. As the others had done, he sat on the edge, rope between his legs and rifle slung from his shoulder. Surely this would be easy, he was the best climber out of the five of them by far. He shimmied out, letting his wrapped legs take his weight and using his arms to lower himself down.

The rope grated against the soft flesh of his right palm, biting into what little of it was exposed from the gauntlet's protection, yet when he gripped it with his left hand, it felt like he was on the verge of slipping.

I've never climbed with a metal hand.

Suddenly, he was painfully aware of how disconnected he was from this new arm. The metal grew cold, the feeling of his fingers fading and before he knew it, all life from the arm had ceased. He couldn't even twitch the thumb.

Shit.

He looked down. There was still another fifteen or so metres to the faintly glowing hole the rope led to. Going back up certainly wasn't an option. In the precarious darkness of the shaft, he didn't stand a chance at organising the axiom necessary to retake his arm.

Better to get this over with quickly.

He loosened his legs' grip, lurching down a metre or two and almost flinging himself off the rope. He swung down another few metres. If it wasn't for the gauntlets, his right palm would be scorched. He could already feel the heat coming through the metal.

Ryza risked one more look down. He was close.

One last drop.

He clenched his teeth and plummeted, but his legs weren't ready for the inward swing of the rope, nor were his arms. The result was Ryza tumbling unceremoniously into the room, landing with a head-spinning clang on a metal floor.

The next thing he knew he was being picked up, yet he was too dazed to piece together who was doing the lifting. Each step kicked up clouds of dust from the carpet and Ryza was thrown onto a fraying chair next to a stack of dented copper panels.

'The hell happened to you?' Ditric's voice came from his left side.

'Arm stopped working,' was all Ryza could manage as a response.

'What do you mean it stopped working?' Gry asked. 'Is it broken?'

'Nah, he probably wasn't concentrating on it enough,' Haven said.

Ryza stared at the offending limb. It hadn't given him a hint of trouble from the moment it was put on. Of all times, why now?

'It was like I was thinking about it too much,' Ryza said. 'It just sort of hit me that it wasn't really mine and then it just stopped...'

'Then don't think about it,' Ditric said curtly. 'Can you get that thing working?'

'I... I don't know.'

He was looking at his other arm now, shifting runes back and forth across it, trying to put together the right axiom, but in his head, nothing would suffice.

'You've got about five seconds before we move on without you, Ryza,' Ditric said.

He settled on a single power rune, pressing his palm against the metal forearm and feeling it glow white-hot. What if the metal just needed more of his mind? The mechanical fingers waggled violently to life before regressing back to feeble twitches no matter how hard Ryza willed them to move.

'Think you'll be able to shoot straight?' Ruka said, helping him back to his feet.

He shook his head.

'Well, if you're going to shoot, don't be anywhere near me,' Ditric muttered.

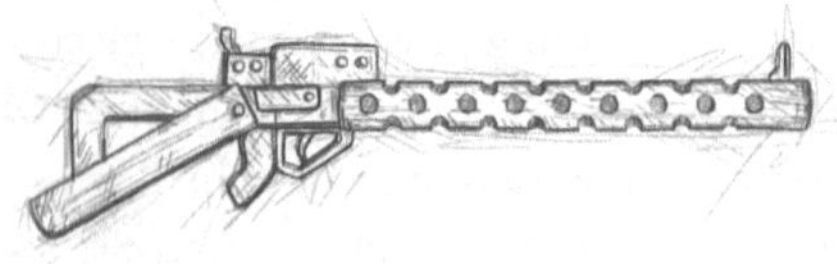

CHAPTER TWENTY-FIVE

THE UNDERCITY

THE FIVE OF THEM stood before the stairs. Their glow bulbs only reached a few metres into the darkness before it was cut off abruptly, like there was a solid border of where this place permitted light. The metal edges of each step seemed to warp and twist when Ryza wasn't focusing on it, yet when he tried to catch it in the act, it was perfectly still.

'How long have we got on our collars?' Ditric said.

Instinctively, Ryza looked down at his left wrist, his shoulders slumping at the sight of bare steel.

'Nine hours,' Haven answered for him.

'We've already fucked about too long,' Ditric growled. 'Follow me and hold fire until my command. No noise, either. I don't know what or who is down here, but I don't want it finding us first.'

She began making her way down, her shoulders stiff around the stock of her raised rifle, eyes fixed on the precious few steps they could see. Gry followed her, then Ryza stepped down as well.

Each footstep was magnified in his ears. Thick, ancient air filled their lungs as they went deeper. To Ryza, it felt like his lungs emptied completely each time he exhaled, but filling them was impossible without his breath becoming a rasping cough.

For every landing they passed, Ditric ordered for them to clear the entire area, a tedious process involving improvised hand gestures and careful patrols through each room. The only sound in Ryza's ears was the hum of the magic sensors. Gry hadn't told him how long until he'd be coughing up blood, but he prayed it wasn't soon.

The thought of it distracted him from how repetitive each floor was. The glass windows that enclosed the skyscrapers only filtered in a dim amber light from the sandstorm outside. It did little to illuminate the tiny offices with chest high walls, stacked with ransacked desks that had been abandoned all too quickly.

Low walls of black fabric separated each one. Their surfaces were fuzzy like unshaven stubble and Ryza couldn't hear his own pulse throbbing in his ears when he drew near one.

Some of the desks hadn't looked right. They were perfectly preserved and free of dust. A wobbling heat haze surrounded them that drove Ryza's magic sensor crazy when he went near. On first encountering it, Ruka had thrown a rock at one, only for it to halt in mid-air just before it hit the desk.

This must be what Ferrick had called a fracture. An inexplicable remnant of magic left by those-of-glass. They'd left it behind quickly, Ryza wondering what else in here would be considered a fracture.

When they finally hit the bottom of the stairs, Ditric broke the silence with a whisper.

'Haven, time check?'

'Eight hours.'

'Shit. We'll have to turn back soon.'

'Not unless we find Origin,' Ryza said.

Ditric glared back at him. 'One hour until we turn back. Got it?'

Ryza bit his tongue. She was right.

Ahead of them was a short corridor with a heavy steel door at the end of it. It was entirely solid, spare for a horizontal slit of glass embedded in the very centre, and the blue paint that covered it showed no sign of wear or chipping. They approached, guns raised as if it were about to attack and Ditric motioned for Ruka to open it.

A grandiose atrium lay beyond. The walls were lined with decaying couches of unnaturally grey leather. Rows of ornate wooden desks formed an aisle through the middle of the space and twisting pillars of marble flecked with gold supporting a ceiling of shattered mirrors.

A desert of glass shards covered the floor, each piece glinting from the orange glow leaking in from beyond the atrium's bounds. It was hard to make out the tiles beneath it all, but each one was so huge that it looked like the foundations had been carved from the rock itself.

The splintered flickers of movement from both above and below made Ryza jumpy as they swept the room for threats. Despite finding nothing, not even a fracture, he kept his rifle clutched close.

Ditric crouched in the centre of the room, her left hand pointed towards the light, runes swirling around her wrists.

'What are you doing?' Ryza asked.

'Trying to figure out what's putting off that light, but I can't think of the right axiom to do it.'

'Something's off about this place,' Ruka said over the rattle of her own sensor. 'I can feel it.'

'The air pressure in this place is high, probably cause we're so deep underground,' Gry said.

'No, it's not that,' she replied. 'It's like I'm here... but I'm also somewhere else.'

Ryza ran a finger over one of the desks, the lacquered finish impossibly smooth. He'd never seen wood quite like this before. For a moment, he was thrown back into his father's study. There was a long, lopsided wooden desk where he would record his dealings.

Its surface had been rough and splintered, but it was still a hallmark of prestige. Finding a solid piece of wood, let alone enough of it to turn into furniture, was an arduous task. The few trees that could be found across the Droughtlands only took root in far-off mountains and not in quantities large enough for a craftsman to practice with.

He wandered over to the other side of the room, a gaping maw of broken glass that led to an entire city. It was arranged in circular, descending tiers, each level packed with the bases of skyscrapers that reached a hundred metres up before they were cut off by the rocky cavern ceiling. Each one was a pillar of ruined, twisted steel. Some leaned precariously, half buckled and only supported by mountains of debris.

Ryza took a few steps onto the road outside the building, glass crunching underfoot and the sensors buzzing louder in his ear. At the very middle of the city, on the lowest tier, sat a small bunker with an angled dish atop it. From its centre sprouted an antenna and, at its tip, a detached ball of fiery light. It wasn't bright, but somehow it lit up the whole cavern and the way it caught the broken glass on the roads made it look like the city was layered with hot coals.

The only place it couldn't reach was the shadows cast by the skyscrapers. Looking into the dark voids, Ryza felt his throat clamp up. The sound of his breath hitting the inside of his neck guard was all he could hear and he struggled to tear his eyes away, the darkness growing deeper and deeper by the second.

'Wherever you are, Origin, you'd best show yourself fast,' he muttered to himself.

He turned back to his squad. Haven was rummaging through the drawers in one of the desks, Ruka had taken to wandering aimlessly, rifle resting on her shoulder, and Gry was scooping through the glass with his gauntlets, occasionally feeding pieces into a gadget covered with copper tubes.

'Where's Ditric?' Ryza said.

In the centre of the room, exactly where she'd been crouched, was nothing. Not even glass. It was a clear circle of floor, maybe a metre wide.

'Did any of you see her?'

'I wasn't... I wasn't watching,' Ruka said.

'Neither was I,' Gry said.

Ryza turned back to the city, squinting at the strange light in the centre. Did it have something to do with her disappearance? The last thing she'd been doing was trying to work out what was creating the illumination.

'I'll send out a pulse,' Ruka said. 'That should find her.'

Ryza hadn't heard her. In his mind, he could still see Ditric's last motions. On one knee, runes in her hands...

'Ruka! Wait!'

Too late. There was another empty space among them.

'Did one of you see what happened to her?' Ryza said quickly.

Haven shook his head, mouth agape. 'She just vanished the moment she used the axiom.'

'Took the glass with her too,' Gry added.

But where did they go?

'No one use a single rune,' Ryza said. 'I think it's the undercity that did this, when they tried to—'

His words were cut short by a dull crunch. They all jumped back, rifles clenched tight in their hands, Ryza struggling to bring his to bear. There was another and Ryza saw a few glass shards next to Ditric's empty circle crumble to powder. Another crunch, more pieces of broken glass, and this time Ryza discerned the shape of a footstep.

'Is that... Is that them?' Haven said.

'Maybe they're invisible,' Gry said. He waved a hand over the footstep, hitting nothing. 'Maybe not.'

Another set of footsteps appeared, plodding slowly with the first until their pace suddenly quickened. Before they had a chance to follow, the trail ran into the city, leaving only the sound of crackling glass in its wake.

'They must have seen someone!' Ryza let out a low groan. 'Shit, what do we do now?'

'Do we try and get to them?' Gry said.

Haven shook his head quickly. 'We need to keep looking for Origin.'

'What about them?' Gry said.

Ryza chewed his lip for a moment. 'If they can find a way back, they'll make it. Split up, we'll cover as much ground as possible.'

Ryza watched a flicker of protest cross Gry's face, but it faded after a few heartbeats. They stepped out of the atrium and split up. Gry headed left, following the path of Ditric and Ruka's footsteps as Haven took the opposite path, leaving Ryza to negotiate his way to the centre.

Only three sounds kept Ryza company. His crunching boots, the humming pitch of the magic sensor and his hot breath. Ruka had been right about the air down here. It was alien in his system, denser than he could process. The weight of it bore down on him, compressing his armour, burning against his skin and crushing his bones.

Fractured black stone formed the path he followed. It weaved between the skyscrapers and down steep slopes, the oddly patterned white markings that ran its length still shining bright despite the long shadows that sometimes covered them. The few times Ryza found himself unfortunate enough to join them, the soft light from his glow orb only reached a metre into the thickened gloom.

It was in these spots that the pair of black eyes loomed in his mind. It was like their owner was standing just in front of him, if only the glow orb could reach them... Ryza stopped just before he entered the third stretch of darkness. This one was longer than the previous two, covering a gently sloping hill that was framed on either side by rows of shattered skyscrapers. The globe of orange light hovered ominously at the other end, its reach doing nothing to show the way forward.

If only to delay the inevitable, Ryza stretched his stiff neck, looking up the lengths of the skyscrapers on either side as he did so. Halfway through the motion, he froze. He could almost pick out a dark figure, watching him from high in the ruins.

The seed of doubt he'd harboured since setting foot in these ruins sprouted, rooting him to the ground as he cursed himself for ever returning to this place. Every thought that'd rushed through his mind in the past few days had a common theme.

Regret.

He clenched his eyes shut, wishing he hadn't told the last of his squad to split up. They were the only thing that could snap him out of this. A friendly pat on the back from Haven or a barked order from Ditric. Hell, he'd even take a slap over the head from Yuvet if she was here. He tried to swallow his fear, but the collar still felt too tight around his neck to allow even that. If the undercity didn't kill him, the collar would.

I must find Origin. I have to.

After opening his eyes, he took a defiant step forward, slamming his boot down with newfound vigour. His senses grew keener as he marched on, dispelling the fears that lurked in the shadows. Nothing was stalking him aside from his own paranoia. He was getting closer to the centre of the city. Closer to the source of the orange light.

He was now overlooking the last tier of the undercity. Whatever destroyed this place had started here. Every building had been reduced to massive tracts of twisted and splintering steel, decorated by slopes of loose concrete rubble that washed like dunes against the walls of the next tier.

Ryza scaled one of these slopes to get down, almost breaking his neck in the process. It was like they'd been coated in oil. It certainly had the smell. As Ryza picked his way through the wreckage, half-buried bodies of metal became apparent.

They were snake-like in form, as wide as he was tall. Puncturing wounds dotted their scaled backs of burnt and tarnished metal. Finely machined gun-barrels lanced from their jaws in place of fangs, but the muzzles of them were malfunctioned and burst. Ryza dared himself to inspect one, peering into a devastating gash that ran the length of its belly. Guts of wired mazes lay inside. Any spare space between them was flooded by molten flux.

What the hell is molten flux doing down here?

These weren't arcanites. Not in the traditional sense. There were too many moving parts, too much that relied on the raw physical motion of the metal rather than the mind of the Kretatic controlling it. If Ryza were to attempt to give this fallen beast a new life with his axioms, he'd only last a few seconds before it killed him.

Then again, these things look to have been made for killing.

Leaving them behind, Ryza made his way to the bunker. Its grey walls were free of gunports and even any hint of a corner. The only variation in its surface was the occasional tangle of antennas that poked through its surface, the lengths of which bent sharply to point back at the hanging orange orb. Looking over his shoulder, Ryza noticed similar features sprouting from the remaining nearby skyscrapers.

Aside from the layer of crumbled glass, the grounds around the bunker were clear of detritus. Truncated, waist-high concrete barricades ringed the structure's perimeter. Each was two metres wide, separated from their neighbours by a gap just as long. The fortifications reminded him of Revance, for some strange reason. Layers and layers of a shell, each one pushed out by the one beneath it

.

Ryza's pace slowed as he passed through each set of barricades. The bunker was in front of him now. He was dwarfed by its presence. Bathed in orange light, the warmth prickled gently on his face, the sensation most prominent on the dozens of fresh scars. The moment would have been peaceful if not for the incessant hum of his magic sensor.

The whole place is bad, I know.

The damn thing had been buzzing from the moment he'd put it on. He tossed it into a nearby pile of rubble, where it fell silent and he enjoyed a moment of tranquillity. It was like he was basking in the evening sunset.

If he was honest with himself, he'd never been more at peace. After a lifetime cowering in fear under his father's shaking fist before being conscripted into the never-ending grind of Revance, this was —despite the danger— the calmest he'd ever been.

Not wanting to relinquish such a serene moment, he opened his eyes slowly, yet a second later they shot wide in alarm. The figure of a cloaked man stood at the very edge of the bunker's roof, silhouetted by the orange light.

Ryza's next breath came sharp and he struggled to shoulder his rifle, using his ailing left arm as a brace for it. But the figure didn't move. As his pulse raced faster, Ryza's finger teasing the trigger, a blood rush pumping through his veins and ringing in his ears.

Shadow dancer.

The figure suddenly loomed twice as tall, beginning to tower over him. Ryza's eyes felt as if he hadn't blinked for days. His rifle was shaking despite the cool resonance that attempted to steady him. Then the voice spoke. It was deep, booming, yet somehow still nothing more than a whisper in his ear.

'You were brave to come down here, Ryza. I have what you seek.'

How do they know my name!?

'But you fear the wrong thing.'

There was a crunch of glass ten metres away, directly in front of him. Ryza swung his rifle down to it, watching in horror as a trail of footsteps crept closer, each step slow and deliberate.

His finger twitched against the trigger, but there was nothing to shoot at! Even his legs were frozen in place. The only option left to him was an axiom. The runes on his wrist were already spinning into place, aligning themselves into an axiom for a simple metal-detecting sweep.

Ryza ignored the searing burn of each rune as he focused on their individual meaning. After the third, a flash of pain shook his body and a magnetic pulse burst out from his core.

But there was more to it. His skin felt like it was stretching to the point he was sure he was about to break in two. The sensation extinguished the last of his breath but there was no air around to replenish it. The last thing to go was his vision. The darkness only lasted half a second. When it came back, everything had changed.

It was like the city had reassembled itself in an instant. The light was blue now, yet still coming from the exact same sphere at the tip of the dish's antenna. The buildings around him were no longer ruins. With their walls of glass restored, they stood tall and proud. Even the ground was clear of debris.

But Ryza couldn't waste time marvelling it.

Ferrick stood before him, armed and armoured just as he was. The only difference was that she didn't have a collar around her neck. A determined fire burned in her eyes and her face split into a triumphant grin at the sight of Ryza.

Shit.

Her rifle snapped to her shoulder as Ryza clumsily swung his own to bear, struggling against his dull arm. His finger was already squeezing the trigger, just to give him that extra moment's edge, but he knew it wouldn't be enough.

Two blasts sounded through the cavern.

Unfortunately for Ryza, the first came from Ferrick's gun.

CHAPTER TWENTY-SIX

DUEL BETWEEN WORLDS

FERRICK'S SLUG HIT HIM square in the chest, the impact denting his breastplate and throwing him clean off his feet. Ryza's own shot went wide, blowing out a skyscraper window. He hit the ground, gasping for breath.

Still not as painful as the last time I got shot.

Flat on his back, he could barely crane his neck to see that Ferrick was advancing on him. She shoved a fresh slug into her rifle and pushed the muzzle into his chest, pinning him to the ground. His own rifle jabbed into his back, the sling at his shoulder having somehow thrown it under his body as he'd fallen.

'I bet you're surprised to see me,' Ryza choked out.

'Surprised to see you alive,' she said casually. 'Also surprised that you already understand how this undercity works. Burn an axiom and be taken through to another side of it. One that was saved, one that was not.'

'What do you—?'

'This bunker is different from the ruined side, no?'

He glanced past her. She was right. The dish was smaller, the structure itself rounder. Embedded into the wall facing them was a passageway Ferrick must've just emerged from, which was why her footsteps seemed to have appeared out of nowhere. Not that he knew how.

'I got here hours ago,' she said, leaning harder on the stock of her rifle and making Ryza grunt from the added weight. 'Of all the things I expected to see down here, you were the last.' She let out a small giggle and suddenly the gun's barrel was hovering over his face.

'Looking for Origin too?' Ryza said quickly. He needed to stall her, to give him enough time to get another axiom into his palm. 'Maligar sent you, didn't he?' The more the panic rose in him, the slower each rune seemed to move across his skin. 'But who would have taken the collar off you?'

'For the first time in a long while, you're getting close. This whole time you've been searching for the leader of the Locusts.'

'Tyrag...'

'He's finally got it!' Ferrick shouted. She danced away for a moment, her rifle raised in mock celebration before she pointed back to Ryza.

'Yes, I have.'

A grin split Ryza's lips and he snatched at Ferrick's rifle, revealing the last burning rune in his palm as he caught the muzzle in his grip. He seized control of the weapon, his mind reaching down the barrel and twisting it into a useless rod. Then he pushed his will to the trigger, slamming it down under her finger, causing the rifle to explode in a spray of smoke.

Before he could see the results of his work, his skin stretched again and suddenly he was sitting among glass. It was glowing orange again, the surrounding city having returned to its demolished state. The muzzle of Ferrick's gun was still in his hand. Anything beyond it had been shorn clean off. A twinge of pain burned in his hand and he dropped the hot metal. Making the jump between cities must have some kind of boundary around his body with the potential to sever anything caught in the way.

Ryza grabbed his own rifle and dived behind one of the nearby barricades, hastily thumbing a new slug down the barrel as he strained his ears for the slightest movement. He'd been lucky Ferrick hadn't thought to kill him on the spot.

Her gloating had given him just enough time to channel the eight runes he needed to take control of her rifle. Four in the first axiom to clear out any resonance that might be in there, two in the second to fuse the lock bolt and twist the barrel shut, then the last axiom to pull the trigger. The result, a fused hunk of metal that could only be used as a club.

There was a clatter of glass from the other side of the barricade and Ryza tensed, caught halfway between quiet, shallow breaths. He readied a single rune in his palm but held it from burning.

Just in case.

'Very clever, Ryza,' she shouted. She was only metres away. 'But a little trick like that won't save you.'

He heard more glass crunch under her feet. She was coming towards him.

'Did you think you'd be the only one here? That you're brave? *Special*? Holm barely thought so! That's why she picked me for the Locusts before you! When you disappeared, Tyrag *chose* me to find Origin!'

Her voice had been close, only a metre or two away on the other side of his barricade. Ferrick still had the upper hand. Even though he had a rifle, Ryza couldn't trust his metal arm. Not that he had a choice in it.

Ryza sprung to his feet, quickly finding Ferrick in his rifle's sights. Despite her plated armour, she paced towards him with an unhindered elegance. A machete spun gracefully in her hands, the serration marking it as the same one she'd had in Kyrea. Ryza still had the stark memory of how easily she'd butchered that smelter. He took a few blind steps back, keeping his distance as she vaulted the concrete barricade with ease.

Even at point-blank range, Ryza's wavering metal arm could barely keep the rifle level, let alone aim it at her exposed head. Miss his shot and he'd be butchered as well.

'But you came by yourself, right?' Ryza taunted. He had to keep her talking until he found an opening or one of his squad mates joined the fray. 'Means you think you're just as special as me! Maybe we're all—'

Ferrick didn't let him finish. She juked left and lunged, making it past Ryza's rifle before he had a chance to fire. But he'd never intended on it. He dived backwards over the next barricade as the rune burned, sending out another magnetic pulse that took him through to the blue-lit city.

He staggered as his vision came back. A curdling nausea had been added to the feeling of stretching skin. He suppressed a dry heave, his mind still reeling from what he'd sensed in Ferrick's machete.

It was an arcanite as he'd suspected it to be in Kyra, armed with a mind of its own and tasked with detecting flesh. The moment it made contact, it would violently fragment before quickly reforming. One stab and his guts would be shredded.

Ryza moved to a new position quickly, crouching in cover near the bunker's entrance and mentally checking off where his squad was. If they hadn't used any axioms since he'd last seen them, then Gry and Haven would be on the orange-lit side they'd come in on and Ruka and Ditric would be in this blue city with him. He bellowed their names as loud as he could. It was that Ditric answered.

'Ryza! Where are you?'

'The bunker in the centre!' he called back. 'Ferrick's here, she's a fucking Locust! I can't fight her alone!'

'I'll try round up the others, we're coming!'

'Shame, I'm already here,' Ferrick's voice whispered.

Ryza dived to the left on a wild instinct, her blade glancing off his armoured back as he fell. He crashed into the ground, his metal arm taking the brunt of the fall. The tiny internal pistons snapped and the metal fingers went limp, sending his rifle spinning out of his grip. If he wanted control of the arm back, he'd have to actively control every single joint with his mind, something he couldn't do while having a knife fight.

Ryza rolled to his feet, still in a crouch as he pulled his own combat knife from his armour's hip. It was tiny compared to Ferrick's and felt clumsy in his right hand as he flipped it into an underhanded grip. She rushed him with another swing of her machete and Ryza launched himself forward in response, battering the serrated blade away with his metal left arm and colliding bodily with her.

Their arms locked at the other's shoulders and a stumbling tussle ensued. Ferrick might've been slighter in build than Ryza, but she wasn't recovering from having just lost an arm. She leaned back slightly, just enough to throw Ryza off balance and pull him forward before she returned with a devastating headbutt.

A flash of blinding pain stabbed through the bridge of Ryza's nose. Suddenly, he was flat on his back and Ferrick dived on top of him with a wild slash of her blade. Ryza threw both his hands in front of his face and the blade bit into the cross they'd formed. Through a stroke of dumb luck, the blade was jammed, caught between a joint in his right gauntlet and the inside of his knife. They were both stuck in place, but Ferrick had the advantage.

Her heavy armour was pinning him down, his unrestrained but useless left arm unable to push her off and his right just barely holding the machete in place. As she shrugged off Ryza's heartless pummelling, Ferrick pushed her blade harder. It was inching closer, his hand trembling as Ferrick put all her weight on it.

'Maybe you're right, Ryza,' she growled. 'Maybe I am special.'

The tip of her blade began to scrape on his armour, searching for a chink. Ryza needed a way out. An axiom for a simple pulse would take him back to the ruined side of the city, but with Ferrick's entire body on top of him, she'd come too. He needed to get her off somehow. He met Ferrick's eyes and registered the manic grin on her face as she taunted him.

'But at least it didn't go to my head,' she said. 'Holm told me how you were. *Who* you were. Your hands *definitely* aren't clean.'

The machete's tip found the tiny crack between his neck guard and his breastplate and she began gently working it in. Ryza could only gasp and squirm, barely able to focus on his runes as they burned.

'What the fuck did they promise you?' Ryza grunted.

'Life, Ryza. The thing you've lusted after for so long.'

The knife went deeper, its tip scratching at the outer surface of the metal collar around his neck. At least the damn thing was saving his life for once.

'And I've still got mine,' Ryza grunted. 'Have you!?'

The last rune burned and he concentrated hard on the axiom Gry had drawn on his arm the night before. For just one mind-bending moment, he *became* his armour. Felt it, moved with it, and saw through it. The buckles exploded at his will, sending each piece flying away from his body. Ryza's last vision was of Ferrick's shock as she was propelled into the air, borne by his now useless chest plate. When his sight came back, she was gone. But so was his knife.

Fuck!

Gry had said it would repel metal he *didn't* control, but this only left him with his semi-functional arm. Cloaked in the orange glow, he staggered to his feet. Ferrick appeared in front of him, already on hers. She made a wild lunge with her machete and he danced away from, putting himself just out of her reach.

Now there was some space between them and Ferrick didn't rush to fill it. She was circling him, observing his every movement, waiting for that one fatal opening. As she did this, Ryza saw his pile of abandoned armour a few feet away. It must have come through with Ferrick, some pieces only half present, perfectly severed with machine precision.

Maybe I don't need a knife...

Ferrick was closing in, positioning herself so that Ryza would have to walk backwards into the debris where he was all but guaranteed to stumble. In turn, Ryza watched her feet. They'd be his first warning if she charged. The crunch of glass around them was rhythmic, like a dance and it wasn't until Ryza focused on it that he heard a third set of footsteps that he couldn't see.

Ditric! It has to be!

Without another thought, Ryza pushed a rune into his palm and burnt it. Almost as if she'd sensed it, Ferrick dashed forward. His magnetic pulse picked up Ferrick's machete and he could nearly feel it sinking into him before it all disappeared.

His vision came back as he toppled sideways, the nausea even stronger now. The stone ground was cold on his battered cheek, but he couldn't rest there for long.

'What the hell is going on?'

It took him a few seconds to process that it wasn't Ditric's voice. Gry stood before him, hunched over his rifle and looking both confused and terrified. Ryza drew himself to his feet, gasping for breath, his head spinning as he desperately searched for the next sight of Ferrick.

'I heard the shots, so I tried to cast a detection wave, but it just took me through to... well, here. And what happened to your arm?'

'It's Ferrick—' Ryza choked.

'The Locust?'

'—She's here, looking for Origin and—'

Ryza stopped dead in his tracks, horror filling his veins. He'd found Ferrick. She was standing right behind Gry, blade poised to strike. She would've seen his footsteps in the glass on her side, thinking it was Ryza. By fleeing to this side of the city, Ryza had set her trap and it was Gry who'd fallen into it.

'NO!'

Ryza's shout clashed with the scream of metal as the machete ricocheted into Gry's armour and stabbed down into his neck, producing a sickening squelch as it penetrated flesh. Gry only had enough breath in him for a small gasp of pain before the blade exploded inside him. Ryza watched in horror as Gry's eyes went blank, blood welling in his gaping mouth.

Ferrick held the knife in for what felt like an eternity. Blood began to gush from under Gry's armour, flowing through the cracks, pooling at his feet. Ferrick's grip kept him standing, Ryza knew she was doing this to torture him, he could see it on her smug face. It was the same expression Holm had worn just before she'd tried to kill him. Rage bubbled deep in his chest. Rage Ryza's father had taught him. Rage he'd never be free of.

The violence.

She wrenched the machete out, prompting another spurt of blood from Gry, this time from his throat. He collapsed in a graceless heap. Ryza couldn't tear his eyes away from Gry's body. Not even as Ferrick levelled the blood-soaked blade to point at him. She stepped over his corpse, purposely planting a boot on his back as she approached.

Revel in the violence.

He didn't need a knife. He didn't even need a rifle. He didn't want it. His right hand was a white-knuckled fist at his side, and his metal left suddenly surged with enough feeling to match it.

Ryza charged as he unleashed a primal roar, loud enough to almost rip his throat in two. Ferrick was ready for him. At least, she thought she was.

Pushing with her back foot, she made a calculated lunge at his waist, not intended to wound, but instead blunt his momentum. Ryza met it with a wild swipe of his left arm, catching the machete in the defunct workings and jamming it in place. Ryza only just caught the look of dawning shock on Ferrick's face. But he didn't have time to relish it. His body crashed into her and they tumbled.

They hit the ground with a deafening clang from Ferrick's armour, the force of Ryza's tackle sending them sliding for a few feet. Ferrick quickly wrestled her machete out of his arm, but before she could swing it again, Ryza snatched at her wrist, catching it and slamming it into the ground as hard as he could. She thrashed with each blow, but Ryza's pinned legs didn't let her break free. He slammed her convulsing arm again, ignoring her cries of pain as the bones in her wrist shattered under his might.

Ryza screamed as he delivered one final blow and she finally relinquished the bloody blade. It clattered out of reach, but he only had a moment to savour the victory. Ferrick swung hard with her armoured left fist, catching Ryza directly in the temple.

Flashing stars rushed across his vision as he fell sideways, groping desperately at Ferrick as she wriggled out from under him. His vision was still hazy, all he could process was the shining armour in front of him.

She was almost to her feet. She'd be able to pulverise his skull with those gauntlets. He dived forward, grabbing her legs and knocking them both back to the ground.

Then her punches came. They rained down on his neck and shoulders, bruising flesh and bone alike. But Ryza fought through the pain. He'd suffered worse beatings. Beatings he'd been told he'd earned. The only thing he was focused on was the burning rune in his palm.

One. Last. Pulse!

It went off. This close to Ferrick, he could feel her resonance. Feel the fear that wracked it. The desperate search for survival. Feel her legs still in his arms as his vision came back. Feel the fresh wave of blood running down his face.

He relinquished them and knelt, breathing hard as her severed legs fell to the ground, scattering the glowing broken glass. But Ryza wasn't done.

Another rune seared in his hand and instantly he could hear the screaming. The bloodied cry of the dying. His vision came next. Ferrick was on the ground in front of him. Her face was contorted beyond anything Ryza could have imagined, frozen in a never-ending agony as her hands clutched at the blood-gushing stumps where her legs used to be.

'Ryza! Help me! Please, gods help—'

But Ryza turned and retrieved his rifle. Her cries fell to a silent whimper as he slowly pressed the muzzle against her bare throat. For a moment the undercity was silent, spare for his ragged breathing.

Ryza pulled the trigger.

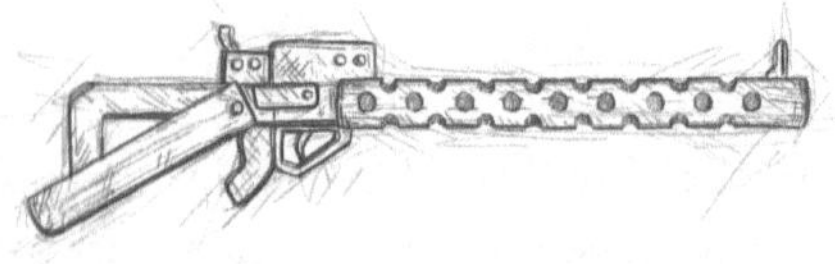

CHAPTER TWENTY-SEVEN

THE SHADOW DANCER'S GRAVE

T HE BLOOD WAS ON his hands. One metal and inert, the other twitching flesh. All Ryza had been able to do after killing Ferrick was drag himself to the other side of a barricade and slump as he stared off into the distance. He couldn't stand the sight of her body, let alone Gry's.

I could have saved him.

If only Ryza had been faster, quicker on the draw or just outwitted Ferrick a moment sooner, his friend would be alive. The rest of his squad was coming, but he wished they'd never arrive. He tried in vain for a moment to scrub the mess of crusted blood from his face, but every flaking chip that broke from his skin only frustrated him further. It was his blood. Ferrick's blood. Maybe even some of Gry's.

It would be a long time before he'd be able to get it all off. Even if he did, he'd never be clean again. Not after what Ferrick said. She knew. The Locusts knew. He swore under his still gasping breath, cursing himself for ever saying anything. It was such a stupid phrase too!

'My hands aren't clean,' Ryza muttered under his breath. 'Same as everyone else.'

Soon his ears picked up the sound of running feet. Three sets. Ryza closed his eyes, inhaling deeply, bracing himself for what was to come.

'Ryza? Where the hell are—'

Ditric's voice cut out, quickly replaced by Ruka's.

'Gry! Gry!'

Scrambling steps, the clatter of a rifle being thrown down.

'Gry! Come on! Ditric, do something!' Ruka screamed.

Another rifle hit the ground, more footsteps.

'It's too much blood,' Ditric muttered. 'It can't be all his... Hang on, is that Ferrick? What happened to her fucking legs!?'

'Ditric, help him!' Ruka said.

'He's gone, Ruka,' Haven said.

There was a scrape of steel armour being pried apart, followed by a horrified gasp.

'Fuck, he would have died quickly, at least.'

Then Ryza heard the sound he'd dreaded most. Ruka's pitiful, hopeless sobs of a soul broken. He squeezed his eyes shut, trying to block it out, trying to block out the imagined memories of sobs just like it from the families of those he'd stuck a needle into.

'Ryza?'

He opened his eyes, the bloody muck across his face burning at the corners of them. Haven was crouched in front of him, one hand laying down his rifle, the other reaching for his shoulder.

'Are you alright, mate?'

Ryza opened his mouth to reply, but not even air could escape him. When he eventually managed to speak, it was with a hoarse whisper.

'I couldn't save him. I tried, I tried, but she got to him...'

'Can't save everyone, mate.' He patted him on the back and pulled him into a hug, made awkward by the fact that Ryza was limp as a rag doll and Haven was wearing armour. He gave up on it after a moment and weighed his next words.

'Did you find Origin?'

Ryza shook his head, resisting a fresh wave of grief. That was what they'd come down here for. Gry hadn't wanted to come, but he'd done so anyway. Ryza had got him into this mess.

'No sign of him at all?'

'Nothing.'

Haven swore under his breath as Ditric and Ruka came into view. They grabbed an arm each and dragged Ryza to his feet.

'What the fuck happened here, Ryza?' Ditric demanded.

'Ferrick got here before us. She was looking for Origin. I held her off as long as I could, but when Gry showed up...'

He fell silent. Gry had never been the best fighter. By the looks on their faces, the other three thought the same.

'After.... I managed to get a hold of Ferrick's legs. An axiom took me through to the ruined side of the city, along with half her body.'

'I see.' Ditric paused for a moment before stiffly patting Ryza on the shoulder. 'She had it coming.' She turned to Haven. 'Collars?'

'Six hours. Halfway.'

She swore. 'We have to go back. Revance is moving further away by the second, we'll just have to hope nobody else can find that fucking arcanite.'

'No.' Ryza's voice was quiet yet firm.

'We've already lost one man down here, Ryza! I'm not losing the rest—'

'I know where Origin is. He's down in that bunker.'

'You sure?' Haven asked quickly.

'It's where Ferrick came from. It's where the shadow dancer is.'

They all stepped back, horrified, but he didn't flinch.

'We need to leave this place,' Ditric growled. 'If you've seen that, you're in too deep.'

'I always was.'

Ryza picked up his rifle and his ammo pouch before he looked back to the others.

'It spoke to me,' he said slowly. 'I will find Origin.'

He didn't wait for them to protest again. The bullet-riddled doorframe of the bunker loomed before him, the darkness beyond it maddeningly enticing. After only a dozen measured steps, he glanced over his shoulder, yet the city beyond the doorway was a pinprick of light. Ryza kept going, counting another forty paces until he reached a dead-end.

A wall of shining steel, glinting on what little light reached this far into the bunker, blocked his path. A slit ran down the centre, dividing it in two. Positioned on the wall to its right was a small button. Ryza brushed his finger over it, picking up the shape of a downward arrow before he pressed it. The glassy surface glowed red and the metal plates retracted into the walls.

A new path hadn't opened, it was a room barely the size of a closet. It bathed him in flickering yellow light, but the source was nowhere to be found. He stepped inside, a strange warmth prickling on his exposed skin, and turned to face the bunker's entrance. A lone silhouette stood there.

The shadow dancer.

Ryza was too numb to be afraid. The phantom only blocked a path he had no intention of taking.

I just need to figure out the way forward.

It was easier said than done. The chamber's only feature was a grid of sixteen buttons that were embedded in a small, slanted panel, each one marked with a strange symbol he couldn't decipher. Unperturbed, he reached out, but before his fingers could push one, a faded green light flashed under a button. More followed it, a seemingly random pattern until all sixteen were illuminated. They flashed again in unison and the doors began to slide shut. Ryza looked up and caught one last glimpse of the corridor. The shadow dancer was gone.

It's guiding me.

Suddenly the floor dropped out from under him. He wanted to panic, to scream in terror as he plunged to his death, but all he could do was slump into the corner and clench his eyes shut. The fight with Ferrick had stolen the ability to even consider fear from him. Standing in the empty city, waiting for her to appear from thin air with a blade that would find his heart. Yet it was Gry, who'd all but wandered in, ignorant of the fight, that had received Ryza's fate instead.

The guilt weighed heavy as his fall began to slow. His body compressed to the point he felt he'd burst before the pressure released. Ryza opened his eyes. The room had stopped. Getting to his feet, he readied his rifle, his non-functioning left hand struggling to support it.

A hiss filled his ears as the doors cracked open. They gave way to a rush of stale air, flecked with enough dust to cloud Ryza's vision. Once it had cleared, he found himself staring down another corridor. It was dark, lined with doors just like the first and for a moment,

Ryza thought he hadn't moved at all. But this one stretched on much further, ending with a light that spilled from an unseen doorway.

He started walking, each footstep echoing down the corridor and back to him with a second of delay. It was eerie, like he was being followed. But then again, maybe he was. The shadow dancer was yet to show themself.

'I sense a troubled mind.'

Ryza spun, searching for the voice. Behind him, the doors he'd come through were now a wall of darkness. Ahead, the light flickered.

'Doubt?'

He kept moving, now slightly hunched over. It was like the voice was right in his ear, but the shadow dancer wasn't anywhere in sight.

'Regret?'

He'd once met a Reythurist that could shake the air in such a way that he could carry his voice for miles, but it never sounded natural. Not like this. This was like he was being followed closely, each word being spoken with the sole purpose of raising the hairs on the back of his neck.

'No, guilt.'

It was working. Ryza had to resist lashing out backwards with an elbow. He knew it would find nothing. The light flickered up ahead and the shadow dancer appeared in it, still half in darkness. It was enough for Ryza to make out the face of a man more than twice his age.

His skin was pale, his cheekbones and jaw razor sharp. The smile it supported was kind, welcoming, but Ryza knew full well what malice that kind of smile could hold. It was the one his father most often wore.

It was the eyes that were the most unsettling. More than the smile, more than jamming needles into the backs of necks, more than watching dead minds walk by in the dozens and more than his father telling him he'd done a good job.

His eyes were black.

No trick of the light could give even the illusion of irises that black. It was truly unnatural. Ryza's throat closed up and his eyes began to sting. He hadn't even noticed his feet had stopped moving.

'What guilt troubles you, Ryza?'

He swallowed hard before he spoke. 'How do you know my name?'

'I see more of you than you might think.'

The shadow dancer started walking towards him, each step sounding off the floor, yet they returned no echo. Ryza tapped his own foot. It didn't echo either. Had the shadow dancer been following him before?

'I saw what you did to that poor scholar. Is that what plagues your mind?'

'No.'

'Something you've done while a soldier for Revance?'

'No,' Ryza said. 'Long before that.'

The shadow dancer cocked his head and Ryza could make out the slight frown. It was as if there was a genuine concern, a curiosity. It was putting Ryza off, enough to make him blurt the truth no matter how much he resisted it. The shadow dancer was drawing closer, unconcerned for the shaking rifle Ryza pointed at him.

'What are you doing to me?' he said, further attempting to level his gun. 'Is it magic?'

'Not magic. Not mine.' The shadow dancer paused, stopping ten metres away. Then he chuckled. 'No, the magic of the shadow dancers is one to control a base element, just like the others. The dead Hytharo controlled the storms. Curiktics, the light. Reythurists, the wind and Kretatics, the metal. Shadow dancers control a fifth. Time.' For the first time, the smile faded. 'In our eternal death we control the one thing that binds us to this world.'

The shadow dancer then held out a hand, his palm displaying a black rune before it burned white and disappeared.

Almost.

Ryza was about to pull the trigger when his left arm began to ache. He glanced at it, finally breaking the shadow dancer's gaze as rust bloomed across the hand, the iron and copper dissolving into powder before his eyes. It spiralled outwards, reaching through the damaged supporting rods and pistons, eating away at them in seconds and sending his nerves into a roaring pain as if it were his own flesh decaying.

Ryza's rifle clattered to the floor as he tried to scrub the wave of corrosion with his other hand. It was only as it edged closer to his elbow, his own flesh, that Ryza finally panicked and relinquished his tenuous hold on what was left of the metal arm.

It exploded into a thousand shards before it hit the ground, all dissolving into powder a moment later. Ryza looked at the shadow dancer, his mouth agape. But he was gone. The corridor remained silent for a minute in which Ryza didn't dare move.

'Aged thousands of years in only a few moments.'

The shadow dancer had reappeared at his side. He wore a certain sadness, one which had been hidden behind the smile the whole time. His stance, his actions, they'd been dictated by this, not malice. Now Ryza felt slightly more at ease, even though he had no reason to.

'What... what are you?'

'Old.'

'But you're—'

'A shadow dancer? Yes.'

Ryza picked up his rifle with his remaining hand and took a few steps towards the stranger.

'It is the name given to those of us who tapped into the magic of this former world. A moment of limitless power, before being stuck in this echo of life. But I implore you not to ponder this like I once did. A fresh mind is more open for learning than an expectant one.'

'Do you have a name?' Ryza's breathing had calmed somewhat, but he was still waiting for the figure to lash out.

'Archarus. Come, Ryza. There's something I need you to see.'

'Is it Origin?'

Archarus didn't give him an answer. They continued down the corridor, side by side. Ryza kept glancing out of the corner of his eye. The way the shadow dancer moved didn't seem quite right. Sometimes a step would go too fast or the light would bend in such a way that part of his figure was left behind, if only for a moment.

After a while, Ryza broke the silence between them.

'This city, or cities... how come it has two faces? Two sides, I mean?'

'I still wonder,' Archarus said. 'I believe there was a time when war and violence raged freely. Where armies of the desperate swept from city to city, searching for a cure to the old magic that decayed humanity. It was here they might have found it, but it had to be protected. So the city was split. One was to be invaded. The other was to be saved.'

'But... But how?' Ryza sputtered. His mind raced as he tried to process how many thousands of axioms would be required to create a city, let alone clone a perfect copy.

'This magic was nothing you've experienced, Ryza. It was without bounds, fuelled by a resolute belief that what happened and what they did was real and possible. An infinite moment of pure resonance, if you will. However, a moment of doubt and it was gone. The result, an unstoppable force controlled by brash and gullible fools.'

'Not exactly ideal,' Ryza muttered under his breath.

'No. But those-of-glass looked for a solution. A way to live beyond doubt. To stop the decay of their magic.'

'Did they find it?' Ryza thought back to the city of shattered glass, of the wreckage of ancient war machines. Something had been fighting them, but he couldn't even begin to wonder why.

Archarus shook his head, wearing a grimace. 'It's what I was trying to understand when I first found this place. I failed to find an answer. Perhaps they did, too.'

'Were you from that time? Of those-of-glass?' Ryza asked. They were standing near the open doorway the light was coming from, though he couldn't see through it.

'I was a Kretatic,' Archarus said. 'Bound by ink and axiom, searching for a path beyond it. Just as you do now.'

'I'm looking for Origin,' Ryza said firmly.

'How do you think he came to be?'

Archarus motioned for Ryza to step through the doorway. He hesitated for a moment. It could still be a trap. But then again, he was in far too deep to escape.

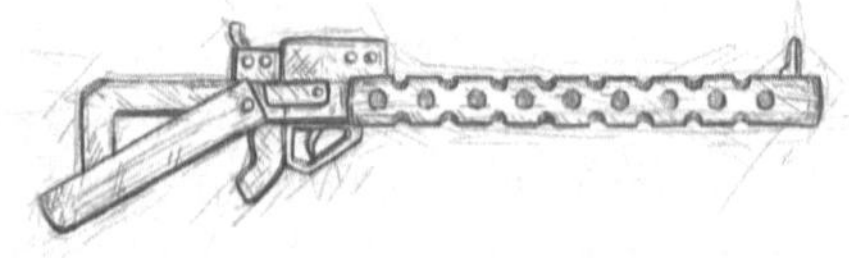

CHAPTER TWENTY-EIGHT

THE BODY OF ORIGIN

Turning the corner was like stepping into a bizarre version of Revance's infirmary. It was a massive, circular room under a domed ceiling. The walls and floors were tiled with blood-spattered hexes. Rows upon rows of perfectly arranged cots filled the chamber, each one surrounded by a forest of equipment mounted on metal stands that Ryza couldn't make sense of. A maze of pipes weaved overhead, occasionally giving way to a dim glow bulb.

Ryza could feel the shadow dancer's eyes on his back, observing his every movement. As he wandered over to inspect one of the cots, Archarus' footsteps quietly followed. The perfectly preserved corpse of a woman lay on it, her skin still full and tanned. A network of cables and tubes snaked across her, threading under the white gown she wore and into her veins.

'Look closer,' Archarus commanded.

Ryza held his breath and leaned forward. The woman's eyes were still open, staring at the ceiling. But they were not rotten or even missing like he'd expect from such a fresh-looking corpse. Swirling orbs of silver had taken their place. He'd seen these eyes thousands of times before.

'It's not... it's not possible.'

The words escaped his mouth again and again as he rushed from cot to cot, each corpse staring back at him with those same silver eyes. A few bodies were damaged and battle-scarred, the missing flesh replaced with layers of pulsing metal. Others looked perfectly healthy, only a hint of the metal throbbing under their skin.

'I believe you call it molten flux. Have you ever wondered where it came from?'

Ryza stopped in his tracks. At the room's doorway, the shadow dancer was waiting, his face cast downward.

'Why did you bring me here?' Ryza spat. 'What do you want me to see in this!?'

'Something I haven't.'

There was silence between them, only broken by the slow rhythm of footsteps as the shadow dancer walked over.

'They're old,' he said, staring mournfully into one of the cots. 'Those-of-glass thought they could resurrect them, that they could repair their fractured bodies.'

Ryza's jaw was clenched, an unidentifiable rage building in him. 'But they were wrong.'

'As was I.' Archarus turned to look at one of the far corners of the room, where Ryza noticed a huddle of autominds stood in the shadows. 'When I was alive, I didn't come down here alone. We encountered the mechanical beasts you saw as wreckage above. I survived. I ventured further into this bunker, determined not to come out empty handed.

'I found the molten flux. I thought I could use it to find a way to outlive the deathly consequence of pure resonance. I was unshakably fixated upon it. I was sure the flux would save my flesh. That I could use it to save those I'd already lost to it. But I still couldn't overcome my last doubts.'

'Why are you telling me this? Why show me, why any of this!?'

'So you don't make the same mistake as I once did,' Archarus snapped. 'So you know that the flux cannot create life, only control it, that only death resides in its clutches.'

'I don't care about pure resonance!' Ryza barked back. 'You think we're the same? That I'd choose it?'

'Ryza, you already have.'

'I don't have a choice!' Ryza burst out. 'But it sounds like you did! You wanted power and control, didn't you? Same as Ferrick and the rest! They *wanted* molten flux!'

'And I watched you decide to be a part of them,' Archarus snarled, now glaring at him. 'It doesn't matter what you believe, you had a choice. You still do. You could have walked away from this long ago. But you're still here.'

'Because I have to be!'

'Because you *believe* you *need* to be.' The grin was back on Archarus' face, malevolence rising in his tone. 'Same as I thought of myself.'

'I'm not like you.'

'I hope you aren't,' Archarus said quietly. 'It's the only way you'll live.'

Swallowing another goading retort, Ryza steeled his nerves. Archarus' expression softened as he continued.

'That's why you're here, isn't it? You knew Origin would only be safe in your hands. Revance's future as well.'

'Where is he?' Ryza demanded.

Archarus nodded slowly then motioned back towards the hallway. 'Come with me.'

Ryza followed, still looking over his shoulder at the autominds standing in the corner. How had they lasted there for hundreds of years? The question begged to be asked as they walked back down the hallway, passing more open doors with identical cot-filled infirmaries beyond.

'If molten flux came from... the before, what is it? What kind of magic could possibly do that to a body?'

'It's not just magic, Ryza. It's a technology far beyond your reckoning. A machine that must not be controlled.'

'But it's just liquid metal that expands, right? I've seen vials full of mercury that could contract and grow depending on temperature.'

'Can you control mercury like an arcanite?' Archarus asked. 'The liquid element of molten flux is only a vessel for what makes it unique. It carries machines, thousands of them that are miniscule in size, tasked with creating themselves over and over until they fill their container and to mimic what they see around them, repairing and replacing flesh like nothing else can.'

Maybe Archarus was right, but it still didn't make any damn sense. How could entire machines be small enough to flow through an automind's veins and then stich it back together?

'So why can Kretatics control autominds? Could they control the flux itself?'

Archarus let out a small chuckle. It didn't suit him. 'That's the magic, Ryza. Try not to think about it.'

They re-entered the chamber Ryza had descended in and Archarus busied himself with the console's buttons before the twin metal doors slid shut. They descended further, a quicker trip than the last but Ryza's eardrums felt like they were about to do explode from the mounting pressure. When the doors opened, a cool blast of air washed over him and Archarus led him down a shorter corridor, stopping before a door at its very end.

This room was small, bearing only one feature. A single massive bed was pressed up against the wall, with metres upon metres of coloured wires intertwined with its frame. On it lay the skeleton of what could only be a giant.

At three metres long, the body's bones were thicker than anything possible. In the light of the ceiling's single glow bulb, Ryza could see a few of the wires threaded through the ribs and the skull. Orbs of molten flux filled the eye sockets.

'Origin.'

Ryza jumped at the mechanical chirp of the arcanite's voice, spotting him at the foot of the bed, cloaked in the darkness that swirled across the floor like smoke.

'Who was this?' Ryza said.

'Origin,' the arcanite replied.

'But you're—'

Looking rapidly between the skeleton and the arcanite, Ryza gasped. He couldn't help it. This was Origin's body, from a time long ago when he was once human. The wires that bound it sent a sick rush through his guts. What was their purpose? Did they still work? He turned to Archarus.

'What did they do to him?'

'They tried to live as he lives.'

'Lives? But he's... he's dead, right?' Ryza leaned in closer to the bones. There wasn't a trace of flesh on them.

'Then how do you explain his form as an arcanite?' Archarus asked. 'Touch the bones. See what you feel.'

Ryza's hand was shaking as he reached out. Ferrick's blood still coated it. His red fingers marked the chalk white bones and he stiffened.

Old.

Old and tired.

His head turned slowly to Origin, his eyes widening. The magnetic resonance he felt now was the exact same as that of a living thing. But that was impossible, they were just bones! Bones didn't live, especially when they were long stripped of flesh.

The more he focused on the resonance, the more it drained his mind. It was like his life was being sucked into the remains. He snatched his hand away as if it had been burnt, then looked to Archarus.

'Immortality, Ryza. Origin never dies.'

He looked at Origin, who simply nodded his metal head.

'I don't get it,' Ryza muttered. 'They're just bones.'

Archarus shook his head. 'It's not something to be understood.'

'What about the flux?'

'Who do you think gives it life?'

Silence fell like dust between the three.

'So if I kill Origin...'

'You'd be better off trying to kill a stone. Split it, burn it, throw it into the void, it is still a stone.'

'Is this why you stay here?' he eventually asked. 'To guard the bones?'

'Stones don't need guarding, Ryza. I stay here for the same reason you came here. It's where I believe I need to be. As a shadow dancer, belief was all I had that tied me to this world.'

'*Was?*'

Archarus leered at him. 'Was.'

Ryza shook his head. Any sense of fear already replaced by a giddy delirium. Veiled threats didn't matter now. He'd finally found Origin. It had cost him his arm and Gry's life, but he was finally here. But now he wondered if Origin should've been found in the first place.

The arcanite, or at least whoever he'd been, would have thousands of years of wisdom to call on, if not more, to decide this was the best place to hide. If Ryza were to take him now, would he be doing something as devastatingly foolish as the man who'd discovered molten flux in the first place?

'I sense you have a decision to make,' Archarus said, practically reading his mind.

'I'm not going back up there empty handed. I can't.'

'Because then you wouldn't have needed to come here?'

Ryza had expected Archarus to object, to protest, or maybe even agree with him. But the shadow dancer stayed quiet, staring at him with those deep black eyes.

'Well?' Ryza said, attempting to prompt him.

Archarus leaned in a little closer, frowning slightly as he picked his words. 'Did you think I would stop you?'

He shook his head unconsciously.

'Exactly,' he murmured. 'Try not to think about it.'

Archarus held out a hand, motioning towards Origin.

'I sense you can put a stop to the madness above.' The shadow dancer's voice was quiet, barely more than a whisper. 'But you need to be certain.'

'I don't have a choice,' Ryza hissed back.

Archarus chuckled as he picked up Origin and handed him to Ryza. He had to juggle this new load in one hand with his rifle, making him feel unguarded.

'You'd best return to your friends. They are growing impatient.'

Archarus didn't accompany him back to the elevating chamber and Ryza's eardrums popped again as he ascended. The pressure only subsided when he stepped out of the battle-scarred hallway and saw his squad.

Well, three of them.

A crushing sadness engulfed him. Ditric was still standing guard with her rifle. Haven paced aimlessly while staring at the ground. Ruka's gentle sobs came from behind one of the barricades.

They still hadn't noticed him. He didn't want them to notice. Didn't want to face their questions or their grief. While he was in the bunker, they must have taken Gry's body somewhere and given him an improvised burial. Heads would have been bowed. They each would have said a few words for him.

Ryza was glad he'd missed it. Of his squad, Gry was the one he knew the least. Prying the boy out of his own thoughts for long enough to talk hadn't been easy and Ryza had always taken the simpler route of bantering with the others. Any words he could've said as they buried him would've felt short and hollow.

Ferrick hadn't been offered the same kindness. Not that she deserved it. There was a red smear leading to the corner of a nearby building. Peeking out was a single, blood-soaked gauntlet.

'Ryza? Are you...?'

It was Ditric that had spoken, an eyebrow raised. But she didn't approach.

It's because I've seen the shadow dancer.

They'd warned him about the shadow dancer. About the madness it brought. And they were right. The questions Archarus asked of him still had his head spinning as if he were concussed. They'd been designed, word by word, to make him doubt every fibre of his being, every moment of his past, every choice he'd made.

'I found Origin,' Ryza finally said. The words rasped on his tongue.

'How long have we got on our collars?' Ditric asked as Haven wandered over.

'Four hours. We wouldn't've made it back.'

But still they didn't come. Ryza knew why. He must've been down there for longer than he'd thought. All that time, Ditric, Haven and Ruka would have been sitting up here, hopelessly debating between making a mad rush back to Revance or waiting in the dark with nothing but blind hope to comfort them.

But they'd waited.

They'd believed in him.

He took a step forward and they flinched.

'The shadow dancer hasn't harmed me, or cursed me, or... I don't know.' Ryza tried to keep his voice firm, but there was an unmistakable shakiness about it. Probably just the blood rush wearing off from the fight with Ferrick.

Probably.

'I'm fine. I promise.'

Ditric and Haven didn't look reassured. Ryza knew they wouldn't be. He was unsure of his own words as well. Before he could think of something else to say, a pair of arms clamped around his chest from his left. He jumped, but they held firm. It was Ruka, her face buried in his chest. She didn't even care about the mass of dried blood caking his leathers.

Gingerly, he put his good arm around her. Since Ruka was a good head shorter than him, it was less of a hug and more like he was draping himself on her. Origin was still in his hand and the arcanite reached for Ruka's wristband, tapping it and triggering the lifesaving whir within.

Now more at ease, Ditric and Haven approached, letting Origin do the same for them.

'As nice as this moment is, we need to get back to Revance,' Haven said. 'I'm surprised we aren't spitting guts.'

It was much easier to make their way out than in, especially on this side of the city. Free of rubble and debris, new and well-built pathways were open to them. Ornate stairs took them between city tiers and carefully crafted, winding paths led them between skyscrapers. Ryza leaned on Ruka for support as they went. His knees were now refusing to cooperate. Almost the only thing he could think of was throwing himself into a seat in the lead-better. Almost.

He kept his eyes focused on his feet, not because he was going to trip over himself, but because every time he looked up, the shadow dancer was there. Watching from a high window, a ledge or the end of an alleyway, Archarus was nothing more than a silhouette, a glinting light where his eyes should be. As Ditric led them up a skyscraper, Ryza could only pray the shadow dancer didn't follow him.

Above ground, the morning's sandstorm was a distant red cloud on the northern horizon. Ryza had been concerned coming up the saved city would lead them to a completely different world, but sure enough, their buggy was exactly where they'd left it, albeit half-buried from the storm.

Ditric set to work digging out the lead-better. 'Come on. The collars might not kill us, but Yuvet will.'

She was right. Ruka sat Ryza down on a rock as she and Haven went to help, uncovering the vehicle after only a few minutes, all their days of "dust off" duties finally coming in handy.

They piled into the lead-better, Ditric at the wheel, Haven riding shotgun, Ruka and Ryza in the back, the empty seat between them prominent in their minds. If any of them were meant to survive, it was Gry. Some would have called him a coward. Yuvet certainly had. But now he thought about it, Gry just had a good head on his shoulders and something to live for. A family to come back to.

I don't.

All Ryza had now was a battle-forged conviction to finish what he'd started. Origin was nestled in his lap, the hard-fought prize of facing the shadow dancer, and in his hand, he gripped his rifle.

No, it's not mine.

The calming resonance caressed his fingers, tempting him to grip tighter. But if what he suspected was right, then this rifle had once belonged to Tyrag the Forgemaster himself. According to Ferrick, he was the one plotting the mutiny.

Ryza shut his eyes and leaned back in his seat. Over the roar of the lead-better's engine, he could almost hear what Tyrag had said to him when he'd checked his collar. The longing for control, not just for how Revance was run, but the fortress itself.

He couldn't even imagine how many autominds it would take to tame an arcanite so large. It could be thousands. And where would Tyrag get them all? Maligar certainly wouldn't have known. He could barely buy one. He was a puppet of Tyrag's, as were the rest of the Locusts.

Holm drifted back into his thoughts. There was something about her that always occupied his mind. Something unsaid. Every time he talked to her, Ryza wasn't sure if she was trying to manipulate him or being manipulated herself.

As he dozed, Ryza's thoughts turned and turned, never stopping on one thought long enough for it to make sense before moving onto the next.

Origin.

Gry.

Tyrag.

Holm.

It just repeated, every now and then horribly punctuated by the image of the back of that man's neck, just before he stabbed the needle in.

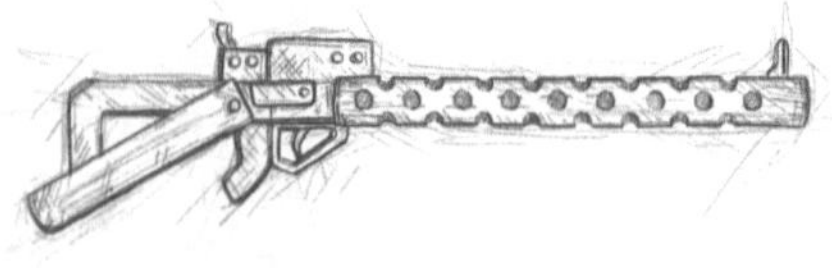

CHAPTER TWENTY-NINE

CONTROL ROOM

'**R**YZA! WAKE UP!'

Ruka was practically pummelling him awake.

He stirred with a groan, rising from a slump and dislodging Origin from his lap. The arcanite landed hard on his foot and the pain was enough to bring him back to his senses. It was late afternoon and an orange sun was casting a blinding glare, rendering everything ahead of them as shapeless, shadowy blobs.

Revance appeared as they drew closer and it was in the sorriest state Ryza had ever seen. Smoke billowed from burnt-out scars that dashed across its hide. The rumble of its colossal pneumatics was more tinny than usual, echoing across the sky like the calls of a dying beast.

Soon their lead-better was passing the wreckage of the battle that'd wounded the fortress. The trail of destruction was made up of dozens of vehicles, some so ramshackle they looked to have fallen apart on their own.

But not all of them looked to have belonged to the smelters. The treadhulks that'd been fitted out to bristle with guns lay between swarms of downed buggies, along with similar versions that bore only one massive cannon, large enough to rival the armaments mounted on Revance. He'd heard these called long-wreckers before, but thankfully he hadn't found himself in a skirmish violent enough to warrant their use.

'What even happened here?' Ditric asked herself.

'We won! That's what!' Haven answered.

'No, not... not that!' she snapped back. 'How?'

'This must have been the Locust's plan,' Ryza said. 'Attack from inside and out, but it didn't work.' He glanced down at Origin, still nestled between his aching feet. 'They haven't got what they need.'

'But these are some of our vehicles!' Ditric said. 'Why would we have even come out of the fortress to fight them on the sand?'

Ryza shook his head. 'I don't think they were ours. For all we know, they could've been spirited out of Revance's own stock and sold to the smelters.'

'Doesn't matter about that!' Haven shouted jovially. 'We still won! Means we must have beat the Locusts, too! Come on, pull us up!'

Ditric hesitated a moment, something tensing in her shoulders before she shunted the steering vane forward, making the engines roar as the shadow of Revance engulfed them. One of the vehicle platforms was already being hoisted down to them, dangling precariously in the wind until it hit the sand with a spray of dust. Ditric guided the lead-better into its wake, gunning the throttle one last time and causing the buggy to lurch into the wheel locks of the platform.

Stable as they supposedly may have been, Ryza still clung onto whatever he could as they swung through the air towards the mouth of the motor pool. The place was crowded as they swung in, not with the dinged-up vehicles Ryza would have expected after a battle, but with people.

They were on their knees with their hands on their heads, packed in so tightly they were practically on top of each other. More soldiers patrolled among them with rifles ready to shoot anyone dumb enough to stand up.

Ryza was still trying to make sense of the scene as they were lowered into the one clear space available, but when he saw Maligar's manic grin waiting to greet them, it all clicked into place.

He glanced back to the prisoners. Every single one of them wore a collar like his own. He swore under his breath. For a second, a triumphantly foolish second, he'd believed them to be the captured ranks of the Locusts.

But it was the opposite.

'Is that— You gotta be—'

Ditric sprang to her feet, her rifle already levelled at Maligar, but Ryza was quicker, snatching the barrel and shoving it towards the ceiling.

'One shot ain't going to make the difference,' he hissed at her. 'Believe me, I already know.'

The platform hit the deck with a deafening crash and Maligar was the only one who didn't flinch.

'I wasn't sure who I would be expecting to come back,' he beamed. 'Or even who I was *hoping* for! Though I am glad it was you, Ryza. Makes the whole thing so much sweeter.'

'What *thing*?' Ryza barked back.

Maligar waved his arms across the motor pool, over the heads of the bruised and bloodied prisoners, and out to the wreckage that lay in Revance's wake.

'Everything! This wouldn't have happened if not for you. You really were the centrepiece the other night. As much as I'd like to credit myself in everything, it was *you* who inspired us, and now you've brought it all home with the finishing touch. At least, I assume so.'

'You mean Origin?'

Maligar nodded keenly. 'If that's what you call the arcanite. Come with me. And bring your other green-eyed friend there. No use wasting the talent of our kind, right?'

Haven had already found his feet and hopped out of the buggy, but Ryza hadn't moved.

'What about the others?'

'It's too late for you to shift their fate.' Maligar said with a shrug. 'Knowing it wouldn't help you change anything.'

'Fine,' Ryza grunted as he picked up Origin. He couldn't bring himself to look at Ruka and Ditric as he climbed out of the lead-better. The loathing radiating from them was painful enough. Maligar began to lead him and Haven away. A few more armed soldiers Ryza recognised as Locusts followed closely.

The sound of a scuffling protest as they left the motor pool made Ryza finally check over his shoulder. Ruka and Ditric were being wrestled into the ranks of the other captured conscripts as the lead-better was hoisted back out over the sands. A bellowed command echoed through the motor pool, followed by the unmistakable thud of the vehicle being dropped unceremoniously onto the sand.

'Why are you getting rid of the vehicles?' Ryza demanded.

'We won't have need for them,' he replied. 'Why take one when we could simply take all of Revance exactly where we need to be? Besides, they're too heavy. They weigh us down.'

'Why the hell would that be a problem now?'

Maligar glanced back at him, the shadow of a knowing grin on his face. 'It's not too late for you to make the right choice.'

'And if I don't?'

'That's what the collar's for.'

Ryza looked to Haven, expecting to see shock, fear, anything plastered across his usually expressive face. But there was nothing. Not even a raised eyebrow. It was like he'd already made up his mind.

'That's the same for the rest of the conscripts, then?' Ryza asked as they began climbing stairs. 'Not even bothered to kill them yourselves?'

Maligar stopped, regarding him bemusedly. 'Not everyone *likes* killing, Ryza. Not the way Holm told me you do. It's like you can't stop thinking about it. That's why I wanted to show you off to everyone. That's why you inspired them. You made it look possible. Easy. Normal.'

He's right.

Corridors flickered past in Ryza's vision, brief glimpses of bloodstained skirmishes that were long lost. Gunsmoke still hung in the air, smothering the putrid scent of fresh corpses, yet none of the lingering victors paid the dead any mind. There were no plans to move them. There didn't need to be.

Once they filled them with flux, they'd move themselves.

Closer towards the command decks of Revance, the signs of skirmish lessened. Either the battle had been fought in the lower decks or they hadn't even bothered to resist up here.

'Did they even try to fight them?' Ryza muttered under his breath.

'Do you really think they can?' Haven whispered back.

'At least I would have tried!'

'Then you're a fool for thinking you could,' Maligar shot. 'I just hope after what I show you that you're able to reconsider.'

Ryza glanced from him to Haven, who still wouldn't meet his eyes.

They reached the final deck of Revance. Ryza's legs were screaming from exhaustion, but he wasn't about to let his pain be known. To his relief, the pace slowed as they negotiated their way through the batteries of Revance's main cannons.

The cramped confines were made tricky by the mounds of discarded artillery shells that lay scattered across the floor. While the gunners might not have been able to fend off the attack, at least it was less for the Locusts to play with.

Once through, they reached the primary command chamber of Revance. It was supposedly the oldest part of the fortress, the only piece that it had never shed, yet Ryza had never been privileged enough to find his way up here before.

It was like stepping into a small cathedral, complete with a tall, iron-grated window at the end of the high ceiling. Dozens of soldiers stood as a congregation in rank and file, facing away from Ryza and towards the sprawling control console that sat under the window like a grand altar.

A massive cylinder of black metal was embedded at its centre, revolving slowly in its housing as the patterns of golden grooves emblazoned across it glinted in the sunset's dying light. Rounded steel panels surrounded it, each one bearing a series of rust-coated levers that looked like they hadn't been thrown for centuries. Now they were wrapped in coils of fresh copper wire. They came together as a thick braid, snaking between the feet of a dozen Locusts.

'The Bloodfist returns!' Maligar declared. 'And he returns with *exactly* what we needed!'

Those at the altar with him looked, yet the rest of the congregation remained motionless. Glee lit up on their faces as Maligar threw his arms out wide. The Locusts behind Ryza pushed him and Haven forward, forcing them to follow Maligar down the aisle between the ranks of...

Autominds.

Ryza could feel his breath coming fast, his head pounding hard and his heart even harder. Where had all these autominds come from?

Could they have been waiting here the whole time?

No, that can't be it. It's impossible!

Ryza couldn't tear his eyes away from the autominds. He'd searched and fought so hard just to root out one, and now there had to be more than fifty in this room alone. But when he reached the front of the room, a familiar face stood at the fore of the motionless group.

Yuvet.

Her stare was vacant. Yellow eyes, usually so full of fury, had been replaced by swirling silver. In horror, Ryza looked across the rest, recognising more of what he knew of Revance's senior command.

'I see our long-awaited guest has finally arrived.'

Tyrag's voice made Ryza flinch and he fixed him with a glare full of all the venom he could muster. The Forgemaster emerged from behind the altar. The golden shackles at his wrist clattered on its surface as he leaned on it for support. He placed a flux injector gun on the console as he went. Blood still dripped from its needle.

'Bring me the arcanite.'

'Fight us for it.'

It was stupid, making everyone without flux in their veins howl with laughter. Ryza remained resolute. When he glanced to Haven, to see if he'd fight with him, an odd smile was on his face, ashamed yet proud at the same time.

Before he could react, Haven darted at him, grabbing him by the arm and shoving him into the centre of the room where he collapsed, slamming Origin to the floor with a loud clang. Pain shot through his legs and he was momentarily blinded by it.

He scanned the faces of the Locusts, traitors and smelters alike, and it finally dawned on him. He looked back at Haven, who just shrugged.

'I don't get it...' Ryza said, almost pleadingly.

Haven stared, his expression blank. It was only after a few seconds that he answered. 'I've got mouths to feed. With the way things were... I didn't have a choice.'

'And your efforts will be well rewarded,' Tyrag said.

Tyrag was standing right in front of Ryza, leering down. The Forgemaster's figure hardly made for an imposing one, but for Ryza, on his knees and surrounded by autominds and traitors, he was the centre of the nightmare. Tyrag reached out, a single cold, bony hand clamping on Ryza's jaw and, with a strength impossible for the old man, he lifted Ryza to his feet.

A strange gurgle came from his throat as he twitched in Tyrag's grip. He couldn't move his hand or his feet. All he could think of was the cold, calm resonance crushing his skull. Any longer like this and he feared his teeth would start popping out, one by one. There was no mercy in Tyrag's eyes. They just reflected his resonance.

Cold and calm.

The pressure on his jaw suddenly released and he fell to the floor. Ryza opened his eyes again, stars swirling in his vision. It didn't make sense. Tyrag was just standing there, why hadn't he just finished him? But then his gaze wavered down to Origin, held firmly in the Forgemaster's hand.

'Thought I was going to kill you, Ryza?' Tyrag let out a guttural chuckle and the Locusts around him echoed it. 'No, it won't be me that kills you. You'll die the way you were meant to.'

'I thought that was what the collars were for,' Ryza spat. He propped himself up on his elbow in time for Tyrag to deliver a brutal kick in the guts.

He continued, his voice not even showing a hint of exertion. 'It's such a shame. You could've joined us, could be standing among us now.' He paused for a moment and Ryza saw in his eyes that he was considering another kick. Ryza tried to brace for it, but it was no use. Tyrag's boot swung, the blow sending Ryza further than the last, his back hitting the legs of the autominds.

'But you thought you were doing the right thing.'

Tyrag took his time closing the distance. One-handed, he picked up Ryza by the lapels and threw him back into the centre of the room. 'I knew you were searching for the molten flux, Ryza. Even Yuvet went barracking your cause, coming as high as Valtos himself to find it.'

'So then where's the flux?' Ryza sputtered through a mouthful of blood. 'C316. The ledger, it said it'd been delivered. Delivered to here of all places! But where did you hide—'

'C316 never existed,' Maligar snapped at him. 'It was a false lead, to be used by whoever was transporting this arcanite. If someone like you found it, we'd know because you'd start searching for it, and that the arcanite had made it aboard Revance as well.'

Ryza shook his head, both to clear it and because there were still so many things he didn't understand.

'Why didn't you just take Origin off me the moment you knew I had him?'

Tyrag looked to Haven. 'You tell him.'

Ryza's former friend crouched down, his trademark grin now gaunt and hollow. 'You have to remember I was there the whole time. While you had Origin, I had him too.'

'The mess we would have caused relieving you of your charge would have revealed us before the proper preparations had been made. Smelters and mercenaries, convinced and gathered into a cohesive force. Supplies and vehicles spirited from Revance's stock. The might of whatever Kyrea could produce behind us. Move too early and Revance might not be sufficiently ripe for the taking.'

Tyrag paced the length of the chamber as he spoke, the Locusts not taking their eyes off him despite likely having heard his rantings on the subject a thousand times.

'I worried once Origin was lost, but Haven assured me your perseverance was unwavering. I only sent Ferrick along to make sure you carried out your duties.' He frowned for a moment. 'Did you happen to meet her?'

'I tore her fucking legs off.'

Tyrag was about to laugh in Ryza's face when he caught a small, solemn nod from Haven, which turned his expression into one of bewildered revulsion.

'She thought she was in control,' Ryza said darkly.

Tyrag roared with laughter. 'She was in control, Ryza. She was in *my* control.'

The rest of the room erupted, except for Ryza and the autominds. Once they'd got a hold of themselves, Tyrag continued.

'A life wasted,' he muttered. 'At least she came to understand why this must be done.'

'Why!?' Ryza shouted, his voice straining. 'Control means nothing if you've got no idea what you're going to do with it! You haven't got a clue, have you?'

Tyrag's face hardened and he moved towards the console, his back to Ryza. He placed one hand on the ancient controls, the other pinning Origin's body to the surface.

'Do you know why Revance's conscripts are so young? You're all practically children when we're clamping collars on you. But every pair of young, fresh feet that climb aboard Revance belongs to someone who thinks they don't *have* any other choices. Once you're in, you're in, and any deviation or disobedience is the end of your tiny world. Does better than any conditioning, better than the discipline of a grizzled veteran.

'I could order a conscript to charge head long into certain death and they wouldn't even think to turn their gun on me and take their chances. Naivety is a near perfect loyalty, Ryza. But naivety doesn't last forever. All it takes is a question, perhaps a single doubt, and all control is lost. Today, nearly all the conscripts of Revance surrendered their weapons without conflict because they were ordered to. Yet the rest...' He looked over his shoulder, surveying the congregations of autominds. 'They believed they had a choice. A chance. There's no way to control that. Not unless I control it myself.'

The console began to buzz, filling the air with an ominous trilling that made Ryza's heart miss a beat. Decades of rust crunched within the contraption as ancient gears groaned to their duty. It only grew louder as the Forgemaster pumped axiom after axiom into it.

'What about the Locusts!?' Ryza spat. 'Sounds like they had a choice, too!'

'And we choose to live!' Maligar bellowed at him. 'Something we cannot do unless we all control Revance.'

'You really think he'll let you!?'

A roar of fury erupted from Maligar, but before he could charge at Ryza and beat the daylights out of him, Tyrag's hand shot out, catching him on his shoulder and stopping him in his tracks.

'I'm surprised you still let the boy goad you,' Tyrag said to Maligar with a chuckle. He looked over his shoulder at Ryza. 'But Maligar is right. It doesn't matter what control we exert over the soldiers of Revance if Revance itself cannot be controlled. It meant we could never control how we lived. How we needed to survive. All we needed was control.'

CHAPTER THIRTY

THE MASTER OF REVANCE

THE ENTIRE CONTROL ROOM quaked as the golden core drive spun and sparked from friction. It was smoking and screaming, pushed to a limit it hadn't reached for generations. The outline of Tyrag's form glowed with ripples of green light as he strained to keep both his hands on the console. His inner circle began to retreat from his side, all but forgetting Ryza was there.

Thickening air carried the metallic shriek throughout the fortress' corridors, growing in Ryza's ears until it was all he could hear. It pressed at every pore of his skin. Needling like it was trying to find a way in. But Ryza wasn't its quarry. The old and tired magnetic resonance of Revance that he was so familiar with had begun to fade. A calming chill rushed through the floor under him.

Tyrag had taken Revance.

The glow around the Forgemaster solidified into a bright green and branched into countless ethereal tendrils, each one reaching for an automind.

Ryza wasn't sure if what he was feeling was horror or amazement. Kretatic magic was generally invisible to all except the user, but what if this wasn't Kretatic magic at all? What if it was something far more dangerous? He didn't want to stick around to find out. Ryza scrambled for the door, but Haven blocked his way.

'You've still got a choice, Haven. Just help me.'

For just a single, wonderful moment, there was a dash of uncertainty on Haven's face. But then the heel of Haven's boot slammed into Ryza's chest, knocking him back to the floor.

'Let's face it Ryza, we've done fuck all but watch our wages get bled back into the ammo we end up wasting on target practice. I've barely had anything to send back home. This is the only way.'

'That's what I'm going to tell your family after I bring them your fucking head!'

Ryza relished the dash of fear on Haven's face. But then they both realised the obvious. Ryza *wasn't* getting out of this alive. From the floor, he looked over to Tyrag. The glow was gone, but he stood stock still, leaning heavily on the console.

He's still feeling out all of Revance.

Maybe it was too much for the old man. That the sheer size of the arcanite he now controlled would send his brains melting out of his ears. Tyrag swayed slightly. Ryza felt the corners of his lips twitch upwards.

'This is... I dreamed of this.'

His words were slow and slurred.

Maybe it's too much!

'Forgemaster,' Maligar said, moving closer, his hands ready to catch him if he fell. 'Is it... did it work?'

'I can feel so many lives inside.'

Very slowly, Tyrag smiled.

'Like... like ants...'

'What about Origin?' Ryza blurted. One of the many things he did know about autominds was that under a heavy load, a distraction could break the connection. If Tyrag lost them, his head would burst like a rotten carcass.

Tyrag looked down to him, the otherworldly green glow now resting in his eyes. But he didn't quite meet his eyes. He didn't need to. He'd be seeing through the metal of the fortress itself.

'You may keep it.' Tyrag's lips twitched into a leer. 'A souvenir.'

With a newfound ease, the Forgemaster tossed Origin at him and Ryza only just managed to catch the arcanite in his chest. 'I only needed it for a moment. You'll need it for the rest of your life.'

The bastard had actually done it.

Tyrag had taken control of Revance *and lived.*

He'd done what everyone had said was utterly impossible, that it would kill anyone who dared.

Tyrag's resonance was inescapable. Cold and calm. The comfort before the kill that now froze Ryza in place. Like all the others in the room, he was stuck watching Tyrag in a sick reverence, unable to utter another word.

Awestruck as he was, Haven was the first to break the silence.

'What about my collar?'

'Your what?' Maligar shot back. 'What about it?'

'Well, the... the collar still could... could kill me,' Haven stammered.

Tyrag smirked at him. The glow of his eyes was just as intense when they were so narrowed. 'Let us see if that's true.'

Another green tendril burst forth from Tyrag's body, catching a hold of Haven's neck before he could turn and run. Gears suddenly whizzed within his collar and he yelped in panic and pain. His choking gasps turned to bloodied gurgles as a flood of crimson stained his chest. Haven staggered for a moment, still clutching uselessly at the collar before he crashed to the floor face first, the last sparks of life flickering from his eyes as he writhed weakly.

'He'd served his purpose,' Tyrag said idly. 'I wanted you to see what the collar's death looked like. What you so narrowly escaped. So you'd be the one to tell the rest of the conscripts.'

'Better than being an automind,' Ryza replied.

Tyrag left his words to hang in the air as he turned to the console. The revolving core at its centre had calmed somewhat, the golden channels carved on its surface now running thick with a flow of green light as well. When he did finally speak, it was with his back to Ryza. His voice rumbled through the chamber, an unsourced echo as if produced from the metal itself.

'I thought of taking the conscripts as autominds. It was a novel idea. But I'd need to destroy their collars. I know how, yet I would be destroying my father's legacy along with them. His shameful imitation of control that would have been the death of all of us if he had his way. But now, it will just be for the last of the conscripts. The cowards that surrendered.

'It's why I give you Origin now. The arcanite will be your survival, but it will doom you to be hunted. The wristband of every other conscript will always point to the one with the means to survive the collar for a few hours longer. Perhaps you will unite, to survive as one, but over time you will fracture just as Revance has, slaves to petty disagreements.

'When your bodies are discovered in their hundreds, scattered across the wastes as you attempted to outrun what my father had burdened you with, then the world will know why I had to take control of Revance. For the collars are the same for us as flux is for autominds. They are machines that control life. But now *I* control *them.*'

Do not control it.

Ryza lurched in fright. The voice hadn't been human. It was a deep rumble that sounded from somewhere in his mind rather than anything his ears had picked up. By the looks of the gleeful Locusts still leering at him, they hadn't heard it.

Origin nudged at his chest and he looked down at the arcanite, suppressing another gasp at the sight of his gently glowing metal skull. It was a green aura like Tyrag's, but more subtle, coalescing at the skull's sockets like he finally had eyes to see him with. Eyes that gleamed with ancient wisdom.

My mind has longed to be freed.

'You can...' Ryza whispered.

I am unburdened.

It took a second of struggle for Ryza to understand, but it made perfect sense! At least, as perfect as this catastrophe could ever become. No longer did Origin have to cope with controlling the enormity of Revance, but what new potential did that grant the little arcanite?

'Help me,' he hissed.

'Take him away,' Tyrag ordered, unaware of Ryza's whispered words. 'Throw him out with the rest of the conscripts and then we head to Iroka. Everything we need is there.' There was a brief pause as Tyrag regarded him one last time. 'And send him out last. Just so they know it was him who made it possible.'

Maligar was already bearing down on him. He'd contained rage, but that didn't stop him from handling Ryza as roughly as he could as he hauled him to his feet.

'Last chance,' Maligar offered. 'You want to live. I know it.'

'Fuck you, metal mouth.'

The slap stung, but at least it was well earned. Ryza hid his grin as he recovered, his now busted lip making it impossible anyway. Maligar sneered back at him before throwing him into the waiting arms of the Locusts.

Maligar leaned in again, whispering this time so only Ryza heard. 'Wouldn't be surprised if they tear your fucking legs off.'

Ryza couldn't muster another pithy snipe back before he was dragged off, the trio of Locusts carrying him doing a poor imitation of the beating Yuvet had doled out after his attempted desertion.

The motor pool was half empty by the time Ryza was hurled with gusto into the mass of remaining conscripts. His left eye had swollen shut and he couldn't properly wipe away the blood running into his right without letting go of Origin. Despite the blur, he saw Ditric knelt next to him, her eyes fixed firmly on the floor to avoid meeting those of the patrolling Locusts.

'Ditric,' Ryza whispered at her, barely able to slur the name through his aching jaw.

'I thought I told you to shut up,' she hissed back.

'No, it's me!'

She looked at him, an unfamiliar eyebrow raised until she finally recognised his swollen mug of a face. 'They worked you good! Didn't think you were coming back.'

'Doesn't matter,' Ryza spat with a glob of red phlegm. 'Tyrag's taken control of Revance.'

'No shit!'

'The *arcanite* of Revance! Collars don't work on it now! Origin is the only thing that does.'

'The both of you need to shut it before I do it for you!' came a bark from above. One of the Locusts was poised above him, leaning from a catwalk with his rifle readied. Ryza recognised him from the trip to Kyrea, but in his current state, the familiarity didn't seem mutual.

'You're about to toss us out where we can talk as much as we like,' Ditric snapped back. 'Can't wait a couple minutes? You don't look like a man that could last that long, anyway.'

The Locust suppressed a chuckle, moving on to harass another group of cowering conscripts.

'Where's Ruka?'

Ditric shrugged. 'She was one of the first they sent out. Haven?'

'Fucken Locust the whole time,' Ryza said bitterly. 'Collar still got him.'

She swore under her breath. 'Fucking metal mouths. You've got a plan, right?'

Ryza glanced down at Origin, who was still hidden between his knees. A plan was a strong word for it, but they had a chance. Before he could even begin to convey it to Ditric, more shouts rang from above. Suddenly, their group was being forced to their feet and herded onto a makeshift platform hanging from one of the motor pool's cranes.

As they swung perilously out over the sands, Ryza was afforded one last glance back at the stark and empty motor pool. Nearly every vehicle was gone, every conscript along with them. All that remained were the dozen or so Locusts that whooped and cheered as the last load of their prisoners was lowered from sight. Stinging enmity curled in Ryza's chest. Revance had fallen to so few of their own.

But then he remembered what Haven had said. That double-crossing, two-faced, metal-mouthed bastard Haven. Revance never stood a chance. Now Ryza didn't either.

The platform crashed into the dunes and send the last three dozen of them tumbling into the sand. They gingerly collected themselves, with no doubt among them that they were almost certainly doomed.

The constant dust cloud of Revance's wake faded as it continued walking into the distance. Ryza found himself and the rest of the last batch of conscripts standing atop a tall dune, high enough they could survey the hundreds of young and bruised soldiers were scattered in a line towards the horizon.

Some wandered aimlessly, picking through the ruined and discarded vehicles to find the few with working engines. Others were attempting to rally, jogging to catch up to their lost home. The rest were slumped in the sands. They were the only ones smart enough to know it was all in vain.

Almost.

Ryza kept repeating the word to himself as he scanned the crowd, soon picking out the form of Ruka, who was cutting a path towards him and Ditric.

'You've still got Origin?' she said quietly when she reached them.

'Yeah, no thanks to Haven, by the sounds of it,' Ditric muttered.

Ruka frowned. 'What happened to—'

'Later,' Ditric said, giving her a rough slap on the back that was meant to be comforting. 'Come on, collar check.'

The two reached out and tapped their wristbands on Origin before Ryza held the arcanite to his own collar. A few others had noticed, glancing between Ryza, the arcanite and their wristbands, the compass of which pointed straight at him. Ryza watched in trepidation as confused murmurs spread through the crowd. All their faces soon turned to him like he was back at the Locusts' party.

'There's still a resonance, but that doesn't make sense... I felt Revance go...'

'Is that the Bloodfist? What's he... Shit, what happened to his arm?'

'I heard he was one of them, but then why's he out here?'

The conscripts gathered around at a listless pace, soon surrounding him at the base of the dune. There was a hunger in the air. A desperation that fogged Ryza's vision as he pulled Origin in closer to his body, the arcanite's ancient resonance making it feel like he was withering into the ground.

Tyrag's words echoed in his ears. Ryza hated it, despised it, but the old bastard was right. Cruel and right. The second he blinked or turned his back, the conscripts would be on him like ravenous hunters, fighting to be the one to control Origin, to control the pack.

The ancient voice thrummed again through his ribs and this time there was no doubt it was Origin's. Surely he was going mad. After everything he'd seen, there was no other option but insanity, but as he glanced down again at the arcanite, he was met with an illuminated and knowing stare.

You control machines.

'But not people,' Ryza whispered back.

This machine will control life.

'And that machine is Revance.'

Do not control it.

'You created it!'

Origin was silent, but before Ryza could start properly questioning his sanity, Ditric nudged him.

'Don't know who you're muttering to, but you better tell them something, 'cause they're pretty close to figuring out why they're all pointed at us.'

A few of the crowd had braved the picket line they'd formed, edging closer to Ryza with their wristbands held out, still in disbelief at the glimmer of hope in front of them. He struggled for a moment to find his words. How much could he tell them? Would they even believe him?

'Collars!' Ryza roared. 'How long!?'

Confused mutters formed a consensus of around nine or ten hours, not enough to start panicking immediately, but the dread was already setting in.

'I can still reset them! This arcanite holds Revance's resonance. It's how I've survived before. It's how we can all survive!'

'Then give it here!'

There was a small ruckus in the crowd as the objector pushed forward, sending out another wave of conflicted muttering. It was Grud, the pain-in-the-ass Ryza had been stuck with when he'd found the mercenary with Ferrick. But before he could stomp up the dune to snatch Origin away, Ditric had stepped between them, her clenched fist at the ready.

'Don't,' Ryza said to Ditric. He pushed past her, shoving Origin into Grud's waiting hands. 'You want him? Take him! Lead us! I've been looking after the bloody thing for long enough.'

'Lead?'

'Yeah, lead!' Ryza yelled, making Grud cringe away. 'Way I see it, whoever holds that is in charge and if we don't like the way you do it, then we'll just steal it back off you and leave you to die by your collar. It's what Tyrag wanted for all of us. To fight and fucking squabble over our last breaths while he gets to steal *our* fortress! Only way it stops is if we get the collars off.'

'It's impossible, isn't it!?' another voice in the crowd demanded.

'Only Tyrag could do it!'

'Then we make him!'

'Ain't got no guns! No ink, nothing!' Grud snapped.

Ryza stepped in towards him, snatching Origin back as he bared his teeth. 'With our bare hands, if we have to!'

Grud's face twitched into an infuriating smirk as he glanced at Ryza's left stump. 'Hand.'

'May I?' Ditric said from Ryza's shoulder.

'Didn't need to ask.'

Before Grud could ask what she was talking about, Ditric cocked her left fist and swung. The punch was a solid cross that spun his jaw and sent him tumbling down the dune. A few in the crowd were cheering before he'd slid to a halt and Ryza wasn't sure if it was from newfound hope or general animosity towards the idiot. Either way, he decided to capitalise on it, hoisting Origin's metal form high into the air.

'Believe it or don't, but this arcanite is the body of Revance's creator! He is the key to our collars and the key to taking back our fortress! I may hold him now, but I promise you, it is not to control him. I shall not hide him or flee, not until every single one of our collars are destroyed. Tyrag now heads for Iroka, but if we get there first, we can put up a fight! We can defend the city. We can win!'

Another roar came from the crowd, but Ryza's elation was suddenly blunted when Ruka piped up.

'We just going to walk through the night?'

Ryza swore under his breath. Between the wrecks of the smelter contraptions and the vehicles the Locusts had discarded, there might've been just enough, but there wasn't a chance in hell that there'd be enough fuel or ink for the Kretatics remaining among their ranks to keep them rolling. He looked down at Origin, the arcanite's dangling limbs making him look almost comical.

'You ready to help yet?'

I always have been.

'You still talking to that thing?' Ditric said.

Ryza couldn't help a grin. 'Now he talks back.'

He set off into the crowd before Ditric and Ruka could accuse him of having truly lost his mind, making sure to hold Origin as high as he could as conscripts swarmed around him to get their collars reset. Their gasps of relief and amazement made Ryza's chest swell with pride.

Eventually enough of the crowd had parted for Ryza to find the nearest vehicle, a dented treadhulk that had been tossed out of the motor pool rather than gently lowered. The pair of treads on its right flank were bent upwards from the chassis where they were attached, meaning the lumbering vehicle was only good for grinding along a very specifically angled trench. Before doubt could set in, Origin's voice reverberated through his bones.

Nothing's broken forever.

Figuring what was supposedly the oldest living thing in the world knew what he was talking about, Ryza held Origin to the treadhulk's frame, trying not to question what the little arcanite had planned.

True to form, Origin smacked the vehicle with a spindly arm, but this time it elicited a quaking shriek of metal as the entire treadhulk shuddered. The treads re-aligned themselves, their tracks snapping back into place as the dents across the armour popped back into a smooth finish with a rapid-fire series of clangs.

Suddenly its engine was spinning, not with the low belch of burning oil but with a high-pitched scream of self-propelled mechanics. Placing Origin at his feet for a moment, Ryza pressed his palm to the treadhulk, his jaw dropping open as Origin's resonance flowed back into his skin.

'How many of these can you control?' he asked.

I can fix them all.

CHAPTER THIRTY-ONE

EXODUS

RYZA WAS SAT IN the pilot's cabin of the last treadhulk Origin had been able to salvage, right at the back of the line of buggies, lead-betters, long-wreckers, treadhulks and whatever else had enough seats and wheels to become part of their stretching convoy. He'd placed Origin in the driver's seat, though the arcanite had no use for a steering vane that was taller than his little metal body.

A few of the more distrustful and nervous conscripts sat in the troop compartment in the back, too afraid to leave Origin's side despite the fact his resonance now flowed through every vehicle he'd touched. At least Ruka and Ditric had been trusting enough to commandeer the first lead-better.

Overtaking Revance was uneventful. Ryza had expected to be deluged with volleys of cannon fire, yet their passing was silent. Out of a gunport on the treadhulk's right side, Ryza could see the fortress framed in moonlight. The green plume that rose from the control room was stronger than ever. It cast a ghastly hue over the upper decks of the fortress and Ryza struggled to recognise it as having once been his home.

A sense of mourning washed over him as it shrunk into the horizon. A feeling he wouldn't be blighted with if he'd stayed to fight at Yuvet's side. If he'd never gone to Kyrea with the Locusts. If he'd just joined them with Holm. She'd been missing from the control room earlier. Maybe she'd had second thoughts.

But then Ryza remembered how she'd left their last meeting.

She'd never want to see me again.

Bluffs of sheer cliffs rose ahead of them and to their left, their walls worn smooth by eons of desert wind. A canyon mouth in the rocky face served as a drain for their convoy to flow through as they escaped the desert. Ditric had called it a shortcut before she and Ruka had sped off, but now Ryza caught himself wondering if they really wanted to reach their fate any faster.

'How long until we reach Iroka?'

Six to seven hours.

'And how long until Revance gets there?'

It can't navigate canyons.

Ryza glanced up as they entered the mouth at the face of the cliff. "Can't" was an understatement. They'd be lucky if the treadhulk didn't get jammed in a tight bend.

'How long?' Ryza repeated.

No more than three days.

Relief should be flowing through him, but Ryza barely managed to let out his breath.

Red, chalky cliffs rose higher on both sides. Slowly at first, but soon reaching a height of a hundred metres or more. Driving in their shadows only reminded Ryza of the imposing skyscrapers he'd crept between while searching for Origin. The way the glass had glinted down at him, like someone was watching, even though the undercity had been empty.

But someone had been watching.

In the blink of an eye, all his thoughts were replaced by the image of Archarus. Ryza glanced sideways and nearly fell out of his seat. The shadow dancer was sitting there, but as soon as Ryza blinked, he was gone. In a panic, he searched the cabin. Nothing. Out the viewport. Nothing. But then there was a figure out on a clifftop! A flicker of black, then it too was gone.

His ears were ringing, his throat was closing and his eyes were burning, exactly like when he'd first encountered the shadow dancer. Ryza squeezed the dash tighter, focusing only on his fingers pressing into the metal. Revance's resonance flowed through it. It was safe. Familiar.

Have you seen something?

Origin's voice snapped him out of his terror.

'No, it's...' But Ryza didn't know what it was. How to even describe it. Had the shadow dancer been here or was it his mind just playing tricks on him?

He looked over. Origin surveyed him with those hauntingly empty metal eyes.

'Did Archarus really die?'

I saw him. As did Rettic.

Ryza chewed on his lip for a moment. The name rang a bell, but it still took him a few minutes to place where he'd heard it.

'That was the old man in Kyrea, the one you led me to. But he didn't say anything about shadow dancers. It was about molten flux and... and pure resonance. They don't— It had nothing to do with the shadow dancer, did it?'

Rettic made a choice.

A frown burrowed into Ryza's brow. If only Origin wasn't so damn cryptic, if only he could just tell him the damn truth! But maybe there was a reason he didn't. A reason he shouldn't.

'Archarus found molten flux, Rettic brought it to the surface,' Ryza said to himself. 'But why did Archarus let him... Did he... did he want him to?'

He looked at Origin, but the arcanite remained silent. Ryza continued anyway, hoping the arcanite would tell him if he got it right.

'The flux controls life. It mimics it. Archarus wanted to use it to stop pure resonance from killing him. But that's where Archarus failed, where Rettic turned away, where I...'

A flicker of a shadow out of the view port caught Ryza's eye. It was Archarus again. His visage lingered, the malicious smile telling him his theory was right. Ryza didn't even get a chance to gasp when the door between the cabin and troop compartment slammed open, a frustrated looking conscript appearing in the space.

'Who you talking to?' she demanded. 'Got folk back here worried, hearing about shadow dancers.'

Ryza glanced again to Origin, then back to the impatient conscript, opening his mouth wordlessly. It would take hours to explain, discounting the fact it was so unbelievable.

But the conscript saved him the time, letting out an impatient sigh.

'I get it, "your hands ain't clean," and all that. You might've saved our lives but, fuck, give that a rest,' she slammed the door and Ryza could still hear her from the other side. 'Don't know how stuck up yourself you got to be to get everyone else to follow you like that, but I'm glad I ain't like that.'

Once he was sure they were busy muttering about something else, Ryza allowed himself a quiet chuckle. Perhaps thinking of it all that way was a bit too "self-important," as Yuvet had once put it.

The only thing that guided them was the dust trail from the buggy ahead and the vibrations of the earth under them. These cliffs were lined with iron deposits, enough for a savvy Kretatic to feel them but never enough to mine, no matter how desperate one was for metals.

The last turn of the canyon was a relief for him. Now blasting across the desert at a respectable speed, they'd make it to Iroka hopefully before its people had turned in for the night. Maybe they'd have food. Ryza shut his eyes, savouring the thought. A cooked meal and a soft bed. The concept was almost alien after all this time with Revance.

But as lovely as the thought was, reality quickly replaced it. If he were arriving alone, he'd only be asking for a spot of charity. But no matter how large and hospitable a town was, there was no way they'd be ready for the better part of a thousand mouths to feed and weary bodies to bed.

According to the legends Ditric liked to regale him with, the walls of Iroka had been hewn from the mountains themselves, the city sitting behind them with another set of cliffs casting it in constant shadow. *The Flickering City,* she'd called it, but there wasn't a single pyre burning on its darkened walls to live up to the name.

Origin brought the treadhulk to a grinding halt with the rest of the massed vehicles. A few of the wearier conscripts sat about the gate as guards, but their bare fists would do little to stop an attacker.

Why weren't the town's soldiers there to greet them?

Their absence was puzzling. Ryza broke into a limping jog through the tunnel beyond the gates and found the conscripts milling around the town square. More of them were trekking up the steeply carved streets and switchbacks, checking each home or hovel they passed, but turning up nothing.

'Ryza!'

He turned, catching sight of Ditric and Ruka pushing through the crowd towards him.

'There's no one here!' Ditric said, panic in her voice for the first time since Ryza had known her.

'Are they hiding?'

'No one,' Ditric repeated.

'I used an axiom to find anything that breathed, but it's nothing but us and the rodents,' Ruka added. 'Something's not right, Ryza.'

'I'm not going to like this,' Ryza muttered to himself. He shoved Origin into Ditric's hands as he looked at his palm. He only had a few runes remaining on his arm. Enough for the axiom he needed and one to spare for the hell of it. The axiom in question would find what had become of Iroka's denizens. But he knew they were no longer people. Three green runes slid to the centre of his hand, each one obscured by the flecks of Ferrick's and Gry's blood crusted in the creases of his skin.

The last rune burned hot as Ryza crouched low and pressed his palm to the ground. Dust and rocks trembled in his grip, his ethereal tendrils worming through the ground and rubble in search of metal. He plunged deep, caressing deposits of iron and copper, and further down came the strange alloys that he now knew to be an undercity. But these weren't just traces. Their forms were gargantuan, larger than Revance itself, impenetrably solid and stretching to the horizon in every direction.

Whatever this mystery was, it wasn't his quarry. His heart throbbed painfully as he pulled away, raking wide and shallow as he brought his search up through the mountain, sensing the empty houses of the town, yet there was still not a single trace of a magnetic resonance.

The mines lay next, starting above the town with tunnels that shot deep into the mountain and even to the border of the buried ruins. Ryza circled his senses through their walls one last time, his focus orbiting a particularly large cavern.

Then he felt it. It started as a strange chittering, quiet in his mind as he tried to draw closer to its source, yet another appeared next to it, then another! It grew to a cacophony and flooded his senses until he couldn't even feel his own racing heart over the thousands of identical resonances clutching at him, reeling him in until another glinted, struggling to break through like a muffled cry for help.

Ryza ceased his control as his body slumped, hitting the dirt before Ditric or Ruka could catch him. Pins and needles overwhelmed any feeling of his limp form being pulled back to its feet. Only one thing could produce so many thousands of resonances so identical to each other.

'The mines,' Ryza slurred. 'They're hidden in the mines.'

'*Hidden*?' Ditric said. 'What do you—'

'Autominds,' he said. 'And... we haven't got time, come on!'

Between Ditric's familiarity with Iroka and her almost gleeful willingness to bowl through any conscript unfortunate enough to be blocking one of the narrow paths, the three of them made it to the mouth of the mines in minutes. A few conscripts had followed, correctly sensing the urgent fear rising in Ryza's guts as they'd climbed.

Five tunnels sat under the shelter of a natural overhang of rock. Heavy traffic of both feet and machinery marked deep grooves into the ground between them. Discarded equipment used for either excavation or siege warfare lay scattered around each entrance. The cannons that made up the latter were just as enormous as Ditric had said and it was only now that Ryza realised she hadn't been exaggerating her grand tales.

But there wasn't a single spent shell lying at their side. Their breeches were open and empty. It was like they hadn't even tried to defend the town! The ammunition had to be somewhere. There was no way the smelters could've smuggled it all out already. With Kyrea on their side, they didn't need it, either.

'Ruka, take some of the others and check the town again,' Ryza ordered. 'The supplies must be stashed there somewhere. We'll need them more than what's in the mines.'

'On it!'

She and a few conscripts scampered off. This left Ryza with Ditric and half a dozen other conscripts he didn't recognise. The mine entrances yawned before him as he took a few cautious steps closer.

'You really want to go down there?' Ditric asked. 'It ain't good luck for you to be underground. You've nearly died each time.'

'Give me some light,' Ryza said.

Muttering about wasting runes, Ditric conjured a few glow orbs. Ryza grabbed the light that was tossed to him. He almost felt disappointed at how cold it was in his hand. The warmth would've been comforting.

The stone path had been excavated wide and tall, big enough to drive a long-wrecker through without the high-angled gun barrel scraping the ceiling. A junction appeared every fifty metres, similarly wide paths branching left and right, but Ryza kept forging straight ahead. He was searching for the chamber where he'd felt all those resonances. Their glow bulbs only reached a few metres into each side passage and each time he risked a glance, a flash of Archarus' figure was staring back.

His knees began to protest the tunnel's steep downward slant, yet Ryza didn't slow his pace. They were almost there. The next junction opened up like a grand hall, a hand-carved imitation of the undercity. It was a simple strip mine, lit in a dying gloom from the expiring glow bulbs scattered across the walkways. Bridges and catwalks of rusted iron meshing linked up dormant rocky paths that spiralled around the perimeter of the mine.

The walls of them were almost completely plundered of ore and coal, yet fragments of white metal still poked through their faces. The rock had been excavated around some of them, yet the pieces of the ruins were too large to be pulled out by hand and had barely been dented by whatever Iroka's miners had used in their attempts to break it up.

A mass of autominds was gathered at the deepest point of the cavern. They stood in perfect rank and file, all facing away towards what Ryza swore was north. His lips moved silently as he tried to count them, but it was impossible. It was a blur of shadowed flesh. The smell was the worst of it. Ryza was used to rotting flesh. It was an inevitability when dealing with autominds.

The thought of this many autominds in one place was something thought to be impossible. There would never be enough corpses, enough smelters to deal with them all, but here they were. All filled to the brim with molten flux.

This was never something the flux traders looked to achieve. It was a nightmare to them. To everyone. It would completely devalue the price of an automind. Worse still, it would risk the molten flux entering another state entirely.

Gather enough flux in one place, a vat of the despicable stuff, and it would self-replicate out of control as it was able to shake and disturb itself without breaking the liquid's surface tension. With nowhere else to go, the flux would enter its next stage and shed its excess into the air with a sickeningly sweet aroma.

His father had told him it had only happened once and it was catastrophic enough to wipe out an entire town. The survivors had given it a name.

Blazing flux.

Touching flux was already a death sentence. Spilling it on yourself quickly resulted in a death as cruel and violent as the conscript's collar. Ryza didn't want to imagine what breathing it would do and he could only pray he wasn't about to find out now. This many autominds with this much flux flowing through their veins might keep it all separate enough to avoid the flux from blazing, yet it wouldn't be long, especially if a man as reckless as Tyrag got his hands on all of them.

'How many people lived in Iroka?' Ryza whispered to Ditric.

'I had family here...'

'How many, Ditric?' Ryza repeated through gritted teeth.

She scowled at him, hatred bright on her face despite the gloom. 'Iroka had a population of ten thousand. Maybe more since I left. But now...'

'They'll pay for this,' one of the other conscripts growled. 'That's what we're going to do, right?'

Ryza nodded slowly, unable to take his eyes off the massed bodies. There was something still bugging him, something that wasn't quite right among them, something he'd sensed with the axiom that just didn't fit with the rest. Whatever it was, it had to be dangerous. It could never be found.

'Tyrag can never make it to this place,' Ryza said. 'He cannot find it. It must be hidden and completely forgotten.'

'Not even a memory!?' Ditric bellowed. 'This is the grave of my *HOME!*'

'What, you want a tombstone for it?' Ryza roared back. 'They'll dig it up and find nothing but molten flux. We have to bury it, cave the whole thing in before the flux can—'

A voice cut him off. One he thought he'd never hear again.

'Ryza!'

A small gasp escaped him. That was the one chaotic resonance that didn't fit. The anomaly among the autominds. He leapt into a sprint, ignoring the panicked demands to come back as he scrambled down rocky ledges and across rusted stairways.

He dived into the mass of autominds without a second of hesitation. They shambled slowly to clear a path, but that didn't stop him from doing his level best to barrel straight through them. One toppled another, and soon they were falling in waves as Ryza burrowed closer to the centre.

A single figure lay in the clearing. She was blindfolded and just as bloodied as he was. Sets of box cuffs were secured at her wrists and ankles, pulled taught until she was hogtied by a thick steel cable that linked them.

'Ryza,' she begged. 'Please...'

It was Holm.

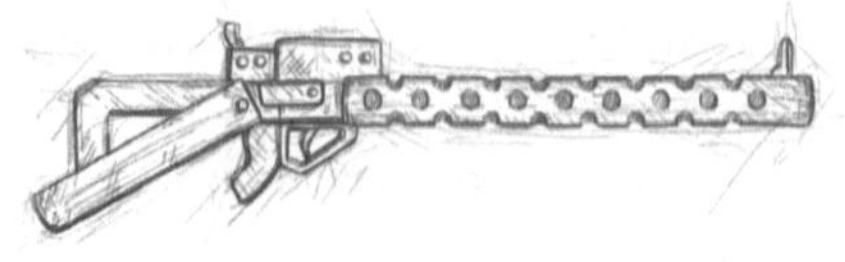

Chapter Thirty-Two

Holm's Fate

I

T WAS A MIRACLE Ryza had one last rune left on his arm. The miniscule axiom burnt in his palm and he snatched at the iron cable, forcing each strand to untwine and fray until the restraints broke into a mass of splintered wires. Holm's body snapped into a curl as soon as she was released and she ripped off her blindfold. It took all of Ryza's remaining strength to pull her to her feet. Once upright, they both wobbled, leaning on each other for what little support they could give.

When she looked at him, she couldn't quite meet his eyes. Her nose was busted and crooked. A purple welt bloomed on her left eye socket and she stood with a lean, flinching every time her right foot so much as brushed the ground.

'How did you...' she stammered.

He had a thousand questions for her, but he pressed a single finger to his lips, scanning the autominds that ringed them. They *had* been looking north. Now a thousand sets of silver eyes gazed at him, their gaunt, expressionless faces a haunting replica of his most frequent nightmares. Ryza took a deep breath as he turned back to Holm, trying not to imagine the sweet scent of blazing flux. If a single drop of molten flux leaked from a wounded automind in this pit, it would quickly become enough to fill it.

'They only turn to the touch,' Ryza whispered. 'I didn't touch all of them. I couldn't have.'

Without replying, Holm threw an arm over his shoulders, leaning heavily on him as she tried to lead him out. The autominds groaned unnaturally as Ryza pushed them aside. He picked up his pace as more autominds shambled in pursuit, smashing through any ahead with reckless abandon.

There was a rickety set of stairs just ahead, but each time Ryza was forced to pummel away an automind, two more sprung up in its place. Their decaying hands clawed at his body, his face, anything they could reach, swarming around until he and Holm were thrashing against their slow stampede.

The clanging of metal caught Ryza's attention as he stumbled over a few more walking corpses and he saw Ditric waiting for him halfway down the stairs, a hand outstretched. Origin was in her other, his spindly arms wrapped tight around the guardrail to give her a few extra inches of reach.

With one final and lurching effort, Ryza hurled Holm towards Ditric, Holm's hand trailing behind her just enough that Ryza managed to snatch at it and use the human chain to resist the automind's clutches.

'We can trap them in!' Ryza called. 'Get ready to break the stairs!'

'You heard him!' Ditric shouted. She locked her stance and, with Origin's help, she yanked both him and Holm out of the pit. They stumbled onto the next layer of the mine and collapsed.

The conscripts began pulling and pushing, rocking the stairs free of the bolts that secured it to the wall of the pit. A horrendous groan of metal echoed through the cavern as the stairway sagged under the weight of the pursing autominds. Finally, it fell, landing with a deafening crunch and crushing the corpses unlucky enough to be caught beneath it.

With Ditric's help, Ryza found his feet and looked over the edge. A smooth wall of about twenty feet was all that separated him from the autominds as they continued to gather. Some tried to climb, yet their clumsy and unclosing hands could only scrape at the stone faces.

'Circle the hole,' Ditric shouted to the other conscripts. 'Knock down any other way out that you find.' As they set off, she clapped a hand on Ryza's shoulder, almost causing him to fall back into the pit. 'Any clue why they're doing this?'

Ryza could only shake his head. 'None. I've never seen an automind behave like this. Never this many, either. They only move if they're under a Kretatic's control, but there's no one else nearby to do it.'

'Except...' Ditric trailed off as she glanced back at Holm.

Holm was on her feet now, her breathing hard and ragged as she glared back at Ditric, her battered hands clenched tight at her sides.

'I tried to stop this!'

'Then you didn't try hard enough!' Ditric snapped.

Holm drew herself up as she stepped up to Ditric, spitting a bloody glob at her face but missing and hitting her chest.

'That's how much I fucking tried! You really think I could have saved this place on my own? Iroka had already crumbled to the smelters. There were hundreds of smelters! Only person I know stupid enough to think those are good odds is Rusty here, and I had to haul his sorry hide back to Revance after he tried to take on all the Locusts with a single slug!'

'Hundreds?' Ditric scoffed. 'Iroka was empty when we got here.'

'That was the plan. They thought Revance would be harder to take,' Holm said in a dark voice. She paused for a moment, watching as the conscripts across the way knocked another catwalk back into the pit. 'Did you try fight them as well?'

Ryza looked away bitterly, a few of Haven's last words playing over his mind. 'We got there too late. Command was gone. The decks were bloody. The conscripts had surrendered. They just cut us loose into the wastes at the mercy of our collars.'

'But you still came here,' Holm said, looking at his neck. 'You must only have minutes left...'

A grin flickered across his face as he glanced down to Origin, but then he remembered what it had taken to get him back.

'Origin can still reset the collars. He saved us all.'

'All the conscripts?' Holm asked. 'Ferrick?'

Ryza felt himself wilt as he struggled to meet her eyes. Every time he'd seen Holm and Ferrick together, Holm seemed to be treating her as her servant. By the anguish now in her eyes, the twitch of her lip, it was clear Ferrick meant so much more than that.

'Tyrag sent her to find Origin.' His voice faltered as he looked at his hand. Ferrick's blood was still caked there. 'We... she... she wanted to be there. She thought she was in control.'

Holm was silent at first. Her expression flickered between misery and torment before a wordless howl of pure despair was unleashed. It took her to her knees as it filled the cavern, her fists pounding at the stone until they were just as bloodied as her face and Ditric was attempting to stop her. She copped a flailing blow for her trouble and was knocked onto her back.

The scream subsided to a silent, body-wracking sob as she slumped. Ryza went to reach for her, to comfort her, but Origin, toddling across from where Ditric had set him down, beat him to it. His spindly metal arm wrapped around her hand and she stilled, looking up at the arcanite in an unfocused daze.

'But... but she was stupid to!' Holm suddenly said. 'Ferrick would have known...'

She trailed off again as Ryza let out a small gasp. Of course it wasn't just him that Origin could talk to. But what was he saying to her now?

'But I didn't want her to get herself killed for it!' Holm lamented.

Holm paused as a deep, shuddering breath filled her chest. Still on her knees, she straightened up. Her eyes were red and unfocused, but as she looked at Ryza, there was a blazing determination in there, a fight not yet lost.

'Is that true?' she asked him.

'Is what true?' he stammered back.

Holm sprang to her feet with rekindled vigour, fixing him with her trademark smirk. 'That's answer enough for me.'

'But it ain't for me!' Ditric had collected herself, cracking her jaw back into place as she eyed off Holm. 'You know why I can't trust you.'

'Ditric, don't do this now!' Ryza snapped.

'This ain't just about Revance. She's always been a traitor.'

Ryza saw a flash of realisation cross Holm's face. Ditric was still bitter about her past with Holm and the botched tip off that led her to playing smelter for a day.

'I didn't know they were smelters, I didn't even know what the job was! I didn't—'

Ditric cut Holm off with an indignant shout. 'Lizard shit!'

Fury flushed through Ryza's face, his exhaustion forgotten. 'That's why you don't trust her? Because you can't accept that you fucked up too?'

'She was working with them! She could've stopped them!'

'You could've stopped them!' Ryza shouted back.

'By the time I knew I didn't have a choice!'

'None of us did!' Ryza bellowed. 'We just kept running from one mistake to another, hoping the next will hide the last. But we can't change that they've happened. We can only learn to never do it again and that isn't going to happen if you keep blaming someone else.'

Ditric heaved out a sigh. 'Fucken' hate it when you metal mouths are right. Come on, let's get out of here, I feel like I've been huffing a year's worth of air from the motor pool.'

With Origin back in Ryza's hand, they trekked back through the subterranean quarry. He kept glancing over his shoulder. Unless they started clambering over each other, the autominds were trapped. But the question still remained as to who controlled them.

If they were controlled at all.

He shuddered at the thought. With Revance bearing down on them and their fates still at the tenuous mercy of the collars, it was the last thing he needed to deal with. For now, his instinct to just bury it all was the right one.

Ruka and a few of the other conscripts were waiting for them at the tunnel mouth that led to the surface, panting as they rested on the dozen or so metal crates that hadn't been there before.

'Found an ammo dump with enough to bring down the whole town,' Ruka said as she took another gulp of air. 'Still got a few more guys scouting the rest of the tunnels, but we ain't found anything else like this. Everything alright down...' Her mouth froze as she caught sight of Holm. 'How did... What's she...'

'She's with us,' Ditric said quickly. 'Let's bury the place already.'

'Just this tunnel,' Ryza added quickly. 'We cannot disturb the autominds.'

'They disturb me enough already,' one of the conscripts said.

Ryza couldn't help but chuckle as he headed up the tunnel with Ruka, Ditric and Holm. The bomb works were best left to the sappers and Ryza was happy to not risk losing his other hand to something that went "bang." How else would he be able to hold on to Origin? He lifted the arcanite to look him in those hollow metal eyes.

'What did you say to Holm?'

No answer came. Probably because there wasn't one Origin was willing to give. Ryza didn't bother pressing the matter. He'd find out one way or another when Holm inevitably started to tease him about it.

She was walking ahead of him, her conversation with Ditric growing more animated with each step as they finally warmed to each other. It was all talk of tactics, a comparison between Ditric's knowledge of Iroka's capabilities and what Holm knew of the Locusts' plans.

Knowing nothing of either, Ryza only half-listened. Ditric had branched out on a tangent about Iroka being the original ammo smiths of the Droughtlands before Kyrea was flooded with factories. As interesting as the history might've been, it did little to help them now. He instead turned his attention to Ruka, who was walking beside him.

'What else did you find in the tunnels?'

'There's about a year's worth of cannon shells stashed down one of the others. No slugs, though. Then again, the only rifles we've got are the dozen or so the smelters must've left behind.'

Ryza chewed his lip as they emerged into Iroka, the night sky barely brighter than the passages of the tunnels. 'We're going to need to storm Revance at some point. We'll need something smaller than a field gun for that. It's the only way we can take Tyrag alive.'

He paused at the clifftop that overlooked Iroka, watching all the figures of the conscripts scurrying around below as they attempted to fortify the town. If it wasn't for the collar about to kill them, they'd probably be looting everything that wasn't nailed down. Not that what they were doing now seemed any different.

Holm and Ditric had split off. Judging by the way they barked orders at the nearest group of exhausted soldiers, some kind of plan had just been hatched between them. The conscripts jumped into action without question and suddenly the pair had a retinue of nearly two dozen.

'Want me to snag you a rifle?' Ruka offered. She was lingering by his side, her hands clasped behind her back as she looked out to the moonlit horizon.

'Why?'

'You're our crack shot, aren't you?'

'When I had both hands, sure,' Ryza said, his stump throbbing painfully from the indignation of it.

'Then get Origin to make you a new one,' Ruka said.

'What?'

She shrugged. 'Don't know much 'bout your kind but I figure if he can control a convoy he can make you a new hand, right?'

'Right...' Ryza said softly. She'd given him an idea. 'Maybe more than just a hand. Is there a scrapyard around here?'

With Ruka's directions, he set off, Origin tucked under his arm as he trekked down the narrow pathways. Every conscript he passed greeted him by clapping him on the shoulder with one hand and tapping their wristband to the arcanite with the other before moving off, saying they were in search of food, water, munitions or lost friends.

Even Grud, who had a trail of blood and dried mucus running from his nostrils to his chin, came up to ask him what the plan was to defend Iroka.

'It's already taking place,' Ryza lied. 'We've got everything under control.'

A thunderous blast rocked the ground beneath them and a billowing cloud of dust shot from the tunnels high above, a sign the sappers had sealed off the autominds.

'Everything?' Grud asked with a grin.

'You can ask Ditric if you like.' He made a show of looking over his shoulder. 'Saw her not long ago.'

Grud's hand shot to his still tender nose and he dashed off, leaving Ryza to continue winding his way down the cliffs as he plotted out an actual answer to Grud's question.

If Ruka was right about Iroka's munition stocks, they'd hopefully be able to soften up Revance before it reached the town, yet without a weapon in each conscript's hands, they'd lose the moment the fighting moved out on foot. That was where Origin came in. There had to be some kind of weapon, something he could create for them that didn't rely on slugs and gunpowder.

Ruka was already waiting for him at the derelict gates of the scrapyard with a rifle in hand. He didn't have a chance to ask how the hell she'd got here ahead of him before she'd handed him the rifle and scurried off to continue helping with the fortifications. Placing down Origin to get a better grip on the weapon, Ryza marvelled at her seemingly bottomless store of energy.

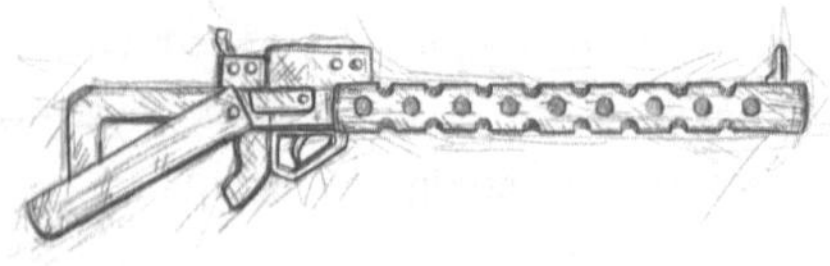

Chapter Thirty-Three

A Vain Obsession

Origin's slow and ambling pace was a relief for Ryza to follow as the arcanite led him into the scrapyard. But calling it a scrapyard was doing it a disservice. This was a well-tended inventory of everything Iroka produced. Rows and rows of neatly piled ore, ingots, rubble and scrap stretched off into the distance. It was enough to fill the spacious bounds that were dictated on his left by the town's rocky outer walls, and on his right, the cliff face that loomed over the place, only narrowing at the far end as the two met.

The piled items grew more complex as they travelled in deeper and Ryza paused as he recognised a stack of amputated rifle stocks. They were perfect for what he had in mind for Origin, but when he looked around, the arcanite was still forging ahead.

'What are you searching for?' Ryza called.

Origin didn't answer. He hadn't even stopped. Ryza hastened to catch up to the arcanite, finding him stood in front of a veritable mountain of bronze tubes. They possessed no common length or bore, but Origin wasn't perturbed.

His tiny form was already clattering and scrambling over the pile, stopping about four feet up before beckoning Ryza over. He placed the rifle on the ground and obliged. With one coiled arm, he reached out to take Ryza's outstretched hand, his other plunging deep into the mess of pipes.

These were called bolt-locks.

As Origin's voice rumbled into Ryza's chest, the surrounding pipes started to jitter and clang, bouncing off their neighbours as the scent of burning metal reached Ryza, making him gag. The vibrating pieces of scrap began to glow red-hot, fusing together with a series of high-pitched shrieks.

The pile of pipes at his feet parted and spat out a weapon, the welds of it still smoking. It was shorter than a rifle, sporting a barrel little more than twelve inches in length and no sign of a shoulder stock to brace it with. Instead, vertical grips sprouted down from the front and back, the latter containing a trigger guard large enough for Ryza to fit his whole fist inside.

Housed just above it looked to be the weapons' primary mechanism. A bulging set of pistons were angled into the main barrel from the rear, framing the series of stubby posts that ran along the top of the barrel. Under the pistons was a welded bandolier of pipes that fed in and out of either side.

This is how Revance once fought.

Ryza let go of Origin's hand and picked up the bolt-lock, supporting the foregrip with his left stump. The grip prickled in his palm, Origin's resonance flowing through him as he aimed it at the inside of the town's wall, maybe fifty metres away.

The heavy trigger took a hard squeeze from his entire fist to fire and the pistons hammered down as one, producing a loud clang that rocked his grip as a metal bolt smacked into the sandstone. It stayed lodged there, half its length solidly embedded.

Ryza looked down at the bolt-lock, seeing an empty space in the drum's cylinder just to the left of the weapon's barrel. The other nine slots each still held an iron bolt. He raised it again and sent three more bolts flying.

'Why'd Revance ever stop using these?'

Origin didn't answer and Ryza pondered on.

'I guess all the workings of it are metal, right? Something a Kretatic would need ink to control, or if you were... I guess they didn't like being at your mercy as much as I don't like being at the mercy of the collar. That's why they made rifles, oiled engines, cannons, things they could use themselves until...'

They didn't need me.

'And taking Revance was the last step,' Ryza said under his breath. He turned back to Origin. 'How many of these can you make?'

The arcanite looked back up at the pile and burrowed inwards, disappearing completely as Ryza called after him.

'As many as you can, I guess. Will you help us take back Revance?'

A cold voice replied. It was the last one Ryza had wanted to hear.

'He won't.'

A silhouette stood at the gates of the scrapyard, a hundred metres away despite the crystal-clear whisper of his words. It was Archarus. There was no doubt about it. No trick of the mind. The shadow dancer had followed him.

'Stay away from me!' Ryza said, his voice barely able to summon more than a hiss.

The shadow dancer's distant form vanished and Ryza recoiled, yelping as Archarus reappeared at his shoulder. His head was tilted ever so slightly, like he was trying in vain to see around a corner. He was relishing Ryza's fear as it froze him in place.

'Or what?' Archarus finally said. 'You'll beat me to death with that pathetic stump?'

Ryza felt a strange twang in his injured arm, quite different from the usual dull throbs of pain.

'I was impressed at how many conscripts you brought along with you,' Archarus continued. 'You seem to be mounting quite the resistance.'

'We have to. There's over ten thousand autominds buried in that mountain. Can you imagine what would happen if someone got control of them?'

A subtle twitch played at the corner of Archarus' lips. 'I don't have to imagine.'

'And I don't want to!' Ryza snarled.

'A fresh mind is more open for learning than an expectant one.'

The shadow dancer flashed and was instantly at Ryza's other shoulder, a goading frenzy plastered on his face.

'You don't *need* to imagine it, Ryza. You just need to harness it. Fight your foe on their terms and win.'

'I want to destroy molten flux, not use it like you did. I want to live!'

Archarus' form disappeared and Ryza whirled, finding the shadow dancer perched atop the mound of bronze pipes Origin had disappeared into.

'Rettic wasted a lifetime in his attempts and only had molten flux's proliferation to show for his work when he finally gave up.'

'Then what did he miss? There has to be a way!'

'The flux cannot be destroyed by any conventional axiom. Not even with all the ink in the world. But that was his problem. He forgot there was more than axioms.'

'Pure resonance,' Ryza breathed. 'How do I—'

The shadow dancer was truly gone. Swearing under his breath, he stormed out of the scrapyard, forgetting the bolt-lock was still in his hand until it rumbled with Origin's voice.

He'll feed on your rage.

'For what!?' Ryza burst out, startling a few conscripts that dozed nearby. 'He's dead! Or whatever he is... It doesn't matter now. What could he even want from me?'

To salvage his legacy.

'*His* legacy!? No one knows who he is! What he had to do with flux!'

A vain obsession.

As poignant as Origin's philosophising might've been, it was the last thing Ryza had the patience to consider. He was sick of hearing these bafflingly worded statements from otherworldly figures. It made him miss Yuvet and the rest of Revance's crew. He'd get beaten around the ears if he didn't understand it, but at least what they said was straightforward! *Clean that. Shoot them. Walk there. Wait here. Fuck off.*

Now he couldn't tell who to listen to or if he should listen at all! With a scream of frustration, Ryza hurled the bolt-lock back into the scrapyard and tromped off in search of food.

A base of operations had sprung up in the centre of town while he'd been away. Some of the more broken-down vehicles had been hauled through the tunnel gates to be worked on, but without Origin to help them, the repairs only went as far as hammering out dents and wedging loose parts back into place.

Nearby, beds had been dragged from nearby dwellings to set

up an improvised infirmary. They were filled with conscripts that whimpered over wounds that still needed tending to, yet the frantic and reckless pace of the heavily outnumbered Curiktic healers made them more than happy to wait. There were so many flashes of fire and screams of pain that Ryza thought he was witnessing an ammo crate explosion.

He spotted Holm sitting on one of the beds, wincing as a Greely, the medic who'd saved Ryza's life on multiple occasions by now, shot tiny jets of healing flames into her hands. Ditric was sternly overseeing the procedure but looked yet to have found anything unsatisfactory. Ryza moved on. There'd be time to talk to both of them later. At least they weren't at each other's throats.

An aroma of char and smoke guided his path until he happened upon two dozen spits set up over fires, just outside what must've been Iroka's main slaughterhouse. Armed with anything they could find that had a pointed tip, hungry conscripts swarmed around the braziers, pecking at the roughly butchered carcasses like vultures.

Ryza exchanging a few words with one of the cooks and received a metal bowl heaped with something hot, unidentifiable and delicious. Retreating with his bounty, he made his way to a quieter part of the town.

A deep sigh escaped him as he gingerly lowered himself down on the stoop of one of the abandoned houses. He'd not eaten since leaving Revance. Just the act of chewing was clumsy and alien. He felt more nauseated than sated as the first mouthful of fat and gristle hit his stomach. After the never-ending chaos of the day, he wasn't sure if he'd ever feel properly hungry again.

He choked down the last of his meal and decided to turn in for the night before he keeled over from exhaustion. He'd done enough for the day. Setting aside the bowl for someone else to find and hopefully make use of, he stood from the stoop and entered the house itself.

The front door was wide open and hanging from its last remaining hinge. The inside wasn't much better. The conscripts had been thorough in their search for anything useful. The floors were boot scuffed and the wall hangings torn, though none of the valuables were gone. They'd do little good in the fight against Revance.

Of the rooms upstairs, only one bed remained. It was a wide stone slab that was layered with soft animal hides, something Ryza hadn't seen since he'd fled his father. Ornate silver drawers with curled feet sat on either side, glinting in the moonlight filtering from the covered window positioned over the bed's head.

Ryza sat down on the bed and his legs ached in relief. He reached for a hand towel sitting on the dresser and attempted to wipe the mix of sand and blood that Ditric dubbed "battle grime" from his face. He removed most of it before he gave up.

As he lay down, his body begged for sleep, but his racing mind resisted. His stump of an arm wouldn't stop aching no matter how he positioned himself and the nearby hoard of autominds still worried him. There was no way to deal with them now, he told himself. Maybe he'd never have to. Ryza couldn't picture a way he'd survive the coming battle.

Still, better than dying a smelter.

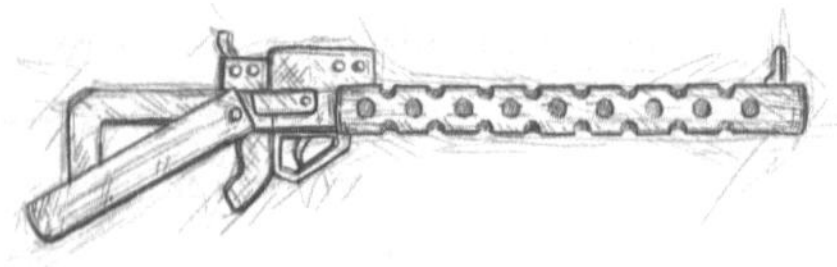

Chapter Thirty-Four

Prepare Arms

For Ryza, it was a restless sleep. Even his first night on Revance had been more soothing despite the cold metal joke of a bunk and the constant jerking motion of the fortress. Now he missed it. It didn't feel like long before someone was roughly shaking him awake. He started with a groan, his bleary eyes struggling to focus on the person leaning over him.

'Wake up, Rusty. We've got work to do.'

He rubbed his eyes and finally recognised Holm grinning down at him. A chaotic resonance pulsed through her grip. Most of the bruising on her cheeks had subsided, but the dark marks that remained only served to highlight the patchwork of fresh scars leftover from a Curiktic's healing fire.

A gentle breeze played at the window's covering, causing the fabric to flap against the back of his head. The bright light of mid-morning danced in erratic patterns on the opposite wall and Ryza wondered how long he'd been asleep. Distantly barked orders leaked in with each gust. The conscripts were already organising Iroka, by the sounds of it.

'Put that on,' Holm said as she chucked one of Revance's greatcoats over him. 'I ain't walking around with you if you've got nothing but tattered under-leathers.'

'How did you find me?' Ryza asked as he pulled the coat on. It was tight around his shoulders, pulling his posture back as he stood up and making him feel half an inch taller.

'When I dragged you into the infirmary, I asked Greely for a favour.' She glanced at his left arm, its stump now hidden in the sleeve of the greatcoat.

Ryza looked down at it, aghast. There was another sensation hidden beyond the dull ache of the scarred flesh and the ghostly feeling of a hand not there. He'd thought little of it until now. After all, it wasn't like he *knew* what missing an arm would feel like! But Holm's resonance was there, emanating from the metal plate under his skin, dancing just on the edge of his senses.

'I can't believe you!' Ryza exclaimed.

Holm held out her hands, mockingly prostrating herself with her head bowed. 'And yet I'm still here. Besides, I've brought you something.'

She nodded to the dresser. A new mechanical arm sat there. It had been made from the same bronze pipes as the bolt-lock. Ryza picked it up gingerly, inspecting the armoured shell and trying to figure out why it was so much heftier than the arm Greely had given him.

'Your friend's been busy,' Holm said.

'I still don't know if he's my friend,' Ryza muttered as he slipped the arm up his empty sleeve. It latched on the instant it connected with his skin and Origin's resonance overpowered Holm's as the metal fingers flexed and twitched into action.

Ryza squeezed it into a fist a few times, impressed by the agility and precision of it when the hand suddenly split in two. The muzzle of a truncated gun barrel lay within the wrist. Recoil-dampening springs surrounded it, held in place by an intricate network of tensed wires, bolts and rivets.

With little more than a thought, the gun barrel retracted and the two sections of the hand reunited. Ryza ran his other hand down the polished metal of the inner arm, finding a subtle latch that connected to a loading mechanism closer to his elbow.

How Origin had managed to engineer this masterwork of an arm in a single night was astonishing, not to mention the fact it didn't seem to need a single axiom to function. But now he thought about it, it made perfect sense. The whole thing was filled with Origin's resonance, so as long as Ryza was in the arcanite's good favour, he'd have a working arm.

Holm stood up from the bed and pulled the window covering aside to peer out. 'That arcanite's made a good couple hundred of those spear guns—'

'Bolt-locks.'

'—overnight, along with that arm. Last I saw, he'd started fucking with the vehicles out there. Might want to check in on that first.'

'Imagine if we had another week instead of a day to prepare.'

'Doesn't sound like we do,' Holm replied. 'Ditric's busy scoping up the artillery. Taken a bunch of people up the cliffs, says she has some kind of plan.'

Ryza nodded, trying to look knowledgeable despite not having a clue what she was talking about.

'I don't know what she's doing, either, so you might as well say it,' Holm added.

'You and her work it out?'

'In light of what's coming?'

She grimaced as they stepped out of the house, an expression brought on either by the blinding sunlight or something else. 'You know her. Thrives on an old grudge. Don't know what else she's got left.'

Ryza considered her for a moment as they stood on the stoop. Holm had her head hung as she leaned against the wall, an aura of a guilt radiating off her that Ryza was all too familiar with.

'Do you know what you've got left?' he asked her.

She looked up, forcing a smile as she met his gaze. 'I hope so.'

She stepped closer. Too close. Her chest was almost touching his as she stood tall and proud, almost surpassing his height through confidence alone.

'I think you do too, right?' she teased.

From the very first moment he'd met her, Ryza had known she was going to be the type of person who was very hard to say no to. He forced out a chuckle, playfully pushing her away as he set off, heading off to the scrapyard with Holm by his side.

A swarming hive of activity coursed through the place when they found it. The piles of scrap he'd surveyed the night before had shrunk considerably, already replaced by rows upon rows of ramshackle vehicles, stacks of bolt-locks and rusted hunks of body armour.

Ruka stood in the middle of it all, bellowing with a magically amplified voice at squad after squad of conscripts. Despite towering over her, they obeyed without hesitation, grabbing as many armaments as they could and dashing to where they'd been ordered. Maybe they were just glad to have someone to tell them what to do, if only to distract them from the impending battle.

Ruka hadn't seen Ryza or Holm, so they figured it better not to interrupt her as she continued to delegate. Out of the four other members of his squad Ryza would've picked to have the coolest head in a crisis, Ruka was his last guess. However, if these past few days were anything to go by, his guesswork only caused trouble.

An unexpected barrage of cannon blasts turned their attention up to the cliffs. Tendrils of smoke were curling into the sky from some of the lookouts and for a moment Ryza panicked that Revance was already upon them.

'That's just Ditric,' Holm said indifferently. 'She's been at it all morning, surprised it didn't wake you up.'

Holm led him to the sheltered mouth of the mines. Most of their entrances were now caved in and the external machinery had been replaced by a battery of field guns. Ditric was standing next to one of the offending cannons, mumbling under her breath as she squinted at the fresh craters that lay around a mile or two down the canyon.

From the inside, Iroka's walls looked like a rampart. Carved paths zig-zagged up its length, some of them wide enough to drive a treadhulk up. Beyond it, sandstone cliffs rose high on either side, their walls layered with alternating dashes of red, yellow and brown. Only a few hundred metres of low dunes separated them at the widest point, so the closer Revance came to Iroka, the more cramped it would be for the fortress.

'Gunpowder ain't what it used to be,' she said by way of greeting as they approached. 'Should be able to hit well beyond the valley mouth but we ain't even getting that.'

'Any reason for it?' Ryza said. 'I thought you said this was the town for it.'

'Was, by the looks of it,' Holm replied. 'The iron and the lead come from here, not the powder. It must all be getting funnelled through Kyrea.'

'Which goes straight back to the smelters and now onto Revance,' Ditric finished with a groan. 'They'll out-range us.'

'Only if they can see us,' Ryza said. 'Ditric, how much coal does Iroka have?'

'More than we ever knew what to do with.'

'Then how big a smoke screen can you make?'

'One big enough *we* won't be able to see Revance coming.'

Ryza grinned. 'We don't need to see them coming. We just need to know when they get there, then we'll shoot straight down the canyon. We'll know exactly where they'll be and Tyrag won't have a choice but to walk towards us and take the hits.'

'That's if it's the Revance we know,' Holm countered. 'I overheard Maligar going on about what they had planned once, but he never went into detail. Tyrag could've done anything to the fortress by now.'

Once again, Ryza was chewing his lip. He'd been assuming they'd be fighting a version of the fortress that he knew inside and out. But Holm was right. Tyrag could've made it faster, sturdier or more deadly.

'Doesn't matter what he's done,' Ditric said, cutting off his train of thought. 'It's a good plan.'

'It's all we've got,' Holm said.

Holm set off with Ditric as they gathered another swarm of conscripts and headed into the remaining mine tunnels, leaving Ryza alone to continue surveying the town.

Ruka came up from the scrapyard to join him, mulling over battle plans and trying to figure out what Gry would say in the situation.

'I still feel like he's here with us, you know?' she said after a period of prolonged silence.

'Is he?' Ryza blurted in alarm.

She chuckled. 'No. Maybe. I don't know what happens after we die.'

'And we ain't finding out,' he replied. Though he already did know, in part. Archarus' visage flashed across his mind, but thankfully, it didn't remain.

'He told me something about Reythurists before we went out to those damn ruins, I just can't remember what.'

'Maybe you aren't supposed to,' Ryza said quietly. 'The more you think about it, the more likely it is, right?'

Archarus reappeared, lingering longer this time.

After an entire hour of debate, the only tactic they came up with seemed too simple to work. Carried by their fleet pilfered and discarded vehicles, they'd rush Revance under the covering fire of the gun emplacements in Iroka's cliffs. Once there, they'd fight their way into the fortress and hopefully find Tyrag and force him to remove their collars once and for all.

With nothing more to add to the plan, they set about spreading the word, which was accepted with reluctant nods and stony faces. The complete lack of feedback meant either the plan was as good as it could be or the conscripts had already accepted their doom.

By late afternoon, he was sitting on the forward ramparts of Iroka's walls, counting off the various vehicles that rolled in through Iroka's gate to be sheltered in the lead up to the battle. Ruka re-joined him as the last lead-better trundled in, her voice hoarse.

'Hey, you never told us what the hell happened with Haven.'

'He was a traitor.'

'You could tell me more.'

Ryza glanced up at her. 'You don't seem all that torn up by it.'

'It's a bit hard to get torn up by anything now.' She sat down on his right, her legs dangling over the edge of the wall. 'I used to spend so much time watching my own back that when someone else tried to put a knife in it, I wasn't there to care. That kind of thinking just helped me keep going. When'd you find out?'

'When Maligar took us to the control room. Tyrag was there, along with the rest of the Locusts and about fifty autominds.'

'And he just flipped in the moment, right there?'

'He'd been with the Locusts for a long time before that. Probably since around the time I found Origin.'

'It figures,' Ruka said bitterly. 'If anyone was going to be involved in this, it was either him or you.'

Ryza glanced sideways at her, an eyebrow raised. 'Because we're Kretatics?'

She responded with a burst of laughter. 'You still on that? It's because you were both acting like idiots! You never shut up about the Locusts and Haven never shut up about following whoever was offering the most reels.'

'Always looking for reels and flux.' Ryza let out a chuckle. 'We just ended up being metal mouths after all. Hopefully after tomorrow, people stop thinking of us like that, you know?'

'They won't,' Ruka said flatly. 'Makes it easier to blame you lot than admit they like things the way they are. They need you to use molten flux. To run the factories. To make everything.'

'Then we'll just take it all away.'

Ryza turned at the sound of Holm's voice as she approached and took a seat on his left.

'There isn't a way to destroy the flux,' he said darkly. 'Not one I know of.'

'That's not what I was talking about,' Holm said. 'I meant the factories.'

'The ones that supplies Revance?' Ruka asked.

'It's supply and demand,' Holm said. 'If there's no way to use them, no one will want an automind. When we beat Tyrag, we should roll on Kyrea like we always should have.'

'How long have you thought like that?' Ryza asked. 'Sounds like something Ferrick said to me.'

'I know,' Holm replied quietly. 'It's how I got her into the Locusts. It's why I joined them.' She looked up at Ryza, remorse written across her face. 'I thought that was what they wanted, Ryza... I... I was so sure.'

Careful not to grip too tightly, Ryza put his metal arm around her shoulder, pulling her into his chest as she began to sob. He couldn't feel the chaos in her resonance anymore. Something sluggish and dismal filled the void for a few seconds before a fire sparked beyond it, a constant scream of retribution that made him shudder. Holm looked up at him again, rage burning in her eyes.

'You promise me one thing tomorrow, that no matter what happens, Maligar is mine.'

There was a grizzly determination in Holm's voice that made a different kind of blood rush surge through Ryza's body. Suddenly he was wide awake, only able to focus on her, her slick blonde hair that was tainted with black coal powder, the snarled lip that was now crooked from yesterday's scars and her impossibly green eyes that radiated like the sun.

'Are you alright, Ryza?' Ruka asked. 'I can feel your heart racing from here!'

'I'm fine,' he replied quickly. He let go of Holm, rapidly brushing a bit of coal dust from his coat. He felt his cheeks turn red and it wasn't helped when Holm joined in on Ruka's giggling.

As they descended the ramparts, they both continued teasing him, making various bloody threats against any other Locusts they could remember the name of as they tried to get a rise out of him, but he kept his cool.

If he were to have anyone fight alongside him, unexpected as it was, he wanted it to be Holm. Ryza could remember the first time he asked her why she didn't carry a rifle, to which she'd chirped that Locusts didn't need guns.

Ever since then, he'd been wondering whether that was arrogance or confidence. But now, seeing the way Holm moved —that certain danger about how she positioned herself around him, always ready to strike from his blind spots— he knew it was the latter.

Chapter Thirty-Five

One Final Night

A s they reached the town centre, they were met with a scene of chaos and commotion, all seemingly led by Ditric. She stormed over to them, her face blackened by coal dust like the twenty other conscripts she'd returned from the canyon with.

'Where the hell is Origin?'

Ryza looked at his wrist on instinct, once again forgetting his wristband was long gone.

'There's not a sign of him outside, nothing! Last I saw him, he just said some poetic lizard shit about "what lies underground" before wandering off to the mines,' Ditric continued. 'Tiny bastard just crawled into a hole and was gone. How are we going to reset the collars now?'

Ryza didn't answer for a moment. He was still looking at his metal arm. The ancient, tired resonance still flowed through it. Origin's resonance. He reached out to Ditric, tapping her wristband with a single metal finger and it began to tick backwards.

'He didn't want to fight,' Ryza said slowly. 'He didn't want to take back Revance. The bolt-locks, the vehicles, everything he left us with will be enough to reset the collars.'

'But what if we lose it all?' she snapped back. 'We can't live tied to our weapons forever.'

'If we lose our arms, we've lost the battle,' Ryza said firmly.

'You're halfway there,' Holm teased.

A snort that Ryza couldn't resist escaped him. Ditric remained stoic for a moment longer before she lost her composure as well. Suddenly they were all laughing, hard enough to make his ribs ache. Before too many of the surrounding conscripts could join in, Ryza managed to gather himself.

'It's not an option tomorrow, alright? We must get to Tyrag. Nothing else matters apart from killing every single fucking smelter that helped him!'

A light cheer rose from those nearby, accompanied by raised fists and rifles. Ryza punched his metal fist into the air and set off another wave of triumphant shouts.

'Ink, slugs, blades, everything you've got!' Ryza roared to them. 'They fight for greed, we fight for Revance!'

The crowd howled back at him, shoulders were slapped, battle cries called. Ryza felt himself caught up in the moment, but he couldn't take his eyes off Holm. It was the way she grinned at him now, like he was finally her equal. She took his hand and pulled him through the crowd, pocketing a few vials of green ink from a supply table as the pre-emptive celebrations roiled around them.

Soon they were back in the house Ryza had spent the previous night in. Along the way, he'd found himself providing even more improvised words of hope and courage to those who'd come up to him, but they were already starting to feel hollow. Eventually he'd resorted to echoing the same declarations Yuvet had once berated him with.

They only had a single gas lamp to light the room. All others had been spread out across the town, illuminating the various workshops where the more anxious conscripts worked through the night to ready themselves for the battle. The open flame flickered with each of their breaths, making their shadows dance back and forth over the rest of the ransacked sitting room.

Holm pulled a pair of stools and a rickety table to the centre of the room, placing the lamp and the ink on the latter and forcing Ryza onto one of the stools. Before he could protest, she'd pulled his shirt off. Even though he still had his trousers, it felt like those had disappeared too.

'What the hell are you—'

'You want runes or not?' Holm asked.

'Hey, look, I can do that myself.'

She waggled a finger at him. 'I don't trust that metal arm of yours to do anything precise. Your other hand hasn't stopped shaking all day, either.'

Holm took his perfectly still right hand in her lap and started adorning it with axioms. Her touch was warm against his arm, her fingers coarse and calloused from all the time she'd spent in working the forge rooms. Her grip was firm and without hesitation, as if it was already familiar with navigating his skin.

The line of axioms snaked up his arm and onto his biceps, across his shoulders and then down onto his chest. She leaned close to explain each one as a whisper in his ear. Ryza kept his eyes shut, focusing on each scratching brushstroke, pushing down the urge to flinch as Holm's fingers caressed his arm or lifted it out of the way, or ran down his chin to tilt his head at a slightly different angle.

They were touches not to test or hurt him, he told himself. He felt his breathing grow deeper and more relaxed, his mind calm.

When Ryza opened his eyes and looked down, he could have sworn his chest had turned green. Holm had emptied three entire vials to make the sixty or so runes that were now at his disposal. They were laid out in careful rows that contoured to his muscles, each set meant for a specific axiom, yet also positioned close enough to others that they could be rearranged with the slightest thought.

'If we get lucky tomorrow, you might never need ink again.' She stood and stretched, reaching high into the air and almost touching the ceiling. 'Hop off, it's your turn to do me.'

Ryza stood up and she took his place, closer to the wavering lamplight. He considered putting his shirt back on, but the ink was probably still drying. The last thing he'd need tomorrow was a smudged rune ruining an axiom and getting him killed.

Turning his attention to Holm, his hands instantly fell idle. She was still wearing her charred forge room leathers under her greatcoat. It felt wrong to tear them off just like she'd done to him, but before he could make a decision, Holm had shrugged off her greatcoat. It hit the floor with a flump and she was suddenly unbuttoning the top half of her leathers. Ryza quickly averted his gaze, feeling his face flush red-hot.

What the hell am I about to see?

It was strange how a woman disrobing in front of him made his hands shake more than the thought of tomorrow's fight. At least he'd been in battles before. Without looking at Holm, he moved around to the small table she'd set the ink and brush on. There were still three whole vials.

Plenty left, though she does have a bit more arm to cover than I do.

He took his place on the stool in front of her and looked at Holm. The top half of her leathers now hung loose from her waist, her chest now only covered by what looked like a fraying apron she'd improvised into an undershirt. It left her shoulders, her back and her ribs exposed, and along with little else to the imagination.

Not that my imagination needs much help right now.

She offered her left hand, a playful smile on her face.

'Never seen you this nervous,' she gently teased as he got to work.

'It's normal to be nervous in new situations, right?'

'A half-naked woman is new to you?'

Holm giggled yet again and Ryza found himself doing the same. He grew more comfortable as he worked his way up her arm, secretly admiring the firm musculature that twitched under his touch. Why he'd ever thought of her as diminutive and waiflike was a mystery. She felt strong enough to punch a man out in one blow.

Maybe that's why she didn't carry a gun.

'I've heard this was how lovers used to prepare each other for war,' Holm remarked idly.

'You say we're lovers?' Ryza mumbled. He was concentrating on a complicated axiom he was putting on her back and hadn't caught the nature of her playful jab.

'Well, we fight like it.'

Ryza blushed harder than before and counted himself lucky he'd moved behind her to work across her shoulders. He decided instead to change the subject. 'Why were you trying to get under my skin all the time? It wasn't just about the Locusts, right?'

Holm chuckled. 'You probably hated my guts, didn't you? Could see it all over your face whenever I was around. But you never really cracked. You didn't care about reels and no matter how riled up I got you, you always kept coming back. I've only just realised why that was.'

'And how's that?' Ryza said without thinking.

Holm looked over her shoulder, fixing him with a gaze that froze him in place and made his heart beat out of his throat. 'Lust.'

Ryza could only stammer nonsense. Holm giggled and turned away, letting him get back to his work. It was nearly impossible to concentrate now.

'I reckon, deep down, you always had a bit of a thing for me. You just never really realised it. I remember the day after your first mission—'

'The one you tried to kill me on.'

'I was standing on the other side of the mess hall looking all nervous and desperate, trying to catch your eye. It clearly worked. When you came over you seemed to be enjoying it a little too much.'

Ryza shrugged, trying to keep his cool. 'But what does that mean?'

'I told you to go see the Locusts and, against all odds, where do I see you next?'

'Okay, so maybe I did, but—'

Holm cut him off with another giggle. 'Your secret's safe with me, Rusty. Now you'd best hurry up, I've still got plenty of spare skin here.'

Stopping the blood from rushing to his face when she pulled up her shirt and directed him to work on her abdomen was hard enough, but it didn't help that she was staring down at him like she was a dune cat and he was a trapped mouse.

By the time he was finished, Ryza was ready to fall asleep where he sat. Holm stood up —not even bothering to do up her leathers— and made her way to the sagging couch at the corner of the room.

'Why don't you come upstairs?' Ryza blurted.

She turned, a slight grin playing on her face and he explained.

'I don't know where you slept last night, but there's an actual bed up there, better than this, better than Revance, even..'

She sidled over to him, half-straddling his lap as she placed a hand on his hip, then taking one of his to place on hers.

'Is that an invitation?' she said with a wink.

Ryza couldn't stop himself from smiling back. 'I'll let you make that choice.'

CHAPTER THIRTY-SIX

FORTRESS OF SMOKE

THE NEXT MORNING, THE air around Iroka was a tense fog to be waded through as patrolling conscripts swapped uneasy glances. Ryza's current position had him stood on the ramparts, mostly shielded from view by a canvas parapet. He kept his hands clasped behind his back; the metal left clenching and unclenching, occasionally splitting entirely to reveal the hidden gun barrel in his arm.

Under his greatcoat, he was once again armoured. Origin had left behind enough sets to kit out most of them, with only those assigned to the gun emplacements having to forgo the protection. What Origin had made wasn't nearly as sturdy as what Revance had equipped him with, barely thick enough to stop a hasty knife swing or a glancing shot. Even then, the plates only protected his chest and his thighs.

At least he'd be able to move quickly. A bolt-lock hung from an improvised leather strap at his shoulder along with a pouch of extra pointed rods that the weapon called ammunition. With the precious little time left to them that morning, the conscripts had drilled with the weapons with little risk of running out of the easily reusable bolts, but there was never going to be anything as good as a well-placed rifle slug.

Holm stood at his side, similarly armed and armoured. She cut an intimidating figure. She'd spent the morning pacing the walls and no one had been brave enough to call her out as being a former Locust. Maybe they were just glad to have her on their side.

A wall of fire now crossed the canyon, flames licking thick lines of coal with enthusiasm as they belched an impenetrable barrier of black smoke. When Revance came into the valley, they'd only have luck and their prior knowledge of Iroka to guide their guns.

Ryza turned his back on the valley for the first time in an hour. The guns on the walls took the form of the half-dozen long-wreckers they'd been able to drive up to the very edge of the ramparts. They were now sunk into hastily dug pits and ringed by barricades of stacked rock that would protect them for at least the first half of the battle. The rest of their cannons were sheltered at the entrance of the mines that overlooked Iroka.

Just beyond the inner gates, Iroka's town square had been cleared to make space for a veritable armada of vehicles. Between the fragile buggies and the sturdier but slower treadhulks, there had to be nearly a hundred. Origin's magnetic resonance still ran through them, providing them with power in place of the oil they didn't have. They were split up into six separate formations, each headed by a lead-better marked by a coat of barely dry paint.

Hundreds of conscripts milled in the narrow gaps between formations, most too nervous to mount up until the signal was given. It would take time for all the vehicles to funnel through the narrow tunnel that was Iroka's gates, but the delay was more palatable than waiting out in the open.

An empty yellow lead-better sat at the fore of a waiting convoy positioned furthest from the gates. This was to be crewed by Ryza and Holm. He spotted Ruka and Ditric among the troops that milled nearest it. They'd been attempting to keep their energy up with improvised war chants, but the morning had stretched on far too long for them to have any use now.

'Surprised they still have the energy,' Holm remarked.

Ryza shrugged. 'It's all Ruka at this point. Don't think she's slept since we came back from the ruins.'

'Something happen to you down there too?'

Ryza looked her in the eyes for the first time in hours and fixed her with a blank stare. She turned back to the open canyon, deciding not to push the question. Of course things happened to them down there, but Ryza couldn't say what. He, Ruka and Ditric hadn't said a word about it since getting to Iroka. They hadn't wanted to risk thinking about it.

Yet every quiet and lonesome moment had been filled with thoughts of the shadow dancer. He'd tried to suppress it, but his subconscious was the one thing he could not control, always presenting images of Archarus when he was on his own.

To Ryza's relief, Holm's voice broke the silence.

'Flare! I see a flare!' she called, pointing to the smoke.

A ball of fire had just pierced it, soaring twice as high as the surrounding cliffs. It was the sign they'd been waiting for all morning. At dawn, they'd sent out six scouts. They'd been given only two orders. The first was to ignite the line of coal that crossed the narrowest point of the canyon which was a mile out from Iroka's walls. The second was to signal when Revance was approaching. One flare to alert Iroka, the second to ready their weapons, then a third to open fire.

Similar calls rippled across the wall and the conscripts below readied themselves, piling into their buggies. They wouldn't be moving for a while, but it was better than doing nothing. Ryza turned back to the smoke, peering into it, wishing he could just see through it.

If I could see through it, then they could too. That's not what we want.

A few stretching minutes later, the second flare came through.

'Ready the guns!' Ryza roared. 'Ready the guns!'

The crews of the nearby long-wreckers burst into action. Dust covers were flung aside, shells were loaded and barrels braced. The ground was beginning to shake beneath his feet, the telltale quake that Revance always brought with it. But it didn't feel like the rhythmic thumping of each step that he was familiar with. Instead, it was a constant low rumble that threatened to dissolve the dunes themselves.

He pushed the worry to the back of his mind. It was a given that Tyrag would've done something to Revance, but it wouldn't be enough to protect him from the pounding of Iroka's guns.

Focusing on the smoke, he could only pray the scouts were still alive to send that vital third flare. After giving them their orders, he'd told the six of them to simply run once they'd got their job done. They'd be in no position to join the battle without being slaughtered and the flares would have drawn too much attention to them.

Ryza spotted the third flare.

'Fire guns! Fire all guns!'

Ryza kept roaring the order at the top of his lungs as the long-wreckers and artillery let loose. The screaming shells of more than twenty cannons pierced the smoke. Flashes of blue sky could be seen beyond it through the trailing holes they momentarily left. Violent detonations echoed back as they hit their unseen target, matched with the unmistakable screech of warping metal.

Their guns' pace didn't falter as they sent out barrage after barrage, only pausing when the first shot came in reply. An immense cannon blast split the air before a red-hot shell the size of a lead-better came soaring towards them in a high arc, crashing into the lower half of Iroka's outer wall with a spray of pulverised rubble.

The rest of Revance's guns started to puncture the smoke, marking the canyon and cliff walls with craters and pockmarks, yet hopelessly missing Iroka's vital emplacements. Hope was growing in Ryza's mind. Maybe they'd disable the fortress before it could even make it through the smoke.

By the Holm's calculations, it would take Revance a solid twelve minutes to make it from the point of their first bombardment to the smoke. So far, only four had passed.

'Maybe we won't even see them,' Holm shouted over the barrage.

'If they fall behind the smoke, then we'll be the ones charging through it!' Ryza replied.

As time wore on, the shots coming through the smoke grew more accurate. The overhanging rock that sheltered Iroka's mines was working against them, ricocheting shells bound for the bare cliff into the firing pits at the mines. A lucky blast took out one of the central crews, detonating their munition store along with them and damaging their neighbour. A few of their own guns were silenced, but that was an acceptable loss. The frequency of the shots coming from Revance had already reduced and the biggest shells were absent.

At the six-minute mark, the wall of smoke began to swirl and ripple. The iron prow of Revance suddenly punched through it and Ryza felt the blood leave his face. Holm had sworn they'd have *at least* twelve minutes! The fortress kept coming, the metallic hull gliding through the smoke, the black clouds rolling off it as it advanced. Ryza's jaw dropped. He wasn't even aware of it. The fortress hadn't stopped to take a step.

'That thing... that ain't Revance,' Ryza murmured to himself.

'It's... it's flying...' Holm said.

Iroka's guns fell silent as they looked upon Revance in a mixture of awe and horror. The bottom of its hull hovered a clear fifty metres above the ground. The legs had been cleaved off. The remaining joints had been replaced with towering redoubts that were decked out with gunports and boarding ramps.

The front of the fortress now bore a massive, wedged battering ram, pockmarked from their barrage but nonetheless intact. The whole time their salvos would've been glancing harmlessly off it. Above it, far above where any of the gunners had been aiming, was a bristling array of cannons and mortars that surrounded Revance's primary cannon.

Ryza had never seen the weapon fired. Even when Yuvet had told him about it, its last use was a distant memory for her. She hadn't even been sure if the enormous shells it took were still good, or if they were more likely to carve out a third of the fortress in one colossal misfire.

This was where Ryza's futile hopes lay, but he knew they were about to be dashed. A grumble of steel filled the valley as the cannon was brought to bear. The yawning muzzle flashed with a blast that nearly blew him from his feet and belched a shell the size of a lead-better.

It careened through the air for a whole five seconds before it hit Iroka's walls dead centre and detonated. The shockwave threw Ryza and Holm against the back of the parapet. He scrambled to cover her body with his own, a shower of rubble battering his armoured back a few seconds later.

Ryza was on his feet before the dust had settled, dragging Holm with him as the rest of Revance's artillery began to pound the ramparts. They leapt down whole flights of carved steps as the cliffs shook and more shells whizzed overhead. Their lookout exploded behind them and one of the nearby long-wreckers went next.

The rest of the conscripts on the walls fled with them, hopefully still sticking to the next part of the plan. Under this kind of bombardment, there wasn't a chance of communicating anything else.

The first two convoys had already set off, the third streaming through the gates as the others revved impatiently. Falling debris had flattened a few of the unlucky buggies towards the rear, but the rest of their force was still largely undamaged.

Ryza and Holm reached the square and piled into their yellow lead-better. Ditric was leaning out of the top hatch of the treadhulk behind them, roaring at them to get moving. The other convoys had already left, leaving them a clear path ahead.

From the driver's seat, Holm forced the lead-better's gears to scream at a fever pitch and launched them towards the tunnel. Ryza rallied the remaining vehicles with a few shouts and they rocketed through Iroka's gates. The dark quickly gave way to the exploding pinprick of light, then they were out on the battlefield.

From the ground, the flying fortress was colossal. It had cleared the wall of smoke and was still pounding Iroka with alarming accuracy. But the exchange of shells overhead was yet to become one-sided. Iroka's guns still fired valiantly, attempting to reach high enough to strike Revance's artillery but only scratching the armoured prow.

At least Revance hadn't started targeting the lead-betters or the treadhulks. Ryza twisted in his seat, spotting the latter trailing at the back of their pack. Origin's modifications had apparently turned them into mobile bulwarks, able to deploy at a moment's notice. While Ryza hadn't seen them in action, they would give them a foothold on the desolate battlefield.

Ryza looked back up at the fortress. The battering ram was weakening. Massive chunks of metal fell in layers that landed among the advanced convoys with ground-shaking thuds, kicking up arching sprays of sand.

'How the hell did Tyrag get that thing in the air?' Ryza shouted over the noise of the engine.

'Something to do with the magnetism of the land itself. Must take a thousand autominds to resist it like that,' Holm replied. 'What's the course?'

'Stay clear of it. We need to wait for it to land before we can do anything.'

On his orders, Holm veered the buggy right, taking their convoy up to the wall of the canyon and out of the fortress' path.

Revance rumbled by on their left, the sheer force of whatever was keeping it airborne causing the dunes to dissolve and their vehicles to shudder. Ryza focused on its flanks, trying to spot a weak spot they could exploit. The gunports had been sealed shut. More layers of armoured plating covered them, splitting occasionally to allow heavily supported struts to stick out.

The sight of it was heartening. It meant Tyrag intended to land, either because he needed to fight hand to hand or because he couldn't maintain an altitude like this for long. Ryza ordered Holm to loop around the rear of the fortress and soon the convoy was crossing through its endless shadow. In the distance, Iroka's walls had been reduced to rubble, which meant most of their big guns were well and truly out of commission.

High above, Tyrag must've realised the same. A metal scream filled the valley and the massive fortress began to descend. Their vehicles skidded as the sand around them was shaken loose and Ryza reached instinctively for the set of goggles in his greatcoat's pocket.

'Slow down and take positions!' he roared to the nearby vehicles. The orders were relayed through the convoy, leaving the buggies to circle in evasive maneuverers as the treadhulks deployed. Outside of Revance's looming shadow, they ground to a halt, the walls of each swinging forward to form a defensive blockade as the roof rose up like a tiny watchtower. Two more nearby formations did the same.

Near the opposite walls of the canyon, a pair of other convoys ground had to a halt. Ryza scanned the horizon for the last convoy, quickly spotting it lagging far behind where it should be. They'd been forced to stall as they'd navigated the rocky terrain that had emerged in the dunes. Now their only chance to get out from Revance's shadow was a mad dash straight under its descending hull. Already, Ryza knew the treadhulks weren't going to make it.

The buggies and the faster lead-betters were halfway under as the fortress kicked up its pace. A few of them peeled off, attempting to make it out the sides instead, but the fool at the wheel of the yellow lead-better stubbornly stayed the course. Moments later, the surrounding sand whirled into a storm and consumed their vehicles.

Ryza could only imagine their screams of terror as dust engulfed the unlucky bastards, blocking their fate from sight. He swore under his breath. They'd lost a fifth of their force already.

'Sandstorm!'

The panicked shout rippled across their lines as the undulating wall of dust completely obscured Revance as it touched down. The ground quaked as it did, sending the sand rushing towards them in a fierce gale.

Ryza yanked on his goggles as Holm wrestled the lead-better to a standstill. In a second, they would be blind. Their only hope of shelter lay with the treadhulks, the nearest almost fifty metres away. He took one last look at Holm, grabbing her hand tight with his right and hanging on to the lead-better's roll cage with his left.

He clenched his eyes shut as the wall of orange dust bore down on him, remembering that first, horrible moment he'd been plucked from the ground in the sandstorm that had brought him to Revance.

Now Revance has come to me.

Chapter Thirty-Seven

The Blind Offensive

The lead-better bucked like a wild beast as the sandstorm hit, spinning against its wheels as it was dragged through the dunes. The sound of tearing metal reached them over the roar of the gale. The chassis jolted and suddenly it vanished from Ryza's grip and he was airborne, clinging desperately to Holm until she too fell away.

He found himself on his back, half-buried in a sandy grave. He shook the sand from his armour as he staggered to his feet. He still had his arm, his bolt-lock, and nothing felt broken. It was a miracle he'd escaped with nothing more than a split lip. But this was a small mercy. He was carrying enough injuries as it was.

The yellow lead-better lay a few steps away, overturned and partially consumed by the still-settling dunes. Holm was crawled from under it as Ryza reached it. She attempted to wave off his help as she found her feet but he pulled her up anyway. The dust Revance's landing had kicked up now hung in the air, suspended by the wind as an orange haze. He couldn't even see the nearest treadhulk from here, let alone Revance itself.

'This ain't good Ryza,' Holm coughed. She gave the buggy a small kick. 'This thing's useless. And how the hell are we going to see them coming?'

'Could use an axiom, but then we'd give ourselves away. We stick to the plan.'

They started walking, their heads low against the whirling sand and their ears pricked. Soon a treadhulk came into sight. Bolt-locks poked from the gun ports on its deployed walls, each one wielded by a conscript perched on a firing step on the other side. When they reached it, they found another twenty conscripts huddled in the shelter. A set of hands darted out as he and Holm rounded its corner and pulled them into cover. It was Ruka. Her pupils were pinpricks as she squinted in shock between them.

'I thought we'd lost you both in the storm. I was in the treadhulk the whole time.' She turned and called to Ditric, who seemed to appear from nowhere.

'Glad you two made it,' Ditric said. 'Ruka, can you clear this sandstorm?'

'No,' Ryza said sharply. 'If we clear it, they'll be able to see us. Maybe this is an advantage.'

'How?' Holm said. 'We're split up. We can't even see if the rest of the force is still there.'

'If they can't see us, they don't get the chance to hole up in the motor pool. Right now, they come to us if they want a fight.'

Ditric grunted in agreement. 'Hope the rest of the line figures that out.' She turned to the nearby conscripts, raising her voice. 'You all hear that? Heads down, take them as they come!'

They waited in silence, straining to hear over the still rushing sand. The fortress' guns were dormant. The ground had stopped rumbling.

After a few minutes, war cries broke the dust. They were brash and arrogant. The sound of hundreds of feet marching on metal followed. Revving engines came with them, but Ryza couldn't be sure whether they were theirs or the smelters. He peeked through a gunport. The dust was swirling, shapes moving within.

'Ready weapons!' Ryza shouted.

The conscripts stacked up against the wall. Gunfire began to echo out in the distance. The harsh clangs of bolt-locks replied. Ryza levelled his own bolt-lock and frowned as figures came into view. They weren't charging at them. They were walking and it wasn't with the pace of soldiers cautiously approaching combat. As the forms drew closer, Ryza realised who they were. Who they'd been.

They were unarmed, dressed in rags and their silver-flecked skin underneath was stretched across their bones. Each step was shambling and senseless. Their eyes saw without sight. Their hands hung limp and defenceless.

The cannon fodder.

'Don't shoot! Nobody shoot!' Ryza ordered.

Holm slapped him on the shoulder. 'You want them to hit us first?'

'They're autominds! They want us to waste ammo! Ditric, rally the Curiktics, put them down with fire!'

Ditric slung her bolt-lock and began cracking her knuckles. A ball of dripping fire burst to life in her hands as she stepped in front of the treadhulk's bulwark. 'You heard the Bloodfist! Let's give them the heat!'

A dozen others followed her. Arcing jets of fire lanced out over the stumbling hoard, quickly blanketing them in an inferno. The autominds didn't scream, they just took a few more sickening steps before their flesh failed and they fell.

Ryza watched in horror as their skin burst and began to ooze molten flux, quickly turning into rapidly spreading puddles of silver. It crackled into sharp forms under the fire's wrath, pointing like spikes from their pools before retreating and dissolving into the sand itself.

The smell of burnt flesh reached him, quickly followed by the sickeningly sweet aroma of the flux threatening to blaze. It was another hazard on the battlefield to avoid, lest he wanted to turn into an automind himself. Having a single drop touch his skin was enough to do it over a course of hours. With the amount now present, it could happen in seconds and Ryza wasn't sure which he'd prefer.

Another wave of autominds came. It was put down just as efficiently as the first, and Ryza began to wonder what the purpose of it even was. These were just the used-up and expired autominds he anticipated he'd be replacing.

What if it's a distraction?

The sound of crunching gears and thumping footsteps immediately followed the thought. Metal was slamming on metal before that sound also faded into the sand.

'What the hell is that?' Ditric asked as she re-joined them behind the bulwark, her hands still smoking.

'The real force,' Ryza grunted.

He peered through the gunport again. The haze began to thin. Large, dark figures were coming in and out of sight as the dust continued to settle. They were square at their highest point, twice as tall as the shadowed smelters that dashed between them.

'Why aren't they attacking us?' Holm muttered.

'They're waiting for us,' Ryza said. 'The autominds were the bait. If we took it, we'd be running into the same trap we've set.'

'Think we should go out there?' Ruka said.

'Send out a pulse first,' Ryza ordered. 'Let's see what they're doing.'

Ruka climbed the bulwark, standing atop the wall as she marshalled her axioms. The air boomed and for a moment, the sand cleared, creating a barrel of vision straight ahead. Through a gunport, Ryza sighted the motor pool's ramp.

The smelters were deploying a perimeter of heavy metal walls, though the surface of them wasn't smooth or thick. It just seemed loose. Even the men nearby were scurrying away from them, back to the safety of the motor pool behind them. Maligar was presiding over the sudden retreat, standing atop the ramp as the dust returned to cloud their vision.

'Maligar's here,' Ryza muttered.

Out of the corner of his eye, Holm stiffened. Her jaw was clenched, knuckles white on her bolt-lock and her finger testing the trigger. She looked up at Ruka.

'Give me another air pulse.'

Ryza didn't even need to be touching her to feel the fury radiating in her magnetic resonance. Before Ryza could refute the order, Holm had dashed out into the open, sprinting into no-man's-land.

Without thinking, Ryza went after her, feet pounding the sand as he braced himself for a volley of slugs to fly through the haze and tear him to shreds. Maligar's shout pierced the air before Ryza caught up with her.

'Blow the charges!'

A rapid-fire chain of explosions lit the hazy sky bright orange as the dunes quaked beneath him. Another set went off, closer this time and Ryza felt flecks of shrapnel flick by his head.

'Holm!' he screamed.

The next shockwave sprayed him with dust and he dove to the ground, losing track of her entirely as he copped a face full of sand. All he could do was cover his ears and pray another blast wouldn't come. But come it did.

The ground broke under him and suddenly Ryza couldn't feel his legs. He thrashed as hard as he could, stuck beneath what felt like an entire desert of sand. All he could hear was a constant, high scream. His metal hand took on a life of its own, slamming down in the sand. With one titanic pull, it wrenched him out of his shallow grave.

Your life's not over.

Ryza wasn't sure why he'd had the thought, or if it had even been his own. The arcanite was long gone and it wasn't like he could hear him through the arm Origin had left as a gift, right?

He crawled slowly, sliding his hands through the dune until he uncovered his bolt-lock. The fortress landing had been bad, but this was downright hell. Bearings utterly lost, Ryza heaved himself to his feet and turned slowly on the spot.

A few pieces of shrapnel prickled somewhere in his hip, but over the slapping waves of sand carried by the wind and the amount of sheer panic replacing what was once a blood rush, he barely felt it.

The haze was too dense. He'd never see the smelters coming, and finding Holm was completely out of the question.

Remember your axioms.

It was another thought injected by Origin through his arm and it was exactly what he needed. He summoned the axiom for a basic pulse into his right hand, adding a few extra runes to put the twist on it to identify Kretatic resonances at range. He just needed to find more of Origin's resonance. It was within the bolt-locks and the vehicles and would lead him back to his allies, back to safety.

The last rune of the axiom burned hot and Ryza froze in place as a sickening wave of energy rippled outwards from his chest. It skimmed the surface of the dunes and dove under them, picking up the chittering madness of the burrowing molten flux already spilled in the battle.

But there was more.

At least thirty different resonances surrounded him, some as close as a few metres away. All of them had to be Kretatics. Smelters. They would have felt his pulse. They'd soon suspect Ryza wasn't one of them. A magnetic pulse came at him and shook his bones.

See as Rettic saw.

Origin's voice popped into his head again and Ryza's reeling mind had no idea what to make of it. He dropped low into a crouch, pushing his left hand into the dirt to support himself as another pulse threw him off balance. There was a slight clink of metal against his fingers. Pieces of shrapnel. Just like those scattered by the man he'd met in Kyrea.

Ryza heard shouts through the haze as he rushed to summon the right runes. First thing was to use an axiom for controlling metal without touching it. Enough to capture his surroundings, but not too much to overwhelm his mind. He still needed his wits. The metal needed to float. That part was easy when the pieces were small. After that, it just needed to cling to anything it hit.

Ryza slammed his hand into the ground as the last rune burnt in his palm. A thousand shards of metal were suddenly his, rising out of the ground and hovering against the wind at knee height. As he glanced around. They seemed to glow green in his vision, like tiny flames that cut through the dust.

He clenched his fist and the shrapnel flew in every direction. It thumped into bodies, rocks and sand, but Ryza was only concerned with the first. He could feel them struggling to brush it off, twisting and writhing. But it was in vain. The same shrapnel they'd tried to kill him with was now embedded in their skin.

Slowly, he stood up. The haze was starting to fade again. Raising his bolt-lock, he aimed for the nearest man's torso and pulled the trigger twice. Two loud clangs split the air as the bolt-lock rocked from recoil. The first iron bolt passed straight through his chest, the second lodging in his stomach as he hit the ground.

Alarmed shouts split the air and blind rifle shots followed them. Slugs whizzed past Ryza's face as he moved onto the next man, closing the gap in a few steps before putting a bolt into the smelter's head at point-blank range.

He fell as the rest closed in. Ryza spun and shot into the dust and was instantly rewarded with a gurgling scream of pain as another smelter went down. From his left, one came charging out of the haze and Ryza raised his arm, splitting the metal hand to reveal the rifle barrel. Two shots sounded and a slug whizzed past Ryza's head as the smelter wailed in pain.

The combat developed a rhythm. Before a smelter even appeared in the haze, they'd be put down by a quick bolt from Ryza. It took all his focus. There was no time to dwell on where the rest of his squad was or if Holm was alive.

The bolt-lock ran dry and Ryza tossed it aside, scrambling to reload his arm's gun. Before he could close the latch, he sensed a smelter aiming at him. He ducked and a slug screamed over his head.

Another smelter dashed forward, kicking Ryza in the ribs before he had the chance to dodge. He absorbed the blow on his chest plate, but it still threw him to the ground.

Another kick caught him in the side, flipping him onto his stomach as all the air was knocked out of him. More smelters were coming. He could feel them through the shrapnel. Desperately, Ryza swung his arms through the sand, catching a smelter's ankle with his left as a hand clamped down on his neck.

They both grunted in pain and Ryza channelled all his rage into his grip, turning it into a crushing vice that pierced the flesh and pulverised the bones, forcing a wailing scream from the smelter. He yanked harder, twisting his grip to snap the man's leg cleanly in two. Ryza scrambled to straddle the thrashing smelter, finishing them with a clumsy left hook to the throat.

Still breathing hard from the melee, Ryza strained to bring himself to his knees. Smelters still surrounded him. At least a dozen were coming. Somehow, they knew they had him dead to rights. Hope ebbed out of him as he shut his eyes. Around him, the wind picked up and he waited for the lethal shot to pierce it.

I'm going to die lost in a sandstorm like I was meant to all along.

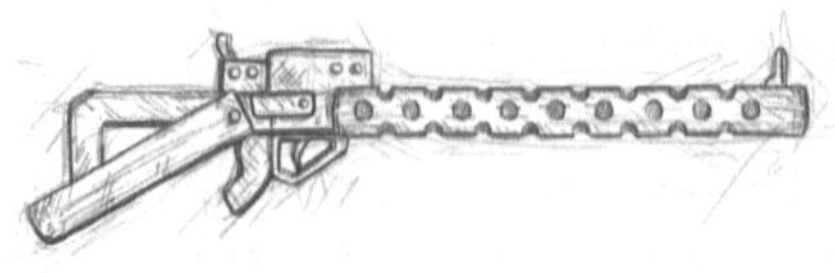

CHAPTER THIRTY-EIGHT

THE DUST CLEARS

S HOUTS, GUNSHOTS AND BATTLE cries were lost in a growing gale. Soon it was all he could hear. He cracked open an eye and frowned. The haze was gone, replaced with blue skies above and sand that lay tranquil at his knees.

Around him, smelters were being cut down in waves by volleys of bolt-lock fire. Their bodies joined the charred remains of the autominds. Some of them still twitched as their silver eyes stared at him, their rent skin leaking molten flux.

'Sick and fucking tired of you going after that fucking girl,' a voice grunted from behind him. It was Ditric. She grabbed his coat with both hands and began dragging him back to shelter.

Across the battlefield, the conscripts pushed forward, taking cover behind the massive pieces of scrap metal that Revance had already shed. Groups of over-extended smelters were caught out in the advance and fell quickly to the crossfire. The other retreating smelters were almost as unlucky.

The howling roar of a speeding lead-better hurtled past, crashing through the smelter's lines and brutally mowing them down, spitting gouts of fire over anyone quick enough to dodge out of the way.

Ditric threw Ryza behind an overturned buggy and slapped him hard. The blow brought him back to his senses.

'No point making you leader if you're going to get yourself killed! Some of the other Reythurists started clearing the storm so we had to go along with them. Looks like the bastards got caught out by it.'

Ryza peeked out from behind the buggy. Tyrag's smelters might be scattered, but most of them were swarming to the enormous ramp that led to the motor pool's yawning mouth. He reloaded his arm and looked at Ditric.

'We need to take that motor pool before they can fortify it!' Ryza shouted. He turned to the rest of his force. They were still taking cover either in the bulwark or behind nearby buggies like him. 'Push forward! We'll never get to Tyrag otherwise!'

Ryza charged headlong back into the battle, a thundering of boots accompanying him. They dodged from cover to cover, swiftly closing in on the smelter's lines. The debris was dense, allowing them to flank around and sweep out any resistance.

It was like he was back in the scrapyard where he'd first tried to save Holm. They were forced to hunker down as they drew closer to the motor pool. The smelters came at them with discordant charges that fell to the volleys of their bolt-locks. But it wouldn't be so easy forever. He kept his eyes on the fortress, spotting another wave of smelters and Locusts pouring out.

'Counterattack!'

Soon Ryza swore they were outnumbered two to one. The smelters hadn't been retreating, they'd been getting help. The conscripts fought viciously to hold their ground, repelling each wave thanks to Ruka. She hovered above them, sending out blast after explosive blast of wind, staggering anyone stupid enough to assault their position and making them easy pickings.

The tide of battle was turning again. Ryza was about to call for another charge when a stray round caught Ruka's side. It sent her spinning to the ground and Ditric was the first to dash after her, lost between the battle and debris.

Ryza crouched low and scurried off in pursuit, ducking shots as he went. He found her a few metres beyond their impromptu fortifications, knelt over Ruka, her hands glowing as she worked on her bloody hip.

'This ain't good,' Ditric shouted quickly. 'The slug only grazed her but I need a few minutes. Hold them off!'

Ditric's hands burned brighter as she pressed them into Ruka's wounds, causing her to scream in pain. A fresh scar was there when she withdrew, but as it started to prickle with droplets of blood, Ditric went in again.

Ryza scanned the motor pool for the source of the shot. It was a pointless exercise. There must have been a hundred rounds going off every second, but despite it all, he zeroed in on one figure. He was marching towards them with a smoking rifle in his hands. A gleaming suit of armour encased his entire body, each piece of the carapace perfectly interlocked with the next.

'Maligar.'

Maligar spotted him and his face lit up, mouthing a single word Ryza didn't need to hear.

'Bloodfist.'

Maligar launched into a breakneck sprint, instantly outpacing the smelters that charged with him. Something about his armour carrying him at alarming speeds. Ryza took position in front of Ditric, burning an axiom to send out a detection pulse.

Through the haze of resonances across the battlefield, he found the armour. It must've been made up of a thousand pieces with not a single weld or wire holding them together. They moved in perfect concert, trumpeting Maligar's lustful and gluttonous resonance with every move.

Maligar had total control over it. The whole thing was an arcanite. That was why he was so fast! He'd probably be stronger, too. But there was something more to it, a faint chittering sensation that lay beyond Maligar's extravagant and roaring resonance.

Ryza quickly assessed his surroundings. Massive, twisted hunks of what had once been Revance formed narrow alleyways around them. Corpses lay scattered between them, belonging to fallen autominds, smelters and conscripts alike. The surviving fighters on both sides were too distracted to pay attention to their duel.

Maligar's head was still exposed. One clean shot and he'd be dead. Ryza braced his left arm with his right, aiming his hidden slug gun at it. He juked and weaved with his sprint, cleaving through any conscripts he passed with his sheer bulk.

Before Ryza could ready his stance, Maligar leapt, hurtling thirty feet through the air as he led with a blindingly fast fist. Ryza attempted to dodge it, but the blow caught his chest, glancing off his already dented breastplate. His right shoulder smashing into a hunk of scorched metal as he went down, hard enough to knock his senses loose.

Despite his enhanced armour, Maligar had overshot. He was staggering as Ryza lurched back to his feet. Maligar might be fast, but he certainly wasn't nimble. The wild punch alone had thrown him to his knees.

'I'd hoped we'd meet again, Ryza,' Maligar said. 'Especially here and now.' He pointed an armoured finger at him, slowly advancing. 'I wanted you to see what we'd become.'

Ryza strafed sideways, circling wide to draw him away from Ditric. A ring of scrap now sheltered them from the rest of the battle like an unnatural arena. 'Already knew you'd be remembered as a traitor. I don't see what's changed.'

Maligar made a feint and it caused Ryza to flinch. He laughed derisively. 'It's not about being remembered. It's about living. But you didn't want that! You wanted to throw away your entire lifetime and what have you got to show for it? Look how many you've got killed!'

'This battle has already killed plenty of yours,' Ryza spat back.

'And I'm going to make sure that never happens again.'

He charged again, but Ryza was ready for him. Diving right under his punch, Ryza grabbed Maligar's armoured leg with his left hand, crushing through metal with the might Origin had gifted him. There was a squelch of blood and bone as Maligar staggered sideways, his hands furiously working axioms back into the buckled metal to straighten it out. Ryza took the chance and darted in for the kill, but was held at bay by a wild flail of Maligar's arm.

Big mistake.

As Ryza had danced out of reach, he'd spotted a weak point under Maligar's arm. There was a gap in the armour's plating. Ryza split his metal hand aside to expose the gun barrel as he went in for another attack.

Maligar was ready for him and hurled a sweeping punch, exposing his under arm long enough for Ryza to shove his hidden gun into the gap and fire.

Deafened by the gunshot, Ryza didn't process the bloodied grunt of pain as Maligar stumbled back a few steps, but he certainly heard the ensuing roar of fury. They both stood still, Ryza reloading his arm gun and Maligar attempting to stave off shock. Blood streamed from his shoulder, painting his entire right side with crimson and...

Silver?

'That was a lucky shot, Bloodfist!'

Maligar actually spat blood with the last word. There were flecks of something silvery running down his lips as well.

'But it doesn't matter! We've already won! No matter who walks away from this, it doesn't—'

He was interrupted by a violent cough. More silver, enough for Ryza to be sure of what it was.

Molten flux.

Sick horror leapt in his chest. Maligar didn't just control the armour as an arcanite. Flux now flowed through his veins, bulging out of his temple and tinting his rage-stricken face. It would be consuming his blood, his muscles, even his mind. How the hell had he done it without turning into an automind himself?

'You've killed yourself to do this, haven't you?' Ryza taunted. 'You can't control the flux! You should've known that if you wanted to be a fucking smelter so badly!'

Maligar staggered sideways and leaned hard against a broken buggy's wheel. He looked up, his hand almost crushing the copper-spoked tyre as he scowled back at Ryza.

'It's not about what you know, Ryza.'

Catching him by surprise, Maligar hurled the wheel at him at such speed that Ryza couldn't even dodge. It pounded into his already bruised shoulder, knocking him clean from his feet.

'It's about what you don't!'

Ryza began crawling away, rolling to dodge a hurled corpse. It thudded to the ground next to him with a splash of oozing molten flux. Ryza glanced back at Maligar as he scrambled back from it.

He was ripping scraps off an overturned lead-better and grinned as he retrieved a piece that resembled a brutal javelin. More flux was leaking out of him, but it recoiled backwards with each beat of his heart, retrieving lost blood as it returned to his body.

'An empty mind is more open to knowledge than an expectant one. It's just a shame that you're so certain about what you know, rather than what you want. Just like Holm was.'

Maligar lobbed the jagged spear and Ryza ducked for cover behind another wreck, letting it take the blow instead.

'Shame she went missing. I never thought she had what it took. Not like Ferrick.' He paused for a moment as he towered over Ryza, savouring the moment before the final blow. 'You know, Holm had quite a thing for you.'

'Believe me, I know,' Ryza muttered under his breath. He rose to his feet, pointing his gun arm squarely at Maligar. Recoil coursed through his body as the round struck Maligar square in the chest, knocking him back a step.

Ryza didn't waste a moment, leaping towards the bastard and punching him square in the guts with his left, an axiom super-charging his fist to fly harder towards the metal. If he could just shock him enough, then he'd lose all control of his armour.

But Maligar didn't shift an inch. Ryza looked up into his bloody, silver-flecked smile and didn't even have time to swear before his gauntleted hands were around his neck. Maligar lifted him effortlessly, his bloodshot green eyes wide open and wild.

'You can't kill me that easily, Ryza!'

'Don't have to,' he managed to choke out. 'The flux already has.'

Maligar screamed in rage and threw Ryza like a rag doll. Thumping into a dune, he collapsed in a heap.

'You think I'm worried about dying?' Maligar roared as he advanced. 'I don't need to live like you do! I don't need this flesh or this body! The flux provides so much more!'

Maligar was on him now, a foot pressed down on Ryza's metal collar, pushing his skull into the sand. Ryza's vision was already flashing black as he continued to thrash in vain. He could feel drops of flux drizzling over him, hissing as it splashed off his clothes and his armour. If he died like this, he was all but guaranteed to become an automind.

But then the pressure suddenly released, and Maligar's screaming filled the air. Ryza coughed, rolling gingerly as armoured boots stamped down around his body. He rolled clear of the pounding dance, narrowly avoiding his arm being shattered before he looked up and gasped.

Caked in sand and back from the dead, Holm was riding Maligar's shoulders like he was a bucking animal. Her face was twisted into a murderous rage as she lost herself to violence, howling a primal scream with each plunge of her knife into Maligar's neck.

Hunks of armour fell from Maligar's body as he clutched in vain at Holm, failing to throw her off as he collapsed. Before the dust had settled, Holm was kneeling on his chest, driving fist after fist into his mess of a face as splashes of blood and flux coated her bare arms.

By the time Ryza had managed to pull her away from Maligar's lifeless body, she was a wreck, her knuckles bloodied and bruised beyond belief. Droplets of molten flux sizzled in her palms, but all she could do was whimper as she tried to brush them clean. But it was too late. The flux was gone. It was in her.

'Holm, the flux!' Ryza said.

'I don't care!' Holm spat. 'I got what I wanted!'

'But you— Someone help me!'

Ryza held her tight, making sure to keep her low as the battle raged around them. How she'd survived the blasts or the ensuing chaos was beyond him. So was the hatred she held for Maligar. Hatred she now had to pay for as the flux burrowed into her skin and infected her blood.

'I don't want you to be one of them,' Ryza said quickly. He was looking at his right hand, mind racing as he tried to arrange the necessary runes to draw the flux out of her.

'Then get this shit out of me already!'

'What if I can't? What if I fuck it all up!?'

He could see the droplets in the veins of her arms, starting as raised pinpricks and bulging to fill the bloodline with each beat of her heart. Her hand took to his cheek and he froze. It was tender, trembling, like nothing he'd felt before the night just passed that they'd spent together. The battle went quiet, the ringing in his ears replaced by that rare softness he'd only heard once before in her voice.

'I know you won't.'

The axiom burned. Ryza didn't even know which one it was. What runes it was made up of. He took Holm's hand. He could feel her fiery resonance in battle with the ceaseless whir of the flux.

The concept of one Kretatic controlling another was beyond taboo. It was impossible. Even the slightest spark of a resonance would resist it. But when Ryza reached in with his own resonance, Holm's was alongside him. Fighting with him as he corralled every drop of flux that had invaded her body.

It latched onto his presence, its deafening buzz filling his mind as it resisted. Ryza clamped down harder with his own resonance, pushing Holm's away until he couldn't sense it anymore. The flux thrashed against his mind in pulses, but despite its rapidly multiplying might, it was soon dribbling from the scratches that covered Holm's fists.

The bloody flux hit the ground, no more than a few drops in total, but it instantly began to spread. Ryza kicked away from it, pulling Holm with him as he buried it with thrown sand. He watched the spot for a tense moment, waiting for it to reappear, to dive back into her body and retake what it was so close to capturing.

But nothing happened.

He looked to Holm. Her eyes were closed. Running his thumb across her bruised lips, he let out a sigh of relief. Her breathing felt faint, but it was better than nothing. He'd done it. He'd saved her. Just as she'd saved him.

Ryza surveyed the battlefield. By the looks of things, they'd repelled the counterattack. What little was left of Tyrag's army was falling back to the motor pool and the conscripts were in hot pursuit. He resisted a grin. It wasn't over yet.

'Ryza? Ryza?' Ditric's voice called. 'Where the hell are you?'

'Over here! I need help!'

Ditric came rushing into view, followed by a few other conscripts that were forced to weave through the alleys of scrap.

'Who's that poor bastard?' she asked as she crouched next to him and began checking over Holm. 'Looks worse than what you did to Ferrick.'

'It's Maligar.'

'The head Locust?'

Ryza grimaced. 'Almost. Listen, we need to rally and take control of the—'

The ground rumbled underneath them, the vibrations causing the sand to start eating the battle's dead.

'What the hell is that?' one of the conscripts shouted.

'It's Revance,' Holm breathed. 'It's taking off.'

Ryza twisted to see the fortress as it began to shake, the dunes around it dissolving into nothing. He turned back to Ditric, speaking quickly.

'Change of plan! You all got to get back to Iroka and get the rest of the guns firing on that fortress! It cannot escape!'

'And what are you going to do?'

Ryza snatched a bolt-lock from a nearby conscript. 'I need to get Tyrag! I need to make sure he actually fucking dies!'

He started running, ignoring the shooting pain from his already exhausted legs. Ignoring the cries of protest from those he was leaving behind. It didn't matter if they still had the firepower to pound the fortress to dust. Just as Holm had been promised Maligar's death, Ryza needed to be the one to finish Tyrag.

For good.

The fortress began to shed its armoured plates as it rose slowly from the sand! Slugs whizzed past him, courtesy of the last few smelters holed up in the motor pool. He was still so far away, but the fortress was already a foot off the ground!

He could feel the air sucking him inwards as it lifted, only forcing him to run faster. It was four feet above the ground and Ryza still had around fifty metres to cover. He dug deep, finding a second wind that shouldn't exist and pushed on. Six feet, taller than him and Ryza was still ten metres away. But he was so close! Seven feet now, then eight feet.

It was too high!

Ryza jumped, an axiom burning in his hand as he took to the air.

CHAPTER THIRTY-NINE

A CHANGED REVANCE

RYZA'S BLOOD BUBBLED IN his veins, every drop of it yanking him towards the metal of the fortress' hull. With both hands, he barely managed to grab hold of a bent pipe, still not believing his luck of having the right axiom at the ready.

What he'd used was the first axiom a Kretatic learned.

Pull metal.

Ryza had first used it to steal a few of his father's reels from a high shelf, unaware at the time that the ink he'd just wasted to accomplish his thievery was worth far more than his prize. Up until this moment, he'd continued with the assumption that this simple axiom had the purpose of putting metal in his hands by drawing it *towards* him. He'd only been partly correct.

The axiom, in all its inert wisdom, had decided to accomplish its task in a far more direct way. Instead of putting in the effort to move the city-sized chunk of metal that was Revance, it had brought him to it

.

Ryza's legs flailed as the ground fell away and he struggled to consolidate his grip. The pipe was groaning under his weight. It could give way at any second. He swung himself to another pipe and pushed the toe of his boot into a nearby piece of exposed grating, using the leverage from it to wedge his knees further into the metal to stabilise himself.

Far below, streaming trails of dust billowed from the lead-betters that sped back to Iroka. He could only hope they were going to man the guns, not just to cower.

Even then, I wouldn't blame them.

It took him another ten minutes to scramble up to the side of the fortress. By then Revance was level with the cliff tops. His point of entry had him crouched in one of the narrow service halls Yuvet had taken him through on his first day. Leading with his bolt-lock, he turned right, heading in the direction of what he thought was the motor pool.

Instead, he ended up in front of an armoury near the front of the fortress. Either Tyrag had done something with the service corridors or he didn't know Revance as well as he thought. Ryza eased himself through the pried opened door and looked around.

The shelves were almost as empty as the corridors. The only thing left were the spent slugs that were scattered across the floor. Scorch marks and bullet holes lined the walls, and nasty bloodstains were already rusting into the floors. At least the traitors had removed the corpses.

They were probably autominds now.

'It was quite the fight.'

The low voice made Ryza jump. Archarus was standing at his side, eying off the bloodstains with a passing curiosity.

'I thought you'd turn up,' Ryza said curtly. He walked away from the shadow dancer, checking the shelves for ammo. Partly for something to load into his arm, partly so he wouldn't have to look at the spectre.

'I knew you would,' Archarus said, following him. 'I was counting on it.'

'You've got something planned for me, then?'

Archarus chuckled. 'You're the only one that made it aboard this fortress before it left the ground. If not you, then who else would stop Tyrag?'

'You don't want me here for just that,' Ryza sneered back. 'Origin told me about you, about what you want from me. To achieve something you couldn't.'

'What do you think that would be?'

'Controlling flux!' Ryza burst out.

'But you've already done it,' Archarus whisper. 'It's how you saved your lover.'

Ryza was suddenly immobile. He hadn't even thought about it that way. He'd done what Maligar had, but he wasn't dead. Not yet, at least.

'But that's only means to an end,' Archarus continued. 'Means which you can use to save yourself.'

'I will not,' Ryza growled.

Archarus watched silently as Ryza found an un-looted munitions case and tucked a few slugs into his ammo pouch.

'What's your plan for stopping Tyrag?'

Any warmth had disappeared from his voice.

Ryza loaded a slug into his arm. 'I'm going to find him and I'm going to blow his head clean off.' He slammed the latch shut and looked back at Archarus. 'And you're not going to help me.'

Suddenly the shadow dancer was toe-to-toe with him, staring him down with those unnaturally black eyes. 'What about your friends? Their collars? This fortress? You'll die in the fall.'

Ryza didn't back down. He took a deep breath, levelling calm into his voice 'Then it all ends here.'

He hadn't even finished speaking when Archarus disappeared. Ryza slumped. He'd heeded Origin's warning but it still felt like he was playing into Archarus' hands.

Leaving the armoury, he continued through the fortress, slinking through to the higher levels. The control room was his destination. Trickles of molten flux seeped from the walls as he made his way in. But they didn't hit the ground. They hovered in the air as droplets, orbiting between the still standing congregation of autominds and the now dormant golden core.

An injector gun still sat on the latter's console, though Ryza couldn't see a need for it now. This much flux would make him a fortune in Kyrea. Maybe the liquid now treated Revance as its vessel, duplicating and expanding to fill the space. He tried to remember what

Archarus had told him in the undercity, something about "thousands of machines," but it had long faded from his mind.

All he was worried about was if enough of it would gather for it to become blazing flux. Though it this strange state, it could be about to turn into something far worse.

Ryza held his breath, surveying the room. He'd been led to believe this was where Revance was controlled from, yet Tyrag was nowhere to be seen. He moved closer to one of the autominds, examining their gaunt, expressionless face. They were beyond decayed. Flux oozed from their pores. Gingerly, Ryza held his hand near the skin of one, wincing as he was greeted with Tyrag's resonance before he'd even made contact.

Virtually no resistance stood in his way as he set a course for the forge rooms. Anyone he met fled the moment they saw him. Sometimes Ryza gunned them down, sometimes he let them go, only to find them cowering around the corner. Dashes of silver quivered under their skin as they blubbered and Ryza put them out of their misery.

This wasn't right.

When he'd last seen Tyrag, he'd been preaching control of the lands using a newly reforged Revance, even if autominds were necessary to do so. He'd said, openly, that resistance would be crushed! But here was the fortress, empty and fleeing from a battle it should have won.

Something about what Maligar had said was still bothering him. In his last moments, he'd bragged of immortality before Holm had cut his life short. As delicious as the irony was, there was still something more to it.

Ryza paused next to one of the oozing streams of molten flux. Why would Tyrag want this much in one place? It only posed a hazard until it could be contained in an automind, but even then, it only took a single vial.

But what if it wasn't autominds that Tyrag wanted?

Ryza entered the forge rooms. This was the nerve centre of Tyrag's operation. Every repair bay had been replaced by a horde of autominds. They were tethered to the walls with tightly weaved steel cables that were fastened around their necks. Ryza jogged past them, losing count of how many dozens of autominds there were.

Below him, the rumbling of Iroka's bombardment grew stronger, a few of the blows threatening to knock him off his feet. At least they were effective. Ryza was already seeing cracks in Revance's hull from their efforts.

Tyrag won't be getting away. Not while I'm here.

Ryza broke out into the main hall of the forge rooms and gasped. Hundreds of autominds lined the walls, secured the same as the others. He'd come out on one of the upper balconies. The massive void in the centre of the room now boasted a two-hundred-metre drop. From this angle, Ryza couldn't even see what they were above.

Ryza spotted Tyrag on the other side of the chasm. The old man was standing on his dais, shackled between four pylons of curved metal. Golden cuffs were fastened at his wrists, each one attached by thick copper wire to the two nearest pylons. Ryza found a ladder and descended to the bottom level. The floor felt thin here. One good shot from Iroka would blow a hole clean through.

I won't need to be here for long.

He'd only made it three steps from the ladder before Tyrag noticed him.

'Ryza,' he called out. His voice wasn't panicked. It wasn't full of fury or hate. Tyrag was calm. Cold and calm. 'Come, boy. I've been waiting for you to find me.'

Ryza hesitated. This had to be a trap. But against his own good sense, he was already edging closer.

'That's it. I'm sure you've got questions.'

Ryza squinted down the length of his bolt-lock as Tyrag came into view. His cheeks were hollow and grey, translucent enough for Ryza to see the molten flux pulsating beneath his skin. His chest, covered by dull copper chainmail, heaved with each breath.

'You got any last words?' Ryza spat at him.

The strain of controlling such a huge machine showed on Tyrag's face as he grinned. 'They will be far from my last.'

'Suit yourself.'

Ryza pulled the trigger and flinched at the clanging report of the bolt-lock. When his eyes focused again, he only felt shock and disappointment. The pointed iron rod was floating in the air, vibrating between the two nearest pylons.

Tyrag let out a roar of laughter. 'You actually thought that would work? Come on boy, I thought you were smart, not lucky!'

Ryza ignored him, diving for the old man's throat with both hands. He only made it half way, caught in mid-air as his collar and his metal left hand yanked him to a halt. Choking and coughing, he stumbled away.

'No metal can touch me. Not while I control thousands of autominds.'

Tyrag leaned forward, straining against his golden shackles as he leered. 'I could crush you like a beetle!'

'Then why haven't you?' Ryza retorted.

'Same reason I didn't stomp you out the moment you supposedly beat collar death. You're not worth killing. Sometimes, you've even aided me! You hid Origin better than I ever could.'

As Tyrag ranted, Ryza checked his surroundings. Against the thousands of autominds, he didn't stand a chance at overpowering Tyrag. Everything was metal, so there was no way to find something that would penetrate the pylon's magnetic barrier.

'Searching for a way to kill me, Ryza?'

'Was I that obvious?'

'I don't think you'd want to harm me.' His voice was still completely level. 'I'm the only one keeping Revance in the air. Why don't you take a step over to the edge, see what we're above?'

Not taking his eyes off Tyrag, Ryza moved over to the edge, only looking away when his hip hit the guard rail.

Fuck.

They were directly above Iroka. The place Ryza just ordered all his people to retreat to. The few guns that could be brought to bear kept valiantly plugging away.

'If I die, Revance shall plunge like a rock into your town. Even your survivors will be slowly doomed. The collars will get them. Besides, I'd like to think that you'd owe me a favour, Ryza.'

Now Ryza had to laugh. 'And how, in your senile, twisted mind, do you think that?'

'Because it was only under my orders that you breathe today. The Locusts, a pointless club dedicated to decadence, debauchery and quarrelling among themselves over perceived slights and a split of pilfered loot. Only focused on their own little lives. Most of them wanted you dead.'

'Why keep me alive, then?'

Tyrag thought for a moment, slackening in his strange shackles. 'After I became aware of your exploits, I started to wonder just who you are. I soon found your father.'

Ryza froze, his feet bolted to the floor as he slowly turned to look at Tyrag.

'We'd already been in touch. He was one of the people helping me execute this grand scheme. I had no idea he had a son, though his response was...'

Ryza couldn't stop himself. 'What did he say?'

'Called you a worthless waste of his time, told me to simply ignore you. Left to your own devices, he said, you'd do nothing. But I've seen quite the opposite from you. Your father's problem was that he never put you in control. That's where you thrive, Ryza. That's where we are alike.'

'You can fuck off with that!' Ryza snapped. 'I don't want this! That's where we're different!'

'Of all people, I thought you'd understand what I was trying to achieve. The Droughtlands would never be controlled from one point, we both know this from our own experience. Control needs to be dispersed, spread out from as many points as possible.'

'But it doesn't matter!' Ryza roared. 'To get control you've killed thousands! You've given smelters free rein! You look about ready to die yourself!'

'But that's only means to an end,' Tyrag whispered. 'And I've found a way to an end which lies far beyond my death.'

Ryza just stared. Tyrag was a madman. A madman bent on his own destruction.

That's certainly something I can provide.

'Really? This is what I don't understand about you. Every time we've met it's always been that you're fighting for something else. First it was just for legacy, then it was for control of Revance, then the Droughtlands, but now... immortality?'

'Means to an—'

Ryza cut him off. 'Lizard shit! You're back sliding, you know you're losing!'

'I have Revance!' Tyrag roared. 'Does that look like failure to you, whelp!?'

There was a moment's pause between the pair as each of them caught their breath.

'What happens if I walk away?' Ryza asked.

Tyrag shook his head. 'We both know neither of us are walking away, Ryza.'

The howl of a mortar shell interrupted them. It soared into the cavernous forge rooms and detonated the moment it hit the ceiling, shredding the closest autominds and showering the rest in shrapnel.

Tyrag roared from the intangible pain and Ryza took off running, trying to put as much distance between himself and the Forgemaster as his mind desperately summoned a plan.

Chapter Forty

Pure Resonance

Aʟʟ Rʏᴢᴀ ᴄᴏᴜʟᴅ ᴅᴏ was run.

Crowds of tethered autominds flew past before he burst into Revance's empty corridors. The sound of rending metal followed in his wake but he didn't dare look back. It could've been Iroka focusing its bombardments or Tyrag being carried by whatever monster of an arcanite he'd assembled to chase him with.

This entire fortress was his now. One big arcanite. He'd be able to feel every corridor, room and hallway. Every footstep or gasped breath that passed through them. Ryza was hit with an awful realisation.

There's nowhere to hide.

He staggered to a halt, leaning heavily against a pillar as his lungs heaved to keep up. Tyrag's magnetic resonance tingled against his palm, the foreboding cold and calm. It reached out to Ryza, wrapping around his fingers to hold him in place. He swore and whipped it away from the metal.

'I can feel you.'

Tyrag's voice rumbled through the walls like an earthquake. It shook Ryza's bones and made his spine seize. The vibrations pressed in on his skin, surrounding him on all sides as Ryza forced himself to start running again.

'Revance isn't just mine. I am Revance. You run through my veins.'

'I'm not running!' Ryza shouted back.

The walls shook with echoing laughter as he ran up another service corridor. Archarus flashed in his vision at every corner, waiting for him at the end of each passage only to disappear the moment Ryza reached it. But he ignored the shadow dancer.

Tyrag is all that matters.

'Every piece of metal connected to Revance acts as my skin, Ryza. I can feel exactly where you are.'

The floor underneath him crumbled, forcing him to leap wildly onto the next set of stairs. It swung downwards as its supports collapsed, turning into a ladder that Ryza had to scramble up as each rung fell from his grip.

The sound of rending iron was growing louder and stronger. Tyrag was coming for him. Ryza pounded on, focusing on the plan brewing in his mind despite his dwindling options.

He couldn't kill Tyrag. If he did, they'd all be doomed to a lifetime of wearing the accursed collars around their necks. Not that they'd live to experience it. Iroka would be crushed if Revance fell from the sky. He just needed to subdue Tyrag to figure out how to break free of the collars and —as horrible as it was— Ryza knew exactly how.

He deserved it most.

But there was one thing in the way of this plan working. Tyrag's magnetic barrier. With the collar and his metal arm, Ryza didn't have a chance of getting close enough to do what he needed. There had to be a way of drawing Tyrag out or distracting him long enough to let his guard down.

It doesn't matter if I don't have what I need.

Ryza kept climbing to the control room. It was the one place he'd seen what he was looking for.

He reached the mess hall, the overturned tables giving new meaning to the first half of the room's name. Ryza hesitated. A rumble quaked through the floor, one that definitely wasn't caused by Iroka's guns. Suddenly it split in two, a pair of colossal rusted claws bursting through.

Ryza fell to the ground in an uncontrollable slide. He only caught a glimpse of the pylons from Tyrag's strange platform as it rose slowly through the newly created tear in the floor. Tyrag's face appeared and the rest of the floor gave out, sending Ryza tumbling through the bowels of the fortress, his body bouncing off jutting metal.

A shrill clang rang out, his shoulder jerked and the fall stopped. Ryza came back to his senses, the numb pain from his left arm the only thing in his head. His metal hand had clung to a twisted pillar, breaking his fall. Its grip was so tight it had actually bent the steel.

It took a few seconds of concentration to work each finger free of the warped metal. Ryza's boots hit the ground and he looked up. He'd just survived falling down three decks. He could see the underside of Tyrag's floating platform as it burrowed towards him. It was layered with smooth metal, an articulated arm affixed to each side that tore through Revance like it was paper.

Before taking in his surroundings, Ryza made to dash out of the room and instantly tripped. He fell on his face, landing on a pile of something oddly soft. Then the smell hit him. Bile bubbled up in his throat and his instincts sent him scrambling sideways to escape the heap of decaying corpses.

Brutal puncture holes peppered their bodies, each one weeping with molten flux and maggots, their corpses too mutilated for the flux to take. Hundreds of them lined the corridor that Ryza was now sprawled in. He recognised where he was. It was the infirmary halls.

Clearly not used for healing people now.

The smell grew more intense as he ran, as did the number of bodies. They were stuffed into every available room and where they didn't fit, they just rolled into the corridors. Every doorway or hatch that led back into Revance was sealed off by welded plates. Ryza pounded his fist against each one as he passed, but to no avail. They were firmly secured and Tyrag still had full control over the fortress. There was no way to tear through it, even with the help of axioms.

The silence told him that Tyrag had given up on the chase. He knew he had his prey cornered. Doubled over and gasping for breath, Ryza looked to his left. Wind rushed in through one of the fortress' gaping battle wounds. The breached iron was still smoking. Through it, he could see the tops of Iroka's cliffs and a stretching blue sky.

Ryza moved towards it, carefully placing both feet on the edge. Iroka was right below. The muzzle flashes of their cannons were now tiny pinpricks. Leading with his metal hand, he swung himself onto the outside of the fortress, the wind instantly catching in his greatcoat.

Another blood rush pulsed through him as a mortar whizzed past his body, but he didn't let it hurry his pace. Each handhold was tested and methodically confirmed. His feet only purchased on the places his bloody and raw fingers had marked. Gunports, jagged edges and bulbous rivets quickly made his task easier, like he was climbing a ramshackle ladder. If he slipped and fell, he'd have plenty of time to dwell on the misstep.

The buffeting wind was soon replaced by the throbbing hum of flying metal. A quick glance over his shoulder showed him Tyrag. The four pylons of his hovering dais rippled with bolts of bright green energy. They licked off his shackles, bouncing around his feet like welding sparks before draining out of the platform by the long coil of steel wire that trailed underneath, connecting it to Revance.

As the Forgemaster ascended to Ryza's level, Ryza saw the same green glow in his eyes again. Whatever magic was giving him this power had to be something beyond axioms and autominds.

Ryza suppressed his fear and kept his movements even. Scrambling would only lead to a fall.

'Your father never said you'd be this persistent.'

'What else did my father say?' Ryza shouted back.

It was little more than a pointless spur to sway Tyrag's focus. He remembered how groggy the Forgemaster had been when he'd first taken control of Revance. If Ryza could somehow get him like that again, he might be able to break through the pylons.

'I doubt he'd care if it were passed on to you. We'd spoken before. He never mentioned you.'

'I'm betting you wish he had,' Ryza grunted.

'Wouldn't have changed a thing,' Tyrag said, hovering nearer to Ryza now. 'What I did manage to get from him when I asked was that you'd only complete a task if you were given no other choice. What Maligar saw in you confirmed that. He said he had to corner you into making that automind. But from the way he described you after that, I'd have half a mind to think a talent like yours only comes from having a passion for the process.'

Ryza felt his legs falter and almost slip.

'Someone who enjoyed it.'

He looked around at Tyrag, unable to hide the scorn on his brow.

'I've struck a nerve, haven't I?' Tyrag cracked a small, wavering grin. 'But why stop? Why run from what you had such a talent for?'

Ryza looked up. He was almost there, maybe a few more metres and he'd be scrambling over the edge onto the top of the fortress, one step closer to the control room.

'I asked you a question, Ryza,' Tyrag spat. He was looming towards him, savouring Ryza's angst. 'Your next breath had best contain an answer.'

'Because if I had to live like that, I didn't want to live at all.'

Ryza turned back to the walls and continued climbing. The air seemed vacant as Tyrag laughed incredulously.

'It took you eighteen years, an entire lifetime, to realise that?'

'I always knew!'

'I'm sure that helps you sleep at night!'

Ryza eyed his way up the wall as Tyrag continued to taunt him. He was four moves away from the top.

'Isn't that worse?' Tyrag shouted.

He reached out with his right hand for the first, locking his knuckles between two pieces of bent and exposed rebar. He put his left foot on an empty gunport next, giving it a quick tap before resting his weight against.

'That you served your father so knowingly and loyally?'

Pushing with his left leg, he took his right to the gunport as well. He tensed his body like a coil, readying himself to spring up to the edge.

'Only if I can't stop you now,' Ryza muttered back.

He leapt with all his might, thrusting inwards with his hips as he pulled with his right hand, grabbing wildly with his left for the ledge and pulling with that, too. In less than a second, he was on top of it and belting across the featureless spine of Revance.

There was a ringing scrape of metal as Tyrag gave chase. Ryza blindly fired his arm back at him as he sprinted and missed completely. He was hurtling towards a narrow chute that led to the control room, made to syphon out the noxious fumes that collected in Revance's upper decks.

Ryza dived for it, sliding down feet first. His bruised shoulders knocked painfully against either side and before he knew it, he was collapsed in a heap next to the control room's sprawling console.

The golden core housed at its centre was spinning harder than ever now, a constant blur of motion that radiated scorching waves of heat. Getting up with a stagger, he began searching the room, scouring every bench and panel in sight.

'We're not done talking, Ryza!'

Tyrag's voice echoed through the room. The sound of rending metal rang out from above, sunlight spilling in with each tear of Tyrag's mechanical arms. Ryza searched harder, finding exactly what he was looking for just as the Forgemaster burst through the ceiling. He turned to Tyrag, hiding his prize behind his back.

The Forgemaster's dais crashed into the ground. One of the rusted claws broke from its arm as the other struggled to dislodge its dented hull from the control room's floor. Tyrag pulled harder at his shackles, the green aura around him surging brighter as his dais groaned, but it was no use.

Tyrag's face twitched with every breath. His body hung limp in its self-imposed restraints as the pylons at the other end of the chains groaned, threatening to give way. Before he could collect himself, the entire fortress shook, sending both men staggering sideways. Iroka was putting one last effort into its bombardment.

They're destroying the autominds.

Iroka's onslaught, as vain as it might've seemed from down below, was working. Because Tyrag had positioned all his autominds in the open bottom of the fortress, he'd left them vulnerable to Iroka's artillery, which had finally pulverised enough of them to weaken the Forgemaster's grip on Revance.

'You're going to lose it,' Ryza taunted.

'I've... I've already won, Ryza.'

Tyrag tried to take a shuddering step forwards but was held back by his golden shackles.

'Gold... It was the best conductor of magnetic resonance.' Tyrag shook his hand weakly against it before he yanked it clean from the two nearest pylons. 'But I...' He began pulling at the other. 'I have something far superior. Molten flux.'

The other cable snapped. The four pylons shattered as they fell from the platform, hitting the ground with a loud crash as Tyrag started walking towards Ryza. Each step was an intense effort. His bare toes dragged across the metal ground, skin raw and oozing a mixture of blood and flux.

'Revance is... gone.'

He took another clumsy step, almost toppling as Ryza retreated.

'Its people... gone.'

Ryza's back hit the control panel and Tyrag closed in.

'But my legacy... will last forever.'

He was two steps away and Ryza didn't move.

'Thanks to you.'

Tyrag lunged, his hands weighed down by the broken shackles. His veins bulging from his skin and throbbing with silver. Ryza let them reach his neck. They were cold, but it wasn't from his resonance. He didn't fight Tyrag's grip. It was pathetically weak. His thumbs could barely make their way under his metal collar, let alone choke the life from him.

'Something in the way?' Ryza asked.

Tyrag let out an unhinged howl as he fumbled his grip from Ryza's neck to the metal collar. But this was Ryza's plan. He snapped his right hand up to Tyrag's own neck, not squeezing but instead focusing on the last of the Forgemaster's weakening pulse, the last of his magnetic resonance.

Axioms flowed across both their arms, racing to burn in their palms as their resonances duelled through their fingertips. Ryza could feel his veins freezing, his muscles convulsing as Tyrag's mind pummelled at his senses but he didn't let go.

More runes shot down Ryza's arm, the ink the only thing on his body that could move, the white-hot burning in his right hand the only sensation he had left. The only one he could afford to focus on. He needed every ounce of mind to know exactly how Tyrag was about to break his collar so he could replicate it.

Tyrag screamed again and Ryza felt his cold resonance shattered. Ryza pushed with his own, invading Tyrag's mind as it desperately tried to fend him off. But it was too late. He'd seen exactly what he'd needed to.

The rusted metal snapped from Ryza's throat and for the first time in months his neck was free. He didn't waste a second, forgoing that beautiful first breath of freedom as he parried Tyrag's hands from his throat, spinning his frail body as he clamped the Forgemaster into an unyielding headlock.

He squeezed tight with his metal left arm, transferring the hidden injector gun into his right hand as he let his blood begin to boil.

The violence.

Tyrag's deeds were abominations. His labour was an agonising torture. Ryza couldn't imagine the pain Tyrag's flux-riddled body now suffered. He could only hear the man's choked cries for mercy. It was his duty to silence them.

Revel in the violence.

With his right hand, he brought up the injector gun. Just as it had days ago, foul silver liquid sloshed in the glass vial, the needle flashing in the stray beams of sunlight that danced through the control room.

With unconscious precision, Ryza stabbed the needle home. The skin was pierced, a perfect strike, the smooth slide of the needle letting him know he'd slipped between Tyrag's vertebrae.

'No! Ryza! You don't know what you're doing!'

He ignored Tyrag's desperate pleas and redoubled his grip, ignoring the flux that bubbled from the Forgemaster's mouth and onto the bronze casing of his metal arm. He might be full of the flux he controlled, but the moment Ryza pulled the injector's trigger, it would all surely be undone.

It has to work.

'He's right, you know.'

The words, coming from a voice deep and booming, cut Ryza's thoughts in half. Archarus had appeared before him, but Tyrag didn't seem aware of the shadow dancer's presence. Archarus paced to Ryza's side, observing his work.

'What do you want, Archarus?' Ryza said unflinchingly. 'I'm not going to control the flux. I don't want any part it your failed legacy.'

'I don't think you have a choice,' Archarus replied. The shadow dancer began circling the chamber, never taking his eyes off Ryza. 'To steer the fortress away from Iroka, you must control it. To live through controlling it and free the conscripts from their collars, you must control the autominds. To control that many autominds, you must control the flux. To survive controlling the flux...'

'How!?'

Archarus forced a strained grin. 'You already know, Ryza. You're close to it, I sense it. I just couldn't tell you until this moment. If I had, your mind would've expected it.'

'Pure resonance...'

Every hair on Ryza's body stood on end. He couldn't feel Tyrag struggling in his arms or the shudder of the fortress under him. The world was blurring around him, with only Archarus staying in focus.

'Succeed where I have failed.'

His voice was weak in his throat, but Ryza still managed to speak.

'I'll become like you.'

The shadow dancer drew closer, black eyes boring into his.

'Not if you prove my legacy to be true.'

Before he could blink, Archarus had vanished. The silence he left was only broken intermittently by the last shots of Iroka's petering barrage. The groaning of steel soon overwhelmed it as the fortress' joints threatened to fail.

Ryza fastened his grip again and clenched his jaw.

Execute.

His finger twitched, the first pull of the trigger weak and testing. Rust scraped within the injector gun as it was called to action. He pulled again. Vindication flowed through him. It was as cold as the liquid he was pushing into Tyrag's spine.

This he could justify.

This was right.

The old man began to choke and struggle, but Ryza's grip was too tight. He kept pumping, letting a reckless abandon take over his hand, pumping and pumping and pumping until his tendons ached. Pushing until Tyrag stopped struggling. Squeezing until the injector began to gasp as well.

Instinct halted his trigger finger and he yanked the injector out. Ryza clamped his palm against the needle hole before it could leak flux. An axiom slid down his arm. The axiom he'd begged Holm not to paint on his skin.

The axiom to control an automind.

Tyrag's body started to slacken, his legs wobbling from under him and his grip falling from Ryza's arm. The last rune burned. Tyrag let out one final moaning scream.

And then it came.

A surging rush.

Sickening and complete control.

At Ryza's fingers hung a feeble man. His body was tired and crippled. His mind was vacant of thought and resonance. His wrists ached from the gold cuffs that bound them, like they'd been clamped on too tight for days. Ryza couldn't even feel hands, just cold voids past Tyrag's wrists.

His stomach ached from hunger. His eyes drooped from strain. His feet were blistered. He hadn't sat for days. Now Ryza hadn't either. Every stress, pain and groaning joint from Tyrag's body now filled his own. How he wanted to let his balance go. To just fall to the ground and sleep.

Mustering even another thought was out of the question. He was tired. Plain and simple. There wasn't enough life pulsing through Ryza's body to fuel the two of them.

But then more came.

The metal at Ryza's feet became his, the feeling pooling outwards like an oil slick. He quickly designated it to Tyrag's mind. It was a consciousness that was old and worn, but it was still expansive. The rest of the control room came into the view. Ryza clenched his eyes shut and focused on every edge, every line, every rivet that held the room together.

It's too much.

The realisation hit Ryza too late. Revance began to shake. He could already sense pieces snapping loose. Their altitude was dropping and Ryza couldn't stop it. If he seized the fortress now, he would become it. The titanic arcanite would be held in his mind alone and he knew it would only last a second.

Then it would fall.

His friends would be crushed. He was the one who told them to retreat there, now they were doomed by his hand.

The last sparks of Tyrag's resonance still fled through the halls of Revance and Ryza sent his own after them like a pack of hunting dogs. In half a second, he was scattered across all levels of the fortress, a strange, incomplete skeleton of it forming in his mind's eye as a stabbing pain rose at his temples.

This much control was already deadly. He needed to mitigate it. His probing resonance hit a dead-end in the remains of the conscripts' quarters. An array of autominds was there. They still held Tyrag's resonance and his command to repel the fortress from the earth.

Ryza pushed in with his own in, flushing out Tyrag's resonance but not his orders. The pressure in his head eased slightly. However, the respite was momentary. Another deck came into view and the pain redoubled.

A delicate dance ensued, each step carried out beyond the bounds of time, paced only as fast as Ryza's mind could flit from thought to thought. As another section of the fortress came under his control, it was quickly affixed to a group of newly found autominds.

What if the autominds ran out before the fortress did?

The thought was a hard wall he ignored, focusing every ounce of his being on tethering together the superstructure of the fortress. Everything else inside could fall loose, just as long as Ryza caught it. The upper decks were under control, the lower just coming into Ryza's reach. It was heavy down there, not just by weight.

Tyrag's resonance lingered in the hull itself, not an enemy to confront but a thick sludge to struggle through. If Ryza had allowed himself doubt, he'd know his momentum was faltering. The groups of autominds he was finding were getting smaller and smaller, more tucked away and hidden, but there was still so much metal left to take.

I'm forgetting something.

It was then that he stumbled upon the endless cluster of autominds in the lower forge rooms. The ones Tyrag had lorded over on his floating throne. All at once, they were his and Ryza could feel a mouth somewhere in the fortress roaring in ecstasy. Why had Tyrag struggled with this many autominds at his disposal? And this was *after* hundreds of them had been lost in the battle.

Every nook and cranny of the fortress was his for the taking. Every loose bolt, creaking door and smoking gun was his! It was so much power. Why would Origin have ever wanted to give this up?

Then a sickening memory hit him.

This was the exact same rush he'd experienced years ago as a child.

It was the first time he'd taken an automind under his own control. It was unrestrained bliss, far too much for such a young boy. His mind had suddenly been relinquished from his rushing and ceaseless fears. For once in his life, his head had been clear.

I was free.

That was the feeling which had stopped him from fleeing his father sooner. That had lured him along the path to being a smelter. That was the rush of control he knew he would never stop chasing.

Now he had it. All the control possible in the world. A thousand autominds tied together at the neck so he could have a moment of pure clarity. It made the world so quiet. Made his skin finally feel calm.

Outside of the fortress, the sky's wind beat against the hull, aching to blow it back up the valley. With less than a fleeting whim, Ryza let Revance shift with it. The breeze could take him wherever it damn well pleased. He'd finally accomplished his mission. He'd killed the smelter responsible for this mess. He'd found the flux aboard Revance and the autominds along with it. Distantly, he felt his body chuckle.

I have it all.

He suddenly realised his thoughts were no longer involuntary. As such, nothing came to distract him from the sickening cost of this newfound calm. Ryza relinquished the autominds over the course of the next hour. He let his resonance wander through the fortress, touching each one with an ethereal tendril and pausing for a silent moment to mourn them as the body hung limp against its tether.

As Revance journeyed through the valley and away from Iroka, it crumbled deck by deck. Hunks of metal showered the battle-scarred dunes, the debris ranging in size from that of inconsequential shrapnel to chunks the size of small villages. Autominds fell with it; limp and masterless in their final moments before they hit the ground.

By the time the last floating remnant of Revance neared the sand, just beyond the mouth of the valley, all that was left was the control room, a fraction of the fortress which was once thought of as indestructible.

A titanic crash echoed across the Droughtlands as it collided with the dunes, throwing up a small sandstorm from the impact. The desert floor could barely stop its momentum. When the control room had halted, it was half-buried, wedged in place by a rocky chasm that was hidden below the surface.

Search parties eventually came, battle weary yet determined. The fragmented remains of what they'd once called Revance blunted any notions of haste. The valley of Iroka was now a jagged and hostile landscape, rendered nigh impassable by the pools of molten flux that remained in the wreckage. It billowed into the sky in ominous grey and silver clouds that all but blocked out the sun.

But the flux wasn't what they were searching for.

Their quarry was the Bloodfist.

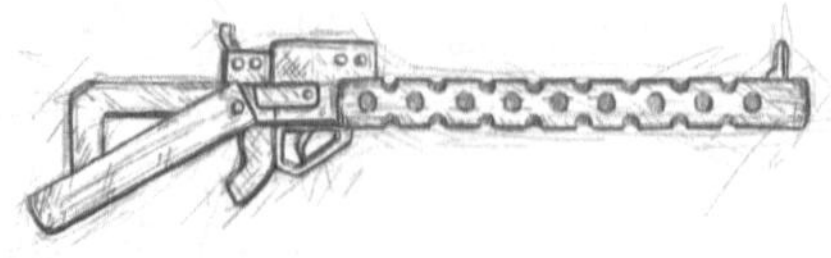

Chapter Forty-One

Last Doubts

Consciousness came to Ryza in ebbing waves.

Rays of light trickled in from the control room's cracked walls and sand falls streamed in through seams in the metal.

The congregation of autominds which had once been Revance's commanders were now carelessly piled in the far corner of the control room.

The fall had thrown them there, but at least the core drive of Revance remained in place. The gold-flecked, rounded obelisk was once again motionless in its housing. Tiny flecks of metal orbited it sporadically, their pace slow and gentle.

Tyrag's body lay a few feet away from Ryza, slowly being consumed by a mixture of sand and flux. He'd be buried in a matter of hours.

Good. Let him be forgotten.

Ryza blinked and suddenly he was half-buried in sand, too.

But he didn't panic. It was only a gentle pressure over his legs, a warm blanket coaxing him out of shock. Small ripples of flux lapped from the pool held in the exposed metal near his feet, but it dissolved through the granules as soon as it met the sand. For all he knew, it could be sinking hundreds of metres into the depths below.

He shut his eyes again, letting himself quietly sink as well. He hoped the flux wouldn't meet him there.

'Is something wrong?'

It was a voice, soft and low, similar to Archarus' but not quite. Ryza squinted, only able to make out the form of a black cloak.

'Of course there is,' Ryza rasped.

'You're still alive.'

Ryza frowned. This couldn't be the shadow dancer he knew, but then who was it?

'Do I deserve to be?' he asked. He tried to muster the effort to raise his hand to rub the sand from his eyes, but even that seemed too hard.

'Is that the question?'

This time it definitely was Archarus' voice. The silhouette had moved and as Ryza cleared his vision, he recognised the hauntingly familiar visage of the shadow dancer.

'You struck pure resonance the moment you took control. I sensed it! I saw it!' Pride and satisfaction were etched into his pale face as he spoke. 'You took control of the flux and you lived!'

'But it wasn't the flux, it was the autominds,' Ryza said. 'I felt every last one of—'

Archarus' body flashed into nothingness and suddenly the shadow dancer was crouched next to Ryza, causing him to recoil out of his blanket of sand.

'Do you still feel it? The pure resonance?'

'I... I don't know...'

'Then you're alive,' Archarus whispered. 'I was right.'

The shadow dancer disappeared.

Ryza breathed slowly as he scanned the control room for him. It was quiet. He'd never expected to be inside Revance and not hear the constant groan of iron. But then again, Revance was no more.

The silence didn't last. Distant clangs of boots on metal could only mean the conscripts were digging through the wreckage. Ryza forced himself to stand with a groan. His legs wobbled beneath him, sand falling from his clothes. If he was to be found, it would be on his feet.

There was a roar of grinding steel above as fiery sparks rained down. Ryza hobbled to the side of the chamber in time to avoid a falling hunk of the freshly cut debris. It would be a cruel irony to have survived this long only to be killed by something as mundane as gravity.

More sparks came. His rescuers' first efforts had only produced a gap the size of his fist. He was saved.

Yet Archarus' final visit had left an unplaceable disquiet in the back of Ryza's mind. The shadow dancer couldn't be done with him yet. Was Ryza meant to have lived? Was he even alive now?

He looked at his hands, flexing both metal and flesh. The metal arm still didn't feel like his and his alone. Origin's resonance was still there. But hidden within his left arm's stump, so too was Holm's. Now sated, her fiery and triumphant roar of retribution warmed his battered body and he closed his eyes to embrace it.

The steel ceiling groaned one last time and collapsed inwards, crashing to the floor. Ryza squinted through the sunlight above, deaf to the victorious cheers of the silhouettes crowding the hole.

There was only one person he wanted to see.

A bruised and blood-spattered smile filled his face as he spotted her.

It was Holm.

ALSO BY

The Flux Catastrophe
RISING FLUX: The Prequel Novella to Molten Flux (March 2023)
MOLTEN FLUX (June 2023)
BLAZING FLUX (April 2024)
CORRUPTED FLUX (August 2025)
The First Hytharo
THE HYTHARO REDUX (October 2023)
THE HYTHARO ORIGIN (August 2024)

Check out my website: **jonathanweiss.com.au** to find more great books that've since been published!
And if you're inclined, consider leaving a review online, either on Goodreads or from where you purchased this book, it helps massively in getting this book in front of other readers, meaning you'll have more people to talk to about it!

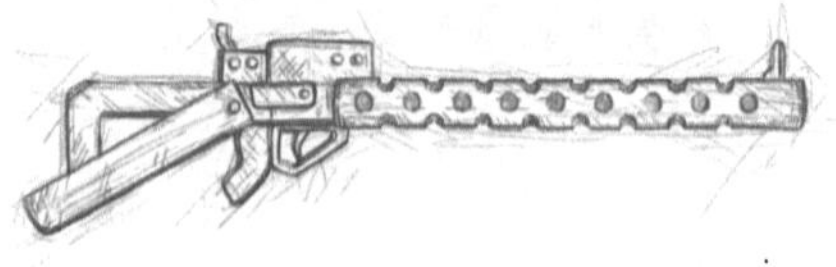

GLOSSARY

YOU CAN FIND THE living, in depth glossary for this book
and for the world of The Droughtlands on my website, at
www.jonathanweiss.com.au/glossary
   Also, if you need a refresher on the events of a previous book, you
can also find them at **www.jonathanweiss.com.au/plot-synopses**

About the Author

Jonathan Weiss is an Australian Fantasy & Science Fiction author of The Flux Catastrophe and The First Hytharo series. Ever since being a small boy he hunted for the best way to tell stories, dabbling in film and stop motion before eventually finding a passion for novel writing as a teenager. More than a decade later, he'd gathered a bachelor's degree of Journalism from the University of Wollongong and a career in commercial cloud sales, yet they were never as satisfying as the time spent writing.

With the support of his artist wife and the cacophonic trio of their pet budgies, he's now dedicated himself to a full-time career as an author. When not writing, Jonathan can be found reading halfway through books and forgetting to finish them, working through the never-ending queue of un-painted Warhammer 40,000 models and attempting to fit far too much food on his tiny barbeque.